Medusa's Gauntlet

New Eden – book 3

KISHORE TIPIRNENI

ISBN: 978-1-7364562-3-1

DEDICATION

For my teachers and all those who infuse knowledge to the next generation.
You know not the power you yield and the influence you have.

ACKNOWLEDGMENTS

The cover illustrations for the book were created by Guillermo Herrera.
The audiobook for this novel was narrated by Lee Goettl.
Thanks to Stephen Ripple for help in editing this novel.

PREFACE

I'm thrilled to be able to present to you the last installment of the New Eden series. There has so much that has happened in the first two novels that I cannot do this story justice by repeating the storyline from the previous two novels. Therefore, I've written this novel from the standpoint of someone who is familiar with the previous two, and I've made minimal attempts to refresh the reader with past events and concepts.

On with the story . . .

Chapter One
Rebirth

Bhumi started her second life as a seed planted in a cavern deep underground. She was not the result of any natural process, but the result of purposeful creation by beings of extreme intelligence. The intelligence that had designed her new physical form had imprinted her design onto the DNA of a watermelon-sized biological seed from which she grew.

Her seed was a miniature, compressed version of her final self—one that, given the appropriate conditions and resources, would expand and grow into her final design. Like many seeds, the instructions in her DNA first caused a root, a taproot, to emerge from one of its sides. This root grew thicker and longer—eventually miles in length—as it slowly crept through crevices in rock that encompassed the walls of the cavern in which her seed was planted. Her root slowly navigated its way through fissures in solid rock towards its destination—a large bay that contained the material that Bhumi needed to grow further. The tip of her root eventually emerged from the floor of the bay like a hollow straw that would suck in seawater and deliver the needed resource to the seed to which it was connected.

While Bhumi's taproot had been growing, other changes were happening inside of her seed. Her DNA instructed the cells of her seed to create highly dense black spheres that would be integral in allowing her to achieve her final form. The spheres had a critical function—a fantastic ability. They could squeeze individual atomic nuclei together until the strong nuclear force came into effect, allowing the nuclei to fuse, forming larger elements. This fusion process produced both energy and new elements, which were both necessary for Bhumi's growth.

As seawater flowed through the continually enlarging taproot from the bay to her seed, the fluid was split using electrochemical processes into its four principle elemental components: hydrogen, oxygen, sodium, and chlorine. When these elements reached her seed, three of the four elements were stored for later use in three of ninety-eight expanding cellular cysts that grew inside of herself—all except the hydrogen, which was fed into the newly created spheres.

Bhumi was a master of the atom. She had the ability to control not only the nucleus made of protons and neutrons, but also the outer shells made of electrons. She was both a master nuclear physicist and organic chemist, although at that time she had no knowledge of her innate abilities . . . she was not yet sentient.

The spheres fused the hydrogen nuclei fed to them, forming heavier elements: helium, carbon, nitrogen, phosphorus, and others. As dictated by the instructions encoded in her DNA, these newly created elements, along with some of the elements she had stored in her cysts, were chemically combined into larger, more complex organic molecules: amino acids, nucleic acids, and lipids. Some of these larger molecules were chemically bonded further to create proteins and other biological structures. The energy released from the fusion process of the spheres was captured into the chemical bonds of still more complex molecules like carbohydrates, lipids, and adenosine triphosphate that Bhumi would use to power her life processes.

The newly created nucleic acids joined together into long chains of double strands in a specific sequence that was an exact copy of her original DNA which allowed her cells to start dividing and multiplying at an ever-increasing rate. As her cells multiplied, Bhumi grew larger, and she quickly encompassed the space of the cavern in which her seed had been planted—a cavern known by its previous occupants as the Bat Cave. The rocks surrounding the cavern were no impediment to her growth as the hydraulic pressure inside her body created by osmotic gradients easily pushed away the surrounding rock as she grew. There were small seismic quakes in the rocks above as they split from the pressure of her growth. The surface of the land above became stretched and fissured as it expanded upwards into a giant dome to accommodate her expanding mass. The abandoned buildings of the scientific lab that occupied the land above her crumbled into ruins.

Bhumi's cells differentiated further into various structures that were designed to perform specific functions. She developed a circulatory system that allowed bright red blood to flow that transported nutrients and materials for Bhumi's rapidly growing body. She developed a sensory system that could sense and focus light through numerous eyes into both her interior and exterior. She developed a plethora of other senses such as touch, hearing, orientation, balance, and advanced levels of electromagnetic and chemical detection. These sensory organs were all connected via neural bundles to an immense brain, a nexus of neural cells, that had grown near the center of her body.

Bhumi became enormous as she grew both deeper into the ground and taller into the fracturing rock above. As she grew into an oval shape, her interior started forming multiple spherical chambers, the largest of which filled with an atmosphere consisting of nitrogen, oxygen, argon, and trace carbon dioxide—identical to the atmosphere that existed above the fractured landscape of the planet inside which she grew. As she grew even larger, these chambers expanded into enormous spheres, the largest eventually becoming a kilometer in diameter. The floor of this largest sphere was not uniform. It was mostly flat but undulated in small hills and valleys. The low-lying valleys of the chamber filled with water forming freshwater ponds and even small streams that connected a few of the ponds. The ceiling of the chamber, a kilometer above, was dark except for a single point at the center, which emanated a white-hot light produced by a collection of the black spheres that were fed hydrogen at immense pressure in order to convert it into helium. The energy and light created by the hydrogen fusion created a miniature sun that Bhumi could turn on and off by modulating the flow of hydrogen flowing to the spheres. This modulation created day and night cycles in the chamber below.

The energy and heat given off by this artificial sun caused some of the water of her lakes and streams to evaporate and rise high into its enclosed atmosphere. Some of this moisture contacted the relatively cool, dark portion of the chamber ceiling—the portion not occupied by the artificial sun. The water vapor condensed back to liquid form as it cooled on this surface. Bhumi collected this water in the sponge-like material, which composed the dark portion of the ceiling. When this material became saturated, she would squeeze it to release the moisture in the form of rain droplets that sometimes poured as torrents, sometimes as a gentle mist on the hills and valleys below.

The ground of the chamber not occupied by the ponds and streams sprouted small green shoots that got their energy through photosynthesis from the artificial sun overhead. The shoots grew themselves into numerous types of flora, including grass, shrubs, and even in areas, tall hardwoods that arched skyward as they yearned to get closer to their energy source. There were other structures that grew from the ground. These were living buildings that were meant to house other intelligent creatures separate from herself.

When Bhumi was almost fully grown, her creators injected into her brain information that gave her consciousness and self-awareness. It was not an entirely new consciousness, but one that had been inadvertently preserved on the planet of both her birth and eventual rebirth for millennia. She learned that she was now an enormous living entity designed for a renewed purpose, and that she would be tasked with that purpose soon. Her brain was also injected with the language, knowledge, and culture of the living organisms that would soon take occupancy inside of her. Like the child that she was, she waited with anticipation for the creatures that would soon be her occupants—creatures with which she had an ancient kinship. She yearned for companionship.

Now in the adolescence of her growth, Bhumi started producing numerous hollow tentacles that arose from evenly spaced areas on the exterior surface of her egg-shaped body. She found that she could move these tentacles and have them point in any direction she chose in a coordinated fashion. She began melding the intelligence inside of her with the sensory input and motor output of the nerves that connected her brain to her extremities. She tested and experienced these connections, thereby becoming more aware of her own body. She was now a complete, intelligent entity a kilometer wide and two kilometers tall—an enormous ovoid creature comprised entirely of living cells.

During the final stage of her growth, the occupants for which she was designed were delivered to her and took up residence inside her. They were also conscious beings both similar and dissimilar to herself—living beings that took some time to get accustomed to living in her main chamber. Bhumi was relieved to be free of her loneliness.

Soon, Bhumi was fully mature. She had achieved the design and purpose for which she had been created. Impatient as any adolescent, and in preparation for the time of her emergence, Bhumi pumped hydrogen, under high pressure, into numerous black spheres in her interior that fused into heavier and heavier elements until they created iron which she stored in one of her cysts. The enormous amount of energy that was created during this fusion process, she stored in an internal organ composed of bioelectric membranes, which stored vast electrical charges.

Finally, on the day of her rebirth, her creators gave her the signal she had been anxiously waiting for—the signal for launch. Bhumi released massive amounts of her stored-up iron atoms into an internal organ that contained long tubes lined with magnetic membranes that she controlled with an automated portion of her brain. She used the electric charge stored in her bioelectric membranes to create magnetic fields in the tubes of the organ that accelerated the iron atoms. The atoms traveled faster and faster down the spiral tubes of her organ as she injected more and more energy into the magnetic fields. When the atoms had achieved a speed close to that of light, she ejected numerous streams of iron through the tentacles on her exterior, which she had all pointed downward.

The force exerted by the downward ejection of the iron from her body lifted her upwards. The ground around her shook and cracked in a thunderous rumble as it fractured further as her enormous form started moving upwards. The connection with her taproot—her umbilical cord—became severed. The land above her burst open in an explosion of boulders and dirt as she blasted out of the ground and into the atmosphere of the planet above. She continued ejecting the iron streams downward as she moved faster and higher as the resistance of the rock she had been created in was released from her body. She was flying now, tunneling straight up through the atmosphere of the planet on which she was created.

The sky above was gray and lined with dark clouds saturated with moisture which rained down in sheets washing the soil from her exterior. As she blast through the low-lying cloud layer and felt the warm rays of the sun for the first time, a bolt of lightning struck her side and traveled down her iron exhaust, and dissipated on the land below.

Her occupants looked out in wonder through the transparent, thick membranes that made up her external shell at the planet beneath them. It had been their homeworld not so long ago.

Bhumi continued upward, her speed increasing still, as she left the confines of the atmosphere and burst into the vastness of empty space. She was free now . . . she had reached her new home—the environment she had been designed for.

I am Bhumi. I am reborn . . ..

Chapter Two
Graduation

(one month earlier)

Richard Miller walked out of Feynman High School with throngs of other students. It was the last day of school, which, for Richard, meant the last day of his high school education. Richard was a tall, handsome, twenty-year-old with long dark brown hair that fell close to his blue eyes. On Earth, most students graduated at eighteen, but students on New Eden were two years behind their Earth counterparts due to the delay caused by the early years of the "Transition."

Richard chatted with and congratulated many of his fellow seniors before taking the short walk to the elementary school next door. The day was bright and sunny as he waited by the entrance of the two-story school, watching for the exit of Ava Andrews. The school was newly built, as were many buildings on New Eden, those that were not created by the petrins.

Richard spotted Ava in the crowd of children exiting the school. "Ava! Over here," Richard shouted over the din of the other children as he waved his hand.

Ava, a typical nine-year-old girl with short curly brown hair, skipped over to Richard with a beaming smile and grasped his hand. "Hi Uncle Richard."

"How was your last day of fourth grade?" Richard asked.

"Over," Ava responded with a scrunched smile.

"You want to walk or take the tube home?"

"Tube. My backpack's too heavy. Got all my stuff to take home packed in it."

Richard led Ava the short distance to the tube entrance and walked down two flights of stairs to the underground station along with numerous other students heading home. The station was an extended platform adjacent to which were multiple clear transport capsules of varying lengths meant to transport a varying number of people. Depending on their lengths, the capsules could accommodate anywhere from two to eight people at once. The capsules were transparent cylindrical objects ten feet in diameter with hemispheres at each end of a horizontally placed cylinder. Richard and Ava waited in line as students in front of them loaded into empty capsules.

When they had reached the front of the line, Richard led Ava to a control panel which asked, "occupants and destination?" in a disembodied female voice with a British accent.

"Two traveling to 1390-7236," Richard answered.

Shortly, a two-person capsule with a circular opening in its side slid up to the platform in front of them. They entered the capsule, and Richard pushed the green close button on the wall, which caused the opening in the capsule to close concentrically from the outside towards the center, sealing them inside. The closure of the opening left the couple in complete silence, a welcome relief from the cacophony of the other students conversing and shouting at each other. Richard and Ava each took a seat on the two reclined chairs and fastened their safety belts.

The chairs were made of a leather-like material that, along with everything else in the tube transport system, including the capsules and the tunnel along which they traveled, were made of living biological cells—a gift from the advanced race that had allowed humans to inhabit this planet. The luminous ceiling above them glowed a soft white as the capsule moved silently and laterally away from the platform, and along with numerous other capsules, moved forward into an airlock, the door of which closed silently behind them. The group of capsules paused only slightly as the atmosphere from the airlock was evacuated. There was no change in air pressure inside the capsule even though its exterior was now a complete vacuum owing to its completely rigid walls. The capsule moved forward, both levitated and accelerated by magnetic fields generated by the walls of the tube. It picked up speed and was eventually injected into one of the tributary branches of the tube system.

The capsule moved silently and swiftly forward as it automatically navigated numerous branch points and curves, rotating automatically along its long axis to make sure that its occupants only felt varying downward acceleration and no lateral pressure as it made its way to its destination.

Richard and Ava stared out the transparent walls of the capsule at the tube to the left of them. This tube ran in the opposite direction. Varying length capsules shot by at high speed as their occupants were transported to their destinations.

The capsule had only traveled for a few minutes before its occupants felt the force of deceleration. Now moving slowly, the capsule entered another airlock, one much smaller than the first, that rapidly filled with air before the capsule stopped its forward motion and then moved vertically upwards, ending in an enclosed room—a garage of sorts. Richard and Ava exited the capsule through the now opened hatch and entered their home.

"Mommy, we're home," Ava exclaimed as she entered the home through the garage door.

"I'm upstairs in the bedroom," Rachael Miller, a tall attractive brunette in her late thirties, shouted.

Ava ran through a circular hallway and up a flight of stairs to the bedroom to her mother, who was folding some clothes and placing them into a suitcase when her daughter ran in.

"I'm done," Ava said as she hugged her mom.

"Done?" Rachael asked whimsically. "Done with what?"

Ava gave her an inquisitive look. "Done with fourth grade."

"Oh," Rachael replied. "I forgot. Is this the last day of school already?"

Ava pushed away from her mother's embrace with an annoyed expression.

"Just kidding honey," Rachael said with a smile. "You've done an amazing job this year in school. We're all very proud of you."

"Hey Sis," Richard said as he entered the room.

Rachael walked over to her brother and gave him a hug. "You're done too. What does it feel like to be finished with high school?"

"I don't know. It feels good to be done, but I feel like I'm going to miss it somehow."

"Where's daddy?" Ava asked to try to regain the attention in the room. "I have something to show him."

"He'll be home soon," Rachael said. "We have reservations for dinner tonight to celebrate both of your graduations. What do you have to show him?"

"It's my art project. I made a painting of the home solar system."

"Wow, I'd love to see it too."

"I'll show both of you when daddy gets home."

"Still daddy's girl, I see," Rachael muttered.

"Where're we going for dinner?" Richard asked.

"I made reservations at an Indian restaurant. It was Vinod's recommendation."

"Uncle Vinod's going to be there?" Ava asked excitedly.

"Yes, Uncle Vinod, Ms. Liz, and Mr. Ted are all going to be there. They didn't want to miss out on the celebration. Why don't you go and get changed into something nice—maybe that yellow dress that Ms. Liz got you for your birthday?"

"Okay," Ava said as she exited the room.

"When do you think we'll be finished with dinner?" Richard asked.

"Why?" Rachael said as she resumed packing clothes into her suitcase.

"Our band has a gig tonight starting at ten, and I was going to hang out with my friends after."

"Hang out? I don't suppose that alcohol is a part of this hang-out?"

"Maybe."

"How late are you going to be out?"

"Late enough," Richard replied curtly.

Rachael paused her packing and looked at Richard, annoyed. Many years ago on Earth, they had been twins. They had grown up together as best buddies until the age of ten, when Richard had died from cancer. When the petrins were able to revive him on New Eden shortly after humanity had been relocated there, Rachael was almost twenty years older than him. Due to their age difference, Rachael had become less of a sister and more of a guardian. She and her husband, Dr. Joshua Andrews, had taken on the responsibility of raising him since she felt that her parents were beyond the age that they would be comfortable raising another child, even though Richard was indeed their child.

The concept of one's age had been radically changed on New Eden due to the "Relocation." The Relocation was the name given to the process by which the petrins had transferred those humans who wanted to leave Earth for New Eden. The Relocation was essentially an evacuation of humanity from Earth by the petrins. The petrins were a highly advanced alien species who operated as a collective of minds interconnected by spookyons—entangled particles created by the Big Bang that allowed for instantaneous information transfer between any two points. The petrins had spread primordial cells on Earth millennia ago that eventually resulted in humans through evolution. However, Medusa, the individual petrin who had invented the cell, split from the petrin collective, and formed her own collective comprised solely of clones of herself. Medusa and the petrins were locked in a battle for control of life in the cosmos ever since. Earth was the latest staging ground for this battle which had necessitated the Relocation.

The process of the Relocation had involved a three-stage process. The first stage was to scan each individual human on Earth to catalog their information. This information included not only the DNA sequence of their cells, but also the arrangement of neural connections in their brains. The scanned information was temporarily stored as data on one of the petrin data nodes. The second stage was growing a clone of the person on New Eden. This was done by injecting their DNA sequence into a primordial cell which was allowed to grow given the proper nutrients. When the clone was mature, the final stage was to replicate the neural connection data stored during the scanning process onto the clone's brain.

The relocation had been seamless for the participants. When one awoke on New Eden, the last thing they remembered was entering the scanning station on Earth. There had been no indication of the passage of time, although many months had passed.

There were, however, some side effects to the relocation process. Unlike children whose clones were grown to the same age as they were on Earth, the petrins gave adult humans the ability to decide what physical age to grow their clone on New Eden before their neural information was transferred to it. This meant that a seventy-year-old human could occupy their body as it was at age twenty. It was a veritable fountain of youth. Therefore, for many humans, the correlation between mental and physical age had been broken.

Rachael's parents were a part of the rare group of older humans who had decided to maintain their Earth age when transported to New Eden. People that had decided to maintain their age during transport were nicknamed "continualists." Rachael's parents were unusual for their generation. Most people of their age had decided to have their clones only age to their early twenties or thirties, and as a result, the average age of humanity had skewed drastically towards younger people. Older humans who had decided to only age to early adulthood were nicknamed "resetters" since they had reset their physical age. The resetters were an unusual portion of humanity. Physically they were in their twenties, but mentally, they had the maturity and wisdom of someone much older.

There was a group in between the continualists and the resetters: those that decided to shave a few years off their physical age, but not quite to the point of being in their twenties. This group was nicknamed the "hedgers." It had become accepted practice on New Eden when someone met another person for the first time to ask, "What's your maturity status?" This had become just as socially acceptable as asking, "How old are you?" on Earth. The proper answer to this query was two-fold. One was expected to give both their mental age as well as their physical age. The difference between these two numbers revealed whether someone was a continualist, hedger, or resetter.

Interestingly, it was not so much the physical age that determined whether two people would be compatible with each other as a couple. Although physical age was important for initial attraction, it was the mental age that most reliably determined whether two people would be compatible in a relationship. As a result, the resetters were the most unusual group in humanity. They had difficulty forming lasting connections with humans in other groups. They mostly liked to congregate together. Therefore, it was unsurprising to see a group of twenty-something-year-olds reminiscing about "the good old days."

Joshua and Rachael had decided to be continualists in that they wanted to be the same age as they were on Earth. The most significant factor in this decision was the fact that they would be raising a newborn, and they felt more comfortable being their natural age.

At times, the role that Rachael had taken to be Richard's guardian resulted in the usual friction between parent and child. This was especially the case when Richard had been in his teens. Things were improving on this front as Richard had gotten older and more mature, but Rachael was still very protective of Richard. Some of this protectiveness was due to their current roles, but some was because of the almost twenty years that Rachael had thought that she had lost Richard. She certainly didn't want to lose him again or have anything detrimental happen to him.

"You remember that I'll be leaving at eight AM tomorrow for Paris for my meeting, right?" Rachael asked.

"So?"

"So, you know that I can't sleep until I know you're home."

Richard rolled his eyes. "Come on, Sis," Richard said as he turned to exit the room. "I'm not ten anymore. You don't need to wait up for me. I'll be fine."

Rachael had just finished packing when her husband walked into the room. In his early forties, Dr. Joshua Andrews was a handsome man slightly greying around the temples. He walked up to Rachael and kissed her on the cheek. "You all packed for tomorrow?"

"Just finished." Rachael latched the suitcase. "How was your day?"

"The usual. More time spent trying to reveal the secrets of physics that are already known by the petrins, but they won't reveal."

"Don't feign frustration with me Dr. Andrews. I know you too well. Physics is your passion."

"That, among other things," Joshua said as he embraced Rachael. "I know you've got an important vote coming up in Paris, but we're going to miss you for a few days."

"I'm going to miss you all too," Rachael replied. "By the way, Ava has something to show you. Apparently, it's an art project she painted of the old solar system."

"What does it look like? Did she get the proportions right?"

"I don't know," Rachael replied, annoyed. "She didn't want to show me until *you* got home."

"Ava, I'm home," Joshua bellowed down the hall.

Ava soon ran into the room with a large piece of paper in her hand and wrapped her arms around her father. "Daddy, I want to show you something I painted in art class," she said as she released her embrace and handed the paper to her father. "I painted the old solar system from what you taught me." She eagerly waited for his approval.

Joshua examined the painting, a series of circles, nine in all, of various sizes and colors.

"That big yellow one on the left is the sun, and the other ones are the eight planets," Ava said excitedly as she pointed to the painting.

"It's very pretty honey," Joshua replied, "You've got the planets in the right order, but the sizes of the planets are a little bit off. You see how Earth is the same size as . . .."

Rachael elbowed Joshua hard in his ribs.

"I meant to say that you've done an amazing job Ava," Joshua replied through some pain. "It's very beautiful. I'm going to hang it up in my office."

Ava snatched the paper from her father's hand and displayed it to Rachael. "Mommy, what do you think?"

"It's very pretty honey. I love the colors that you've used." Rachael glanced at Joshua. "I'll have it framed so that daddy can hang it in his office."

"It's interesting," Joshua remarked as Ava sauntered out of the room. "A child of New Eden making a painting of the home solar system—a place we'll never see again. I suppose it's good to know your origins."

Ava was indeed a child of New Eden. She had been the first human conceived on another world. This fact was kept discrete by Joshua and Rachael since they didn't want Ava to receive any unwanted notoriety at such a young age.

"I'm sure you're right," Rachael replied. "I love our new home, and I wouldn't want to leave it, but there are times I miss Earth."

* * *

Later that evening, Joshua, Rachael, Richard, and Ava sat at a large circular table at a bustling Indian restaurant mulling over their menus. There were three empty seats at the table which occupied the corner of the restaurant, the air thick with the smell of masala and the chatter of the patrons.

"Mommy, when are they coming?" Ava asked, squirming impatiently in her chair.

"I'm sure they'll be here soon. We got here a bit early."

"I see them," Joshua remarked as he spotted their three dear friends as they entered the restaurant. The three newcomers exchanged greetings and hugs with those at the table and took seats adjacent to the others. They all congratulated Richard and Ava on their graduations.

The three newcomers were Joshua and Rachael's close friends on Earth, and they had nurtured this friendship on New Eden. They had all been involved in a life-threatening adventure together, and the bonds they shared from that experience had strengthened over the years.

The first newcomer was Vinod Bhakti, a tall, slender Indian man in his late thirties. He was a computer expert and information theorist who had been instrumental in establishing communication with the petrins on Earth many years ago. Rachael and Vinod had been college buddies, and she had known him longer than she had known Joshua.

The second person was Elizabeth "Liz" Yang. Liz, a slender Asian woman, was a physician and exobiologist. She had been busy since coming to New Eden cataloging the new species of flora and fauna that had been introduced on New Eden by the petrins in addition to that which had been transferred there from Earth.

The final person was Theodore "Ted" Johnson. Ted was a large, muscular African American man that had been the commander of a Navy Seal team on Earth. He had continued in the security realm on New Eden and was in command of a local group of elite security forces. The other adults at the table were continualists, but Ted was the exception. He was a hedger since he was ten years younger than he had been on Earth. He was now physically in his late thirties.

"It's so great that the gang's back together," Vinod remarked. "Let's see what kind of trouble we can get into tonight."

"There'll be no trouble," Rachael shot back, knowing Vinod's penchant for overindulgence. "I have to leave at eight AM for Paris for a Global Council meeting."

"What, no trouble?" Ted remarked as he produced a bottle of clear brown liquid from inside his jacket. "Then I shouldn't have brought this."

Vinod's eyes widened. "Is that what I think it is?"

"Yup. My first batch of New Eden bourbon—aged eight years right here on this planet."

"Even across light-years, some things never change," Liz remarked with a smile.

Vinod snapped his fingers to summon the waiter to ask for six empty glasses and a glass of apple juice. Vinod turned to Ava. "The juice is for you. We have to toast your graduation, and you need to participate."

"You should've ordered two juices," Rachael remarked. "I'm not drinking tonight."

"C'mon Rach," Vinod replied. "One shot won't kill you. It's a celebration."

"How many times have I heard that before?"

"Not enough, apparently."

"Fine," Rachael acquiesced. "Just one shot for Richard and Ava's sake."

The waiter retrieved the glasses, and Ted poured a shot into the empty ones. Vinod distributed the glasses around the table and paused before giving a glass to Richard.

"You legal yet Richard?"

"Legal enough," Richard replied with a smile. "I'm the same age as Rach. Remember, we're twins."

"Um . . . not really the same age," Rachael said.

"It's good enough for me," Vinod said as he slid the glass over to Richard. "Josh, do us the honors."

Joshua raised his glass. "To the graduates."

"To the graduates," they all repeated before downing their shots.

"Shit Ted!" Vinod exclaimed after downing his drink. He quickly glanced sideways at Ava. "Ah . . . I mean, shoot Ted. That's some smooth stuff right there."

"Glad you like it Vinod. I'm thinking of starting my own distillery."

"Well, you certainly got a winner with this batch."

The group ordered dinner consisting of samosas, curries, naan, and rice which they ate family style as they got caught up on current events. Joshua, Vinod, Ted, and Liz had polished off the bourbon bottle as they sat contemplating dessert.

"What time's your gig Richard?" Vinod asked.

"Starts at ten. I got to be going soon to get ready. You coming?"

"Absolutely. We're all coming. It's your band's first big gig. Can't miss that."

"Don't speak for me Vinod," Rachael remarked. "You know I have an early trip." Rachael turned to Richard. "You understand, right Richard?"

Richard tried to hide his disappointment at not having his twin sister attend his band's first big concert. "I guess so. It's your decision. Anyhow, I'd better get going," Richard said as he rose from the table. "Got to catch up with the others and get set up. I'll see the rest of you guys there." He walked away from the table.

"Are you kidding me Rach?" Vinod asked after Richard's departure. "You're not going? They're playing the Whisky-a-Go-Go. It's a big event for his band—their first real gig. I heard it's going to be a sellout. You can't miss that."

Rachael shook her head. "If they start at ten, then that means they won't be done until one, which means by the time I go to bed, it will be two, which means . . .."

"Which means that you can sleep in the tube on the way to Paris tomorrow," Joshua interrupted. "It's a big deal for him. You should be there. He looked disappointed when he left."

"What about Ava?" Rachael asked.

"Can I see Uncle Richard's band?" Ava asked excitedly.

"No honey," Joshua replied I'm sure there's an age restriction at the club. "We can drop you off at your grandparents on our way. You can spend the night there."

All eyes turned to Rachael, who sat with her arms crossed. "Fine . . .," she relented. "I'm sure Richard would be happy to see me there."

* * *

The Whisky-a-Go-Go, which was named after the famous club on Earth as many of the establishments in New Eden were prone to be, was standing-room-only as the group entered. Similar to its namesake, it was a club where up-and-coming bands were invited to play. It was a vast, dark establishment with classic rock posters adorning the walls and a bar that occupied one entire side. Patrons ordered drinks and found their spots on the open floor before the band took the stage.

The group entered the club, meandered towards the stage, and got as close as possible to get a good view. Rachael perused the crowd in front of her next to the stage. "This place is packed. Look at that large group of young women right in front of the stage."

"Rach, did you expect anything different?" Vinod asked. "You know that Richard's a pretty handsome guy, right?"

"I'll second that," Liz replied with a giggle. "He's certainly got a lot of fans."

"Fans or groupies?" Rachael asked, glaring at the women.

"What's the difference Rach?" Vinod asked.

"Damn," Ted remarked, scanning the women. "The life of a rock star."

"That's what I'm afraid of," Rachael replied.

The lights dimmed further as the crowd roared. The band entered the stage bathed in spotlights. They were a trio with a female drummer, a male bass guitarist, and Richard, the singer and lead guitarist. The band took their spots, and Richard scanned the audience and noticed Rachael in the crowd. He pointed at her and gave a thumbs-up as the women in the front row looked back in envy to see who he was pointing at. Rachael let out a smile and a wave.

"We're overjoyed that y'all could join us for this evening," Richard spoke into the microphone. "We are the New Classics. Y'all ready for some classic rock from the homeworld?" The crowd roared their approval. "This first song is from another power trio like us. It's called limelight." The crowd roared louder as Richard played the intro cords of "Limelight" by Rush.

"They're really good!" Joshua shouted to Rachael. He turned to Vinod. "Vinod, you should be proud. I know he got his musical influence from you."

"That guitar I got him for his fifteenth birthday was a great investment," Vinod shouted back. "You can thank me later Rach."

The club stayed packed as the New Classics played two, hour-long sets of classic rock with a twenty-minute intermission. As they left the stage after their second set, their performance complete, the crowd started shouting, "Encore! Encore!"

"Man, they love these guys," Ted said. "I bet ya those girls upfront rush the stage."

Rachael looked suspiciously at the group of women that had inched themselves ever closer to the stage throughout the performance. "How old do you think those girls are? They look young, but they're probably all resetters."

"So, what's wrong with that?" Vinod asked.

"It creeps me out thinking that some woman old enough to be my mother is pining after Richard."

"Rach, you worry too much. Let him have his fun."

The band returned to the stage to the delight of the crowd. "Well, I guess we have time for one more song," Richard said into the microphone. "We're going way back with this one. It's called 'So You Want to Be a Rock n Roll Star' by a band called The Byrds."

"Awesome song," Vinod remarked as the band started the song. "I've taught him well."

Chapter Three
A Traverse of New Eden

Rachael awoke early the next morning. She was tired from the late night, but unlike the others, she wasn't hungover as she had curtailed her drinking. She showered, changed, and collected her pre-packed luggage. She glanced at her bed and noted that Joshua was still asleep. She went over to the bed and bent to kiss him on the cheek. "Josh, I'm leaving."

"Okay, have a safe trip," Joshua mumbled, his eyes still closed. "When will you be back?"

"In a few days, I suppose. You never really know for sure how long these Global Council meetings will last."

"Love you."

"Love you too."

Rachael entered the garage and moved towards the control panel, which sensed her presence. "Occupants and destination?" the panel inquired in a female voice with a British accent. It reminded her of the receptionist at the Bowman Particle Research Center all those years ago on the first day she had met Joshua.

"One going to 1930-1239 Paris," Rachael announced.

"Routing . . .," the panel replied.

Rachael wondered how long the tube system would take to present her with a transport capsule. Her destination was a point almost on the other side of the planet from her current location, so it would be a complex routing. The system's intelligence continuously gathered information about the number of occupants and their destinations. From this information, it would determine the most efficient use and routing of capsules in the system. This meant that Rachael could be presented a small capsule that could hold two occupants or one big enough to hold eight. Rachael also wondered if she would have a direct routing to her destination or whether she would have to change capsules mid-trip at some transfer point.

"Direct routing established," the panel stated. "Capsule arriving in twenty-two seconds."

Rachael was both surprised and pleased that she would have a direct route with no need for a capsule change. *The system must not be too busy today.*

The garage floor slid open, and a two-person capsule emerged from the ground and opened its doorway. Rachael placed her belongings into the capsule and took a seat in the left-most of the two empty seats. The door closed, and she heard, "time to destination twelve hours and forty-three minutes," as the capsule descended into the airlock below.

This capsule was different from the ordinary capsules that traversed the city. This one was configured for long-distance travel. In the back of the capsule were a restroom and a food and water pantry that she could utilize during her journey.

The first part of her journey was underground as her capsule navigated the tributaries of the city's tube system into ever more extensive and faster connections. As she neared the outskirts of the city, the capsule elevated above ground as the tube in which it traveled emerged from the ground. Rachael could see in all directions, given the fact that both the walls of the capsule and the walls of the tube were constructed of a rigid, but transparent, material.

Her velocity now increased, but there was no sound at all. She was in complete silence. Since the capsule traveled in a vacuum inside the tube, there was no wind rushing by the capsule. Also, any sounds external to the tube could not penetrate the intervening vacuum since there was no material with which to conduct sounds. Magnetic fields propelled the capsule, and as a result, there were no noisy engines. It seemed strange for Rachael to be moving at such a speed in complete silence.

Even though a trip in the tube system had become routine for humans on New Eden, Rachael still marveled at its design. The tube system was the primary mode of transportation on New Eden. The petrins created it for the transport of both people and goods throughout the planet, but it wasn't actually constructed per se—it was grown. The entire tube system was biological—constructed from living cells. The system was initially created by planting numerous seeds along the path through which the tube would run. From these seeds grew elongated hollow tubes that inched their way through the ground and then increased in diameter, leaving a hollow cavity at the center. The growing tubes would automatically combine and fuse when they contacted the end of another tube from another seed. The result was a completely connected hollow tube system that crisscrossed the planet and could service any location. There had been no need for digging or any other construction method. The tubes had simply grown themselves into the dirt and surrounding rock just as root systems from a tree would do.

As Rachael peered at the world outside, she pondered the material that comprised both her capsule walls and the tube in which it traveled. This polymer, similar to polycarbonate on Earth, had been excreted by living cells and now formed the substrate in which they lived. Rachael had marveled once to Liz how amazing it was that living cells could excrete a polymer. Liz had responded that it didn't surprise her since all plastic polymers were organic in origin. They were based on carbon which forms both the backbone of organic molecules as well as the backbone of long-chain molecules like polymers. Living cells were masters of carbon chemistry. To Liz, producing relatively simple carbon-based polymers seemed much less complex than generating complex carbon-based molecules such as proteins.

"It's very similar to bone," Liz had remarked after studying the organization of the tube and capsule walls under a microscope. "In bone, osteoblasts excrete the solid bony matrix in which they get embedded. This substance is similar, but the cells of the tube excrete a plastic polymer instead of bone matrix."

The walls of the tube and capsule were perfectly transparent but also very stiff, which allowed all the air inside the system to be pumped out, creating a vacuum. This meant that the walls of the tube were under tremendous external pressure while the walls of the capsule were under internal pressure, but the same material could handle both easily.

The vacuum between the tube and capsule allowed the capsules to travel friction-free using magnetic fields for both levitation and thrust. The capsules could achieve speeds in excess of a thousand miles per hour given the lack of friction or sonic booms in the vacuum they traveled in.

The movement of the capsules through the tube system was all controlled by a central neurological brain. Whenever a capsule needed to go to a particular destination, the brain would find the most efficient path along the system and program the capsule to take that path.

Just like any living organism, the tube system was dynamic. It could easily be modified. If a new building or location needed a connection to the existing system, a seed was planted in the building on the ground floor. This would grow into another tube that eventually joined itself to the nearest connection point on the existing network.

The genetic engineering technology of the petrins was absolute. They had, after all, created the cell and its internal machinery. They were masters of the cell and the genetics that underlie its inner workings. They could literally construct any physical entity they chose by simply designing the final product utilizing any of the numerous varieties of physical materials that living cells could produce. This design could then be imprinted into the DNA of a single cell that would divide and grow into the final design.

Yet, the final construction continued to be living, and just like other living entities, was self-repairing. If a tube in the system was damaged or punctured, the tube would automatically repair itself, much like a laceration on the skin of a human would heal. There was no need for any maintenance.

As Rachael stared at the fast-moving landscape at the city's outskirts, she saw numerous buildings in various stages of construction. A plethora of large construction cranes dotted the horizon at the locations new buildings were being erected. The cranes were human constructions, made of steel and not biological in origin. Humans were in the process of transforming New Eden from the original design created by the petrins to one more to their liking. Many of the original biological homes and buildings created by the petrins were being replaced by human constructions. These constructions were being built using techniques that humans employed for building while back on Earth. Humans didn't have the advanced knowledge of genetics and genetic engineering that the petrins employed, and these were deemed off-limits for human use by the petrins. New Eden, even though humanity had been there for almost a decade, was still undergoing the "Transition." The Transition was a period during which control of the planet was transitioning from the petrins to humans.

Rachael reflected on the early days of humanity after it had been relocated to New Eden from Earth. There were numerous decisions that had to be made that mostly revolved around how much influence the petrins would have on human society after they had been relocated. There had been various opinions as to this level of influence. On one end of the spectrum, some humans wanted the petrins to act as complete caretakers with humans living on a planet that the petrins controlled and regulated. These people had absolute trust in the petrins and pointed out that without petrin help, humanity would have become extinct on Earth. On the other side were people who wanted no influence from the petrins whatsoever.

They wanted humanity to be completely independent of the petrins and even advocated for the complete disconnection from them.

In the end, a compromise was reached which would allow for a period during which petrin influence on human society would gradually be diminished until the point when humans were fully self-sufficient. This period was named the Transition, which was still ongoing. But yearly, the technology and influence of the petrins were diminishing.

Even at the end of the Transition, according to agreement, there would still be some petrin technology that would remain on New Eden. Once humanity had experienced them, there were some technologies that they were reticent to relinquish. One such technology was the tube system used for transportation. The system was too convenient and efficient for humans to replace. Why would humanity want to go through the grueling effort of etching roads that required constant maintenance across the landscape just to replace a much more efficient system that the petrins had already created? It simply didn't make sense. In addition to the tube system, there were two other petrin technologies that humans wanted to retain after the Transition.

One of those was something that Rachael's capsule, which now sped along a riverbank, was approaching—an atomic generator. Rachael could see the generator on the horizon as the evening sun glinted off its metallic surface. It was a vast semi-spherical structure a hundred feet high and a kilometer in diameter. Its flat base spanned over the river that Rachael's capsule followed. The generator had numerous transportation tubes both entering and exiting from the sides. These tubes carried the transport capsules that transported the materials created inside.

Rachael leaned her seat back and viewed the structure rapidly advancing towards her. She marveled at the technology that it contained—a technology that was off-limits to the inhabitants of New Eden. The generators were a miniature embodiment of the universe itself. There were forty of these structures dispersed throughout New Eden whose purpose was essentially the same purpose as stars and the universe in general. They were complexity creators.

Each generator, which was built either on top of, or close to, a water source, had the same function—to generate atoms and molecules from the simplest atom—hydrogen. The generators would suck in water from a river, or another nearby water source, and use electrolysis to split the water molecules into its component oxygen and hydrogen gases. Each generator contained a nuclear fusion reactor which would use the hydrogen generated from the electrolysis and fuse it at the nuclear level to form larger elements like helium, oxygen, nitrogen, and others. Any element up to the atomic number of iron could be created via fusion and would release a vast amount of energy in the process. Some of this energy was exported via large underground electrical cables that provided almost limitless electricity to the human population.

The generators could also create elements larger than iron by utilizing some of the energy obtained from the fusion of elements smaller than iron. In essence, the generators could start with water and then create any element in the periodic table with excess energy exported as electricity.

The generators would then use the elements created by the fusion process to export simple raw materials like metals such as iron, steel, aluminum, or titanium. The elements could also further be combined into more complex molecules such as polymers and plastics. Even traditional biological raw materials such as wood and timber were created. The petrins, after all, were masters of genetics. They could grow wood at will given the raw materials needed and the biological cells to transform these materials into cellulose which is the major protein component of wood. Almost all raw materials required by humanity were created by the generators and then transported via the tube system to where they were needed.

The generators, since they contained technology that humans did not possess, were strictly off-limits to humans. Their internal nuclear fusion reactors were massive structures that encompassed most of the volume of the generators. The petrins would have loved to have incorporated the technology of the nuclear fusion spheres that Medusa had incorporated into the arachnid infiltrators back on Earth, but as of yet, the petrins had been unable to reverse engineer the spheres and could not create them on their own.

Since the generators were essential for both energy and raw materials needed for human society, and they provided both without polluting or destroying the ecosystem, the generators were also determined by humanity to be preserved after the Transition.

As Rachael's capsule sped by the hulking silver dome of the generator, she marveled at its power and technology. The petrins had always believed that the cosmos was created to be a complexity-generating machine. It was destined over time to create ever-increasing pockets of complexity which, for them, translated to creating ever more complex life. The petrins had learned the process by which the universe creates complexity and controlled and codified this process into these generators. They had absolute control of two of the four fundamental forces of nature—the strong nuclear force and the electromagnetic force—and used this control to create energy and raw materials from simple hydrogen.

The generator retreated to the edge of the horizon behind Rachael as her capsule sped forward. Rachael's thoughts turned to the final petrin technology that would survive the transition—the health pods. The petrins, due to their absolute understanding of biology, could cure any disease. Therefore, they oversaw healthcare for humans. This was accomplished by numerous health pods located throughout New Eden. Each pod was a self-contained healthcare apparatus. It was a room-sized biological structure that a human could enter. Once inside, they would be scanned by the device, and a diagnosis of any health irregularities was determined. Then the treatment would be rendered by the pod. For some ailments such as cancer or diabetes that operate at the cellular level, the cure would be in the form of an intravenous injection. For others, such as physical injuries like fractures, anesthesia was given to the patient and the fractures mended by a physical process.

Diseases had been eliminated in the human population. Diseases such as cancer, diabetes, infections, and numerous others that had afflicted human society on Earth were no longer present. This was a gift that humanity simply could not give up after the Transition. They could not bear the thought of the suffering caused by these afflictions returning, so it was decided that the health pods would remain after the Transition.

The three petrin technologies that would survive the Transition: the tube system, the atomic generators, and the health pods, due to their self-repairing nature, would last for millennia with no need for petrin intervention, and would therefore survive even a complete disconnection of the petrins from humanity.

Rachael's capsule now entered a tunnel under a mountain range, and her thoughts turned to the upcoming Global Council meeting she was en route to. The Global Council was the top governing board for New Eden. New Eden was divided among numerous local regions determined mainly along cultural and linguistic lines. The city she was traveling to, Paris, was in the French region. Each local region had its own governing body, but the Global Council was tasked with governance of New Eden as a whole. There were thirteen members of the Global Council, all elected by the general population of the planet. It came as no surprise to anyone that Rachael had been elected to the council. She had, after all, been instrumental in convincing the human population of Earth to relocate to New Eden. Her videos describing New Eden to the populations of Earth before the Relocation had been viewed worldwide, making her one of the most famous and recognizable people on the planet.

Many had persuaded Rachael to run for a Global Council seat once the council had been established, and she easily won. One of her other acquaintances from Earth had also been elected to the council—Dina Williams. Rachael was overjoyed to learn that Dina would be on the council with her. In fact, when the time came for the council to elect the chief council person who would act as council leader, Rachael had advocated for Dina, which allowed her to win.

Central to this next council meeting was the topic of healthcare. There was one human health condition that the petrins did not treat—aging. Even though all human diseases had been eliminated, humans still aged on New Eden. Life expectancy had grown dramatically into the late nineties, but humans still died of the aging process. But humans knew that the petrins had the ability to stop even this cause of death. The concept of having the petrins stop aging for those humans who requested it had been a contentious one when the initial agreements for the Transition had been drafted. It was so contentious in fact that it had to be tabled to be discussed at a later date in order to move the Transition process forward. That later date had come. The issue of whether humanity would allow individual humans to not age was the main topic of discussion for the upcoming council meeting, during which a final vote on the topic would be enacted.

Rachael was not looking forward to this meeting. There were strong emotional arguments on both sides of the issue, and there would be no happy compromise. Could individuals, who so chose, be allowed to live forever? Could society ban individuals from living forever if they had the ability to do so? Is this decision an individual decision or a societal decision?

Rachael had hoped not to have to make this decision. She had hoped that Seth and the petrins would not allow for human immortality and hence leave the decision out of the hands of the council, but this had not happened. The petrins had left this decision, as they had with most decisions, to the humans. Seth had promised human control of New Eden and was trying his best to hold to that promise.

Rachael smiled as she realized she would soon see Seth, her close friend, again. He was always present at council meetings as a non-voting representative of petrin interests. Even on New Eden, Seth was the petrin ambassador. Even though he was a non-voting member, his opinions and advice were highly regarded, and he had much sway on council decisions.

Rachael's capsule exited the tunnel, and she noted that the sun had just set on the horizon behind her. Rachael glanced at the screen at the front of the capsule. The lettering read, "Time to destination: 6 hours and 9 minutes. Velocity: 1633 kph." The sun had set much sooner than her body clock was accustomed to. She had been traveling almost due east, so the day had been shortened. It was not her normal time for sleep, but she was still tired from the late night the day before.

Her capsule was fast approaching the shoreline, and she knew the next few hours of her journey would be under the ocean. The tube system operated more efficiently underground rather than through water. In water, it would be jostled by waves and ocean currents which would mean that capsules would have to lower their velocity. For this reason, all ocean crossings of the tube system traversed under the ocean floor which meant for Rachael it would be a good time to get some sleep since there would be nothing outside to see. She leaned her chair back to a fully-reclined, flat position and curled up on the seat. The interior became darker as her capsule dipped underground and into the ocean floor, and Rachael soon fell asleep.

She awoke a few hours later as sunlight streamed through her capsule. She raised her seat back into a reclined position to look at the surrounding landscape. It was a savannah much like the African savannahs of Earth. She could see congregations of elephants, zebras, wildebeests, and giraffes that grazed along the flat plains interspersed by acacia trees. This landscape was familiar to her. She had spent a night near this location on her second trip to New Eden. This also meant that she was near the location that she and Joshua had inhabited on their first trip to New Eden. In fact, up in the distance, she could see the snowcapped mountain, recently named Mount Endeavor, where they had spent the night, warm in their arachnid cocoon where Ava was conceived.

Rachael reflected fondly on both her first and second trips to New Eden where she had explored this land. Unlike other areas of New Eden, this area had largely been unchanged since those visits. There were no cities or permanent human habitats in this region. This region was now a part of New Eden known as the Natural Continent.

The Natural Continent stretched from pole to pole which meant that it encompassed all the climate zones including arctic tundra, deciduous woodlands, arid savannahs, and tropical rainforests. At the insistence of the petrins, the Natural Continent was initially off-limits to humans. It was a natural preserve that would allow the flora and fauna from Earth to evolve and grow without human intervention. The petrins had been keenly aware of the environmental destruction and extinction that humans had caused on Earth and wanted to insulate this area from such devastation.

The Natural Continent encompassed fully one-third of the landmass of New Eden, but recently was no longer devoid of all humans. There was a small group of humanity, after they transitioned to New Eden, who decided that they wanted to be rid of all modern technology and shunned it. They had argued that humans had been on Earth for two hundred and fifty thousand years, and for ninety-five percent of that time, they lived as nomadic hunters and gathers. In their minds, this was the most natural habitat for humanity—the type of existence that human genetics itself had evolved for. They argued that true happiness for humanity would be in this type of habitat without the stresses pervasive to modern society. They had demanded a small portion of New Eden to re-establish this ancient lifestyle.

Since the number of humans requesting this had been small, and the environmental impact of such existence would also be small, the petrins, with approval from the Global Council, allowed for a small number of humans to live in the Natural Continent so long as they used only rudimentary technology like spears and stone tools. Occasionally someone living this existence would want to leave for the more technologically advanced areas of New Eden and vice versa. This was allowed on an individual basis.

Rachael herself had contemplated trying to convince Joshua to move to the Natural Continent. She remembered fondly the time that she and Joshua had spent here. But she also recognized that those trips were aided by the petrin technologies of living habitats, food orchards, and their arachnid transports which were no longer present. Besides, Joshua wouldn't be able to pursue his love of science and physics, so she decided against it. Still, she had a smile on her face as she absorbed the beauty of the natural world that surrounded her.

As her capsule moved to the opposite coast of the Natural Continent, Rachael knew she would have another under-ocean crossing before reaching Paris. Unlike its namesake city on Earth, Paris was oceanside on New Eden. This underwater crossing would only take an hour and a half, so she took out some papers from her briefcase that described the background on the topics to be discussed at the Global Council meeting and began reviewing them.

Ninety minutes later, Rachael's capsule exited the ocean at the beaches of Paris. Like her home area, this area was also filled with construction cranes erecting new buildings. She passed along cobblestone streets lined with houses of French provincial architecture that would have fit right in along the suburbs of Paris back on Earth.

As her capsule got closer to the city center and her tube stop, it dove beneath the ground and navigated the Paris tube system. Rachael grew excited. It was now morning in Paris, and she had scheduled a coffee meeting with a close friend prior to the Global Council meeting. It had been quite some time since she had seen him, but an encounter with Seth was always exciting . . . and eventful.

Chapter Four
The Immortal Choice

Rachael wore oversized sunglasses and a baseball cap as she strode the cobblestone streets of Paris. The glasses and cap were an effort to shield her identity since she was easily recognizable on New Eden. Even if she was recognized, most people simply smiled at her and did not engage, which was a relief to Rachael, but today she was trying to be inconspicuous.

As she turned a corner and saw the entrance of her destination, a coffee shop named Fringe Coffee, she saw Seth. He was standing adjacent to the entrance also adorned in sunglasses and a baseball cap. They both smiled at each other before embracing. Seth was a handsome African American male of average height. Gone was his robotic, android body. He was now fully flesh and blood like any human. However, he was not fully human—he didn't have a brain. Instead, he had a spookyon connected to a neural nest in his head which allowed him to remotely control his body on New Eden from his original location on Petri.

"'sup Rach?" Seth asked with a grin after their embrace.

"'sup Seth?"

The two entered the coffee shop and ordered some pastries and coffee and took a seat at a table in a quiet corner of the shop. After they were seated, Rachael looked more closely at Seth's appearance. "Looks like you've got a few grey hairs poking out at your temples."

"Yup. This body is human and ages just like all humans do."

"Do you miss your android body?"

"Not really. Although my android body is stronger in some respects, it's not self-reparative like this one. Besides," Seth said as he took a bite of his croissant, "in my android body, I can't enjoy the act of eating like I can with this one. I can see why humans derive so much pleasure from it."

It still seemed strange for Rachael to see Seth eating. His android body on Earth was incapable of this, and the act seemed out of place for Seth. "What're your favorite foods?"

"I like everything really," Seth replied. "Although I've decided to follow Joshua's tract and be a vegetarian. If I'd have to pick, I'd say my favorite would be pizza."

"Pizza?" Rachael said with a chuckle. "We'll make a human out of you yet Seth." Rachael took a sip of her espresso.

"Actually, I've been spending more time in my android body back on Earth recently," Seth said.

"Why? Is there some news from Earth?"

Seth paused before responding. "Yes."

Rachael was taken aback by the short response. There hadn't really been any changes on Earth in a few years. The war between Medusa and the petrins was still ongoing, but Medusa had been slowly gaining the upper hand, and less and less territory was controlled by the petrins.

There were no humans left on Earth. Seth had informed the council with deep sadness a few years ago that all the humans, over three hundred million that had decided not to relocate to New Eden, had been killed. Medusa had determined that the only indigenous species on Earth that presented a threat were humans. After scanning human DNA to determine human biology, she had released a toxin into the atmosphere that specifically targeted human DNA. As a result, the remaining humans on Earth had been eliminated. Humanity on New Eden was devastated to learn that no more humans occupied their home world but were grateful for the petrins for providing New Eden as a haven for them.

Since the eradication of humanity from Earth, there had been no significant news from Earth as Medusa gradually occupied more territory. Everyone knew that Medusa would eventually prevail. There was nothing more that could be done. The main reason for the petrins to continue their battle was to give them more time to study the fusion spheres located on Earth.

The spheres were discovered inside an arachnid that humans had managed to kill. They had essentially the same function as the atomic generators on New Eden, but on a much smaller scale. Each sphere could accomplish nuclear fusion and generate energy and larger elements from hydrogen. Even though the petrins could accomplish this using their enormous fusion reactors like those in the atomic generators, they had no idea how to replicate this technology in a sphere the size of a golf ball. They had been working tirelessly on Earth to try to reverse engineer the spheres, but as of yet, had not succeeded. With the invention of the fusion spheres, Medusa had tipped the balance of power in the universal battle between Medusa and the petrins in her favor. The petrins were keenly aware that reverse-engineering the spheres would be paramount in restoring the balance as evidenced by their tireless work mostly happening deep underground in the Bat Cave at the Bowman Particle Research Center back on Earth.

"Is it good news or bad news?" Rachael asked excitedly.

"A little of both, I guess," Seth replied as he took another bite of his croissant.

Rachael waited for more of an explanation, but none was forthcoming. "Are you going to keep me in suspense? Is the information redacted?"

"No. Not redacted. But I'm not quite ready to reveal it."

Rachael glanced sideways at Seth. "Somehow, I don't believe that you're telling me that there's news from Earth just for friendly reasons. There must be some ulterior motives involved."

"Very observant of you."

"You know I was a reporter in my past life. Spill it."

Seth sat back in his chair and laced his hands in front of him. "Because of some happenings on Earth, which I'm still not going to disclose until after the council meeting to only you and Ms. Williams, the petrins require the help of a group of humans. I'd like you to ask Ms. Williams for some private time for me with the two of you after the meeting."

"Private? I see," Rachael said. "Obviously, there's something you want to keep secret from all humans, however, you need our help in some way."

"Obviously."

Rachael now also sat back in her chair. "Okay, I'll arrange for some time with Dina after the meeting, but you've piqued my curiosity. It's exciting."

"About to get to get a lot more exciting," Seth responded with a curious gleam in his eyes.

* * *

"I'm officially calling the sixty-seventh meeting of the Global Council to order," Dina Williams said into a microphone in front of her as she banged a gavel on a table. In her late fifties, Williams was an elderly African American woman who served as the Council Chair. She had been White House Chief of Staff back on Earth and had reprised her leadership role on New Eden.

The twelve other council members were seated on one side of a large, curved table on either side of Williams on a stage in the council meeting room. All local regions of New Eden were represented on the council. There was even a member who represented the population of humans that resided in the Natural Continent. Rachael sat immediately to Williams' right. The council members faced a packed auditorium with people and reporters observing the meeting. Seth also sat at the council table in the right-most seat.

"The first order of business is to hear final arguments from both sides as to the resolution presented before the council on whether or not individual humans should have the decision to not age, and in essence, becoming immortal. This service, if approved, would obviously be provided by the petrins. I'd like to begin by asking Seth if there has been any change in the petrin decision to provide this service if approved."

Seth leaned forward to his microphone. "There has been no change Ms. Williams. If humanity approves this decision, the petrins would be willing to provide it."

"Okay then," Williams said. "We will hear final arguments from both sides, after which time, the council will render a final vote on the matter."

The room was tense. This would be a decision that would have enormous ramifications for humanity and their existence on New Eden. Since the council meeting was being televised world-wide, a large portion of humanity watched the proceedings live.

"Mr. Kahn," Williams continued. "I believe you are first. You have the floor."

A young man in his early twenties of Pakistani descent stood up and walked to a microphone placed on the floor in front of the council. He was the attorney for the coalition of people who had presented the resolution to the council to allow humans to make their own decisions about ending aging. Rachael had seen him before in numerous videos and press conferences advocating for his clients. She had heard him speak eloquently and with passion for his cause. The fact that he seemed so knowledgeable and experienced with public speaking at what appeared to be such an early age gave away the fact that he had been a resetter. It was no surprise to Rachael that a resetter would be the one to argue for anti-aging.

Kahn spoke for over thirty minutes laying out the arguments to allow those humans who so choose to prevent their aging. His arguments equated aging with being a disease. He pointed out that just like any disease, aging was ultimately fatal and should be cured if possible.

"What if we were back on Earth?" Kahn stated as he began his closing statements. He paused for a few dramatic moments before continuing, "What if we were back on Earth and some scientist had found the cure for cancer? Would this council deny that cure for those who desperately needed it? Would it even be controversial?" he asked rhetorically. "Of course not," he stated emphatically. "If you deny this resolution, for me and many others . . . in fact for all humanity which is afflicted by the disease of aging, it would be akin to signing their death warrants."

It was a bold statement. One that was not lost on the councilmembers. Kahn went back to his seat as a round of applause erupted from the audience, although not all members were clapping.

Rachael squirmed in her seat as the gravity of the upcoming vote enveloped her. Would she be condemning those who didn't want to die to an eventual death? She wished even more that the petrins hadn't left this decision to the humans.

"Thank you, Mr. Kahn," Williams said without emotion. "Ms. Kim, your floor."

A graying woman of Korean descent approached the microphone from the audience. She spoke with a soft, but confident, voice about the perils of allowing portions of humanity to be immortal. She pointed out the upheaval already apparent in society by the petrin decision to allow humans to determine their own age when they were transported to New Eden. She stated that a decision to allow for aging to stop would cause much more upheaval than that decision.

"Mr. Kahn stated that he didn't believe that all of society could determine what he felt was a truly individual decision," she said as she began her closing statements. "This is simply not the case. This is not an individual decision that affects only the individual that makes it. A decision to allow certain individuals not to age does not only affect *that* individual, but *all* individuals . . . even those that choose to continue aging. The societal changes would be vast and everlasting. Therefore, we feel that this is not an individual decision, but a decision that should be made by society."

Kim paused and scanned the faces of the councilmembers staring back at her. "We are all the products of an evolutionary process—a process which requires death in order for the next generation to be slightly more advanced and better than the preceding generation. If we allow for the ending of aging, we will stagnate as a species. We will go against the exact process that has allowed for our own existence. For these reasons, I implore the council to disallow this resolution." Kim scanned the faces of the councilmembers in front of her.

Rachael glanced at Seth who was fixed on Kim. He had an expression on his face that Rachael had not seen before—an intense stare of understanding. Kim had obviously struck a chord with Seth although

Rachael didn't understand why.

"I thank you for your time," Kim said before sitting back down to another round of applause.

"I want to thank you both for your impassioned arguments," Williams began. "We have been skirting this issue for quite some time, but I believe the time has come for a decision on this matter. But before I call a vote on this resolution, I'd like one more opinion to be heard." Williams turned to Seth. "Seth, I know that you've told us that the petrins are willing to provide this service if we so choose, but I would like to hear from you whether you and the petrins, knowing what you have gleaned from interacting with humans over the years, think this would be a wise decision. What is *your* opinion?"

All eyes turned to Seth as he adjusted his seat and moved closer to the microphone. He took a few moments to collect his thoughts and those of the collective before he spoke. "The arguments that Mr. Kahn and Ms. Kim have laid out are both valid. I have enjoyed and continue to enjoy my time with humans. Our goal has always been the preservation of the human race. As you know, unlike Medusa, we believe that the universe is destined for complexity, and part of that complexity is humanity. The collective doesn't have a firm opinion on this issue. There are risks and benefits to each side of the equation. However, the collective has allowed me to give my personal opinion due to the fact that I'm the petrin who has had the most interaction with humanity."

The statement moved Rachael. She had known that Seth was part of a collective, and that his actions were always in accordance with the collective. The degree to which each individual in the collective had autonomy to make their own decisions was unknown to Rachael. The fact that the collective was allowing Seth to present his personal opinion on the subject revealed the trust that they had in him on matters related to humanity.

Seth continued his statement. "I personally believe that at its current stage of development, the stopping of aging would be too destabilizing to humanity. I personally am against it."

Seth was abruptly interrupted by Mr. Kahn who shouted out from his seat, "I find it entirely ironic that an immortal individual is advocating mortality for other individuals!" The room erupted in indistinct chatter at the statement.

Williams banged her gavel hard on the table. "Enough!" she shouted. "We will have order in this meeting!" She turned to Kahn. "Mr. Kahn, you will *not* speak out of order, or I will have you removed." The room fell silent at the raised voice of the usually unflappable and stoic Dina Williams.

Williams turned back to Seth. "Seth, Mr. Kahn spoke out of turn, but does raise a salient point. You yourself, as well as the other petrins, are immortal. It does seem somewhat antithetical that a member of petrin society, a society that has chosen immortality for itself, seems reticent to recommend it for another society."

"There's no such thing as immortality," Seth said, his voice measured. "The fact that we don't age doesn't mean that we want to, or will, live forever. We believe that the universe was meant to evolve with each successive generation more complex and improved from the last. We know that we ourselves, in some way, are an impediment to this vision. There are disadvantages to living forever that we have realized. However, we have specific reasons for our existence in our current state which has led to the decisions we have made."

"I understand," Williams stated after Seth stopped speaking. "Can I ask for those reasons?"

"You can ask Ms. Williams, but unfortunately, those reasons are redacted. I, however, want to make it clear that even though this is my opinion, I will abide by the vote of the council."

Redacted . . . a word that Rachael had heard many times in the past from Seth. She and Williams knew that it would be fruitless to press Seth on the issue since no more information would be forthcoming.

Williams turned back to the audience. "I believe the time has come to take a vote on the resolution." The tension in the room escalated as everyone knew the vote was imminent—a vote that had the possibility of changing human society permanently. "I would like a show of hands of those council members who are in favor of approving this resolution. I want to remind everyone that a yes vote would mean that we allow individuals to stop aging with petrin help. Please raise your hand if you are in favor of this resolution."

A total of five council members raised their hands. "Five," Williams stated. "Now, I want a show of hands of those opposed to this resolution."

Eight hands rose, including those of Rachael and Williams. "The issue has been resolved," Williams stated. "Let it be recorded that by a vote of five to eight of the Global Council, the resolution is *not* adopted." Williams banged her gavel as some in the room rose in applause.

Chapter Five
News from Earth

For the remainder of that day and the next, the council discussed less pressing matters of global need. Near the end of the third day, Williams announced. "I believe we have exhausted our docket for this meeting. Anything else that anyone has to bring up before we adjourn?"

No one had anything else to offer.

Williams banged her gavel and announced, "I'm officially declaring the sixty-seventh meeting of the Global Council adjourned."

The people in the room started filing out as Seth, Rachael, and Williams remained in their seats. They waited for the others to leave before Williams said, "Let's move to my office. We'll have more privacy there."

Williams' office was located in the same building. She was the administrative chair of the council and had other duties for the council outside of leading the council meetings.

The trio walked into an office on the fourth floor with a large window that afforded a view of the Paris skyline. Williams took a seat behind a large wooden desk as Seth and Rachael sat in two cushioned armchairs in front.

"Okay Seth," William said turning to Seth. "What do you have to tell us? Rachael has informed me that you wanted a private meeting with the two of us. What's happened on Earth?"

"I have a few things to report to you, and I also have a request of you," Seth said. "I'm happy to report that six months ago the petrins were successfully able to decipher the technology that Medusa was using to create the fusion spheres. We are now able to create them for ourselves. The petrins wanted me to personally thank humanity for their help in this process."

The two women listened intently to Seth. The news that the petrins had been able to decipher the spheres and their technology was welcome news to both. A similar thought simultaneously crossed their minds that Rachael voiced. "That's great news Seth. Does that mean that the tide of the war on Earth will turn in the petrins' favor?"

"Yes, it's great news," Seth agreed. The elation of the women at the news was, however, short-lived. "But unfortunately, it only evens the playing field on Earth. We feel that we have lost too much territory on Earth for this discovery to make a long-term difference. The result of the war on Earth is still inevitable. Granted, we may have pushed back the date, but we still feel that eventually Medusa will still have domain over Earth."

There was silence in the room for a few moments until Williams asked, "Is this the only news?"

"No," Seth said, shifting in his seat. "About nine months ago, Medusa launched an object into space from an area near Singapore. It was a space probe of some type."

"A space probe?" Rachael asked, surprised. "What do you mean? What exactly was it?"

"We're not sure exactly what it was," Seth responded. "It was some type of spacecraft, though, that blasted off from Earth and traveled along the planetary plane of the Earth solar system."

"Do you know its purpose or where it was headed?" Williams asked.

"We don't know its purpose, but we do know its destination. The probe was headed for Planet Nine."

"Planet Nine?" Rachael asked. "Are you sure?"

"Yes," Seth replied. "I'm quite sure."

Williams was confused. "You two want to explain to me what Planet Nine is?"

"Yes," Rachael said. "I've heard Joshua talk about it many times in the past. Planet Nine is a theoretical ninth planet in the Earth solar system outside the orbit of Neptune, the outermost known planet. It was proposed to exist by two Caltech astronomers in 2015 according to some computer modeling they performed on the gravitational movement of the known planets. Their modeling predicted that there should be a ninth planet, a gas giant with a highly elliptical orbit, that they theorized to exist due to its gravitational effect, but which was never actually discovered. Although astronomers tried at the time, the extreme distance to this hypothetical planet was so large that the planet was never observed, so their theoretical findings were never verified." Rachael turned to Seth. "Seth, are you are telling me that Planet Nine actually exists?"

"Yes," Seth replied. "It exists, and we've known this fact for some time.

We've known about its existence since well before humanity was evacuated from Earth, but this knowledge was of no real significance. It's a gas giant similar in size to Neptune, but at such a considerable distance from the sun that it has almost no influence on Earth or the inner solar system. We felt it to be irrelevant. But when we analyzed the trajectory of the probe sent by Medusa, there was no question that it was headed for Planet Nine.

"Three months after the probe's launch, which was six months ago now, a new light source appeared in the Earth solar system. It was a new star, or more precisely, a quasi-star, exactly at the location of Planet Nine."

The two women took some time for Seth's last statement to sink in. Rachael wished that Joshua was with her. He was the physicist and could better discern the implications of what Seth was revealing. "Seth, are you telling us that there are now two suns in the solar system?" Rachael asked. "Has Medusa turned Planet Nine into a star?"

"Not exactly," Seth replied. "The light source is definitely the result of a nuclear fusion source, but there's not enough mass in Planet Nine to allow it to become a star. There's a minimal amount of mass needed to allow gravity to generate enough heat and pressure at the core of a star in order for nuclear fusion to start. Planet Nine doesn't have enough mass to start this process. However, we do know that the light emanating from Planet Nine's location is fusion-related. The light emitted definitely has the spectral signature of nuclear fusion."

"What is its purpose?" Williams asked. "What's Medusa doing?"

"As I have said before. We have no idea what its purpose is, or how a nuclear fusion light source is now located at Planet Nine, but we do have reason to believe that Medusa is conducting some type of clandestine experiment there."

"An experiment?" Rachael asked. "What makes you think it's an experiment?"

"That's what we believe given the information we have available," Seth replied. "I need to explain to you our reasons for this belief." Seth took a moment to collect his thoughts before continuing. "You're both familiar with the concept of spookyons. They're entangled particles created during the Big Bang which allow for instantaneous data transfer between any two points in the universe. What you don't know is that the mechanism that allows for the data transfer between spookyons can be locally blocked. It involves physics that humans are not yet privy to, but the petrins and Medusa have known about it for ages. It's possible to create a dampening generator that can block spookyon transmission for a distance from the generator. This generator requires vast amounts of energy to operate. As far as we know, this amount of energy can only be generated by a process that releases an enormous amount of energy such as nuclear fusion. The more energy that can be utilized by the dampening generator, the larger the volume of space that can be blocked from spookyon transmission. After we noticed the new light source at Planet Nine, we also noticed a spookyon dampening field surrounding this light source with a spherical radius of approximately two billion kilometers."

"You say you can create a dampening field that can block spookyon transmission?" Williams asked.

"Yes."

"Why didn't you use this technology on Earth before Medusa established contact there? It seems to me that if we had such a dampening field in place, humanity might not have needed to be evacuated."

"The dampening field is not possible on Earth," Seth replied. "As I said, the physics is complex. The dampening field can't operate in a powerful magnetic field like Earth has."

"I see," Williams said, her arms laced in front of her. "So then, what do you believe is the purpose of the dampening field that Medusa has placed around Planet Nine?"

"It's a barricade," Seth replied. "All petrin technology is spookyon based. Medusa has put up a barricade in the form of this spookyon dampening field to keep secret and protect whatever she's developing at Planet Nine. With this dampening field, we wouldn't be able to send a probe or other such object to affect or even observe what she's doing there. Because of the field, we can't remotely control or get any data into or out of the volume encompassing the sphere represented by the field. The dampening field is a barricade for petrin technology."

"Quite a conundrum," Williams stated after what Seth had said sunk in. "You obviously want to find out what Medusa's doing at Planet Nine but can't because any probe you send to that region couldn't be controlled or even be able to send back any data."

"It's not that a probe couldn't send back data at all," Seth explained. "The dampening field affects only spookyon transmission via entanglement. Radio transmissions are still possible. However, at the distance that Planet Nine is from Earth, the closest petrin location, radio transmissions would take approximately ten hours for just a one-way signal which would mean a round-trip time of over twenty hours. Since we have no idea what's at Planet Nine, there would be no way for us to program an automated probe to send there."

Seth shifted in his seat and took a deep breath. "We've analyzed this situation since we've had months to work on this problem. We definitely need to find out what Medusa's doing at Planet Nine and have determined that the best way to do this is to send a manned spacecraft there."

"Manned?" Rachael asked. "Manned by whom?"

"Manned by humans," Seth replied calmly.

"Humans?" Williams asked. "What humans? You've told us that there are no humans left on Earth."

"That's true," Seth said. "Let me explain our plan in more detail. For the past six months we've been constructing . . . well, I believe *growing* would be a more appropriate word. We've been growing a spacecraft on Earth. This spacecraft is designed to carry humans from the Earth to Planet Nine to try to figure out what's going on there. We would like to transport a team of humans from New Eden back to Earth to be the crew of this spacecraft. This transport would involve the same process by which humans were transported to New Eden from Earth in the first place. We would grow a clone of each crew member on Earth and then transfer their neural information from New Eden to their clone. Once the human crew was transported to Earth, they could go on a reconnaissance mission to Planet Nine."

The room was silent as the women ingested the new information. "What would happen to the humans who were part of the crew on New Eden while they were on this mission?" Rachael asked.

"As you know, our petrin moral rules do not allow for multiple copies of any sentient entity to be living at the same time. Their bodies on Earth would be randomized. At the end of the mission, new clones of them would be grown on New Eden, and their neural information from the clones on Earth would be transferred back to these new clones."

"Randomized?" Williams asked. She was keenly aware that petrins considered randomization the anthesis to life. For petrins, randomization was the definition of death. "As in destroyed? Why destroy their bodies on New Eden? Why not just simply freeze them?"

"You haven't figured this out yet, but a frozen body can't directly be brought back to life. As you know, when water freezes into ice, it expands. This expansion in a human body, which is two-thirds water, causes the cells in the body to rupture. This damage can't be repaired." Seth turned to Rachael. "When we recreated both you and your brother on New Eden, we did this with a new clone grown for each of you. We simply took the information from your frozen bodies on Earth and then transferred this information to the new clones. There's no utility to freezing the bodies of those humans who would be the crew for our spaceship. To preserve the humans who would go on this mission, we would simply store their information as data and not retain their bodies."

"Buy why humans Seth?" Williams asked. "Why not send petrins or some other intelligent species?"

"For a few reasons," Seth answered. "Petrins in their natural form are not mobile. I remember on my first visit to Earth, your biologists thought us more like plants than animals. Our mobility is entirely dependent on our ability to remotely control the arachnids on Petri that act as our transports. We couldn't do this on a mission that involves a spookyon-dampening field. Besides, we operate as a collective based on spookyon transmission. Our collective would be completely inoperable in a spookyon-dampening field.

"As far as using other intelligent species is concerned, this was considered, but the spaceship we're growing had to be grown on Earth. This meant we had to adapt this ship to Earth's unique properties such as its atmosphere and gravity. It only made sense to us that humans would occupy a ship grown on Earth for these reasons. Besides, we feel that humans are very well suited for this mission. I know that you're not privy to other intelligent species that were the result of our initial cell seeding process, but humans are one of the most creative of these species. This is a mission that has many unknowns. We feel that the creativeness and problem-solving ability of humans would suit this mission well."

"How many humans would you need?" Williams asked.

"Thirty."

"Thirty?" Rachael asked, surprised. "How big is this spaceship?"

"Big enough."

"Will the mission be dangerous?" Williams asked.

"Quite possibly," Seth answered. "We are dealing with the unknown here. We can't make an accurate risk assessment when we have almost no idea of what we'll encounter. However, we can mitigate that risk. Since each human on the crew will need to be scanned for them to be transported to Earth, we will keep a backup copy of that information on one of our petrin nodes. If something unforeseen befalls any crew member, they can still be recreated on New Eden given the backup information. So, there's no real long-term risk."

"How long a mission will this be?" Rachael asked.

"I don't know for sure," Seth replied. "It depends on what we find at Planet Nine. Our spaceship would take a little less than a month to reach Planet Nine from Earth."

"A month?" Rachael was shocked at the time. She knew that a voyage of that distance would have taken years at typical Earth spacecraft speeds. In fact, Voyager One, the farthest man-made object from Earth, had taken almost twenty years to cover that distance. "How fast is your spaceship?"

"Fast," Seth replied. "The round-trip time back to Earth would encompass two months if we accounted only for travel time. Obviously, we would need to add some time to learn what Medusa is doing at Planet Nine. A reasonable estimate for this mission would be about six months, but it could be less than this if we don't need to spend four months at Planet Nine."

"A six-month mission then?" Rachael said.

"That's my best estimate."

"What are the requirements for this crew?" Williams asked.

"We have studied the mission that humans sent to deal with the first infiltrator in Korea on Earth. We were fascinated by how this team was able to kill an infiltrator. To be honest, this was almost an impossible task given the situation and materials at their disposal. Their methods were both creative and ingenious. When we studied this mission, we realized that *that* team had all the components we are looking for on *this* mission. It's another discovery mission into the unknown. For this reason, we would like the team members on that mission to also be on this mission if they so choose."

Seth and Williams turned to Rachael who was in shock. She couldn't believe what she was hearing. "Seth, you want *me* to go on this mission? You want *me* to go to Planet Nine on a spaceship?"

"Yes," Seth replied with a grin. "You and the others. If you're willing, of course. I'd also like your bother Richard to go."

"Richard?" Rachael asked, still in shock. "But why him? He's only twenty and hasn't even been to college yet."

"I have my reasons."

"Which are?"

"Which are redacted."

"Well Mrs. Andrews," Williams stated after a few moments. "It looks like you and your friends have a chance to go on another adventure."

"Except this time, I'll be going with you," Seth said, still smiling.

Chapter Six
The Crew

"Are you kidding me?" Joshua shouted excitedly as he and Rachael were seated at the dining table in their home. His voice echoed through the house. Rachael had waited to tell Joshua about the mission until she was back with him. She wanted to be face-to-face with Joshua to discuss the topic.

"No," Rachael said quietly. "Not kidding."

"A mission on a petrin spaceship to Planet Nine?"

"Yup. So, you want to go?"

"Hell yes, I want to go!" Joshua shouted as he jumped up from his seat and did a little dance. "It's the adventure of a lifetime. Not that we haven't had a couple of those already, but this is next level." Joshua sat back down on his chair as he sensed Rachael's lack of enthusiasm. "Why? Don't you want to go?"

"I'm conflicted Josh," Rachael said, head down. "Obviously, it'd be a great adventure, but we're older now. We have responsibilities here." Rachael looked back at Joshua. "I'm a member of the Global Council, and aren't you forgetting about Ava? How will she manage with the two of us gone?"

"She'll be fine Rachael," Joshua said dismissively waving his hand in the air. "I'm sure she'd be happy staying with your parents for a few months. Sure, she'd get a little bit spoiled, but no long-term harm. As far as the council is concerned, they can manage for a few months without you. Besides, Seth said that this is probably a six-month mission. That's his best guess. It could be much less for all we know."

Rachael was not convinced. She felt that Joshua's desire to go on a once-in-a-lifetime adventure was clouding his judgment. "The mission could also be longer Josh. Seth said so himself. There are many unknowns. I couldn't forgive myself if Ava was without either of her parents for an extended period of time." Rachael sat quietly for a few moments. "How about if you go, and I stay?"

"Absolutely not," Joshua shot back. "We're a team. We're all a team. I'm not going on this mission if you're not there. It would be meaningless to me."

This was the reaction that Rachael was afraid of. Joshua had, in effect, left the decision up to her. She had worried that this would be the scenario she would be left with, but she hoped that Joshua would agree to go without her. Her thoughts reflected on the time when she and Joshua had first met. She was a different person then. The younger Rachael would have leapt at this chance, but with age comes wisdom and responsibility. She was definitely not as impulsive as she had been in her younger age.

Rachael looked up at Joshua who stared at her waiting for a response. She remembered that day when she and Joshua had first tested the Bowman sphere in the Bat Cave that was connected to the petrins. It was an event that would not only change the course of her life, but that of humanity in general.

Rachael looked down at the table and instinctively reached for the cross pendant that dangled at the bottom of the necklace she wore—something she was prone to do in times of stress. She rubbed it as she contemplated her decision. She had always believed, as Seth did, that her existence had some purpose. Maybe this mission was destined for her. Perhaps this mission was part of that purpose. She looked up at Joshua. There were many things she could not live with, but the largest of these, she realized, was disappointing him. "Josh," she said solemnly, "You know I could never be the impediment for you going on this mission." Rachael let out a sigh. "You're right," she said with conviction. "We are a team. Are you absolutely sure you want to go?"

"Yes," Joshua replied. "But it'd only be meaningful for me if you were there to share it with me. Otherwise, what's the point?"

"I understand," Rachael replied, sitting straighter in her seat. She looked directly at Joshua. "Then let's do it."

"Yes!" Joshua shouted again as he ran around the table and embraced Rachael. He kissed her and then looked into her eyes. "You know how wonderful you are?"

"Of course I do," Rachael said with a smirk.

"We really are a great team, aren't we?"

"The best! But I'm not going to feel comfortable going unless Ava's fully settled and taken care of. We still have to ask my parents if they're willing to care for her while we're gone."

"Absolutely, Ava's welfare comes first," Joshua said, trying to tamp down his excitement. "How should we tell the others?"

"Let's invite them over for dinner, and we can ask them then," Rachael said as she released Joshua from their embrace.

"Sounds like a plan."

"Oh, I forgot to tell you. Seth wants Richard to be part of the crew."

"Richard? Why?"

"Don't know. He was evasive on that point."

"Evasive? Does that mean redacted?"

"Precisely."

"How do you feel about Richard coming along?"

"Does it really matter how I feel? We both know that Richard would jump at this chance."

"Quite right," Joshua said. "Oh well. The more the merrier."

* * *

Rachael, Vinod, Liz, Ted, and Richard sat around the dinner table at Joshua and Rachael's home. They had just finished dinner, and Rachael was serving some apple crisp à la mode that she had made. She also poured everyone a glass of grappa to go with their dessert.

"Damn girl," Ted remarked as he took a bite of the crisp. "This dessert's the bomb. You need to give me the recipe for my parents' restaurant."

"Sure," Rachael replied as she took a bite. "The secret is I added in some of your homemade bourbon when cooking the apples."

Joshua came down the stairs and joined the others at the table.

"Is Ava asleep?" Rachael asked.

"Yes, sound asleep."

Rachael looked at Joshua who gave her an affirming nod. "There's a specific reason that Josh and I invited you all over for dinner tonight," Rachael said. All eyes turned to Rachael. She proceeded to tell the group about what Seth had revealed about the events on Earth. She told them about Seth's request to be the crew of a petrin spaceship on a discovery mission to Planet Nine.

The group listened intently to Rachael's story without interruption. After she had delivered the news, she ended with, "Seth made it plainly clear that this was only a request. Josh and I have agreed to go on the mission, but no one here is obligated to go. The decision is up to you."

No one said a word as they let the incredible request Rachael had relayed from Seth sink in.

Ted was the first to speak. "Y'all can count me in. A journey into space across our old solar system? Absolutely I'll go."

"You can count me in too," Liz replied. "It's an amazing scientific opportunity. There's no way I'd miss that."

"I'm in too," Richard stated. "It's an adventure of a lifetime. No way I'd give that up."

"Ted," Rachael said. "Seth said that he needed a crew of thirty humans. There are six of us here, but for the remaining crew, Seth wanted humans experienced with dealing with Medusa. He requested that the remaining crew have military training and have experience with controlling the defender arachnids on Earth."

"Why?" Ted asked. "We're going into an area where these spookyons can't work. That means no remote control of arachnids."

"I don't really know," Rachael said. "Maybe he's covering all his bases. You were the commander of the defender control facility on Earth. You recruited and trained the people that remote-controlled the defender arachnids. Do you think you can pick twenty or so people from their ranks here on New Eden for this mission?"

"I think so," Ted said after some reflection. "There're both men and women, actually more women now that I think about it, that were great at controlling those defenders on Earth. I think I can scrounge up twenty folks to go along with us. They'd love the opportunity."

"I'd like you to get on that right away," Rachael said. "Seth told me he wanted the crew ready to go in a month. He needs a list of all crew members in a week, however, so that he can start growing their clones on Earth."

"I'll get on it first thing tomorrow."

Everyone slowly turned to Vinod. They were keenly aware that he had been the only one in the group who had not agreed to go on the mission.

"Jesus," he said. "Another goddamn dangerous mission? More potential military bullshit? I don't know."

Some members of the group recollected Vinod's anxiety while on the mission in Korea. He had lamented the fact that he had agreed to go on a mission which he had regretted at the time as being akin to a suicide mission. They had gotten out of that predicament, but the emotional scars of that time were now apparent on Vinod's face.

"Look, Vinod," Joshua said. "There's no obligation for you to go. We realize the trauma of what you went through . . . what we all went through in Korea. Everyone here would understand if you decided not to go. There's no pressure."

Vinod looked down as he nervously twiddled his fingers. In Korea, he had agreed to go on the mission without knowing the risks involved. This was a different situation. He was keenly aware of the unknowns here. The unknowns *were* the risk. Anything, including dying, were possible outcomes.

"So, Rach," Vinod said. "Our boy Seth said that we would be backed up before we go? We could be recreated on New Eden if we croaked on this gig?"

"Yes, that's what he said."

Vinod looked up and scanned the faces around the table. "You all are committed to going?"

"Yes," the others said in unison.

Vinod picked up the glass of grappa in front of him and rolled it between his fingers as he contemplated the mission. "Well then fuck it," he said after some thought. He raised his glass. The others also raised their glasses. "Let's do this bitch. Fuck Medusa."

"Fuck Medusa," they said in unison before downing their drinks.

*   *   *

A month later, the group of six from the dinner party arrived at the scanning building that Seth had requested the designated crew should meet. As they approached the entrance to the building, Seth greeted the group. "'sup humans?"

"'sup bro?" Vinod said as he gave his friend a bear hug. "Damn man, never a dull moment with you, is it?"

"No bro," Seth replied as he and Vinod exchanged the special handshake that Vinod had taught him back on Earth many years ago.

Seth addressed the group. "Hello fellow crewmembers. There're a few people who were invited on this mission but declined. However, they wanted to greet you before you get scanned. They are waiting for you inside the lobby."

The group entered the building. In the lobby of the building, they encountered General Mitchell Porter, Robert Langdon, and Dina Williams waiting for them.

General Porter was in his late sixties with weathered skin and a full head of grey, short hair. Vinod walked up to his old nemesis and remarked, "Damn Porter, I can't believe that you didn't want to come on this trip."

Porter smiled at Vinod. "Bhakti, believe me, I considered coming along so that I could keep you in line, but I decided against it. I'm retired from the military, and I'm getting too old for this shit."

"Too old?" Vinod asked. "I'm sure Seth could have cured that ailment."

"Too old as in mentally retired from the military," Porter explained. "Besides, I have faith in you all. You people go get this bitch."

As the two men stared at each other, Vinod became emotional as he remembered the time that Porter had ordered him to move away as he detonated the explosive in the process of killing the arachnid in Korea. His sudden well of emotions left Vinod nearly speechless. "Yes sir," Vinod said as he stepped back and offered Porter a military salute with his hand. Porter was taken aback by the salute, the first sincere salute he had ever received from Vinod. Porter slowly reciprocated the gesture.

The magnitude of the incident was not lost on the others observing. Vinod and Porter had had much disdain for each other on Earth, but over the years and their experiences together, they had each grown an understanding and respect for the other.

Joshua walked up to Robert Langdon. He had been the director of NASA on Earth but was now also retired like Porter on New Eden. "Robert, I would've loved to have your insight and wisdom on this mission."

"You don't need it," Langdon replied. "You're not the inexperienced scientist from Berkley anymore. I have the utmost confidence in you and your team."

"I appreciate that Robert," Joshua said, holding Langdon's hand in his. "It means a lot to me."

"I know," Langdon said. "I wish your entire team a safe and successful mission."

"Thanks."

Dina Williams addressed the group. "I want to personally thank you for volunteering for this mission. We all realize the uncertainty that you'll confront, but we all recognize its importance to not just humanity, but to life in general. I wish you the best of luck."

"I think it's time," Seth said after a moment. "Ted, the military personnel that you have chosen for this mission have already been through the scanning process. You six are the last remaining." Seth motioned to a door behind him. "Please enter this way to get scanned."

The group entered the door, and it closed behind them. Porter, Langdon, and Williams watched as they left and turned to exit the building.

"Can you please stay for a moment," Seth requested of the trio. "I have a request of you."

The three turned back to Seth. "What kind of request?" Williams asked.

Seth lifted a small wooden box that he had been holding. "I need you to take care of this," he said as he lifted the hinged lid of the box. The three peered inside. There was a single oval white object the size of a marble inside.

"What is it?" Langdon asked.

"It's a seed," Seth stated. "I need you to plant it in a large, secure area. It will grow into a large structure, but I need your assurance that you'll allow it to grow undisturbed and that you'll protect it."

"But why Seth?" Williams asked. "What will it grow into?"

"I can't explain it to you," Seth replied, his voice uncharacteristically emotional. "But it's of the utmost importance that you allow it to grow undisturbed. Please trust me on this."

"Grow undisturbed, you say?" Porter asked. "Then it will need security which will require some effort, but we have to know at least *some* reason. We have to know what we're protecting."

"I understand," Seth replied. "Just consider it as insurance for this mission. Something that I don't know whether or not will be needed, but I need to have in place before this mission starts."

The trio glanced at each other. They all had faith and trust in Seth. He had helped humanity escape their homeworld at a time of peril. He had given humanity haven on an entirely new planet so that their species could live and thrive. Now, Seth was earnestly asking for human help albeit without providing a reason, but they were all willing to comply.

"Okay Seth," Williams said as she took the box from Seth and closed the lid. "We'll take care of it."

Chapter Seven
Starship

Joshua awoke and slowly opened his eyes. He was lying on a bed and noticed that Rachael was lying beside him, eyes closed. He had gone through the scanning process before Rachael and figured she would wake momentarily. Joshua noted that he and Rachael were dressed in the white fabric suits they had worn on their initial trip to New Eden. *The petrins were never really ones for fashion*, he thought to himself.

Joshua looked around the room with its curved walls and instantly recognized it as a petrin abode, not unlike the ones on New Eden initially grown to house humans. One wall of the room, though, seemed different. It was flat and seemed to be made of a smooth, transparent material outside of which appeared to be some type of dark, almost black, gravel. To Joshua, this wall seemed to be a large window of some sort. Joshua got up and walked over to the window. He ran his hand along it, and it was indeed smooth and somewhat warm.

"What are you looking at?" Rachael said from the bed, now sitting up.

Joshua turned to Rachael. "You're awake. How was the transition?"

"Seamless."

Joshua turned back to the wall. "I was looking at this wall. It seems to be some kind of window, but there seems to be some rock and gravel outside it. Strange."

"Have you been up for long?"

"No, only about a minute. We should probably go and find the others."

Joshua and Rachael exited the bedroom through the only door in the room. It was the same circular opening that they were accustomed to in petrin abodes. They entered a living room with two couches and a table with the same window wall as in the bedroom on the backside. It seemed to

Joshua that the windows of the two rooms were contiguous with each other.

"Hello," Richard said as he entered the living room from another entrance. "Looks like we made it here okay."

"Seems so," Rachael said. "Did you just come in here from a bedroom?"

"Yes."

Joshua, Rachael, and Richard explored their abode. They found that it consisted of two bathrooms, three bedrooms, the living room, and a small dining room. There was no kitchen.

"No kitchen," Joshua remarked. "Guess we'll be getting our food elsewhere."

"I wonder why there's an extra bedroom," Rachael said.

"I'm sure we'll find out soon," Joshua replied. "Let's go find the others."

The trio walked out of what appeared to be the main entrance to their home, a door that exited from the living room. The scene that appeared before them was something they were wholly unprepared for. They stood in awe as they took in their surroundings.

They were in an enormous cylindrical space about a kilometer in width and height. The walls of the space were bounded by the same window-like material that Joshua had seen in their home. The circular wall was divided into thirty-two vertical panels separated by vertical white support structures that arched skyward. Just like in their home, outside the window-like material was only dark dirt and gravel. The transparent walls soared upward and converged slightly as they rose. There was sunlight streaming down from above, but the light was not coming from the sun. On the center of the flat ceiling, a thousand meters above them, shown a bright light source. It was so bright that they could not directly look at it. Surrounding the light was a flat ceiling made of some type of matte black material. It was circular in shape and met at right angles to the soaring, transparent walls.

What lay in front of them was also astounding. It was an immaculately manicured landscape of grass, trees, shrubs, and flowers. There were ponds and small lakes dispersed throughout. Some of the ponds were interconnected by slow-moving streams. They were in some type of immaculate park or garden. The scene was so beautiful and awe-inspiring that no one said anything for a while as they took it all in.

"What is this place Josh?" Rachael asked, still looking around, her mouth slightly agape.

"I don't know," Joshua said, "but it's beautiful."

"Where are we?" Richard asked. "Is this even Earth?"

"It must be Earth," Joshua said. "The gravity matches Earth, and all of that vegetation seems Earth-like. The atmosphere in here is definitely like Earth. It's completely breathable."

"I wonder where the others are," Rachael said looking around. "I think I see more of the petrin houses like ours at the edges of this space." Rachael pointed in the direction she was looking.

"Yea, I see them," Joshua said. "But I don't see any people."

"There they are," Richard said, pointing to an area near one of the lakes. "One of them is waving their arms at us."

"Guess that's our destination," Rachael remarked.

The trio walked a distance of five hundred meters from their home to where the other people had congregated. They were now near the center of the enormous space next to a pond. At one edge of the pond was a large two-story building. This building, however, was not of the biological construction that the abode they woke up in was made of. It seemed like human construction made from brick-and-mortar walls with flat glass windows.

A group of thirty people had coalesced to an area of grass at the edge of the pond. They were all dressed in the same white outfits that they wore. Rachael recognized Ted, Liz, and Vinod in the group.

"Nice of you three to join us," Vinod remarked as they approached. "We've been waiting for you. Typical Rach, late as usual."

"How long have you been waiting for us?" Rachael asked.

"Not long," Liz replied. "Vinod's just being dramatic."

"Ted," Joshua said, looking at the people surrounding them who were quietly chatting with each other. "Are these your people? The military crew?"

"Yup, that's them. Fine folk. Well trained."

"Where's Seth?" Rachael asked.

"He was just here," Vinod answered. "He went into that building and said he'd be back in a few minutes for a briefing. He's back to his old self."

"What do you mean by that?" Joshua asked.

"You'll see."

"What is this place Vinod?" Rachael asked looking around. "Richard was questioning whether we're actually on Earth. Some things like the vegetation seems familiar, but that up there," she said, looking at the ceiling, "is definitely not our sun."

"Beats me what this place is," Vinod said. "Seth hasn't told us anything yet. And what's with these crazy white getups," Vinod said as he looked down at himself. "Not something from my wardrobe."

"They're petrin clothing," Joshua answered. "These are the same outfits that Rachael and I had on when we went to New Eden the first time."

Seth walked out of the building and moved to the edge of the pond in front of the group, but this was not human Seth that everyone on New Eden had grown accustomed to. This was android Seth. He was back in his android body. Seth was not dressed in the white outfits of the others. His skin-tight suit was a dark blue color which seemed to shimmer slightly in the overhead light as he walked. To Rachael, he looked to be wearing some type of blue wetsuit not unlike those worn by divers.

The group gathered around Seth and stood quietly.

"Back in android form I see," Rachael remarked.

"Yup. I'm always in android form while I'm on Earth. This body you've built has weathered the years well."

"Yea, and it doesn't age like we do," Vinod quipped.

Rachael was strangely happy to see Seth in his android form. It reminded her of their days on Earth during the time when they were first learning about the petrins.

"Looks like we're all here," Seth said, looking over the group.

"Yea, but where is here?" Vinod asked. "Are we even on Earth?"

"Of course we're on Earth."

"But where on Earth?" Vinod asked. "I've never seen anything like this place."

"You don't recognize it?" Seth said coyly. "I can assure you you've spent much time in this place."

"You're crazy," Vinod said, looking around. "I've never seen this place before."

"Ladies and gentlemen," Seth said, addressing the entire group. "Welcome back to Earth. We're currently underground, underneath a section of a city you know as Berkley California. This place is a cavern located underneath the Bowman Particle Research Center."

Rachael's jaw dropped. "Seth, are we in . . . *the Bat Cave*?"

"Yes," Seth responded with a grin. "Don't you like what I've done to it?"

"What the hell *have* you done to it?" Joshua asked. "I can't believe this is the Bat Cave."

"Oh, it definitely is the Bat Cave," Seth replied. "Although not as you remember it. This entire structure," Seth continued as he raised both hands in the air, "is a living creature that we grew from a seed planted in the Bat Cave. As it grew, it pushed away the surrounding rock forming this enormous space."

"You grew this?" Liz said, shocked. "This entire structure, this . . . this cavern is a living entity?"

"Yes."

"Amazing," Liz whispered under her breath. She had always been in awe of the tube system on New Eden and how the petrins had grown it, but this was next-level genetic engineering. As Liz looked around, she realized that the petrins had grown an entire ecosystem underground using only genetics.

"How can something grown from a seed push away all this rock?" Rachael asked, still in disbelief that she was in the Bat Cave.

"Osmotic gradients," Liz answered. "Cells use osmotic gradients to expand. The pressure of these gradients caused by the exchange of ions across cellular membranes can generate tremendous forces. Just think of how tree roots can snake through solid rock. It's a similar process."

"What's that light source?" Joshua asked, pointing at the ceiling.

"It's actually something that you discovered Dr. Andrews," Seth answered. "The light source is a collection of the nuclear fusion spheres you originally discovered in the infiltrator. We have now been able to reproduce them. Those spheres in the ceiling are being fed hydrogen at immense pressure, allowing them to enact nuclear fusion. The light is a result of this fusion process."

"So, you've created an artificial sun?"

"We needed a light source since this structure was built underground. All this vegetation in here needs light to perform photosynthesis in order to live. So yes, we've created an artificial sun." Seth paused and scanned the faces looking at him. "Would you like a tour of this place?"

"Yes," many in the crowd responded.

"Where would you like to start?" Seth asked.

"I'd like to see the spaceship," Joshua said. "If we're going to be cramped up with thirty people on a six-month mission, then I'd like to see that first."

"Spaceship?" Seth asked, puzzled.

"Yes, spaceship," Joshua replied, also puzzled, and somewhat annoyed. He felt that Seth was being unnecessarily evasive. "You told us we're going on a space mission to Planet Nine. Where's the ship that's going to take us there?"

"Don't you understand Josh?" Seth asked.

"Understand what?"

"This," Seth said, raising his hands in the air again. "*This* is the spaceship. You're standing in the spaceship."

Joshua's eyes grew wide. "*This* is a spaceship?" Joshua scanned the kilometer-wide space surrounding him. "This entire structure is a spaceship?"

"Yes."

Joshua's mind reeled at the thought. He imagined the physics, energy, and technology required to launch and move such a massive object through space. He became overcome with emotion. He became weak, and he bent over, hands on knees.

"Josh, you okay?" Rachael asked, laying her hand on his back.

"Yes," Joshua said, standing back straight a few moments later. "Just overwhelmed by the thought of a spaceship the size of a small city."

"Goddamn Seth," Vinod said, looking around the enormous space. "This thing's gargantuan. You just gave a whole new meaning to the phrase 'go big or go home.'"

"Why the need to make it so big?" Liz asked.

"Why not?" Seth responded. "We knew that we would have a human crew. We wanted the crew to be as comfortable as possible. We wanted you to be in your natural environment and hence this ship. Size for us isn't an issue. There are no manufacturing costs for us in building this ship. We simply design what we need and implant the design into the DNA of a seed that grows into this structure. Size is only a matter of how much time we have. We were able to grow this structure over a period of six months. In fact, it's not quite complete in its growth. It has a few more days left before it's fully mature—before it can be launched into space. I figured these next few days you can all familiarize yourselves with each other and your surroundings."

Joshua looked around the enormous structure to try to get an overall picture of what the ship looked like. "What's the external shape of this ship? I'm assuming there must be some more structure above that ceiling and possibly beneath the ground as well."

"You are correct Dr. Andrews," Seth replied. "The overall structure of this vessel, I think, is best described as egg-shaped with the more pointed side up and the rounder side down. Under our feet are where all the mechanical systems of the ship are. That includes the energy source and raw materials needed for maintenance and propulsion. Above the ceiling is mostly empty space, but a dome covers that area to give this the ship a more aerodynamic shape."

"Aerodynamic?" Rachael asked. "Why aerodynamic? I thought we're traveling through empty space. There should be no need for aerodynamic effects there."

"Space is not completely empty," Seth responded. "Did you know that there's an average of one hydrogen atom per cubic centimeter in space? There are also dust and micrometeorites we may encounter. The dome is designed to handle these. Besides, there are many unknowns on this mission. We wanted to make sure the ship would flow smoothly through an atmosphere if needed."

Joshua was still trying to wrap his mind around the fact that this enormous structure was a spacecraft. He was confused by its design and how it worked. "I still don't understand how this is a spaceship," he said. "It's not really designed for space."

"How so Josh?" Seth asked.

"You've got lakes and trees in here for chrissake. There's no gravity in space. All this stuff would simply either break off or lift off and float in a zero-G environment. It'd be a mess in here. How does this make sense as a spaceship?"

"You're absolutely right," Seth said. "It'd be a mess in here with a zero-G environment. That's why this area and this ship will never be exposed to a zero-G environment."

"Never be exposed to a zero-G environment? But . . .," Joshua didn't finish his sentence as a thought crossed his mind. Seth's words echoed in his brain. *This ship will never be exposed to a zero-G environment.* He realized the implication of Seth's statement. "You're going to accelerate at one-G the whole way, aren't you?"

"Precisely."

"But that means you'll have to do a 180-degree rotation at the halfway point."

"You catch on fast."

"What are you two talking about?" Richard asked. "You two want to explain to us non-physicists what's going on."

"You want a shot at that Dr. Andrews?" Seth asked.

"I'll try my best," Joshua said and moved next to Seth and addressed the group. "It has to do with gravity. When you're standing on Earth, you are in its gravitational field. The amount of acceleration that you experience on the surface of the Earth we refer to as one-G or one Earth gravity. When a spaceship takes off from Earth, it must accelerate upwards to escape Earth's gravity. The rocket engines of the ship achieve this acceleration. Astronauts from Earth typically experience about three-Gs when their rocket blasts off. This is a combination of the one-G from Earth and an additional two-Gs of thrust produced by the engines. Once a spaceship is in space, and it's out of the influence of Earth's gravitational field, it coasts. The rocket engines are turned off, but it maintains its speed indefinitely.

This is according to Newton's First Law—an object in motion with no forces acting on it will continue in motion indefinitely. This is how the Apollo astronauts got to the moon. They blasted off the Earth with their engines, but during the transit to the moon, their engines were shut off—they coasted. However, when a ship's coasting, there's no more acceleration. This means that they're weightless. They're in a zero-G environment, and everything simply floats about since there's no gravity or acceleration. But that's only because the engines are turned off. If a ship continues to burn its engines and not coast, then its occupants would still feel a gravity-like force—the force of acceleration that their engines are generating. The side effect of this would be that the ship would continue getting faster and faster since its engines are running and pushing it forward.

"What Seth's saying is that this ship will do just that. It will keep its engines running in a way that the entire ship will continue accelerating at one-G getting faster and faster in the process. It would feel no different for us on the ship than what we're experiencing now on Earth. It will, in essence, be an artificial gravity caused by the engines that will make us, the entire ship, feel like we're in Earth gravity—no weightlessness at all.

"But there are side-effects to this process. The fact that the ship will continually be gaining speed towards our destination does mean we'll get there faster, but it also means that by the time we get to Planet Nine, we'd have so much velocity that we couldn't stop. We'd simply fly right by it. To solve this problem, the ship has to make a 180-degree turn halfway to our destination to point its thrust in the opposite direction in order to slow down. So, during the second half of the trip, the ship would be pointed backwards, but now decelerating at one-G. For us on the ship, the effect is the same. We would still feel like we were in Earth gravity.

"Scientists have known for quite some time about this kind of space travel. It's really the fastest way to get to a destination on a spaceship. But spaceships from Earth had nowhere near the technology or fuel to be able to accomplish it."

"Excellent explanation Dr. Andrews," Seth said as Joshua returned to his place next to Rachael.

"But how does it all work bro?" Vinod asked. "Where are the engines? What's the fuel?"

"The ultimate fuel source is hydrogen," Seth stated. "But the process is a little complex, but I'll try to explain."

"A little complex for a petrin?" Vinod whispered to Rachael. "That means we got no hope Rach."

"Speak for yourself," Rachael whispered back. "Pay attention."

"There are enormous containers of liquid hydrogen underneath our feet," Seth began. "Also, there are numerous fusion spheres. The spheres are fed with the hydrogen and fuse them to larger and larger atoms all the way up to iron which is stored for later use as the propellant. The energy obtained from this fusion process is stored as electrical potential in bioelectric membranes."

"Bioelectric membranes?" Liz asked. "Like some type of biological battery?"

"Exactly. When we're ready for launch, the iron stores are released and heated to form an iron-based plasma. This plasma is injected into numerous ion accelerators that feed off the bioelectric membranes as their energy source. The accelerators accelerate the iron plasma to tremendous speeds. Once the plasma has achieved the appropriate velocity, it's ejected through multiple ejection nozzles on the ship's exterior. The ejection of this plasma causes a reactionary force on the ship which propels it forward."

"Amazing," Joshua commented. "So nuclear fusion is the ultimate energy source, and you're using the hydrogen for both the energy source and the source of the propellant."

"Yes."

"Amazingly efficient," Joshua remarked. "The ash of nuclear fusion, which is iron, is being ejected at high speed to propel the ship. How big are these ejection nozzles you mentioned?" Joshua asked. "Where are they located?"

"They're located all along the exterior of the ship. You can't see them now because they are buried in the dirt outside." Seth pointed to the vertical structures that climbed the transparent walls of the ship. "Those channels transport the plasma to the ejection nozzles which are attached to the outside of the structures."

"I'm assuming that you have nozzles at the bottom of the ship, but why do you need to have those nozzles so high up?" Joshua asked. "After all, the propulsion force needs to be directed upwards, which means that the nozzles only need to point down."

"The nozzles are flexible tubes. There are hundreds of them. They're able to be aimed in any direction. That means that the ship's capable of accelerating in any direction it chooses simply by reorienting the nozzles on the exterior of the ship."

Liz pondered what the entire ship looked like from the outside—a clear, egg-shaped vessel with numerous tentacle-like ejection nozzles emanating from its surface. "It's like a cell," she stated. "The ship looks like a cell from the outside."

"How's it like a cell, Liz?" Vinod asked. "Never seen a mile-long cell before."

"If I saw the shape of this ship under a microscope, it would look exactly like a cell. It has a similar shape to a cell, and the ejection nozzles would be like the cilia on the cell. Cilia are projections that some cells have for various purposes. The shape of the ship definitely reminds me of a cell."

"An apt analogy, I suppose," Seth remarked. "The ship's a mile-long biological entity whose natural environment is space."

"How's the ship controlled Seth?" Joshua asked. "With all of the coordination needed for the energy source, the plasma injection, and the directing of all of these ejection nozzles, you must have one complex control mechanism."

"Yes, that's true."

"So, where's the control center?" Vinod asked. "Where's the bridge on this beast?"

"I was hoping someone would ask that," Seth responded with a grin. "I'd like to show you the control center." Seth turned to the building behind him and said, "Come on out."

A door to the building opened, and a woman walked out. She was dressed in the same skin-tight white suit as the others. She was grinning as she walked and stood next to Seth.

Those in the group were mesmerized by her appearance. She was the most beautiful woman they had ever seen. She looked to be about twenty years old and stood five foot eight with dark brown, almost black, hair that fell in long curls to her shoulders. She had olive-colored skin that was perfect and unblemished. The woman wore no makeup at all and didn't need any. Her body had perfect curves that were perfectly accentuated by her skin-tight suit. But her most remarkable feature was her eyes. They were large, but not unnaturally so. They were a brilliant emerald green that seemed to pierce everything she looked at.

"Everyone," Seth said. "This is Bhumi. She controls the ship."

No one said a word as they continued staring at the woman, engrossed by her appearance—especially the men present. Rachael glanced over at Joshua who stared forward, his mouth slightly agape. Rachael elbowed Joshua firmly in the ribs and whispered, "Josh, you're about to drool."

"Oh, am I?" Joshua said as the pain in his ribs snapped him out of his trance.

Chapter Eight
Bhumi's Story

No one said a word for a few moments until Rachael broke the silence. "Is she human Seth?"

"Yes, I'm human," Bhumi responded in a strong female voice with no accent.

"But how did she get here, Seth?" Rachael asked. "She wasn't part of the crew that was scanned on New Eden, and you told us that all of the remaining humans on Earth were killed by Medusa."

"Yes, that's true," Seth replied. "Medusa did kill all the humans left on Earth. She released a toxin into the atmosphere that specifically targeted human DNA, but Bhumi wasn't affected by that. Let me explain. Around nine months ago, one of our defender arachnids was patrolling an area near the base of a glacier in the Himalayas. The glacier had been melting due to the global warming process that you humans had initiated. The defender came across the body of a young woman that had been frozen in the glacier for quite some time. We believe that she had been caught in an avalanche and trapped in the glacier. The defender brought the body to me. We scanned the body to see if it still contained its life information—to see if she could be revived like I revived you and Richard. We noted that most of her information was intact except for a small area of her brain related to long-term memory storage. Some of her memories could not be recovered, but in our minds, and by our definition of life, she was still alive, albeit in a suspended state.

"As you know, we consider ourselves the preservers of life. Therefore, we started the process of growing a clone of the woman by taking a sample of her DNA. This was happening during the time when we were designing this ship. We were coming up with ideas on how humans would be able to control such an enormous vessel. We're enamored with the human brain. We've been amazed at how humans could so efficiently control the defender arachnids on Earth during the war with Medusa. We wondered if such a mechanism could be employed to control this ship, but we didn't have a human test subject with which to test this interface. That's when Bhumi was discovered. While growing her clone, we developed a spookyon interface via a neural nest in her brain so that she could control the ship. Bhumi, after her reanimation, has tested and has become familiarized with this interface. She has complete control of this ship. For Bhumi, this ship is a part of herself. She can sense and control it just like any other part of her body.

"We knew that Bhumi would have to coexist with humans different than herself. So we've embedded in her brain information regarding modern humans such as language and culture." Seth turned to Bhumi. "Sorry, don't mean to talk about you like you're not here."

"It's fine," Bhumi replied. "I understand."

The group tried to understand the incredible tale that Seth had just revealed. "How old are you?" Liz asked. "How long were you frozen in that glacier?"

"Let me answer that," Seth replied. "Using isotopic testing, we believe that she was caught in an avalanche approximately forty thousand years ago."

"Did you say *forty thousand*?" Vinod asked, shocked, staring at Bhumi. "You brought back a forty-thousand-year-old human?"

"Yes."

"That's incredible," Liz stated under her breath.

The group was dumbstruck. They were seeing a human that had lived during the Paleolithic era. Bhumi grinned back at the group with nervous excitement. Seth had been her only companion over the past few months since she had been reanimated. She'd been anxiously waiting to meet others like her.

"Bhumi, you have control of this ship?" Richard asked.

"Yes."

"How does it work? How are you able to control this ship?"

"The ship is a part of me," Bhumi replied, "just like my hands and feet are a part of me. I can feel it and control it just like any part of my body."

"You can sense the ship?" Liz asked.

"Yes, I can feel it just like I can sense other parts of my body. Like I said, the ship is just another part of me. I'm connected to it. I can make it do whatever I want."

"Bhumi, are you okay if I give a more technical description?" Seth asked.

"Sure."

"This ship is a living entity comprised of living cells," Seth began. "It has a nervous system with senses such as touch, vision, hearing, and others. Neural bundles route these senses to a central brain located under our feet. This brain processes this information and relays it via a spookyon to the one in Bhumi's brain. She's absolutely correct when she says the ship is a part of her body. To her, the ship is just another appendage. Bhumi, would you like to give a demonstration?"

"Sure. What should I do?"

Seth looked around the landscape. "It's a little dry in here. The vegetation in here could use a little rain."

Bhumi looked up to the ceiling, and the group followed suit. The dark material surrounding the artificial sun changed color. It became initially grayish and then turned a misty white. A few moments later, the group felt drops of water on their face and realized it was raining. The rain was a gentle mist that coated them in dew drops that were not absorbed by their suits. Bhumi looked back at the group, and the rain soon stopped.

Bhumi stared straight at the group and said, "This is moonlight." The entire chamber turned instantly dark, but not pitch black. There was still some light emanating from the artificial sun, but only an amount that would have been present on a full moon night on Earth.

"Back to day," Bhumi said as sunlight flooded the chamber.

"Incredible," Joshua remarked. "Absolutely incredible. A human-neural interface to a spaceship."

Seth scanned the group to assess their status. There was much information he had unloaded on them in quick succession. He could see that they were in information overload and needed some time to absorb and reflect on their new surroundings. "You must all must be hungry," he said. "On the other side of this pond, a hundred meters back, is an orchard. It's similar to the orchards we had on New Eden when we moved humanity there. Why don't you all go and get something to eat. Also, spend some time exploring and getting used to your new surroundings. We can continue the tour of the ship later."

The group started walking to the other side of the pond. Richard looked back and noticed Bhumi standing anxiously next to Seth, watching the group as they walked away. He left the group and walked back to her. She was his same age, and he knew that any human at that age needed friendship.

"Hello Bhumi," Richard said as he stuck out his hand. "I'm Richard." Seth watched nervously as he stared at Richard's extended hand. He was relieved to see Bhumi grasp his hand and shake it. *I have taught her well.*

"Hi, Richard. Nice to meet you."

"You want to join us for lunch?"

"Sure. That'd be great," Bhumi said enthusiastically. "Are you coming Seth?"

"You two go. I have to charge my batteries a bit. I'll catch up with you later."

Rachael noticed that Richard was no longer part of their group. She looked back and saw Bhumi and Richard walking together some distance behind. A slight sense of anxiety welled up inside her.

"I've never met a forty-thousand-year-old girl before," Richard remarked as they walked.

"I've never met a man from the future."

"Definitely from different worlds," Richard conceded. "But you know we do have something in common."

"Really? Like what?"

"We were both frozen and brought back to life."

Bhumi stopped dead in her tracks and stared at Richard as tears formed in her eyes. Bhumi had spent the last few months with only Seth as a companion, but he wasn't human. She had been lonely and felt that even after meeting other humans as Seth had promised her she would, she would feel like an outsider. She was, after all, not from this culture or even this millennia. Seth had taught her much about current human culture and language, but even with this knowledge, she worried about her uniqueness. Would she fit in in this new reality? "You were once frozen too? I thought I was the only one."

Richard sensed Bhumi's sudden emotion. "Yes, I was frozen as well, but for only twenty years, not millennia like you."

"Were you caught in an avalanche too?"

"No," Richard replied with a chuckle. "My story's a bit more complicated than that."

"Can you explain it to me?" Bhumi asked as the couple resumed their walk. "I'd love to hear it."

"I had a disease called cancer. Are you familiar with cancer?"

"Yes. Seth explained the concept to me."

"This was when I was ten years old. I died because of cancer, although I wasn't dead according to the petrin definition."

"Yea, I get it. Seth has explained to me their definition of life and death and how I was able to be brought back to life."

"After I died, my parents had my body frozen with the idea that sometime in the future, technology would be available to allow me to live again. This was all during a time before the petrins had made contact with us. When humanity was relocated to New Eden, my sister asked Seth to recreate me there, which he did."

"What was it like for you when you first woke on New Eden?"

It was now Richard who became emotional. He remembered vividly the shock he went through at that time. Everything had changed for him. Everyone was years older—his friends, his parents, even his twin sister. He wasn't even on Earth anymore. His entire existence was utterly foreign. He suddenly realized that Bhumi had also gone through this type of shock, but her situation was much more drastic. No one she knew was around. In fact, no one was around except an android named Seth. No one knew her culture or even her language. Richard understood Bhumi's loneliness. He had gone through it too. "It was hard at first . . . really hard. Everything had changed for me. Nothing I had known before was the same. But over a year or two, I slowly adjusted. I made new friends and adjusted to my new surroundings. I'm thrilled to be on New Eden now."

"So no regrets about being brought back to life?"

"None."

"That's comforting to know."

As the couple approached the orchard, they noticed Joshua, Rachael, Vinod, Ted, and Liz having a picnic. They had gathered some food and were sitting on some grass at the edge of the orchard.

"Why don't y'all grab some food and join us?" Ted suggested.

"Sure," Richard replied. "Let's go Bhumi."

Richard and Bhumi went into the orchard. They were both very familiar with the variety of choices of food there. Richard had experienced similar orchards on New Eden when he first was there, and Bhumi had been eating from this same orchard for months now.

After Richard and Bhumi left, Liz asked, "Well, what do you think of that Rachael?"

"What do I think of what?"

"Richard and Bhumi seem rather chummy."

The others listened intently to the two women's conversation and were interested in Rachael's response.

"You think so?"

"Don't play coy with me. I know you noticed it too."

"You're reading too much into it."

"Gotta say I agree with Liz on this," Ted remarked. "Definitely some spark there."

"What do you think Josh?" Rachael asked.

Joshua raised his eyebrows and let out a sigh. "I think I know the reason Seth wanted Richard on this mission."

Rachael was taken aback by the response. "Are you saying Seth was playing matchmaker somehow?"

"No, not matchmaker per se. It may be nuanced, but did anyone else notice how Seth seems to interact with Bhumi? He seems almost kind of parental with her."

"Yes," Liz replied. "I picked up on that too."

"I must have been extremely difficult for Bhumi—waking up in a world so foreign to her," Joshua stated. "But Bhumi has a critical role on this mission—maybe the most important in fact. She's in complete control of this ship, and to do her job well, she has to be in a good mental state. The rest of the crew is much older than Bhumi. I think Seth wanted someone her own age for . . . companionship."

Rachael pondered Joshua's analysis as Richard and Bhumi returned and sat with the others.

"Bhumi," Richard said. "I want to introduce you to the gang. This is my sister Rachael Andrews."

Bhumi got up and went to Rachael and extended her hand, which Rachael shook. "Nice to meet you."

Richard introduced Bhumi to the others after which she sat back down next to Richard to eat her lunch.

The group was quiet for a few minutes as they ate their lunch. "Bhumi," Liz said. "I can't believe you were alive on Earth forty thousand years ago."

"To be honest, I can't believe it either," Bhumi said.

"I have so many questions to ask you," Liz said. "What was life like back then?"

"I'm not entirely sure. Like Seth said, much of my long-term memory was damaged. What I do remember is like certain scenes and feelings. I remember living in the mountains in a small village. I believe we survived by hunting. I have a vivid memory of hunting a large animal, and from the pictures that Seth has shown me, I believe the creature was a woolly mammoth."

"A woolly mammoth?" Ted remarked. "Damn girl, you gotta be pretty brave to go after an animal that big."

"Well, I wasn't alone. There was a group of us, but as I said, my memories of that time are almost like a series of pictures. I remember almost nothing. I didn't even remember my name."

"So Bhumi wasn't your original name?" Joshua asked.

"No. Something Seth came up with."

"I wonder if your name means anything," Rachael said.

"It sure does," Vinod chimed in. "It's a Sanskrit word. It means Earth."

"Earth," Richard repeated, turning to Bhumi. "Certainly seems appropriate. We're going to be living in this spaceship for a while. It'll be our home. This ship is a part of Bhumi. She will be our Earth."

Bhumi smiled at Richard after the comment. "Yes, it'll be my job to keep you safe. I will be your Earth."

After the group had finished eating, Richard said, "Seth said we should explore this place. Bhumi said she would show me around. Anyone want to join us?"

Others in the group were reluctant to join the young couple. They looked at each other before Joshua finally said, "You two go and have fun. We'll explore on our own. We'd probably bore you with our scientific analysis."

"Suit yourself," Richard replied as he and Bhumi got up and walked away. The couple passed an area where other crew members were also seated, having lunch. They stared at the couple as they passed. Bhumi smiled at them and nodded.

After they had gotten past the group, Bhumi asked, "Why did they stare at us like that?"

"Oh, I don't think they were staring at *us*. I believe they were staring at *you*."

"Why?" Bhumi asked, suddenly self-conscious.

Richard paused before answering. "I'm not sure you realize this, but you're one very beautiful girl. Probably one of the most beautiful they've seen. I think you've piqued their curiosity."

"Beautiful? I don't seem any different than any of the other women here."

"Oh, you *are* different."

Bhumi turned to Richard. "Do you think I'm beautiful?"

Richard blushed at the question. "Yes." He turned to Bhumi. "I think you're gorgeous. But you must have experienced that in your previous life. You must have looked the same back then. Seth built your clone from your original DNA."

"To be honest, I don't know what I looked like back then."

"Because you lost those memories?"

"No, not that. I don't think that I ever looked at myself before being here."

Richard was confused by the statement. "How's it possible that you never saw yourself? How's it possible that you never knew what you looked like?"

"There was no way to see myself."

"What do you mean? You just look in a mir . . .," Richard didn't finish the sentence as a thought suddenly dawned on him. How could a person from that ancient era see their own appearance? There were no mirrors or even shiny metal. Modern humans had taken for granted smooth surfaces that would offer a perfect reflection. There were no such things forty thousand years ago. Modern humans spend so much time looking in the mirror or taking selfies. This was not even possible for humans of Bhumi's era. "I get it now. You really had no easy way to see your reflection."

"That's right, but I'm sure I looked much different back then."

"Why?"

Bhumi paused to collect her thoughts before answering. "For starters, my hair was much different. We didn't have combs or scissors, so it was kind of a matted mess. Also, I don't recollect anything like taking a shower or bath like I can do here. I also think I was a lot thinner than I am now. We didn't have an orchard where literally we could walk in and get food at will. Getting food was hard. We spent a lot of our time trying to get nutrition. I believe there were long periods of time we simply had to go without."

"It must have been a rough existence."

"It may have been, but I can't tell you for sure since my memories are so incomplete. But I have a feeling of comradery from that time. We were social and did many things as a team. We were surviving as a group. There was no such thing as loneliness."

"Well, you won't be lonely with the group of people here. They're very friendly. We're all also a team with a common mission. I think you'll find much comradery with the crew here."

Bhumi smiled and looked at Richard. "I think I already have."

*　　　*　　　*

As the group by the orchard watched Richard and Bhumi walk away into the distance, Rachael remarked, "I think you're right Josh."

"About what?" Joshua asked.

"About Seth's reasons for wanting Richard on this mission."

"Hey Rach," Vinod said chuckling. "Remember at the club when you were worried about Richard hooking up with some seventy-year-old resetter?"

"Yea, what about it?" Rachael replied, annoyed.

"You should've hedged your bets," Vinod said, laughing out loud. "Now you're dealing with a forty-thousand-year-old with Richard."

The others in the group tried only with limited success to repress their laughter.

"I'm glad you all find this funny," Rachael said with sarcasm.

"Don't fret about it Rachael," Joshua chimed in to appease her. "It's fine. No harm, no foul. Richard absolutely wanted to come on this adventure. It's the trip of a lifetime."

"What do you mean no harm no foul?" Rachael said angrily. "Richard's with a forty-thousand-year-old girl! How's that okay?"

"Oh snap!" Vinod said gleefully. "It's a rare moment guys. We get to witness an argument between the love birds."

Joshua became defensive at Rachael's statement. "Why are you so upset? They're just going for a walk. It's not like they're getting married or something."

"Are you really mocking my concerns?" Rachael asked.

"I told you this was going to be good," Vinod said.

"You're not helping Vinod," Rachael snapped back.

"I'm not mocking your concerns Rachael," Joshua said. "But I don't see anything nefarious going on."

"Nothing nefarious? You were the one who suggested that Seth asked Richard to come because of Bhumi. He did so without telling us why or asking our permission."

"Permission?" Joshua said. "Why does he need our permission? Richard's an adult and can make his own decisions."

"Speak of the devil," Vinod said as he saw Seth walking towards them.

Joshua and Rachael stopped their arguing and waited for Seth to arrive. Seth walked up to the others. "How was your lunch?"

"Excellent," Ted replied. "My compliments to the chef."

"Rachael," Seth said, "can I have a word with you in private?"

Rachael squinted at Seth. "Interesting. I was going to ask you for the same thing."

"Guess we should go explore guys," Joshua said to the others as he stood up.

"But Josh," Vinod protested. "We're going to miss the fireworks."

"Let's go Vinod," Joshua said sternly. The group left, leaving Seth and Rachael to themselves.

"You want to go first, or you want me?" Rachael asked after the others had left.

"You go ahead and start."

Rachael pointed her index finger into Seth's chest. "I have a sneaking suspicion as to why you wanted Richard to come on this mission."

"Which is?"

Rachael removed her finger and now stood with her hands on her hips. "You wanted him here to be with Bhumi. Admit it. Don't lie to me, and don't tell me it's redacted."

"Yes," Seth admitted, "that was part of the reason, but I thought you'd be happy about it. I thought you'd be appreciative of the fact that your brother could come with you on the mission. I knew that it'd be difficult for you to leave Ava on New Eden. I thought having Richard here would be something you'd want. I don't understand. You don't want Richard here?"

"No, it's not that," Rachael said in a calmer voice. "I guess I feel that you should have told me about Bhumi first before bringing Richard here."

"I did consider it. But how would you have reacted if I told you that I wanted Richard to meet a girl from forty thousand years ago? I know how protective you are of him. I calculated that you wouldn't allow it, and that fact would have also jeopardized you coming on this mission."

Rachael didn't speak for a few moments. She knew that Seth was right. She had already been hesitant about coming on the mission, and learning about a potential relationship between her twin brother and a woman from millennia ago, she would have viewed as an unnecessary risk. "You know you're pretty sneaky sometimes."

"Only when I have to be, but Richard and Bhumi seem to be hitting it off. You don't know her as well as I do. She's really a wonderful girl. She actually reminds me a lot of you when I first met you. I think you'll like her once you get to know her better."

Rachael's tone softened still. "She reminds you of me?"

"Yes. In many ways."

"Well, she certainly doesn't look like me. That's the other thing. How is it she looks so perfect? The men can't seem to keep their eyes off her."

"Are you . . . jealous?"

"No, not jealous," Rachael said and paused. *Am I jealous?* "I'm suspicious. Did you alter her looks somehow?"

Seth was shocked at the question. "No, absolutely not. You know it'd be against our petrin morals to genetically alter a sentient individual. Her looks are her natural looks, just like she would have looked millennia ago."

Rachael didn't know what to think of the situation. Although she did feel that Seth had been sneaky in his methods of getting Richard to come on the mission, she was glad to have him here. Besides, Joshua was right. It would be the experience of a lifetime for him.

"I don't know Seth. I know I'm acting kind of crazy, but I just don't want Richard to get hurt, emotionally I mean."

"I don't want that for him either—or for Bhumi for that matter."

"It's strange Seth. We sensed an almost paternal attitude you have towards her. What gives?"

"Is it any different than the paternality I've shown to all humans?"

Rachael rarely lost an argument, but she knew she had lost this one. Seth had been nothing if caring of all humanity. He had, in fact, saved humanity from a deadly virus and extinction. He had even saved both Rachael and Richard. Rachael realized that he was doing the same for Bhumi. "I'm a bit overprotective of Richard, aren't I?"

"A bit, but it's only natural for you. You'd thought that you'd lost him for almost twenty years. Now that he's back, some level of overprotection is to be expected."

"Okay Seth," Rachael said, her voice now calm. "I'll try to show more objectivity and give this a chance. Sorry I got upset."

"No harm no foul."

"No harm no foul? Have you been spending a lot of time with Josh?"

"Not really. Why do you ask?"

"Never mind. What was it you wanted to speak to me about?"

"To be honest Rachael, I also wanted to speak with you about Bhumi. You're very observant. I've known that about you. Yes, I was hoping for some companionship for Bhumi when I asked Richard to come on this mission. She's been utterly lonely here on Earth, and I'm sure you can understand the reasons. She would be much better if she was with other humans and not a human-looking android." Seth lowered his head for a moment before looking back up at Rachael. "I was hoping that Bhumi could live with your family while on this mission. That's why I had an extra bedroom grown in your home here. I haven't told Bhumi yet because I wanted your permission first."

Rachael was not surprised at the request. She had anticipated it. She knew about the extra room in their home and could see this scenario coming. "And the other shoe drops." Rachael thought about the request for a while before answering. "Okay Seth. I'm willing to help out, but you do know that I'm putting a lot of trust in you here."

"I realize that."

"But, I have one condition. *I* want to be the one who suggests it to her."

"Perfect."

*   *   *

Rachael and Seth walked along a path near the edge of the ship. The path was a three-kilometer circular trail that circumnavigated the exterior walls of the ship. It was designed to be used for exercise by the crew. They passed many petrin-grown homes that sat at the junction of the land and the outside of the ship. Seth explained that he wanted humans to have a view of the outside when they were in their homes during the mission. The path entered a small grove of trees—deciduous oaks, maples, and beech trees intermixed with tall pines.

Rachael marveled at how Seth had grown a small forest inside a spaceship. "Are the trees and grass part of the ship too?" she asked. "Were they grown from the same seed that the ship grew from?"

"No," Seth replied. "The vegetation is all genetically separate. Only the major structural features are genetically part of the ship."

They soon exited the forest to a large grassy area. "This is the recreational area," Seth explained. There was a tennis court, a basketball court, a soccer field, and even a large swimming pool. "Behind the soccer field is a put-put course."

Rachael was amazed at the facilities. "What, no golf course?" she asked jokingly.

"Thought about it. Didn't have room."

"It's simply amazing."

The couple walked past the basketball court where Ted and some of his crew were playing a game of five on five. They walked to the tennis court where Joshua, Vinod, Liz, and a female member of Ted's crew were playing doubles. Vinod walked to the edge of the court, still dressed in the white suit.

"Jesus Seth," he remarked. "This isn't a spaceship. It's a goddamn resort."

"Glad you like it. I used my knowledge of human enjoyment when I designed it. Like you said earlier, 'go big or go home.'"

"What's up with these outfits?" Vinod asked. "You don't sweat in them at all."

"They're biological," Rachael explained. "They maintain the optimal temperature for humans when you're wearing them. Josh and I noticed the same thing on our trip to New Eden. You guys continue your game. Seth and I will watch."

*   *   *

Richard and Bhumi had meandered to the put-put course. "You know this game?" she asked.

"Sure, we have some of these on New Eden. Do you play?"

"Yes, Seth and I have played many times. He beats me most of the time, though."

"Most of the time?"

"I win occasionally."

"Really?"

"Why is that a surprise for you? You don't think I could be good at this game?"

"I'm sure you're okay, but there's no way you could be able to beat Seth. He has the entire computing power of the collective at his disposal. I heard about a time when he threw dice at a craps game in Vegas years ago. Apparently, he could make the dice come up any number he chose. Put-put for him must be child's play compared to that." Richard looked at Bhumi. "It's obvious . . . he let you win."

"Why would he do that?"

"So you wouldn't get too discouraged."

"I guess it's possible, but I am pretty good," Bhumi said, looking up and down at Richard. "You want to have a go?"

"Sure," Richard replied, retrieving a putter and a ball from a basket located near the start of the course. "But I have to warn you. I'm pretty good too."

"We'll see about that," Bhumi replied, grabbing her equipment.

Bhumi and Richard worked their way around the course. Richard noted that Bhumi was very skilled at the game. They were evenly matched. They both had a competitive streak and didn't want to lose to the other. As they approached the last hole, Richard remarked, "This is the last hole, and I'm up by one. I'll go first." Richard placed his ball and lined up his shot. "You do realize that if I make this in one shot that you can't win, right?"

"I get it. I know how the game works."

Richard took his shot that missed the hole by two inches. Bhumi started laughing. "What's the term for that? I think Seth told me. Oh yes, I think it's called choking."

"I didn't choke," Richard said as he tapped his second shot into the cup. "It's a difficult shot. Besides, I can't lose now. The best you can do is get a hole-in-one, and that'd just tie me."

"So, you don't think I can do it?" Bhumi asked as she lined up her shot.

"I have my doubts."

"We shall see Mr. Miller," Bhumi said as she took her shot. Her ball rolled directly towards the hole but stopped just at the edge without falling in. It was now Richard's turn to laugh. "Tough luck. I win."

Bhumi looked at Richard with a smirk. "I make my own luck."

The ground suddenly shook with a tremor. Richard spread his feet wide and could see the leaves on the trees nearby shaking as they felt the effect of the quake. The tremor stopped. "What was that? An earthquake?"

"Maybe, but have you checked the ball? I believe we're tied."

Richard noted that Bhumi's ball had fallen into the cup. He looked directly at Bhumi. "You . . . you did that. That's cheating!"

"Is it?" Bhumi said coyly, leaning on her putter.

* * *

"What the hell was that?" Vinod asked from the tennis court. "Was it an earthquake?"

"Possible," Joshua answered. "The area around Berkley has numerous faults. If it was, it'd have to be a pretty minor one. Do you think it was an earthquake Seth? Do you think the ship was damaged?"

All eyes turned to Seth. "I don't know. Only Bhumi would know about any damage. She would sense it. Where is she?"

"I saw her and Richard headed to the put-put course earlier," Vinod said.

"Come on Rachael," Seth said. "Let's go."

Seth and Rachael sprinted down the path to where Richard and Bhumi were standing next to the course.

"What was that tremor?" Seth asked Bhumi. "Was it an earthquake? Are you damaged?"

"Oh, you're in trouble now," Richard said under his breath, smiling. "Serves you right."

"I'm not damaged," Bhumi said. "It wasn't an earthquake. I just um . . . moved some of my ejection nozzles."

"Why?" Seth asked.

Bhumi blushed with embarrassment. Richard could sense her discomfort. "It was my fault," Richard said. "I was asking Bhumi how she moved her nozzles, and she was just demonstrating for me."

"Richard, you should have known better," Rachael said, hands on hips.

"You both should have known better," Seth chimed in. "We can't have any unnecessary damage to this ship."

"I was being careful," Bhumi said. "But I understand."

"Why don't you two come back with us to the others," Rachael said. "I think you've done enough solo exploring."

The foursome walked back towards the others. Bhumi leaned over to Richard and whispered, "Thank you." Richard replied with a wink.

When they got back to the tennis court, Joshua asked, "Was it an earthquake?"

"No, not an earthquake," Rachael replied. "Bhumi was just ah . . . testing out the movement of her ejection nozzles. The ship isn't damaged." Rachael turned to Bhumi. "Can you walk with me for a minute?"

"Yes."

The two women walked back on the path towards the forest. "I can't imagine the shock you must have felt when you were revived by Seth," Rachael said as they entered the forest. "What was that like for you?"

"It was difficult. I woke up and had no sense of myself. I didn't know who I was or where I was. It was very disorienting."

"I can imagine. I had a similar experience once on New Eden. How're you feeling now?"

"I'm getting accustomed to this new life. Today's been the best day yet."

"Why?"

"Because you all are here. I was waiting anxiously for you to arrive ever since Seth said you would come. I'm happy to have some friends."

"I understand. You were lonely."

"Yes, I was terribly lonely," Bhumi said, happy that someone else understood her feelings.

"That's exactly what I wanted to talk to you about," Rachael said. "Humans need other humans to interact with. We're social creatures. I'm not sure where you've been staying, but we have an extra room in our home. I was wondering if you'd like to stay with us in our home during this mission?"

Bhumi stopped walking and stared straight at Rachael. Her face lit up. "Really?"

"Yes, please stay with us."

"I will!" Bhumi shouted and jumped towards Rachael and hugged her. "Thank you so much!"

Rachael was surprised by the sudden embrace. She slowly wrapped her arms around Bhumi and reciprocated the gesture.

Chapter Nine
Launch

For the next three days, the crew spent their time becoming familiarized with the ship. They explored every area and got a mental map of its layout. They learned that the large building near the center of the ship was an administrative building as well as a laboratory and medical center. The administrative portion was on the second floor, and the lab and medical area were on the ground floor. Seth had not allowed the crew into the lab, explaining that he would do so after launch.

The ship was divided into five geographic areas labeled from A to E. Four circular quadrants circumscribed the edges of the circular plane that constituted the living area. These were labeled areas A to D. The circular area at the center of the four quadrants, which encompassed the central one-third of their living area, was the final area labeled E. Area E was where the administrative building and lab were located. Areas A and B were the areas where the living habitats for the humans were. Area C was the recreational area which contained the tennis court, basketball court, and soccer field. Area D had a large, tall structure attached to the exterior wall. It was a biological building that displayed the typical petrin architecture of petrin habitats. Seth had referred to this building as a garage, and he would explain its contents and purpose as the mission progressed.

Richard was overjoyed to learn that Bhumi would be living with them during the mission. She had moved into the extra bedroom and was happy to have the company of the others. Richard and Bhumi spent most of their time together over the three days in which the crew was becoming familiar with the various areas of the ship.

"It seems like Bhumi and Richard are growing close," Joshua commented to Rachael near the end of the three days. "What do you think of that?"

"I'm okay with it," she responded.

"Are you okay or just resigned to it?"

"I'm not sure."

The humans were surprised to learn that the transparent outer walls of the ship doubled as video screens. Videos could be displayed on any portion of the walls. Seth explained the process as being some kind of reverse retina. He elaborated that the retinal tissue in the eyes of humans were sensitive to light and translated these to electrical impulses that were transported to the brain by optic nerves. The video screens reversed this process. They took video signals transmitted via neural bundles to a membrane on the inner portion of the walls. The membrane would then output light using light-producing cells according to the video signal. Since the light-emitting cells were much smaller than the pixels on a typical TV monitor, the images produced had incredible clarity.

Rachael and Joshua used the video wall of their abode to have video calls back to New Eden to speak with Ava. As they had foreseen, she was being spoiled by her grandparents, but it gave the couple solace to know that she was in good spirits despite their absence. They also knew that the video calls would have to end once the ship entered the spookyon dampening field since the system was using spookyon information transfer via the petrin network to transmit the video feed.

The crew also learned that there was a ship-wide audio system. The arching support structures that separated the wall panels had membranes that vibrated from neural inputs to create sound.

"Bro, please tell me that I can interface to this audio system," Vinod said to Seth when he learned of the audio system.

"Of course," Seth replied, grinning. "I designed this thing from the ground up. You think I'd leave out an audio interface for you to hook into? Just tell me a song to play, and it'll be blasted throughout the ship."

Vinod was ecstatic with the response. This led to hour-long sessions in the evenings where the entire living area of the ship was treated to a virtual concert from Vinod's vast knowledge of classic rock, which boosted the crew's morale. Seth had also invited other crew members for song requests which resulted in the crew listening to all musical genres, including pop, hip-hop, and classical selections.

The crew's mood was one of cautious excitement the night before the ship's launch. The crew had familiarized themselves with the vessel and had grown comfortable with their accommodations. As Vinod had described before, the ship was a resort, but one which could travel to distant destinations through the vastness of empty space.

Joshua, Vinod, Richard, Bhumi, and Seth finished a round of put-put where Seth had hit a hole-in-one on every hole. Richard glanced at Bhumi with a look of "I told you so."

Bhumi replied with a resigned eye roll.

"Man, you could've at least made it competitive," Vinod remarked as Seth hit his ball into the last hole. "Were you using the computing power of the collective to aim your shots?"

"I'm always using the computing power of the collective," Seth replied. "It's a part of who I am. We're a collective."

"Then we need to have another game when we enter the dampening field," Joshua said. "That'll even the playing field."

Seth picked up his ball from the cup. "Evening the playing field—that's what I'm hoping for. I hope you understand this, but once we're in that field, the technologies of the petrins and Medusa will be severely limited, but humans will operate as normal. Your species is not dependent on spookyon information transfer as we are. That's the main reason I wanted you on this mission. I think that a species as creative and resourceful as yourselves will serve us well."

Joshua and Vinod looked at each other as they recognized the purpose they were tasked with. Seth was hoping that the abilities that humans possessed without the help of information transfer via spookyons would be a benefit on a mission where such transfer would be unavailable. He was counting on them, and both Joshua and Vinod hoped they were up to the task.

Joshua looked around at the immaculate landscape surrounding them and the biological structure that enclosed it. He was still having difficulty believing that a structure as enormous as what he was viewing would soon be traveling at thousands of kilometers per second through the vacuum of empty space. He remembered that some had referred to their home planet as "spaceship Earth" since it too was a self-contained ecosystem that hurtled at tremendous velocity through not only their own solar system, but through their galaxy as a self-contained "spaceship" that nurtured life.

Vinod had asked Seth before why the petrins had made this spacecraft so large, but now Joshua realized the reason. The petrins had built a new "spaceship Earth." It was nowhere near as large as the original, but it was a representative slice of their original homeworld that could travel on a path that *they* could determine. Unlike their original homeworld, the petrins had created a mini-Earth that they could control and use as a home to explore the vacuum of empty space.

Joshua looked at Bhumi. He realized that she was in control of this incredible vessel. Seth had given her control of what would be their home for the next few months. He had wondered why Seth had chosen her for such an important task. She was, after all, a human that had lived on their planet millennia ago. Couldn't Seth have picked a more advanced human? Couldn't Seth have picked someone more learned in the sciences such as himself?

But what was the difference between himself and Bhumi? They were both human. Joshua realized that genetically they both had the same innate ability. Homo sapiens had inhabited the Earth for over two hundred and fifty thousand years, essentially unchanged from a genetic standpoint. Joshua realized that the only difference in knowledge between himself and Bhumi had nothing to do with something innate, but instead was dependent on what information was available to them when they were alive. He knew that Seth also understood this. Seth viewed all humans with the same lens. Humans were humans. The only difference between humans was what information they were exposed to. When Seth had picked Bhumi to control the ship, he was simply picking a human due to a human's innate ability as dictated by their genetics. Joshua knew that his genetics had no superiority to Bhumi's even though she had lived forty thousand years ago. The advancements that humans had made, especially over the last two centuries, had nothing to do with genetics, but everything to do with information that they had stockpiled external to their bodies.

* * *

The night before the launch, Seth called a meeting of what he had labeled the executive committee of the crew. This consisted of Joshua, Rachael, Vinod, Ted, Liz, Richard, and Bhumi. They met in a conference room on the second floor of the administrative building located in E. The meeting was televised to other crew members via a video interface projected on the outer walls of the ship.

Ted's security crew watched the pre-launch meeting while sitting on a grassy area in area B adjacent to one of the walls. The projected video feed was over one hundred feet in diagonal dimension but was crystal clear in resolution.

The executive crew sat around a large conference table. "I want to go over step-by-step the launch process and the initial trajectory the ship will take through the solar system until we get to Saturn."

"Saturn?" Richard asked excitedly. "We're going to Saturn?"

"Yes, we're going to Saturn. It's a refueling stop."

"Refueling?" Rachael asked.

Seth explained the need for the stop at Saturn. "It's not efficient for this ship to launch with its fuel tanks full. It'll require a huge force for the ship to break free of the ground it's now in. By my calculations, if it was fully loaded with liquid hydrogen fuel, the propulsion system won't have enough thrust to get us out of the ground."

"What's the weight of the fuel if we were fully loaded?" Vinod asked.

"The entire mass of this ship, if fully loaded with fuel, would be approximately one million metric tons," Seth explained. "The fuel would represent six-hundred-thousand metric tons of that mass."

"Sixty percent of the weight of the ship is just fuel?" Ted asked.

"It's not unusual," Joshua interjected. "It's actually fairly low as far as fuel to payload ratios are concerned for spaceships. Rockets from Earth typically had over a ninety-five percent fuel to payload ratio."

Seth continued the launch plan. "The ship will be launched with only one-fourth of its total fuel capacity to reduce weight. This will allow for enough fuel to get off the Earth and travel to Saturn. As I've mentioned before, hydrogen is the fuel for this ship. The atmosphere of Saturn is ninety-four percent hydrogen. The ship simply needs to enter the upper atmosphere of Saturn in order to ingest the hydrogen needed for the rest of the journey."

Everyone around the table was excited about the prospect of visiting a planet in their home solar system they had only seen in pictures. "Oh my god!" Joshua said. "We get to go into the atmosphere of Saturn. That'll be an amazing experience. Seth, do you think we can get a close-up view of the rings?"

"With our destination being the upper atmosphere," Seth said, "I don't think we can avoid seeing the rings close up even if we wanted to. But we're getting off track here. I want to explain the entire process, not just our initial destination. When I give Bhumi the signal to launch, she will start ejecting the iron plasma through the ejection nozzles. The initial movement of the ship will require the most force since we'll have to break free of the surrounding ground before reaching Earth's atmosphere."

"I've been wondering about that Seth," Joshua said. "Even with the reduced weight, it seems to me that blasting out of the ground would require a tremendous force. Are you sure the ship will be able to launch?"

"I believe so, but I'm not a hundred percent sure. My calculations do have some margin of error. I'm banking on the fact that the ground above us has been weakened and cracked. Remember that this ship has been growing for six months, all the while pushing away the rock and dirt surrounding it. The soil above us has been expanded and is definitely weaker than normal soil."

"How much propulsion force can the ship generate?" Joshua asked. "It'll take a tremendous force to release a ship this big from the ground."

"The max is approximately forty-Gs."

"Forty-Gs?" Joshua said, eyebrows raised. "That's incredible. That kind of G-force would kill a human. Why the need for so much force?"

"The ship can generate that much force if all of the ejection nozzles are pointed in the same direction with maximum plasma output, but it can't do this for very long. I estimate that most of that force will be required to lift us out of the ground, but we inside will not feel it since most of it will be used to push away the surrounding dirt, and only a small amount will be used to lift the ship."

"But still," Joshua said. "That's a tremendous amount of force. If Bhumi accidentally applied that while we're out in space, we'd all be killed."

"I'm aware of that," Bhumi said somewhat defensively. "I know the fragility of the contents of this ship, especially since I'm one of those contents. The maintenance of proper G forces inside the ship is intuitive to me."

"Intuitive? How?" Joshua asked.

Bhumi thought about how to answer the question for a while before answering. "I'd say it's kind of like picking up a fragile object like an egg with your hand. You can generate enough force with your fingers to crush it, but when you pick up an egg, you know the right amount of force required to pick it up and not break it. You don't have to think about how much force to use. It just comes naturally."

"Josh, I trust her on this," Liz said. "Biological neural systems have feedback mechanisms to prevent self-injury. Remember, for Bhumi, the ship is a part of her. She wouldn't harm herself. She's intuitively aware of how much thrust she can apply to prevent damage."

"Exactly," Bhumi said.

"Point taken," Joshua said. "Continue Seth."

"Once we've broken through the ground, Bhumi will automatically lower her thrust to allow us to rise through the atmosphere."

"How many Gs will we feel during that time?" Joshua asked.

"The net force the occupants will feel will be 1.1-Gs."

"1.1-Gs?" Joshua asked. "We'll barely feel it. It won't be like blasting off on a rocket ship at all. It'll feel like we're going up on an elevator."

"That's right," Seth said. "It'll be very comfortable. But remember, Bhumi will maintain 1.1-G thrust until we're outside the atmosphere at which time she will reduce the thrust to one-G, which she will maintain for the rest of the trip."

"Josh, can you explain what that means we'll feel during the launch?" Rachael asked. "I'm not following this discussion of G-forces."

"I'll try. You'll have to let go of your prior notions of astronauts strapped tightly into seats for a launch. It won't be needed. I suspect we'll slowly move upwards through the ground. Once we break free of the ground, we'll experience 1.1-Gs until we're through the atmosphere. At that acceleration, you'll only feel about ten percent heavier. If, for example, you weighed one hundred and fifty pounds normally, then you would feel as if you weighed one hundred sixty-five pounds. It would be barely noticeable. If the ship is accelerating at 1.1-Gs, its velocity will constantly increase, but remember that it will still be affected by Earth's gravity, which will pull us downward at one-G. So, our net acceleration upwards will be only 0.1-G which means that our speed will be increasing at only one meter per second per second. Like I said before, it'll feel more like we're going up in an elevator rather than like we're blasting off in a rocket ship."

"But once we're out of the gravitational field of the Earth, our velocity will be increasing much faster since we are maintaining one-G, right?" Vinod asked.

"Yes," Joshua said. "But remember, the gravitational field of the Earth extends much farther than most people realize. Many people have the misconception that the astronauts on the ISS were outside the gravitational pull of the Earth since they were in a zero-G environment with everything simply floating around. In fact, they were not. The Earth's gravity was still pulling on them, but the reason they seemed weightless was that they were in orbit. In essence, their spacecraft was continually falling towards the Earth due to its gravity, but never really reaching it. This is the definition of an orbit."

"Once we leave the atmosphere," Seth continued, "we will make a course change so that we will be headed towards the moon. We will use some of the moon's gravity as a slingshot to boost our velocity without using fuel."

"We choose to go to the moon!" Vinod exclaimed, right arm raised. Most listening understood that Vinod was channeling John Kennedy's speech from 1962, but the comment was lost on others.

"At our rate of acceleration," Seth said, "it will take a little more than two hours to reach the moon."

"Wow," Joshua commented. "It took the Apollo astronauts four days to get to the moon, but we'll be there in a couple of hours. That's the power of constant acceleration."

"Absolutely," Seth agreed. "After we pass the moon, we will be directed towards the inner solar system and the sun."

"The sun?" Ted asked. "I thought that Saturn and Planet Nine were outside Earth's orbit. Why the hell are we goin' towards the Sun?"

"Saturn and Planet Nine are currently located at a place in their orbits where they're on the opposite side of the sun from us, so we have to head towards the sun to go towards them. In fact, we're going to use the sun's gravity as an additional slingshot for us."

"How close will we get to the sun?" Rachael asked.

"Within the orbit of Mercury," Seth answered.

"Shit, that's close," Vinod said. "Won't we get fried?"

"The ship was designed with thermal shielding and heat dissipation systems, so we won't. Once we leave the sun, we'll head directly for Saturn."

"When will we make our flip?" Joshua asked, referring to the 180-degree rotation that the ship would have to make to decelerate on the second half of the trip to Saturn.

"Approximately at the distance of the orbit of Jupiter," Seth answered. "Although Jupiter will not be at that location at that time. It will take about five days to get to the rotation point, then an additional five days for the deceleration leg until we reach Saturn. This, in essence, is our flight plan to the refueling stop at Saturn." Seth looked around the table. "Any other questions?"

There were none.

"The ship will start its launch sequence at eight AM tomorrow. I want everyone gathered at the large lawn in the B quadrant next to the external wall at that time. We'll get a great view of the launch from there. Meeting adjourned."

"It's the petrin solar system tour," Ted commented as he rose from the table.

* * *

The next morning, the crew stood on one of the lawns at the edge of the ship in the B quadrant. Seth stood next to Bhumi as the others gathered close. The group's emotions were those of excitement tinged with apprehension as they realized the dangers of the mission they were embarking on. The largest of those dangers was uncertainty. The most immediate uncertainty was whether or not the ship would be able to generate enough thrust to leave the ground. They had faith in Seth and the petrins, but even they were not infallible. Seth had said that he had designed the ship with his "best guess" as to the forces needed. They were about to test these calculations.

"Bhumi, are you ready?" Seth asked.

"Ready."

"You may start the propulsion sequence," Seth said.

Bhumi stood perfectly still with her hands at her side, palms open facing upwards. She slowly closed her eyes as if concentrating. The crew felt a slight vibration under their feet.

"The vibration is normal," Seth explained. "Bhumi is generating the iron plasma. In a few moments, she'll begin ejecting it."

"Plasma generation at full capacity," Bhumi announced a minute later, her eyes still closed. "Starting plasma ejection."

The crew heard a slight rumble from outside the ship as the vibrations under their feet became stronger. The rumble grew louder over the next minute. Suddenly loud thunderous cracks sounded, which caused the crew to grow apprehensive.

"It's the sound of the surrounding rock fracturing," Seth said. "Not to worry."

"Thrust at fifty percent," Bhumi announced. Her face now showed a slight grimace. The ship still had not moved. "Sixty-five percent thrust," Bhumi said a few moments later. "Seventy-five." Bhumi's face contorted more.

"Is she alright?" Richard asked Seth. "She looks like she's in pain."

"She's fine," Seth replied. "Remember the ship is a part of her and gives her feedback in the form of pain when it's under stress. I'd be like you trying to lift a heavy barbell. The more you strain to lift it, the more pain you feel."

"Pain is an important feedback mechanism in biological systems," Liz said. "It prevents one from stressing yourself beyond your capacity."

Joshua noted some heat emanating from the wall he stood next to. He could see areas of the external rock starting to glow a dull red. "The wall's getting hot Seth."

"Yes, it's being heated by the plasma the ship's expelling," Seth replied. He turned to Bhumi.

"Still within thermal limits," Bhumi stated with pressured speech. "Increasing thrust to eighty-five percent."

Richard could see the pain that Bhumi was experiencing by her expression. He thought of going to her to offer some comfort but decided against it. She was concentrating on the task at hand, and he figured that she shouldn't be disturbed.

The sound of the cracking rocks became more frequent as some crew members covered their ears against the noise. The ship suddenly lurched upward as it became dislodged from its location. "Adjust for acceleration," Seth told Bhumi. "The ship has broken free of its moorings."

"Yes," was the only response from Bhumi as she concentrated on the control of the ship.

Rachael wondered whether the crew should sit down on the grass on which they stood. Would there be some turbulence that would cause them to lose their balance? *I'm sure Seth would have told us if we needed to be seated. He's thought of everything.*

The ship slowly started moving upwards. The rocks and dirt scraping the outside created a loud grinding sound. The ship gathered speed as the crew standing next to the wall noticed the rocks outside the ship moving down faster as the grinding grew louder. Suddenly the noise stopped as the ship blasted through the surface of the ground, spewing rocks and dirt high into the air.

"Decreasing thrust," Bhumi announced, her face more relaxed.

Joshua looked down through the clear-walled exterior of the ship and could see he was above the Bowman Particle Research Center, its buildings destroyed into ruins by the ship's exit. He noticed water streaming down the exterior walls of the ship as a heavy rain fell from above and washed the dirt from the surface. There were no more vibrations. The ship slowly and smoothly left the ground behind. As the ship rose higher, he looked to the horizon and could see the bay with the Golden Gate Bridge in the distance. It looked unchanged from what he had remembered. He saw the skyline of San Francisco, its buildings intact, but its streets, however, overgrown with vegetation. *Earth*, was the only thought that crossed his mind. He had missed this place.

The ship slowly rose higher as the crew felt the sightly increased weight of 1.1-Gs. Joshua could now see the ejection nozzles on the ship's exterior that had previously been obscured by the dirt that surrounded them. They exited the ship's walls horizontally and then bent in a curve which pointed them towards the ground. Their ends spewed out the red-hot iron plasma gas that was lifting them upwards. They were much more significant than he had anticipated.

The ship headed upwards towards the grey clouds releasing rain above. There was a sudden blinding flash accompanied by a loud crack.

"Lightning strike," Seth said looking at Bhumi.

"I'm undamaged," Bhumi said, her eyes still closed.

The ship entered the clouds and soon rose above them. Below them was a sea of white clouds covering the landscape below. As the ship rose higher and gathered speed, the sky above turned a darker shade of blue. Joshua could now see the curvature of the Earth below. He recognized the shoreline of northern California as they went higher still. The sky above now grew black, and Joshua could see stars appearing in the blackness.

"Atmosphere cleared," Bhumi announced. "Decreasing thrust and starting course correction."

Joshua felt the reduced weight of the decrease in thrust from 1.1-G to one-G. He also felt a slight sideways motion as the ship started to rotate. This motion only lasted for a few seconds as the Earth below moved from directly underneath the ship to below and to the side. He could see the entire planet now. He was over North America bathed in sunlight. He had expected to see a world scarred by the ten-year war that had taken place between the petrins and Medusa, but it looked perfectly normal to him. It looked placid and inviting with its green vegetation-laden land contrasted by tan desert areas all surrounded by crystal blue ocean. Humans had left the Earth, but the plants and animals of Earth survived on.

No one said a word, and the entire ship grew absolutely quiet as they were no longer hearing the rush of the atmosphere outside. They were in awe of the view outside. There was not a sound.

Joshua was overcome with emotion. He reached out and grasped Rachael's hand, both glued to the spectacle outside. He was an astronaut now, experiencing a view that very few human eyes had directly experienced. But even those humans had a limited view of the Earth through a small portal window of their ship. His view was expansive. Standing next to the transparent wall of the ship, he felt as if he could step off into space.

Joshua stared at the globe beneath him. He knew he was looking at his mother . . . mother Earth.

* * *

The doe walked with her newborn fawn through a meadow in the forest. She found some fresh, green sprouts that poked up from the sodden ground. She started eating the nourishment as her fawn nuzzled up to one of her teats and started drinking. The ground below them shook suddenly, and they heard a loud sound in the distance. The doe immediately ran and led her fawn to the shelter of a nearby grove of trees. They peered out and saw a bright red light ascending in the sky. As the light reached the clouds, there was a flash of lightning, and the red streak slowly disappeared. They waited for a while in their hiding place before the doe gradually led her fawn back to the meadow.

Chapter Ten

The Moon and the Sun

Bhumi opened her eyes as the blue-green orb of the Earth slowly rotated beneath them. Richard walked to her and grasped her hand. "Are you alright?"

"Yes," she responded, looking out the window, seeing the Earth for the first time. "I'm great. It was an amazing experience."

"It looked like you were in pain."

"Yes, there was some pain, and I felt like I was straining at the beginning, but now it feels . . . wonderful." Bhumi tried to think of how to better explain what she was feeling. "It's as if a part of my body had been trapped in something, and now it's been let free." She turned to look at Richard. "I feel . . . reborn." After a moment, she turned towards Seth. "How'd I do?"

"You performed the launch perfectly," Seth said. "Are you sensing any damage?"

"No."

The group stared at Bhumi. They realized the importance of Bhumi's role on this mission. Their lives were in her control. She was in command of their immediate environment and was tasked with ensuring that their vessel would keep them safe through the hostile vacuum of space. Joshua started slow applause that increased as other crew members joined in and grew to a crescendo for a few seconds before subsiding. Bhumi blushed with appreciation.

"Alright everyone," Seth said. "The launch is complete. The transit of the moon will be in two hours. Those that want to observe should meet back here at that time."

The group started to disperse as some still stared out the window at the view. The sun now shone brightly through the walls lighting up the landscape. Bhumi looked up and turned off the artificial sun that had lit their space while underground. The changing of the light source changed the perspective of the landscape from what they were accustomed to. Before, all shadows had been directly underneath objects due to the light directly above. Now the shadows were slanted across the landscape.

"Are you able to go for a walk?" Richard asked Bhumi.

"Yes, my launch duties are done." Richard grasped her hand, and they strode down the circumferential trail towards the forest.

"You said your duties are done, but aren't you still controlling the ship?" Richard asked.

"Yes, but it's more automated now." Bhumi thought of how to explain the experience to Richard. "I guess it's kind of like breathing. Most of the time, you breathe without thinking about it, but if you want to, you can control how fast or how deep you breathe. The ship is keeping its same trajectory and thrust, so I don't really have to think about it. It's automatic."

* * *

Rachael watched as the couple walked away from the group. "It was a perfect launch. Bhumi performed exactly as expected."

"Yes she did," Seth said with an element of pride in his voice. "Her neural interface to the ship worked perfectly."

"Speaking of the ship," Vinod said. "I've been meaning to ask you Seth. Does this ship have a name?"

"A name? No, why?"

"All ships from Earth have names, even spaceships."

Seth thought about the notion for a moment. "If that's the case, then there can be only one name for the ship . . . Bhumi."

"Bhumi?" Vinod asked.

"Yes. Remember that the ship's a part of her. You really can't separate the ship from her. When I refer to you as Vinod, I'm referring to your entire self. It doesn't make sense to name, for example, your right hand as Jason."

"Yea, I get it bro, but referring to both the ship and the girl as Bhumi would be confusing. We need to have a separate name simply to avoid confusion."

"I guess I see the logic in that. Do you have any suggestions?"

Vinod stroked his chin with his hand and thought of a name. "How about Zephyr?"

"Zephyr?" Seth asked. "A westerly wind?"

"Yes. We basted off from the west coast of the US, so it seems to make sense. Besides, I like the word—Zephyr."

"I'm good with it bro."

Rachael looked annoyingly at Seth and Vinod. "You two've got some arrogance."

"Why?" Seth asked, startled.

"You're naming a part of a girl without her input or her even being present? Who do you think you are?"

Seth and Vinod were surprised by the response. "You're right Rach," Vinod said. "It should be her decision, but I'm still going to recommend Zephyr to her."

"My batteries are running low," Seth said. "I'm going to recharge for a while." He headed towards the administrative building that contained his charger.

"I've got a run scheduled with my crew this morning," Ted said. "Gotta keep in shape. I'll catch up with y'all for the lunacy."

Joshua smiled as he grasped that the meaning of the word "lunacy" from Ted's last statement referred to the moon. Ted walked away with his crew.

"We have a couple of hours to kill," Liz said. "What does everyone want to do?"

"I'm going to lay down right here on this grass and catch some rays," Rachael said as she sat on the grass and laid back, her hands laced behind her head. "I haven't been in the light of our home star for quite some time. Its warmth feels nice." The others agreed to stay on the grass and wait there for the two hours until the lunar transit, absorbing the view.

"Man," Vinod said after some time. "Zephyr . . . ah, I mean presumed Zephyr is amazing. We're hurtling through space, and I can feel nothing. No vibration, no turbulence, nothing. There isn't even a sound. It's like we're standing still, and the universe around us is moving past. The only thing that gives away our motion are those red streaks of plasma coming out of the ejection nozzles, but even those don't make a sound."

"The plasma is being ejected into the vacuum of space," Joshua said. "It's not contacting the ship and therefore no sound."

"I've always been humbled by the genetic engineering abilities of the petrins," Liz stated. "But this . . .," Liz looked around the ship, "this is by far their greatest achievement. And to think that it was all grown from a single seed. Genetics and genetic engineering may be the most powerful engineering method in the cosmos."

"How long Liz?" Joshua asked, now seated on the grass with the others.

"How long 'til what?"

"How long do you estimate 'til humans have that ability? How long before we discover the secrets of the cell—why a certain sequence of DNA codes for a human, and another, using the same processes, can code for this ship?"

"That's tough to estimate," Liz replied. "Humanity, especially when we were on Earth, had moratoriums on many forms of genetic engineering. But now, after experiencing New Eden and what can be accomplished with it, those moratoriums are slowly fading away. If I were to hazard a guess, I'd estimate that we could get it done in one to two hundred years."

"But somehow, I don't feel that we could do it simply by using biological science," Vinod said. "We would need the help of computer science."

"Computer science?" Rachael asked. "Why? Computer science isn't biological."

"Remember when I asked Seth how they design something and then encode it into DNA?" Vinod asked. "He said that they have something like a compiler used in computers. It's a program that takes higher-level code and converts it into machine language that a computer can understand. Seth said they design the structure of something like this ship, and their compiler translates that design into a DNA sequence. I can't imagine the complexity of that process as it pertains to DNA, but we as humans will need the help of computers and AI to do it. We're not a collective like the petrins that can instantaneously recruit other individual minds into a networked computer of sorts."

"He's absolutely right," Liz stated. "If or when we do get the power of genetic engineering, it will have been a parallel process of improvements in both the biological and computer sciences."

"Can't say I'm looking forward to that," Rachael said. "I'm not looking forward to humans controlling genetics."

"Why?" Joshua asked. "Surely you've recognized the vast power that genetic engineering can have. As an example, you saw the overwhelming joy of all those people who were paraplegic or quadriplegic on Earth who were able to walk again when they were transported to New Eden. Surely you can't be against something like that."

"That was very moving and powerful," Rachael agreed. "But with vast power comes vast responsibility and vast change. The council decided, and rightly so, in my opinion, that humans shouldn't be immortal, but we were only able to make this decision because the petrins were the only ones who could provide this service. If genetic engineering becomes ubiquitous, if it becomes a process that any human can utilize, we couldn't have central control of it. If everyone had the ability to alter their own genetics so that they don't age, even if we enact laws that say that it shouldn't be done, we could never hope to control it. There would be those humans who would make themselves immortal despite the laws. And that's just with immortality. How about other characteristics like physical ability or mental acuity? Could we prevent humans from altering this if genetic engineering was readily available? I think not. I fear that the entire definition of what constitutes a human would change."

"I see your point," Liz said. "I don't think we as humans are ready to redefine ourselves. I'm glad we have some time to figure that out, but like I told Josh, that time is coming."

"To be honest, I feel we've been lucky with our technology so far," Rachael said. "We haven't had a powerful, easily accessible technology that we've developed."

"What do you mean by that?" Joshua asked.

Rachael rolled her body on the grass and turned to Joshua, her head resting on her arm. "Josh, you remember when we talked a few years ago about the Manhattan Project on Earth and how they developed the technology for the nuclear bomb and later for the hydrogen bomb?"

"Yes."

"That technology, like any technology, could be used for good or evil. We certainly used it for evil on Earth, but that same technology is sitting right under our feet at this exact moment, propelling this ship forward. This ship uses nuclear fusion for its energy source. We were lucky that the technology for building a nuclear bomb wasn't easily accessible. Many understood the science behind it, but it required a source of relatively rare uranium ore and highly specialized equipment to be able to enrich that uranium to create a bomb. But what if it didn't? What if anyone could create a nuclear weapon just as easily as they could make a pipe bomb? How long would humanity have lasted? I don't think we'd have made it out of the twentieth century. Most humans are moral with good intentions, but all it takes is a small percentage of humans with access to a powerful technology to destroy all humanity. That's my fear with genetic engineering."

The group was silent as they reflected on Rachael's statement. "Maybe that's why the petrins formed themselves into a collective," Liz stated. "Maybe they wanted more control over individual petrins as their technology advanced so that no one individual could usurp it."

"Liz," Vinod said. "Are you saying that you think society should curtail individuality in humans? That individual freedoms should be restricted to let the society thrive?"

"I don't know for sure," Liz replied. "But somehow, I feel that that may be the only choice as we increase the amount of technology we possess. Otherwise, we risk our own technology ending our society due to some of humanity's outliers."

"An outlier," Joshua said somberly. "That's exactly who we are confronting on this mission. A petrin outlier—Medusa."

*   *   *

The crew regathered at the lawn area for the lunar transit. Vinod asked Bhumi about a name for the ship, and she approved of the name Zephyr.

The moon would pass on the opposite side of the ship from where they were located, so Bhumi rotated two of her ejection nozzles on opposite sides of the ship ninety degrees so that they now pointed along its circumference. She applied a slight thrust to the two nozzles for only a second, which started the ship rotating on its long axis. As the ship slowly spun, she repositioned the now inert nozzles 180 degrees from their current position. When the ship had rotated to a position such that the moon would pass directly in front of the group, she again applied a one-second thrust to stop the rotation.

"Nicely done," Seth said after the maneuver. "When we reach the moon, due to our constant acceleration since leaving Earth, we will be traveling at over seventy kilometers per second. Unfortunately, our encounter with the moon will only last a couple of minutes at that speed. So everyone get a good viewing point."

The group spread out close to the clear wall. As they looked up, they could see the moon approaching from above. The globe was primarily bathed in darkness, but a crescent portion near the top was in sunlight.

"We will reach minimal distance in two minutes," Bhumi announced.

Joshua studied the approaching orb. It was a patchwork of light and dark grey areas potted with craters. He was familiar with significant landmarks on the moon. "I think I see the area of Tranquility Base," he said, pointing with his right index finger. "It's in the dark portion." Everyone was familiar with the area. It was the location of the first lunar landing, where Neil Armstrong had placed the first human footprint on an extraterrestrial body.

"Do you think we will see anything left from the Apollo 11 landing?" Rachael asked.

"No way," Joshua replied. "We'll be too far away to see anything that small."

"Maybe I can help," Bhumi said. "Please look to the opposite wall."

The group turned their heads and viewed the wall on the ship's opposite side. On one panel of the wall was an enormous video image portraying the moon's surface. The video zoomed in to show a smaller area of the moon's surface. Joshua made out a small white area in the center of the image with a dark trail leading from it. "Is this a live image?"

"Yes," Bhumi replied.

"What are we looking at Josh?" Rachael asked.

"I'm not sure, but I believe that white spot is what's left of the lunar lander from Apollo 11. It's the portion left behind when the crew portion of the lander blasted off back to the command module."

"Let me zoom in some more," Bhumi said. The image zoomed in and gave a crystal-clear image of the landing site.

"My god, it *is* the lunar lander," Joshua said under his breath. "How are we seeing this?"

"I'm using one of my eyes," Bhumi responded.

The group turned to Bhumi and noted that she was facing them and not in the direction of the moon above.

"She means one of the eyes of the ship," Seth explained. "There are eight of them, four near the front and four near the back. They can see in any direction. She can project their images onto the walls of the ship. Like human eyes, two of them can be used in concert to determine parallax and the distance to an object, but unlike human eyes, they can also zoom in on the object they're seeing."

"They're not eyes," Joshua said as he saw the resolution and clarity of the image on the wall. "They're biological telescopes. They have to be in order to see an image of this resolution at this distance."

"I suppose your right," Seth said. "They can see extreme distances with high resolution. Each is more than a thousand times the resolution of your Hubble telescope."

Joshua's mind reeled at the statement. What could they discover with eight telescopes with that much power? "You should have brought an astronomer on this mission Seth," he said, mesmerized by the image. "What science they could have done."

"Not in the mission plan," Seth remarked casually. "We're approaching the moon."

The group turned back to the window in front of them. The moon descended towards them from above and grew larger by the second. The ship entered the moon's shadow, which caused its interior to go dark. Soon they were right on top of it. They could see its surface details like none of them had seen before. The crescent-shaped sunlit area grew larger. The crater's edges in this area cast dark shadows into the interior of the sunken craters.

"We're at minimal distance," Bhumi announced a few moments later. The ship was now once again bathed in sunlight as it emerged from behind the lunar shadow.

The group watched the grey orb as it passed them and started descending below them. Soon it was a small bright circle in front of the blue-green Earth, both slowly fading away. They felt no change in momentum as the ship used the moon's gravitation to gain additional speed and change direction. The ship had curved around the moon and was now pointed directly towards the sun. The landscape inside the ship was in dark shadow as the opaque ceiling above blocked the sun's rays. Bhumi turned on the artificial sun in the ceiling, which gave the appearance of high noon.

It was a strange environment. There was the heat and light of a perfectly sunny day from the artificial sun overhead but surrounding them was a deep back night sky with bright, untwinkling stars. They were on a small disk of Earth accelerating towards their home star.

* * *

The Zephyr continued accelerating at one-G as it left the Earth-moon system behind. It would take a full day to reach the slingshot point near the sun, which would give it even more speed and a course change to direct it towards Saturn.

Bhumi oversaw the day-night cycles on the Zephyr. She could automatically adjust the brightness and duration of the artificial sun to match those of Earth. Currently, her cycle was that of late September in the northern hemisphere of Earth, with the day cycles slowly growing shorter and the nights longer. She could also adjust the intensity of the artificial sun to regulate the temperature of the interior of Zephyr. Crew members noted a slight chill in the air when they awoke the next morning.

"A little cooler this morning," Richard remarked as he and Bhumi left their abode and strode towards the orchard for breakfast.

"On purpose," Bhumi remarked. "It's autumn, so the days will be getting cooler and shorter. I believe the leaves of the trees in here will be turning colors soon."

"I thought that since we're headed towards the sun, the ship would get warmer."

"No, I've got complete control of that. The nosecone of the ship is in direct sunlight now. It's getting warmer as we go closer to the sun, but I've opacified it to prevent the sunlight from getting in and causing a greenhouse effect."

Richard looked curiously at Bhumi as they walked. "What?" Bhumi asked as she noticed Richard's stare.

"Greenhouse effect? You seem to know a lot of modern science for someone from the Paleolithic. How'd you learn all this stuff? It took me years of school to learn concepts like the greenhouse effect."

"I'm not sure 'learn' is the right word for some of the information I have," Bhumi said. "Some of it I simply woke up with because Seth had ingrained it into me. Other information I learned after I woke up, but there's still other information that I can ask for as needed."

"Ask for?" Richard asked. "From who? Seth?"

"No," Bhumi said hesitantly. She didn't elaborate on the response, which caused Richard to look at her with curiosity.

"Boom, you're not going to tell me?"

Bhumi displayed a slight grin at the term "Boom." It was a pet name that Richard had made up for her. The first time he'd used it, she had responded that her name was 'Bhumi.' Richard had explained that it was a pet name he had come up with for her, which signified familiarity and closeness—a fact which made her happy.

"It's not that I don't want to tell you," Bhumi said. "Seth said I can't tell you yet. It's something he wants to show the whole crew at once."

"A secret huh? Okay, I get it. So, what other secrets are you two hiding?"

"A few," Bhumi replied with a sly grin. "There's one that I want to show you this afternoon during the solar transit."

Richard raised his eyebrows. "You going to show the whole crew?"

"No," Bhumi said, turning to Richard. "Just you. As long as you're nice to me."

"I'm always nice to you," Richard replied as he took her hand in his as they continued their walk. "Except when we're playing put-put of course."

* * *

Later that afternoon, Bhumi led Richard to an area at the outer edge of quadrant D. They were at the base of one of the prominent pillars that separated the window panels of the ship. Richard looked up at the ivory-white structure. It narrowed as it soared upward one kilometer, eventually ending as a thin line at the ceiling. "Does this thing actually get thinner at the top, or is it just perspective?"

"Just perspective. It's the same diameter up there as it is down here."

Richard looked behind him. "We're on the opposite side of the ship from where Seth said to meet for the solar transit. We were supposed to meet everyone there in half an hour. Shouldn't we head there now to get there in time?"

"You worry too much Blue," Bhumi said. "We're not going to be viewing the transit with the others. We'll view it together from some other place."

"Blue?"

Bhumi turned to look at Richard. "I made it up. It's *my* pet name for *you.*"

"Why 'Blue?'"

"Because it's the color of your eyes. You like it?"

Richard shrugged his shoulders. "It's fine, I guess," Richard responded with a smile. "Whatever suits you. So, where're we viewing the transit from?"

"Follow me," Bhumi said as she touched the pillar in front of her. A circular door opened on the pillar's surface through which Bhumi led Richard. The door closed behind them, leaving them in total darkness. They were in a small, enclosed space inside the pillar.

"Is this the secret you wanted to show me?" Richard asked in the darkness. "Not much to see."

"Oh yee of little faith," Bhumi said as she turned on a luminous wall inside the pillar with her mind. The space was bathed in a gentle white light. Richard noticed that they were in a small circular room. On one side of the room were climbing rungs that emanated from one side of the circular walls. They were U-shaped structures attached to the wall spaced two feet apart that progressed upwards. Richard turned his head and looked above. He could see inside the pillar now that it was illuminated. It slowly arched inward as it rose in height. The climbing rungs soared upwards, becoming tiny as they ascended a kilometer into the air. Opposite to the rungs on the other side of the enclosure were long circular pipes that also flowed upwards.

"Those are the plasma pipes," Bhumi said, pointing to the structures. "They deliver the iron plasma to the ejection nozzles on the outside."

Richard's sight followed the climbing rungs as they soared up the chamber. "Whoa!" he exclaimed. "That's one tall ladder. Does it go all the way to the ceiling?"

"Yup."

"Are we climbing *that*?" Richard said, pointing up.

"If you can handle it."

"Oh, I can handle it," Richard said. "I was more worried about you."

"Are you saying that I'm not in good shape?" Bhumi asked, hands on hips.

Richard sensed a certain familiarity with Bhumi's posture. He had seen it from Rachael many times before. *Do all women stand with their hands on their hips when being confrontational?* "No, you're in great shape," he said, looking her up and down. He turned his head and looked back up at the endless vertical tunnel. "What's up there?"

"I don't know for sure," Bhumi replied. "I've never been up there."

"You don't know what's up there, but you want us to climb a kilometer to find out?"

"I didn't say I didn't know. I said I didn't know *for sure.* But I think it could be pretty cool."

"How's it cool? How do you know what's up there?"

Bhumi gave Richard an exasperated look. "I know the layout of this ship. I *have* to know it. It's a part of me. I felt the presence of this passageway, and I also know, in general, where it leads. I thought it'd be a fun place to watch the solar transit from. You up for this or not?"

Richard walked over to the ladder and ran his right hand along the surface of one of the rungs. "They seem to have a decent grip, but what happens if one of us slips halfway up. It's a long fall."

Bhumi looked sideways at Richard. "Are you scared?"

Richard glanced at Bhumi and then back up the ladder. He was definitely a little apprehensive. He was not afraid of heights but climbing a kilometer-long ladder did give him pause. However, he wasn't about to show Bhumi his trepidation.

"No. But seriously Boom, is this dangerous?"

"No silly," Bhumi responded. "I have control of the ship. If one of us falls, I'll simply reduce the ship's thrusters and therefore the artificial gravity, and you'll travel all the way slowly to the bottom with a gentle landing."

Richard was still apprehensive. "Turning off the gravity by cutting the thrusters wouldn't be a good idea. There'd be a mess on the ship with the loss of gravity. Remember the trouble we got into with the put-put incident? This would be much worse."

"That's why we have to climb carefully and not slip," Bhumi responded. "But still no permanent damage if it does happen."

Richard recognized a mischievous streak within Bhumi—one that he identified with. His heart beat faster at the thought of what they were about to do.

"You coming with me, or are you going to wimp out?" Bhumi asked. "I'm going whether you come or not."

Richard shrugged his shoulders. "If you can handle it, I can handle it,"

Richard said resolutely as he pointed to the ladder. "Ladies first."

Bhumi started climbing up the ladder rung by rung with Richard behind her. It was a strenuous climb, but something they could accomplish without too much difficulty. They stopped multiple times along the way to take a break when they became winded. They took another rest break when they got about three-quarters of the way to the top. Richard glanced down and noted that he couldn't see the floor anymore. The vertical tunnel simply seemed to end at a point hundreds of meters below. It was a surreal and frightening experience being hundreds of meters in the air. He quickly closed his eyes and took a deep breath to relieve himself of the sight.

The couple resumed their climb, and Richard looked up and saw Bhumi's perfectly shaped hips undulating above him as they ascended each rung. *Certainly a better view looking up than down*, he thought to himself.

They reached the top of the ladder and stepped out onto a dark platform, both sweating profusely and out of breath. "I hope this climb was worth it," Richard remarked, his hands on his knees as he tried to catch his breath. After some time, he stood up and took in the surroundings. The ladder they had climbed ended on a flat surface on which they stood. The space was dark, and they couldn't see anything beyond the surface beneath their feet.

"Let me turn on some lights," Bhumi remarked. The space became illuminated by a luminous ceiling. "We're above the artificial sun and the water vapor collectors of the ceiling of the landscape below," Bhumi explained.

Richard looked around. They were in an enormous space seven hundred meters wide and a hundred feet tall. All the surfaces of the space were black, including the flat ceiling a hundred feet above. Even the normally transparent exterior walls of the space that constituted the ship's exterior walls were black and opaque. The entire space was empty except for four large spherical structures that rose from floor to ceiling. The four spheres were in opposite corners at the edges of the space. The exteriors of the spheres were also black in color.

"It's warm in here," Richard commented, wiping some sweat from his brow with his forearm.

"We're above the artificial sun," Bhumi said. "It must be right under this floor. I'm sure some of its heat is bleeding into this space."

Richard walked over to the closest sphere, which was not far from the top of the ladder. It towered above him. "What are these structures?" he asked as he ran his hand along the sphere, its surface smooth and hard. "They're gigantic."

"One of my eyes," Bhumi responded.

Richard understood what she meant. He knew that this was one of the "eyes" of the ship. Joshua had referred to them as biological telescopes. He knew that he was looking at a housing that enclosed an enormous biological eye that Bhumi could point in any direction to view outside the ship.

"It's a pretty cool place," Richard commented, looking around. "Not sure it was worth a kilometer-long climb, though."

"We're not done climbing," Bhumi said as she walked to a wall a few feet away from the sphere.

Richard realized that there was another set of rungs to climb that ascended a hundred feet to the ceiling above. "After a kilometer, I guess another hundred feet won't be so bad," he commented as the couple began ascending the rungs.

Near the top of the climb, Richard noted an orange glow emanating from the orifice into which the rungs ended. Bhumi disappeared into the bright glow, and Richard soon followed and stepped out onto a soft surface. As he looked up, he saw that the orange glow was from a large orange disk that encompassed most of the ceiling above. He walked next to Bhumi, who was also looking up at the orange light source. Richard saw that the glowing disk was not static. Its edges seemed to undulate slightly as if its surface was bubbling, slowly releasing tiny explosions that marred its perfectly circular shape. The undulations appeared to be moving in slow motion, popping at the surface as its contents slowly raised from the edge and then eventually fell slowly back to the surface. The remainder of the ceiling was pitch black.

"What is that?" Richard asked Bhumi, her body a silhouette against the orange glow from the disk from above.

"It's the sun," Bhumi replied. "We're in the nose of the ship. I've opacified the walls so that only a minimal amount of light is getting through."

Richard was speechless. He was awed by the sight. He felt a small amount of warmth coming from the bubbling disk above, but not anything uncomfortable. He was experiencing a star up close. He had learned much about the incredible role that stars had played in his existence from Joshua. He knew that the material that comprised his body had been forged in the core of a star that extinguished itself in a massive supernova explosion millennia ago. To see the process happening before him made him wonder what would happen to the elements that were being forged now in the glowing object in front of him. Would they simply be scattered through the endless void of space, or would they eventually be combined with other elements in a specific order to create a living entity like himself? Whatever the case, Richard realized that what he was looking at was a crucible of life.

Bhumi led Richard to the center of the semi-spherical space that enclosed them. It was three hundred meters from the edge to the center. They stood side by side as the orange orb of the sun above grew more prominent and moved to the side as the Zephyr moved closer to the star.

Tears formed in Richard's eyes as the magnitude of what they were witnessing engulfed him. He reached out and grasped Bhumi's hand. "Boom, thank you for bringing me here," he murmured, his eyes affixed to the spectacle above.

* * *

"Where the hell are they?" Rachael asked, her right hand above her eyes as she scanned the horizon. "They're going to miss it."

The crew had gathered at one of the ship's walls to view the solar transit.

"Who knows where they are," Vinod commented. "Typical teenagers. Off in a world of their own. Probably playing put-put or something."

"I can't believe that Bhumi's not here," Seth said, also looking around.

"Don't you need her here for the transit?" Joshua asked.

"No," Seth said. "The solar transit doesn't need any course correction on her part. We'll simply use the sun's gravity to slingshot around it. I'm somewhat disappointed that she's not here to see it though."

"I don't know Seth," Rachael commented. "It may have been a mistake leaving control of this ship to a person so young. You may not have realized it, but young humans are unpredictable."

Seth turned to Rachael. "You weren't much older than her when I first met you. Like I told you before, she reminds me a lot of you."

Seth's statement caused Rachael to reflect on when she and Joshua had first made contact with Seth. She had not been much older than Bhumi at that time. She thought back to the time in the Bat Cave when they had first tested the Bowman sphere. She was a brash young reporter that had manipulated her way into viewing the testing of a sphere that would change the course of humanity. It had been fortuitous that she had been there during that time. She had been instrumental in introducing Joshua to Vinod and establishing first contact with the petrins. Seth was right. She was young and impetuous at that time, but somehow, things had worked out. She had been brash, but not irresponsible. "I'm sure they have their reasons for not being here. It's fine," she said without much conviction.

A few moments later, a dark arc appeared near the edge of the ceiling on the wall they were standing next to. As they watched, the arc grew larger and advanced downward towards them.

"What's that dark spot?" Joshua asked.

"Thermal shielding," Seth replied while glancing up at the advancing arc. "The walls of the ship have some photochromic abilities. They automatically become more opaque if a large light source is shined on them. The sun is approaching, and the exterior of the ship is becoming opaquer to accommodate the increased heat and light."

The darkness on the wall grew to eventually encompass an entire half of the ship. Joshua looked towards the opposite wall and noted that it was still clear, stars shining through its surface. Soon a giant orange orb appeared at the ceiling in the center of the dark opacity. It grew larger and closer as the ship continued its acceleration. The orb grew to encompass almost their entire field of view, its surface slowly bubbling with the energy released by its nuclear furnace thousands of miles below.

"How are we only feeling only a small increase in heat?" Joshua asked. "At this distance, the ship must be getting bombarded with intense heat and radiation. How is the Zephyr dissipating all of this energy?"

Seth smiled. "Look to the opposite side Dr. Andrews. See if you notice anything different."

Joshua turned to the other side of the ship. He looked out of the clear walls and noted only the normal starscape. "I don't see anything . . . wait." Joshua spotted the change. The plasma being ejected from the nozzles was no longer glowing red. It was white-hot. Joshua realized where the excess heat was going. "The ship's transporting the excess heat from the sun into the plasma exhaust. It's using the external heat to increase the temperature of the plasma being expelled by the ship. That's why its color changed. The exhaust is much hotter than normal."

"Correct," Seth responded.

"Ingenious," Joshua replied under his breath. He knew that heat dissipation was a huge problem for any spaceship that came close to a star. The Parker Solar Probe that had been launched from Earth many years before had to be equipped with shielding that would reflect most of the radiation from the sun because absorbing the radiation was not an option because there would be no way of getting rid of the excess heat from the ship in the vacuum of space. But Seth and the petrins, who had designed the ship, had come up with a different solution. Instead of reflecting the excess energy, they simply absorbed it and transferred this heat to the ship's propellant. The excess energy absorbed by Zephyr was simply being redirected and ejected into space as part of the iron plasma that was also being used to propel the ship.

The group stared at the orange disk as it descended from above and slowly became a half-circle as it descended beneath their floor.

"I've seen some amazing sunsets from the Louisiana coast," Ted remarked, "but nothing like this. It's beautiful."

Liz extended her arms wide, opened her hands, and closed her eyes as the small amount of heat she felt from the orb invaded her body. "The ultimate power source for life," she said. "We're all children of the sun."

Those in the group understood her statement. The sun was the ultimate power source for the Earth. Its energy output had been absorbed and manipulated by the microscopic cells that had resided on Earth for billions of years. This energy source had fueled evolution and natural selection. They all realized that the ultimate result of this process was their own existence.

"When we were leaving Earth," Joshua said, absorbing the warmth of the glow, "I felt as if I was looking at my mother. Now I feel as if I'm absorbing energy from my father."

"I can't believe that Richard and Bhumi are missing this," Rachael said, mesmerized by the glowing orb in front of her.

"Like I said Rach," Vinod commented, "typical teenagers. They don't know what they're missing."

* * *

Bhumi and Richard held hands as they watched the orange disk grow larger and eventually sink beneath the floor on which they stood. They didn't say a word for a few moments even after the light source had disappeared beneath them, and they were bathed in total darkness.

"My god Boom," Richard said as he turned to her and embraced her in a hug. "What an experience."

Bhumi said nothing and returned his embrace as she laid her head on his shoulder. A few moments later, she released herself from his embrace and said, "Lay down Blue."

Richard complied and laid down on the soft surface, staring up into the darkness. He felt Bhumi lay down next to him on his right side, her body on its left side turned towards him.

"I have one more thing to show you," she whispered into his ear. Bhumi closed her eyes and suddenly changed the opacity of the dome above them that encompassed the nosecone of the Zephyr. An all-encompassing scene appeared above them. Millions of stars suddenly appeared above. The vast starfield was transected by the hazy white band of the Milky Way that extended from horizon to horizon. They were looking on edge into the heart of their galaxy. Richard felt as if he was laying on a field on Earth on a moonless night looking at the sky above, but this was different . . . this was much clearer than any night sky he had ever seen. It wasn't bright but was brilliant in its own way. He felt as if he could see to the edge of the cosmos. He felt small, a microscopic speck floating through the vast expanse of space.

Bhumi moved closer to Richard, and he could feel her warmth adjacent to him. With her left hand, she gently stroked his hair. She reached up with her right hand pointed to the center of the dome above, a light source brighter than all others directly in the center of their view. "That's Saturn," she said. "That's our destination."

Richard focused his gaze on the object. Even at this distance, he could barely make out small projections at either side of the object that constituted the rings of the gas giant. Bhumi and Richard felt as if they were alone on top of a slice of heaven as it hurtled through the vacuum of space towards an alien world. There was nothing in front of them except the vast expanse of creation.

"Thank you so much for this Bhumi," Richard said, his voice breaking with emotion. He turned to Bhumi lying next to him. He reached his right arm under her neck as she turned her head to look at him. Their eyes focused on each other, bright blue gazing into emerald green.

Richard closed his eyes and kissed Bhumi. As the kiss ended, they stared back into each other's eyes and then back at the scene above. They both knew that this was an experience they would never forget.

Chapter Eleven
The Quantum Sphere

The next morning Bhumi and Richard sat at the kitchen table in their abode eating a late breakfast. Rachael walked in and took a seat next to them. "I see you two are finally awake. Looks like you had a late night."

"Yea, we were up pretty late," Richard responded while taking a bite of fruit.

Rachael drummed her fingers on the table. "I hope whatever you were doing was important because you both missed an amazing spectacle yesterday, a once-in-a-lifetime experience. Where were you?"

Richard glanced at Bhumi, who smiled in return. "Yea, sorry we missed that," he said. "We . . . um . . . we were taking a nap and must've overslept."

Rachael shook her head. "You two realize we're on an important mission here, right? I think it was highly irresponsible of you to miss the solar transit." She turned to Bhumi. "Bhumi, you know the critical function you have on this mission, don't you?"

"Yes, Rachael," Bhumi responded, head lowered. "I know my responsibilities."

"Then I think you need to place a higher priority on them. Sleeping through an important event is inexcusable."

"Back off Sis," Richard said, coming to Bhumi's defense. "She knows what she's doing. She's performed wonderfully given what she's had to deal with."

"You're one to talk," Rachael shot back, glaring at Richard. "I can understand her being a little disoriented after the transition she's been through. I can give her some leeway because of that. But what's your excuse? I'm not sure if you realize this, but Seth invited you on this mission to help Bhumi, to guide her and help her perform her duties. So far, I feel you've not been a good influence on her."

Richard grew red in the face with anger. Bhumi grabbed his arm before he could respond. "Rachael, Richard's been absolutely wonderful," she said. "You don't realize how much he's done for me. I'm so grateful that Seth invited him here. He's been more help to me than you realize."

Joshua walked in and saw the others sitting around the table. "What's up?" he asked jovially. "Solving the problems of the cosmos?" He took a seat with the others.

Rachael took a moment to calm herself. "I was just reiterating to these two how critical they are to this mission."

Joshua took a moment to gauge the mood of the others around the table. Everyone was obviously tense. He tried to diffuse the situation. "Rachael, I'm sure they understand their responsibilities. Everyone on this mission is critical. I have faith in everyone on this crew, including Bhumi and Richard."

"Thanks Josh," Richard said, raising from the table. He grabbed Bhumi's hand and lifted her from her seat. "I'm glad someone has some faith in us. Let's go Boom. I think we're done here." The couple left the room.

Rachael watched the couple as they left the room. "Don't forget that Seth wants to meet us at the administrative building at noon," Rachael shouted after them. They didn't reply.

"Well, you weren't much help," Rachael said, turning to Joshua. "You could've supported me in getting them to be more responsible."

Joshua shrugged his shoulders. "I came in in the middle of the conversation. You were all tense. I was just trying to diffuse the situation. Besides, maybe you should lay off them a little. They're young. They'll figure things out."

"I certainly hope so. For all of our sakes."

* * *

The executive members of the crew gathered with Seth in front of the administrative building and lab promptly at noon. "I'm glad everyone's here on time," he said, glancing at Bhumi and Richard. "I wanted to show you some of the scientific equipment we have in the lab. We have four more days until we reach the rotation point and then another four days of deceleration until we reach Saturn. I want the crew to take the next eight days to familiarize themselves with the equipment aboard the Zephyr. I'm going to take you into the bio lab first."

"Man, I feel like he's Willy Wonka, and we're about to be led into the chocolate factory," Vinod whispered to Ted, who stood next to him.

"Think there's a chocolate river in there?" Ted whispered back.

"We can only hope."

Seth led the group through the double doors on the first floor of the large building. They entered a hallway, and he led the group through another set of double doors to the right, which led to a large room. The room was filled with various biological lab equipment. There were microscopes, DNA sequencers, fluidic analyzers, and various chemicals and reagents arranged on the shelves. "This is the bio lab and medical bay," Seth explained. "Liz, I want you to familiarize yourself with the equipment in here and tell me if there's anything you find missing. Nothing's off-limits. There's a medical pod in the next room similar to the medical pods we've created on New Eden. They can handle almost all medical emergencies."

Liz walked up to the chemical reagents neatly arranged and labeled on shelves. She picked up a bottle labeled "hydrochloric acid." She noted that the jar was initially difficult to lift.

"The jars are magnetically attached to the shelf," Seth explained. "If the ship lost its thrust for any reason, I didn't want this stuff floating around. The equipment is also bolted to the floor."

"It'll take me a couple of days to analyze all the equipment and reagents you have in here," Liz said, looking around. "But on cursory glance, it certainly looks complete."

"Man, how'd you do it Seth?" Vinod asked. "How'd you get all this equipment in here? I mean, this stuff isn't biological. You didn't grow it from some kind of biological seed like you did with the Zephyr. How'd you manufacture all this shit?"

"That'll become apparent shortly," Seth replied. "On with the tour." Seth led the group back into the hallway. They passed a few doors and stopped at double doors at the end of the hall. "In here is something I can't explain. You'll just have to see for yourselves."

"Lickable wallpaper?" Ted whispered to Vinod.

"My bet is on fizzy lifting drinks."

Seth opened the double doors, and the group walked in. Inside was a large two-story room. The group noted that the room was much cooler than the hallway. The room was empty except for an enormous sphere that occupied most of the space in the room. White mist flowed from the ceiling and over the sphere and dissipated into the air. The sphere seemed to be luminescent but without a definite color. At its center, it appeared to be a crystalline blue, but transitioned more to white near its edges. The edges of the sphere were not distinct. It seemed that the entire sphere became more transparent as one looked from its center towards its periphery. Joshua approached the sphere.

"Don't touch it Josh," Seth said. "It's not harmful, but it is fairly delicate and extremely cold."

Joshua closely examined the sphere's edge as the mist descending from above swirled around his face. It reminded him of an aerogel. Aerogels were super-light, solid structures created by mixing a polymer with a liquid solvent allowing the polymer to form into a gel matrix. Once the polymer solidified, the solvent was removed and replaced with air. The result was a semi-translucent, solid structure with very low density. "What is it Seth?" he asked. "It seems like it's made from some type of aerogel."

"It does have a similar appearance to an aerogel," Seth conceded, "but it's not made from a polymer. It's made from silica."

"Silica?" Joshua asked. "As in glass?"

"Yes, and also unlike an aerogel, its structure is highly ordered. Every molecule of this machine has been arranged in a specific location for a specific function."

"What function?" Vinod asked as he now stood next to Joshua, close to the sphere, mist rolling down its surface.

"It's made of trillions and trillions of tiny glass computational units. They use photons as their transmission medium. I guess the basic function of each of these units you would consider to be analogous to a transistor."

Vinod's eyes widened. "This entire sphere is made of microscopic glass transistors that compute using light?"

"Yes."

Vinod couldn't believe what he was hearing or seeing in front of him. "Are you kidding me? Seth, are you telling me this is some type of information processing unit? It's a . . . computer that uses light-based transistors?"

"Yes."

Vinod slapped his forehead with his right hand. "That's incredible!"

"What is it Vinod?" Rachael asked. "What's so incredible? I don't get it."

Vinod tried to explain to the others what they were looking at. "You're all familiar with microprocessors in computers. They contain billions of transistors on a tiny silicon chip that allows them to store and process data. Each transistor on the chip must be placed and connected to the others in a specific design that allows it to function. Over the years, transistors have gotten smaller and smaller to the point now that we are reaching the limit of how small they can become. We're almost at the atomic limit where transistors are only a dozen or so atoms wide. We simply can't make them any smaller. Size is important for computer chips. The smaller you can pack transistors together, the less distance the electrons that flow between them have to travel, making the computational power of the chip faster. Normal computer chips are essentially 2D structures with their transistors located on a flat silicon plane. We've recently been able to sandwich multiple layers of transistors together, but only a few layers thick. What we're looking at here is essentially a 3D CPU made up of light-based transistors. It must pack some amazing processing power." Vinod turned to Seth. "Am I right?"

"Yes, that's essentially correct," Seth replied. "Although this is not just a CPU. It is a fully self-contained computing device complete with memory for storage and an IO interface."

"A crystal computer," Vinod said, examining the sphere. "Amazing. What's with this cooling mist? It's light-based, no need for supercooling for the superconducting of electrons. So why keep it so cold?"

"The core of the sphere is near absolute zero," Seth explained. "We need to make sure that its molecules have minimal motion to be able to stabilize its internal quantum effects."

Vinod's mouth opened wide. "Does this thing use Q-bits? Are you telling me that this thing's a quantum computer?"

"Yes."

Vinod gazed up and down at the sphere. Humans had been experimenting with quantum computing for some time but hadn't built anything commercially viable. Unlike regular computers, which manipulated and stored ordinary bits as ones and zeros, quantum computers used Q-bits. They were data represented in the quantum state of atoms which meant that they could be one, zero, or a quantum superposition of both. Vinod understood the informational power of quantum superposition. In fact, it was the exact property that spookyons were based on. "What's its computing power?"

"Around a hundred exaflops."

"A hundred exaflops? You've got to be kidding me."

"How much processing power is that Vinod?" Liz asked. "For us non-computer scientists, that is."

"It's the equivalent processing power of one million human brains," Vinod stated. "It's simply mind-blowing." He turned to Seth. "What's the interface for this bad boy? Is this thing programmable?"

"It wouldn't be of much use if it wasn't," Seth replied. "It can handle any programming language for low-level programming, but its high-level interface is mostly verbal."

"Verbal?" Vinod asked. "What do you mean?"

"Let me demonstrate. Hello Gilead."

"Hello Seth," a male voice emanated from the walls of the room. It was completely natural sounding and not synthetic.

"How're you feeling today?"

"I feel good. No problems."

"How far are we from Saturn?"

"About seven days, give or take."

Rachael was surprised by the responses. They didn't seem like they were from a computer at all. The responses were natural, completely human-like. "Is this a computer Seth?"

"Of course. Why do you ask?"

"The responses seem human-like. I noticed the grammatical error in using 'good' instead of 'well' in its response, something that only a human would do. Also, that approximation of our distance to Saturn seemed most human-like."

"Rachael, I preferred to be referred to as 'he' instead of 'it,'" Gilead said. "Seth gave me my gender and my name."

Rachael was taken aback. "Sorry Gilead. I won't make the mistake again." She turned to Seth. "He seems to have emotions."

"Of course he does. He's very advanced. We find that all advanced intelligence tends to have emotions."

"Damn Gilead," Vinod said. "You're like Siri on steroids."

"Come on man," Gilead said. "You're doing me wrong even comparing me to that mindless troll. Get with it."

"Sorry bro," Vinod said with a look of bewilderment.

"What's his function on this mission Seth?" Joshua asked.

"I'm the central information processing and retrieval system," Gilead answered. "You can ask me any question, and I'll try to answer."

"Go ahead," Seth said. "Give him a try."

"What's the atomic number of Indium?" Joshua asked.

"Forty-nine."

"Where are ribosomes located?" Liz asked.

"On the surface of rough endoplasmic reticulum."

Vinod thought of a question that would require a deep understanding of context and human culture to understand. "What black hole was referenced in 2112?"

"Cygnus X-1."

Vinod was dumbstruck at the response. He knew that Gilead had to understand the context of what he was asking to be able to answer the question. There had been no hesitation in his response. 2112 was an album from the rock band Rush, and Vinod realized that Gilead had to know that Vinod was a classic rock connoisseur to understand the context of the question.

Rachael was unnerved at what she was seeing and hearing. Gilead knew about Vinod's love of classic rock? How much did Gilead know about them? She thought of some questions to find out.

"Where did Joshua and I first meet?"

"It depends on what you mean by meet. You saw him for the first time at a lecture given by Professor Henry Bowman at Berkeley, but the first time you spoke was in his office at the Bowman Particle research center."

Rachael turned to Seth. "Just how much does Gilead know about us?"

"Just about everything."

Rachael wasn't comfortable with a machine knowing so much personal information about the crew. How far did this knowledge reach? She decided to push the envelope with a more private question. "Where were Richard and Bhumi during the solar transit?"

"Are you kidding me?" Richard blurted out, glaring at Rachael.

"Do you want me to answer Richard?" Gilead asked.

"No," Richard responded.

"As you can see," Seth said calmly, trying to tone down the discussion. "Gilead has privacy controls built-in."

"Sorry," Rachael said to Richard. "Just trying to ascertain how much Gilead knows about us."

"Then why don't you ask some questions about yourself and leave us out of it," Richard responded.

"Fine. Gilead, who's my daughter?" Rachael asked.

"Ava Andrews."

Was there nothing that Gilead didn't know? Rachael thought of a personal question that only very few people knew the answer to. "Where was she conceived?"

Joshua turned to Rachael with an inquisitive look. "Seriously?"

"On top of Mount Endeavor on New Eden in an arachnid cocoon."

Rachael's jaw dropped. She turned to Seth for an explanation.

"As you can see, he currently has a spookyon connection to the collective. He's able to access any information we have."

Rachael couldn't wrap her head around what she was seeing and hearing. She wanted to get more information about Gilead but without his presence. "Gilead," Rachael said. "You okay if we have a private conversation?"

"Sure, I'll go into private mode. Catch y'all later."

"He can't hear us anymore?" Vinod asked a few moments later.

"No," Seth responded. "He's in private mode."

"What *is* that thing?" Rachael asked Seth, pointing with her right hand to the mist-laden sphere.

"What do you mean? He's Gilead. He's a quantum computer who's going to help us on this mission."

"Is he a computer though?" Rachael asked. "He seems like more than that."

"I'm not sure I understand," Seth said.

"I mean, is he . . . alive?"

Seth was puzzled by Rachael's question. He looked at her with an inquisitive look. "Of course he's alive. You of all people should know of our definition of life by now. It's purposeful complexity. Gilead has purposeful complexity and is enacting the purpose for which he was created. So, by that definition, he's alive."

"He's artificial intelligence, Rach," Vinod said with excitement. "Our boy Seth here has created an artificial life form."

Seth shook his head. "I really don't understand your human penchant for this term 'artificial.' What does artificial mean in this context?"

"Artificial means something that was purposefully created," Vinod said. "Something that wasn't the result of natural forces."

"Then, by that definition, aren't all of you also artificial life?" Seth asked. "The cells that evolved into you were purposefully created by us."

The last statement caused those in the group to pause and reflect. What made them different than Gilead?

Seth realized that this could be a protracted discussion with many ramifications, but it was something that would be critical to the mission they were on, and he wanted to give it its due deference. "Let's go up to the conference room. I can see we have much to discuss, and I want everyone to be comfortable and to understand Gilead and his function on this mission."

The group walked upstairs and sat around the conference table.

"Are you sure he can't hear us in here?" Rachael asked.

"No, he's in private mode," Seth said. "His sensory inputs are cut off. He can't get out of private mode unless one of us requests it. What are your questions?"

"I have some," Vinod said. He was the sole person in the group that understood at a deep level how computers worked. "What are his data inputs?"

"He has access to all the sensory elements of the ship," Seth explained.

"The information from all sensory organs is routed simultaneously to the central brain of the ship and to Gilead. Bhumi is connected via spookyon interface to the central brain which is how she gets her information. This information is also routed to Gilead. As another input, he also has a spookyon connection to the collective. Therefore, he can access the information stores of the collective, but this connection is temporary. It'll be shut off once we're in the spookyon dampening field surrounding Planet Nine. Bhumi also has a direct connection to Gilead via the spookyon interface in her brain."

"That's right," Bhumi said. "I can ask him anything at any time."

"How does that work?" Richard asked.

"It's hard to explain," Bhumi replied. "I don't have to speak to him. I just have to ask him a question with my mind, and he answers." Bhumi saw the puzzled looks around the table. "Remember during the lunar transit when Joshua mentioned the Apollo 11 landing site, and I was able to zoom in on it?"

"Yes," Richard responded. "I was wondering how you knew exactly where it was."

"That's something I asked Gilead," Bhumi explained. "I didn't really need to know technically where it was. I simply asked Gilead in my mind to focus one of my eyes on the Apollo 11 landing site, and it happened."

"That's one powerful interface," Vinod said. "It's like having the Internet on steroids in your mind."

Richard stared at Bhumi and realized the incredible access she had to information. Her connection to Gilead explained how she seemed to possess a vast amount of scientific knowledge at her fingertips. Since the start of the mission, he had also been wondering what his exact role was. He had felt like somewhat of an outsider. He was surrounded by heady scientists and expertly honed military personnel, but why had *he* been asked to come along? What was his purpose? Richard had already realized the vital function that Bhumi had had on this mission—being in control of the Zephyr. He had not discovered the incredibly intelligent tool she was also interfaced with. A tool that could reference all the known information of the cosmos. It was an epiphany. He now truly understood his role on this mission. He was the caretaker. He was in charge of nurturing the most important component on this mission . . . Bhumi. He was her mentor and companion. He gazed across the table as she looked back at him. He gave her a comforting smile which she returned.

"So, Gilead knows where all the members of the crew are and what they're doing at any time?" Vinod asked. "He must because he's monitoring the sensors of the ship."

"Yes, as long as they're within his sensory range," Seth said. "Most areas of the ship have sensors for various inputs such as light, sound, temperature, and others. However, not every inch of the ship is monitored. For example, your living habitats are private areas that aren't monitored. When he's in private mode like he's in right now, he has no sensory inputs at all."

"Well at least that's a relief," Vinod remarked. "I was beginning to think that he could see me when I was taking a dump."

The remark brought a chuckle from the group. Vinod had always been a source of comedic relief, not at all times unwelcomed as in this case.

"Believe me Vinod," Ted said. "No one, not even some computer intelligence with access to the knowledge of the collective, wants to see that."

"I get it," Vinod said, leaning forward in his chair, elbows on the table as he became more serious. "Okay. What about his outputs? What can Gilead control?"

"He can output audio through the various speakers on the ship, as you've already seen. He can also output video onto the surfaces of the ship that can support this if requested."

"What about ship controls?" Vinod asked.

"He has no direct control of the ship," Seth explained. "He can make suggestions to Bhumi regarding this, but she has ultimate control."

"Another relief," Vinod said, now leaning back. "No HAL-9000 scenario."

"HAL-9000?" Seth asked.

"It's a fictional AI from a novel by Arthur Clarke," Joshua explained. "The AI killed the crew of a spaceship headed towards Jupiter due to conflicting goals in its programming."

Seth now better understood the crew's trepidation with Gilead. He felt that they were reticent to trust an intelligence that they considered to be artificial. He knew that each crew member trusted each other explicitly, but they were hesitant to trust an intelligence based on a substrate different from their own. He endeavored to rectify the situation. "I would like to ask something of you all. You need to let go of your ingrained notions of something that you consider to be intelligent. As I've said before, I don't understand your fixation on artificiality as it pertains to intelligence or life, which is the substrate for intelligence. For the petrins, there's no such thing as artificial intelligence. It doesn't matter to us the processes that create purposeful complexity, or life as we regard it, to come about. Intelligence is intelligence, and life is life, no matter its source. Intelligence is just a product of purposeful complexity. It's an emergent property of life itself. Why does it matter to you if it came about due to the natural process of the universe, or someone purposely created it?"

The question caused the group to embark on some internal reflection. It was a difficult question to answer. Why did they hold what they considered intelligence that came about as a result of natural causes in higher esteem than one that had been purposefully created? The group sat in silent reflection for a while. Seth waited for a full minute before Liz finally gave a response. She was a member of the 103 club and espoused the petrin definitions of life and death. "You're right Seth. It shouldn't matter the source of life. It shouldn't matter if life came about as the natural processes of the universe or if some other intelligence created it. Like you said, life is life."

"I'm happy to hear it," Seth said. "I trust everyone on this crew. For me, Gilead is another crew member just like the rest of you. We're all on the same mission with the same goal, and I believe the best way to accomplish this mission is with mutual cooperation and trust."

Rachael still had her doubts. She did believe that Gilead was some form of life. He was definitely alive, but there was something different about him. "Seth, you said that you consider all life to be the same no matter its source or substrate, but not all life is the same. Not all life is sentient. Is Gilead conscious? Is he . . . sentient?"

The question gave Seth more insight into the crew's hesitancy as it pertained to Gilead. "You're right Rachael," he said. "Not all life is the same. Life can have different goals. Remember, our definition of life is purposeful complexity. Life can have different purposes based on its goals and the source of those goals. Gilead is not sentient because of the *source* of his goals. He's not capable of creating his own goals. He's extremely intelligent but must be told what to do. He's a tool we can use on this mission. I've always been puzzled by your use of the words 'consciousness' and 'sentience.' You don't seem to have a clear definition of these, but you seem to use them as if you do. Our definition of sentience is fairly simple. Any intelligence that is self-aware and self-motivating is sentient."

"Man, what are you talking about Seth?" Vinod asked. "That, that . . . ." Vinod pointed to the door and paused to find the right word. "That intelligence out there has the processing power of a million human minds, but you're telling me it's not sentient? How's that possible?"

Seth was frustrated that his explanation was not getting across. He sat back in his chair and laced his fingers. "Gilead's not sentient because he's not self-programming. Like I told you before, you need to consider him a tool. He's not capable of generating his own goals. He needs to be given tasks to complete to function. He can definitely create tasks for himself if he's given a goal, but these tasks would be steps on the path to complete the original goal he was given, but he can't come up with original goals on his own."

The room was silent as the group reflected on what Seth had told them. The petrins had had millennia to contemplate the moralities of life, something that humans were just beginning to consider. Seth understood their confusion. The petrins had tackled this exact problem ages ago and had come up with their own understanding, and out of this understanding, they had developed their own morality as it pertained to life.

"I want you all to understand something," Seth said. "We view all life, sentient or not, by the same lens. It's all purposeful complexity, but we do appreciate the difference between sentient and non-sentient life. That's why we have different laws for the two. We'd have no qualms about replicating Gilead for another purpose outside this mission, but we understand the power and pitfalls of replication. You all understand that on this mission, we're dealing with replication with no other purpose than replication itself. This is the essence of Medusa. We don't have an issue with the limited replication of a non-sentient intelligence like Gilead for a separate defined purpose, but as I've told you before, we are vehemently opposed to the replication of any sentient life. This, for us, is the main differentiator between sentient and non-sentient life. Sentient life generates its own goals and must be allowed to do so. But also, sentient life should not be directly replicated, which results in the dilution of the goals of the original life. Sentient life is a unique entity unto itself. Its uniqueness is a core determinate of its sentience. Replication of sentient life dilutes its core purpose. We realized this after Medusa separated from the collective and started cloning herself. I hope you all understand this. It was a mistake we made millennia ago to allow Medusa to leave the collective, one that we're still dealing with today. That mistake is at the core of the mission we're presently on."

"We understand," Liz said after a moment. "But I have a relevant question that I've been meaning to ask you for some time."

"What is it?"

"You just told us that the replication of sentient entities dilutes the self-oriented goal of that entity. Medusa has made endless copies of herself and has organized these clones into her own collective. Do you believe she's still sentient?"

Seth's face displayed a grin unlike anything the others had seen before.

He was happy to realize that his thoughts on life and sentience had finally been understood. "No Liz," Seth responded quietly. "We don't know for sure, but we don't believe Medusa is sentient any more. Her endless replication has hopelessly diluted her self-determination. As you have stated before, we believe that she is akin to a cancer, whose only purpose is replication. She is replication without purpose. This is why, like any cancer, she is the antithesis of life. This is why we're on this mission. I don't know what we'll find when we get to Planet Nine, but this mission is to discover what she's doing. It's a step to our ultimate goal. Medusa is a cancer, and like any cancer that attacks life, she must be eliminated. But don't be complacent. Even though we believe Medusa to be non-sentient, she's still highly intelligent. Don't underestimate her. She can be very manipulative in ways you couldn't imagine."

Joshua looked at the others around the table. He could intuitively sense that they understood the gravity of the mission they were all on. "We've all known this, Seth. We wouldn't have come on this mission otherwise. But your explanation has been clarifying. I trust you now as I've trusted you in the past. If you want us to treat Gilead as just another crew member with the same trust and respect we show to other crewmembers, I'm willing to comply."

Rachael scanned the others around the table who didn't speak but nodded in agreement. "Okay Seth," she said. "We'll comply. We'll treat Gilead as part of the crew. We're all on the same mission with the same goals. I guess he's part of the team."

"I'm happy to hear that," Seth responded. "Are you okay if I take him off private mode? I'm sure he's anxious to reconnect with us."

Rachael pondered the concept of anxiety as it related to a computer. It was a thought for later contemplation. "Yes Seth. Ask Gilead to join us."

"Okay, I'm going to take him off private mode. Just treat him as a person that's always with you when you're in monitored areas. You can simply access him by name. But unlike a regular person, even though he's monitoring your conversation, he won't initiate a conversation unless there's an emergency." Seth touched an area of the left forearm of his blue suit with the index finger of his right hand. "Hello Gilead."

"Hey y'all." Gilead's voice emanated from the speakers in the room.

Ted was surprised by Gilead using the term 'y'all.' "You been down south Gilead?" he asked.

"I feel like I've been everywhere."

Chapter Twelve
The Life Printer

The group left the conference room as Seth continued the tour of the lab. They walked back downstairs into a different hallway and stopped in front of another set of double doors like the ones in front of Gilead's room.

Seth paused before opening the doors. "What I'm about to show you is a technology that the collective has just perfected. We consider it to be one of our crowning achievements. It's something that Medusa doesn't have and doesn't know about, so you all must keep this technology completely top secret."

The group exchanged excited looks. New secretive technology from the petrins? "A secret technology that you don't want us to share?" Vinod asked. "What is it? An everlasting gobstopper?"

"A what?" Seth asked.

"Never mind," Vinod said as Ted turned to him with a grin.

Seth led the group through the double doors. Inside was a large room two stories tall. At the opposite end of the room were two cubic chambers forty feet on a side. The chambers were divided by a one-foot-thick wall. All surfaces of the chambers, including the ceiling and floor, seemed to be clad in some type of dark grey metal. There were two large circular push buttons on the dividing wall, one green the other red. Above the buttons was a screen that displayed the word "Ready" in large white text on a black background.

Other than the chambers, the room was empty except for a potted tree in the corner. It was about ten feet tall and was in a tan, ceramic pot three feet in diameter filled with dirt. Liz recognized the type of tree given its fan-shaped green leaves. It was a ginkgo tree that seemed out of place in the otherwise barren room.

"What are we looking at here Seth?" Joshua asked, looking at the two chambers. "What are these cubic rooms with the metallic walls?"

"These two chambers may look similar," Seth said, "but they have two completely different functions." He walked in front of the chamber on the left. "I'll explain this one first. This chamber is a scanner. You're already somewhat familiar with this technology. It's similar to the scanners we used to transport humanity to New Eden. Let me give you a demonstration of how it works." He turned to Ted. "Ted, can you help me with that tree over there. It's a test object. We need to move it into this chamber."

Ted and Seth walked over to the tree and lifted it by grabbing the pot on opposite sides. They carefully walked over to the left chamber and deposited it at the center, and then exited the chamber. "There're only two buttons to operate this machine," Seth explained. He pointed to the green button in the dividing wall. "This green button is for the scan function. When pushed, the machine will scan atom by atom the makeup of the object in the left chamber, which is the scanner. It will then record this information into memory. This information not only includes which atoms are present, but also the position of each atom relative to the others. This information is stored as data in Gilead. Let me show you how it works." Seth pushed the green button on the wall. The message on the screen above changed to "Process initiating. Commencing in 5 seconds."

Nothing happened initially as the timer on the screen counted down to zero. Then the message on the screen changed to "Scanning chamber sealing . . .." The group noted a thick clear wall that descended from a slot in the ceiling and moved all the way silently to the floor, sealing the chamber. The message on the screen now displayed "Scanning . . .." Numerous light-blue beams of light emanated from the chamber's walls near its floor and shone on the base of the pot. To Joshua, they looked like some form of high-intensity laser beams. The group heard a low-pitched whirring sound as the beams started moving in a circular fashion around the base of the pot. The sound grew louder and higher in pitch as the lights spun faster and faster. In a few moments, they were spinning so fast that the beams seemed to form a plane of blue light. The plane started moving up the chamber's walls, as did the line of light shining on the pot. The plane now moved past the pot and crept up the trunk of the tree. Blue lights danced in all directions around the chamber as the light plane reached the leaves of the tree and reflected off its uneven surfaces. The light plane eventually moved past the top of the tree, and the high-pitched sound ceased as the lights turned off. The display read, "Scan complete. Compressing data . . .." After one minute, the display switched to, "Data stored. Storage file 782609-76."

"Do you want me to save the scan?" Gilead's voice emanated from the walls of the room.

"Sure Gilead," Seth answered. "Please name it potted ginkgo."

"Done," Gilead answered. "Total storage size around 1.2 terabytes."

"1.2 terabytes?" Vinod asked. "It's a lot of storage, but it seems small given the trillions and trillions of atoms that are in that tree."

"We use a loss-less compression algorithm to compress the data before storage. The amount of data required for storage is not dependent on the mass of the object but on its complexity. For example, if we scanned a tank of water that weighed two hundred pounds, it would require very little storage. On the other hand, if we scanned a human of similar mass, the data storage would be exponentially higher."

"You can scan a human in this thing and store them digitally?" Rachael asked.

"Sure," Seth remarked. "It's similar to the process of how we backed each of you up on our data nodes before this mission."

Joshua pondered Seth's statement about the data storage requirements for a human versus a tank of water of the same mass. Something about it stuck in his mind. A tank of water would require exponentially much less data storage than a human? Joshua knew that humans were two-thirds water, so why the difference? Exactly what was the data that was being stored? It can't simply be the atoms and in the object and their location as Seth had insinuated because a tank of water and a human contained about the same number of atoms, and each atom definitely had a specific location. Why the difference? Why did Gilead need exponentially more data storage for a human? His mind turned back many years to the discussion he, Rachael, and Vinod had had with Seth in the early days after their connection. It was a time before Seth even had his android body. He was simply a disembodied voice coming through the speakers in the Bat Cave. It was during the infamous session 103 where Seth had quizzed the group about a frozen frog and whether they considered it to be living. Joshua connected the dots and came to a realization. "Seth," he said, "you're not really storing information on the atoms and their position, are you?"

"Why do you say that Dr. Andrews?" Seth said with a curious smile.

"You may be right in that atomic composition and position are the core data that's obtained by the scanner," Joshua replied. "But there's something special about this data compression algorithm you speak of. I'm assuming that Gilead gets the raw data from the scanner, and he's the one who enacts this algorithm."

"Yes, Josh," Seth replied, his smile growing. "Go on."

From the grin on Seth's face, Joshua knew that he was on the right track. "It's not really a data compression algorithm that Gilead is running the raw data through, is it? It's actually a filter of some sort."

"Maybe," Seth said coyly. "But what do you think it's filtering?"

Joshua paused, his hand on his chin, before answering. "It's a randomness filter," Joshua said. "You're taking the data about the atoms and the position of those atoms in an object, and you're removing all data that doesn't have a specific reason for being in that location. You're removing the randomness from the data. You're only selecting the position information for atoms that must be in a specific position for that object to function. You're storing only the data that your algorithm gleans is not random."

"Correct," Seth responded, and then looked at Joshua for a further response. He was giving Joshua time for his mind to expand on the implications of his revelation.

Joshua knew that the petrins considered life to be purposeful complexity, but he also knew that they considered randomness to be the antithesis of life. "You're extracting life," Joshua said. "You have an algorithm that can take the raw data of the composition of an object and then delete out that information that you consider to be random. What's left is the purposeful information. This information by your own definition is . . . life."

"Brilliant," Seth said.

The group was silent for a few moments as the rest digested the conversation between Seth and Joshua. Rachael was the first to speak. "I don't understand Josh. How is the compression algorithm distilling life?"

"It's exactly what it's doing Rachael," Joshua said. "Distilling raw data about the composition of an object to obtain the life information in the data. It has an intelligent algorithm that can differentiate between randomness and that which is non-random. It's only storing the non-random information. This, according to the petrin definition, is life. This machine," Joshua said, pointing towards the scanning chamber, "isn't really a scanner at all. It's a life extractor. It extracts the purposeful information out of any object it scans and stores this information as data. It distills the life of an object inside of it to the minimal about of bits represented as ones and zeros needed to store its life information as data. The amount of data needed to store this information represents the amount of life the object contains. That's why a tank of water of the same mass as a human requires much less data storage. The atoms in the water are in a random orientation.

There's nothing special about their locations. The arrangement of atoms in a human, on the other hand, is highly specified. This specificity is what defines the human. That's why a human would require much more data to store since the data would have to encompass the specificity of the arrangement of the atoms." He turned to Seth. "This is not simply an atomic scanner. Seth, am I correct in my assessment that it's a life extractor?"

Seth stood motionless, grinning at Joshua for a few moments. He had endeavored for years to try to teach humans the petrin notions of what constituted living entities. He didn't know if all of humanity had grasped the concept that Joshua had just revealed, but he knew that his teachings had gotten through to at least one human. "Right," Seth responded. "I'm glad you understand."

Vinod had listened closely to the conversation. Unlike others in the group, he understood how data compression algorithms worked. "I get what you're saying Josh, but for a compression algorithm to work, it needs to understand the data it's compressing. You can't use the JPEG algorithm, which is used to compress image files on a file that represents a word processing file. The compression algorithm must know the type of the data it's compressing." Vinod turned to Seth. "Surely, even the petrins can't recognize all patterns that represent life. I can definitely believe that they understand all biological, cell-based objects like the tree or a human, but what happens with the scanner if it scans something that it doesn't understand?"

"Excellent question Vinod," Seth replied. "You're correct. Gilead's compression algorithm can't absolutely determine if the data it obtains from the scanner is random or not. But, when it encounters data that it knows for sure is random, it strips it. For unknown data or data that it recognizes as purposely ordered, it copies the raw data directly into memory. This means that it'll require more data to store objects it doesn't understand, but still, the essence of the original object is retained with no information loss. It's reliably backed up."

Seth waited a few moments to see if anyone else had any questions about the scanning and data storage process, but no other questions were forthcoming. Seth walked in front of the right chamber. "As I've said before, you're all somewhat familiar with the concept of scanning and data storage. It's the same process that allowed you all to be scanned on New Eden to enable you to be transferred here to the Zephyr. Medusa also has this technology, but as I've said before, the petrins have developed a new technology Medusa doesn't possess and doesn't know about. It's a corollary to the scanning process. We hope that this new technology will turn the tide in our battle with her. This chamber on the right contains this new technology. Instead of telling you what it is, I'm just going to demonstrate it for you. Gilead, please reconstitute file 298703-22."

"Executing," Gilead responded.

The screen once again read, "Process initiating. Commencing in 5 seconds." After the countdown completed, a clear divider lowered from the ceiling and sealed the right camber just like the left one. Two beams of energy emanated from the chamber walls from opposite sides, one glowing red, the other white. They seemed to undulate in brightness in perfect sync with each other. The beams converged at a point on the center of the chamber, which glowed red-hot. The machine started making a sound, but it was much different than they had heard before. This seemed to be a series of clicks or pulses that were in perfect sync with the undulation of the beams. The beams started spinning around the chamber, slowly at first, but spun faster with time. The group noted that the conversion point of the beams was no longer just the center of the chamber. It moved, leaving a glowing substance in their wake that cooled and became solid as the beams progressed. The spinning of the beams became even faster and moved slowly up the chamber.

"What's it doing?" Rachael asked as she saw the material the beams seemed to be depositing on the floor.

"Looks like it's building something," Joshua replied.

"Yea," Vinod said. "But what?"

Richard watched as the beams progressed higher, leaving a three-dimensional object in their wake. *It looks like it's wood*, he thought. "Wait Seth," Richard said excitedly as more of the object appeared. "Am I seeing what I think I'm seeing?"

"I think so."

As more of the object appeared, the others in the group recognized the object that was appearing. It was a wooden classical guitar. A few moments later, the guitar was fully formed, and the screen changed to "Process complete." The clear door slid back into the ceiling. The group noticed a slight burning smell emanating from the chamber.

"Is that a Manuel Rodriguez?" Richard asked.

"Yes," Seth replied. "A Café Ole."

Richard recognized the guitar at once. It was a custom hand-crafted guitar that cost thousands of dollars back on Earth. "Can I touch it?"

"Yes," Seth said. "It's for you."

Richard walked into the chamber and picked up the instrument. He placed his left hand on the frets and strummed a chord with his right. "It's in perfect tune." He looked up at Seth. "*This* is for *me*?"

"Sure. I know you're a musician. I thought you'd like it."

"I love it! Thanks so much."

Bhumi smiled as she sensed Richard's joy.

"What the hell is that machine?" Rachael asked. "What exactly does it do?"

"It's kind of the opposite of the scanner," Seth explained. "I'd guess you'd consider it a 3D printer, but it operates at the atomic level. It fuses layers of specified atoms into a three-dimensional structure."

"How does it work?" Vinod asked.

"It's a little hard to explain," Seth said, "but I'll try. First, it needs a design to print. This design needs to be stored in Gilead's memory from a previous scanning process. A high-energy plasma is created using the necessary atoms that make up the final structure. This plasma is separated into its ionic components. The positive ions consisting of the nuclei of the atoms are separated from the electrons. Using powerful magnetic fields, the two components are injected as two separate streams, one containing the nuclei and the other the electrons. These beams are then focused on a single point where they collide, allowing the atoms to be reconstituted and deposited on the surface. The order of the atoms in the streams is dependent on the pattern. Like I said before, it's like an atomic 3D printer."

"What kind of stuff can it print?" Rachael asked.

"Anything made of atoms," Seth said. "As long as Gilead has the pattern for it."

"But bro," Vinod said. "*Everything* is made of atoms."

"Just about everything."

"It can print *anything* made from atoms?" Vinod asked, not believing what he was hearing.

"Yes."

"How about a laptop?" Vinod asked.

"Easy."

"An electron microscope?" Liz asked.

"Sure. It's how we got all that equipment in your lab."

"A bowl of Louisiana gumbo?" Ted asked.

"No problem."

"A bottle of Grey Goose?" Vinod asked.

"If the need arose."

"Oh, the need may definitely arise," Vinod responded excitedly. "Damn, Seth. It's like it's Christmas morning, and we're opening our presents."

Rachael started to realize the astounding implications of the printer. "Can it print a human?"

"Yes, but only if the original human is non-functional. Remember our moratorium on making copies of a sentient entity."

"But didn't you already have this technology?" Ted asked. "Isn't it how we were transported to New Eden from Earth and how we got here from New Eden?"

"No," Seth said. "It's not the same process. Remember, we had to grow a clone of each of you from your DNA first. That process takes weeks for us. Then the brain of your clone was injected with the information from your original body. This is an entirely different process. It's much more low-level and granular. It works at the individual atomic level."

"I get it," Ted said.

A thought crossed Joshua's mind. One that caused him pause. "How about a nuclear weapon? Can the printer print that?"

"Yes, it's possible," Seth replied. "But it would take more time."

"Why?"

"Remember that this machine needs a source of atoms for it to be able to deposit them in a specific order to print an object. Nuclear weapons require enriched uranium or plutonium as part of their atomic source. It needs time to be able to obtain these."

"What's its ultimate source of the atoms it uses?" Joshua asked.

"I create them," Bhumi answered. The others turned to look at her. "I can create any atoms needed by fusing my hydrogen fuel with the fusion spheres inside me. I store varying quantities of all ninety-eight elements in storage containers located below us. These containers are connected to this machine and are its source of atoms."

"Shit Seth," Vinod said. "Anything this bad boy can't make?"

"Like I said, it can produce anything made of atoms as long as we have the pattern for it. Gilead contains data files on many items that I felt may be of use on this mission, but he only has a limited memory capacity. At present, since he has a spookyon connection to the petrin network and can requisition the data pattern of anything the petrins have data on, this machine can print just about anything. But once we enter the spookyon dampening field, this connection will be lost. That's why over the next few days, I want everyone to query Gilead and make sure that anything that anyone thinks will be required for the mission is in his local memory. But there are some things that the printer can't handle. For example, it's not capable of creating anything containing a spookyon. Spookyons need to be created at the same place and time to be entangled, so the printer can't handle that. Also, remember, whatever needs to be printed must fit in this chamber. Larger objects are possible, but only if they can be printed in parts and reassembled later. Any questions?"

The group looked left and right at the incredible machine. It would take them some time to fully realize its power. "I have a question," Vinod said. "I know that the green button on the wall is used to scan an object. What's the red button for?"

"Oh, I forgot about that," Seth remarked. "The red button is an immediate copy button. It allows you to make an immediate copy of an object. You place the original in the scanning chamber on the left and push the red button. The printer on the right will immediately begin depositing material as its information is scanned in the left chamber. This process bypasses Gilead and his data compression, making the entire process faster. The scanned data is simply relayed to the printer and printed."

"It's a goddam 3D Xerox machine," Ted commented.

"Jesus Seth," Vinod said, glancing at the chambers. "These two chambers look identical. What happens if you messed up and placed the object you want to copy on the right side?"

"The chambers had to be similar because they need to handle similar-sized objects. I assumed that you could remember something as simple as left to right. It's the direction that you read."

"Yea, but what would happen if you did screw up?" Vinod asked again.

Seth rolled his eyes. "Nothing good bro. Remember that the printer chamber's not a vacuum when it's printing. There's an atmosphere in there. When the printer is printing, it's replacing the atoms of the atmosphere with the object it's printing. I suppose that if you did have an object in the printer when it was printing, its atoms would be dislodged and replaced by whatever was being printed."

"Got it," Vinod responded. "No screw-ups. Left to right only."

Seth glanced around the group. No other questions seemed to be forthcoming. "I think you all realize the incredible power of the printer. Like I've told you, it's a technology that Medusa doesn't possess and doesn't know about. I'm not sure how we'll need to use it on this mission, but I think it will give us a competitive advantage. But it's not a toy; it's a tool. It does require some energy to operate, whose ultimate source is the Zephyr's hydrogen fuel. I'd like it to be used for only mission-specific activities."

"Come on bro," Vinod said, laying a hand on Seth's shoulder. "You've got to be able to let us have *some* fun with it. The Zephyr's got a shit-ton of liquid hydrogen. Surely we can spare a little to . . . boost morale."

Seth didn't respond. He simply rolled his eyes again.

Vinod turned to Ted. "Tabasco, we've found the chocolate river."

Chapter Thirteen
The Rogue Comet

Joshua and Rachael stood in front of the main entrance to Vinod, Ted, and Liz's abode. They had a three-bedroom residence a short distance from their own abode.

"Do we just walk in?" Rachael asked.

"I guess so," Joshua replied, scanning the surroundings of the entrance. "The petrins haven't figured out doorbells. Privacy is not one of their strong suits."

"The concept of privacy may not make much sense to a trillion individuals who have formed themselves into a collective." Rachael touched the circular door, which opened concentrically from the center. "Hello. It's Rachael and Joshua."

"Come in y'all," Ted announced. "We're in the dining room."

Joshua and Rachael entered and noted that this abode was similar to theirs. It had the same petrin architecture with curved walls and a luminous ceiling. The couple walked through a living room to a dining room with a large table around which Ted, Vinod, and Liz sat. The back wall of the room was an exterior wall of the Zephyr like their abode. Stars were visible through the expansive window despite the luminous ceiling.

"Sure smells great in here," Joshua said as he and Rachael took a seat around the table, which contained platters of food.

"It was Ted's selection," Vinod said. "A Cajun dinner—gumbo, fried catfish, crawfish étouffée, dirty rice, and bread pudding for dessert."

"Richard and Bhumi aren't coming?" Liz asked.

"No," Rachael answered. "We invited them, but they said they have plans."

"Plans," Vinod said. "I know what that means," he said with a wink.

"You need to get your mind out of the gutter," Rachael shot back. She quickly tried to change the topic. "So I see you've made use of the atomic printer. I'm assuming this spread in front of us wasn't picked from the orchard."

"Right on," Ted said. "Gilead has a ridiculous number of patterns he has access to. All this grub was created in the printer. Oh, I almost forgot." Ted walked into the other room and returned with a bottle of Tabasco and set it on the table. "Now dinner's complete."

"Gilead had Tabasco in his database?" Rachael asked.

"He's got a lot more stuff than that," Ted answered. "Vinod and I started randomly asking different items he could print. There was almost nothing he didn't have."

"Although we don't know if he had that stuff in his local memory or he was getting the data from the collective," Vinod said.

Joshua shook his head. "Remember, Seth told us to use the printer sparingly. We don't know how much hydrogen this dinner cost us."

"Hydrogen?" Vinod asked. "You're talking about the most abundant element in the universe. You worry too much Doc. You're about to embark on a starlit dinner with some amazing food. Live a little."

"You forgot about the drink, Vinod," Ted said as he produced a bottle from the floor and set it on the table. Joshua picked up the clear bottle filled with brown liquid and read the label. "Pappy Van Winkle's? What's this?"

"Only one of the smoothest and most expensive bourbons available," Ted said. "Vinod and I found it when we were perusing the library of items Gilead had in his database. It's aged fifteen years. One bottle of this stuff costs more than a couple thousand dollars back on Earth."

Rachael shook her head. "Seth cautioned us about taking too much liberty with the printer. He told us it was a tool and not a toy."

"Jesus Rach," Vinod said. "Ted, Liz, and I spent hours going over the pattern inventory in Gilead. We looked for everything from RPG launchers to night vision goggles to microprocessors to high-speed centrifuges. We got through the essential stuff. This dinner was our reward. You two need to relax and enjoy. We've got this covered."

"I have to concur," Liz said. "Gilead's library of essential items for this mission seems complete. We're very well equipped. There were a few items that I felt we needed for the lab, and Gilead printed them for us. The bio lab is complete, as far as I can tell."

"I'm sure you all did a thorough job," Joshua said. "Besides, it'd be a waste of perfectly good hydrogen if we didn't enjoy this," Joshua opened the cork of the bottle in his hand. "Who's first?"

Rachael shrugged her shoulders and held up her glass in front of her. "Me, I guess."

The group enjoyed drinks and a gourmet dinner. They were all relaxed and content from the products of the printer. The empty bottle of bourbon sat on the table as Ted distributed portions of bread pudding onto the plates in front of the others and took a seat.

"That was one of the best meals I've ever had," Liz said. She turned to Ted. "Thanks Tabasco. Great choices." Her glance lingered on Ted before she looked away. "This atomic printer of the petrins is amazing technology."

"Oh, I almost forgot," Vinod said as he got up from the table and went into the living room. He returned a few moments later with a rectangular object in his right hand and a hammer in his left. He held the rectangular object against his body. It was a wooden frame with some canvas that occupied the side towards himself.

"What's that?" Rachael asked.

"Something I need to hang up," Vinod responded. He placed the object on the ground and held up a small nail that he had had along with the hammer against the wall. He pounded the nail halfway into the wall. He then picked up the object on the floor, flipped it over, and placed it on the wall, hanging it on the nail.

The others recognized the object immediately.

"You printed a replica of the Mona Lisa?" Rachael asked.

Vinod took a seat back at the table. "It's not a replica. It's the actual Mona Lisa. I figured the walls in here can use some decoration."

"What do you mean the actual Mona Lisa?" Joshua asked. "As far as I know, it's stored in some vault somewhere underneath the Louvre in Paris on Earth. That is, as long as Medusa hasn't destroyed it by now."

"I don't know if that one's still there or not," Vinod said. "Ted and I noticed when we were perusing Gilead's archive of scanned items, some were works of art from Earth. Remember, the petrins scanned some of these before humans were evacuated to New Eden. I printed this from that archive. It's an atom for atom copy of the original."

"Then it *is* a replica," Rachael remarked.

"I don't consider it a replica," Vinod stated. "It has the exact same number and type of atoms as the original in the exact same positions. If you feel that this painting on this wall is of less value than the one in Paris, then what would you consider all of us around this table. Aren't we also replicas?"

The statement caused quiet reflection from the group. Vinod turned and pointed to the painting. "If you had this painting here and the one from Paris in a room together, is there any art expert that could tell the difference?"

Rachael thought about the question for a while. How is an atom by atom copy of something different than the original? The mere concepts of original and replica didn't seem to make sense in this context. "I suppose not," she finally replied. "There'd be no way to tell the difference." She looked back at the painting on the wall. "The actual Mona Lisa . . . on your wall. I can't believe it." She pondered the possibilities. "Do you think that the printing chamber is large enough to hold Michelangelo's David? I never got a chance to see it on Earth."

"I suppose so," Vinod said. "But how the hell would you get it out of there. That's one massive stone."

"Simple," Rachael replied with a grin. "We can simply ask Bhumi to shut off gravity for a while."

"You two are getting way ahead of yourselves," Joshua said. "This atomic scanning and printing technology is a tool, not a toy. It's technology way beyond anything humans have come up with. We just can't use it willy-nilly."

"Relax Josh," Rachael said. "I was just kidding about the statue." She looked at Joshua, who stared solemnly at the painting on the wall. "Don't you think that the atomic printer is some amazing technology?"

"Yes, it is," Joshua said solemnly as he took a bite of pudding. The group stared at Joshua. They sensed that he had misgivings about the technology.

"You don't seem very excited about it Josh," Liz said, also taking a bite of bread pudding.

"It certainly is amazing technology," Joshua said. "Almost too amazing."

"What do you mean by that?" Liz asked.

Joshua put his fork down and leaned back in his chair. He crossed his arms against his chest. "I don't know," he said. "It's almost *too* good."

The others still didn't understand what Joshua was trying to convey. "How's it too good?" Rachael asked.

"I mean, it's a panacea. It can produce anything we can think of. There's something about this technology that gives me pause. It can create anything, literally *anything*, within its size limit. Even the petrins have had this technology for only a short period of time. We don't know the long-term ramifications of it." He turned to Rachael. "Remember a few days ago when you said humanity was lucky that atomic bomb technology was so hard to produce? You felt that if everyone could make a bomb with ease that humanity wouldn't have survived the twentieth century. But isn't that what we've witnessed today? A machine that can produce anything, good or evil, with the push of a button. We don't know the long-term ramifications of that."

"Are you suggesting that someone in the crew could do something harmful with the printer?" Ted asked.

"No, it's not that. I trust everyone in the crew explicitly. I simply fear the long-term ramifications of such a powerful technology for society as a whole. The power to conjure up objects at will seems almost god-like."

"I see your point Josh," Rachael said, "but it's not something we're going to have to worry about. I don't think Seth has any intention of allowing humans to have this technology beyond the scope of this mission."

"I suppose you're right," Joshua said, leaning back in his chair. "But still, something we have to be careful with."

After a few moments, Vinod said, "The printer is really useless by itself. For me, the really powerful stuff is the data that Gilead and the petrins have stored. Without this data, the printer is just a hunk of metal."

"True," Joshua replied. "We always seem to come back to this point when we're dealing with petrin technology. Everything is information."

* * *

Richard and Bhumi climbed the last rungs of the ladder leading up to the area of the eye telescopes. Richard had the guitar slung over his shoulder via a strap. They stopped for a few moments to catch their breath before climbing the short distance to the nosecone.

They moved to the center of the space and took in the expansive view. Saturn shone brightly as a pinpoint of light directly above them. "Let's try it out," Bhumi said.

Richard wanted to try out the guitar in the nosecone area of the ship. The couple had named this area of the ship the "Pinnacle Lounge." It was a private, magical place for them—a place where they had shared their first kiss. Richard had said that he loved the acoustics of the lounge on their prior visit. He could think of no better place to try out his new gift.

The couple sat on the soft floor, and Richard positioned the guitar. He strummed a chord that echoed magnificently through the space.

"It sounds amazing," Bhumi said. "Play me a song."

Richard paused as he thought of a song to play. He started playing an acoustic version of "Sweet Child 'O Mine" From Guns N' Roses. The notes from the guitar were perfectly accentuated by the slight echo of the cavernous space. Bhumi's eyes lit up as Richard started into the vocals of the song. She had known about the concept of music and had also heard a few songs before, but this experience was surreal. She stared at Richard's face and the expressions it made as he sang the lyrics. She was engrossed by the song and Richard's presence.

"That was amazing," Bhumi said after the song finished. She moved closer to Richard, wrapped her arms around his neck, and kissed him. "You've got to play me some more."

Richard played a few more songs for Bhumi, and then the couple laid flat on the ground to take in the view. "Saturn is still just a speck," Richard said.

"Would you like me to zoom in on it for you?" Bhumi asked.

Richard turned his head towards Bhumi. "I forgot that you could do that. Can you project an image on the nosecone?"

Bhumi didn't respond. She simply pointed straight up.

Richard looked up and saw a zoomed-in, rectangular image of Saturn that now occupied the central one-third of the space that represented the nosecone. The gas giant was mainly in the sunlight with only a small crescent in shadow. Its rings shone brilliantly. Richard was overcome by the sight. It was pristine in its clarity. "It's beautiful. Is this image from one of your eye telescopes? Is it live?"

"Of course it is silly. I didn't display some random image of Saturn."

The couple stared at the image for a few minutes before Richard announced, "I thought of another song I want to play for you." He sat up and picked up his guitar. Bhumi rolled on her side towards him, her head resting on her hand, her elbow on the ground.

Richard played "In Your Eyes" by Peter Gabriel. Bhumi smiled as she understood the hidden meaning behind the song as it pertained to the image above and how it had been produced by one of the eyes of the ship. When the song finished, Richard laid down next to Bhumi.

Bhumi looked at the guitar. "Do you think you could teach me how to play?"

"Sure. It takes a lot of practice, but I think you'd be good at it. If you can control a massive spaceship, controlling a guitar should be a piece of cake."

The couple turned back to the image of Saturn. Richard noted a small white spot in the periphery of the image. "What's that white spot on the right? It kinda looks like it's located in one of the rings."

"I don't know. Maybe it's one of the moons. I'll zoom in on it."

The image changed to show a spherical moon, its surface almost pure white crisscrossed by channels of blue with a few craters.

"It's definitely a moon," Richard stated. "But I can't tell you which one. I'm no astronomer."

"Gilead," Bhumi said. "What moon are we looking at?"

"Enceladus," Gilead's replied, his voice echoing around the Pinnacle Lounge.

"Why is it so white?" Richard asked.

"Its surface is mostly water ice," Gilead responded. "It's one of the most reflective bodies in this solar system."

The couple stared at the image for a while, noting the details of the surface of the moon. "I wonder what it would be like to be there," Richard said dreamily.

"What do you mean?"

"I mean standing on that surface—on all that ice with an enormous Saturn up above you. That's got to be an amazing sight."

"I'm sure it'd be amazing, but unfortunately not in the mission plan."

They continued staring at the image. Bhumi noted another white object close to the moon that seemed to be slowly moving towards it. "Gilead, what's that small white object moving towards the moon?"

"I don't know," Gilead replied. "It's not in my database. I've analyzed its spectral signature, and it's also made mostly of water ice. It could be a comet of some type. Its trajectory is directly towards the moon."

"It's going to hit Enceladus?" Richard asked excitedly. "When?"

"In about five minutes."

"Are you recording this?" Richard asked.

"I record everything," Gilead responded.

"How lucky Blue," Bhumi said. "We get to see a comet hit a moon."

The couple watched as the comet grew closer and closer to the moon. Bhumi zoomed in further on the portion of the moon that would be the impact site. The comet impacted the surface and shot a shower of ice in all directions that exploded away from the surface. They watched the image for a few more minutes and noted a deep crater where the impact had happened.

"Wow, that was awesome," Richard said. "Did you see the size of that explosion? It looked like that thing shot right through the surface. We were lucky to see that."

"I have some new information," Gilead said. "I've analyzed the trajectory of the comet. It seems to have originated from Planet Nine."

Bhumi and Richard turned to each other. Neither spoke as they got to their feet. Richard grabbed his guitar, and the two raced for the exit.

* * *

The executive crew sat around the conference table in the administrative building. The video of the comet impacting the Jovian moon had played multiple times on one of the walls of the room.

"It certainly looks like a comet," Joshua remarked. "Maybe it's just coincidental that it emanated from the region of Planet Nine."

"Wishful thinking," Seth said. "I'm certain that Medusa sent it."

"Yea, but for what reason?" Vinod asked. "Smashing one piece of ice into another, although cool, doesn't seem to have much of a purpose."

"I can think of a purpose," Liz stated.

"What?" Ted asked.

"Seeding."

"Seeding? What do you mean?"

Liz took a deep breath and let it out. "Remember how the petrins seeded life on Earth? They exploded an ice-world in their solar system seeded with primordial cells. Some chunks from this explosion eventually landed on Earth as comets and started the process of evolution there. Maybe this comet is a similar kind of seeding process."

"Exactly my thoughts," Seth said.

"Gilead," Liz said. "Anything more you can glean from the spectral analysis? Can you tell us anything more about its composition?"

"Not much," Gilead replied. "The comet is mostly water-ice, with trace amounts of carbon and other elements, but nothing unusual for a comet."

"There's carbon on ordinary comets?" Rachael asked.

"Yes," Joshua replied. "More than just carbon. NASA sent the Rosetta spacecraft to a comet to analyze the composition of its tail. They found amino acids, one of the building blocks for life. Amino acids are derived from carbon."

"Maybe that comet the spacecraft visited was one from the petrins," Vinod said, turning to Seth.

"Possible," Seth remarked. "But amino acids also form from natural processes. Even comets we didn't create have amino acids."

"What do you think we should do Seth?" Rachael asked. "It's definitely something we have to investigate. It's really the purpose of our mission."

Seth nodded his head in agreement as he looked at the image on the screen. "There's no way around it. We'll have to send a crew to Enceladus to retrieve some samples."

Bhumi looked at Richard, who smiled back at her. "I'm sure that'll be an amazing experience for whoever gets to go," she said.

Chapter Fourteen
Second Skin

Seth had the entire crew assemble near the pond next to the administrative building the next morning. He was holding a blue suit identical in color to the one he was wearing in his right hand as Bhumi stood next to him. "I'm sure you've been wondering why I've been wearing a suit that's different in color from all of yours. This blue suit is specialized with different properties than the ordinary white ones you've been wearing. It's biologically based like your white suits, but it's much more advanced. I'd planned on showing the blue suits to you later in the mission, but the news from Enceladus has moved this demonstration up."

Seth held up the suit in his right hand. "This is a spacesuit that's adapted to low or no atmosphere environments. It also has some features to allow you to deal with environments that are different from the one-G environment you're used to. This suit is meant to go directly next to the skin with no intervening layers."

"No intervening layers?" Vinod asked. "You mean we gotta be naked in that thing."

"That's right," Seth answered. "The material's much thicker than the ones you're wearing and therefore takes some effort and practice to get into. Since Bhumi's done it many times before, I'm going to have her demonstrate how to transition from the white suit to the blue one."

Seth turned to Bhumi, who started to pull on the collar of her white suit to remove it, exposing her bare shoulder. Many of the eyes in the group widened, and their pulse quickened—especially for the men of the group.

"Whoa!" both Richard and Rachael said simultaneously.

"Hold on a second," Rachael said to Bhumi, and she pulled her collar back up. "Seth, are you kidding me?"

"What?"

"You're not going to have Bhumi undress in front of everyone, are you?"

"Yes, but it wasn't just going to be her. I wanted everyone to change into the new suits right here."

"That's not going to happen," Rachael said with arms crossed.

Seth rolled his eyes. "I don't think I'll ever understand your human predilection for not being seen as you naturally are. Okay then. What do you suggest Rachael?"

"How about if you just tell us the process without demonstration, and then everyone can get changed on their own. I'm sure we can figure it out."

"Fine," Seth replied with some exasperation. "It'll take more time, but I understand the reasons," Seth explained the process to the group. They had to remove their existing suits, which all crew members knew how to do by now since they had needed to do this for taking showers. Getting into the new suits required them to slip into it from the neck hole and progressively pull it on from bottom to top. They inserted their feet first, then pulled it up over their torso, and then pulled on the sleeves. Seth reiterated that they must be completely naked in the suit. After the explanation, he led the group to a room in the building with two rows of suits arranged neatly on hangers on opposite sides of the room. They were all the same blue color as the one Seth wore. "They're all the same size. They'll automatically adjust to the size of your body once you get them on."

The crew grabbed their suits and noted that they were heavy, weighing over fifty pounds each. They walked back towards their habitats. Rachael, Joshua, Richard, and Bhumi walked on the path towards their abode, new suits in hand. "Were you really going to undress in front of everyone?" Richard asked Bhumi.

"Yea, I was a little uncomfortable, but whatever the mission requires. I seem to remember clothes being more of a functional thing in my previous life rather than anything to hide your body. I feel at times, we were naked around each other when the weather permitted."

"I guess I can see that," Richard responded. "But I suggest you be more careful here. The function of clothes has changed over time."

When they got to their abode, they went to their bedrooms to change. Joshua and Rachael undressed from their white suits in their bedroom and started the process of getting into the blue ones.

"This is much harder than it looks," Joshua commented after he had gotten his legs on. "It's kind of like trying to get into a wet suit with no zipper."

"It is a bit of a struggle," Rachael agreed.

The couple worked for a few minutes pulling the suit over their torsos and then into their sleeves. Joshua noted that the ends of the sleeves were gloved that he slipped his fingers into. When he finally pulled the collar up around his neck, he noted a change in the suit. "Woah, the suit's tightening around me." He noted that any space in the suit quickly vanished as the material of the suit contracted. The suit was skintight, but not uncomfortably so. He moved his arms and legs in all directions and noted that he could move freely despite the skintight material. "It feels good. Not restrictive at all."

He turned to Rachael, who also had finished. He thought that the skintight material accentuated her curves nicely. "You look good in that."

"It feels nice," she replied. "Though it's going to be a pain to take off. The gloves and feet on this suit are a perfect fit." She looked at her hand. "The gloves are strange. I hardly feel them at all." She ran her hand over the bed in their room. "Josh, this is amazing. I can feel perfectly through this suit. It's like there's nothing on my hands at all."

Joshua ran his hand along the wall of the room. "Wow, I see what you mean. I can feel the texture of this wall with no issues even though the material of the gloves seems thick. It's strange, but wonderful. We'll have to ask Seth how it works." Joshua noted a slight bulge in Rachael's suit located at the small of her lower back. He walked over and ran his hand along it. "I wonder what this bulge is. The rest of the suit seems skintight except for this area."

"You have one on your suit too. Something else to ask Seth. Let's see if Richard and Bhumi are done."

Joshua and Rachael found Bhumi waiting for them in the living room. "Any problems?" Rachael asked.

"No, I've done it many times before."

A minute later, Richard appeared from his room. "Did you guys notice these gloves?"

"Yea," Joshua said. "It feels like they're not even there."

The four walked back to the meeting area and waited for the others. Within a few minutes, the entire crew had reassembled, all wearing the suits. "What's with these gloves?" Vinod asked. "I can feel right through them."

"The suits are biological," Seth explained. "They're made of living cells. You can think of them like a second skin. They have sensory areas on the surface of the gloves that transfer the sensations they feel to the inner surface of the gloves. This means that you can feel with your hand just as if you weren't wearing gloves."

"It's pretty cool bro," Vinod said, rubbing his fingers together. "That'll definitely come in handy."

"Seth, how's this a spacesuit?" Joshua asked. "The material seems flexible. How can it keep us pressurized in a zero-atmosphere environment?"

"There are contracting cells in the suit. The closest analogy would be something like tiny muscles, but much more powerful than your own. As the pressure outside the suit gets lower, they automatically activate. The end result is that the suit presses against your skin so that you don't feel the reduced pressure outside. The lower the pressure outside, the more the suit squeezes in on you, but you won't feel any increased pressure. It's perfectly calibrated so that you won't feel anything from the exterior pressure drop at all. There's also a helmet, of course, for your head which I'll give you shortly."

Joshua pondered the mechanism that Seth had described. "Amazing. Spacesuits from NASA were huge, bulky, and heavy, which severely restricted the astronauts' movements. With these suits, it'll feel like we're not wearing anything at all even in the vacuum of space."

"That's the idea," Seth said. "Also, the suits have automatic temperature control. They can operate at a temperature range from a few degrees above absolute zero to four hundred degrees Celsius with no change in the internal temperature of the suit."

"Jesus, that's a wide temperature range," Vinod said. "Doesn't maintaining the internal temperature over that wide a range require a lot of energy?"

"Sure it does," Seth said. "That's why the suit has a powerful energy source. Each suit has a single fusion sphere located in the lower back region. The sphere powers the suit."

"There's a nuclear fusion device on our back?" Liz asked, trying unsuccessfully to look behind her.

"Yes, it's not dangerous. It's operating at very low levels, but it provides all the energy the suit needs."

"I'm assuming that hydrogen is the fuel source," Joshua said.

"Correct. There's only a small amount needed due to the relatively low energy requirements. There's a small storage area for the hydrogen in the region surrounding the sphere. It's located near in the lumbar region of the suit."

Guess that's what the hump is for, Joshua thought to himself.

"Now," Seth continued. "I'd like everyone to take their right index finger and touch the inner portion of their left forearm."

Rachael did as told and noted that some symbols appeared on the suit's surface on her inner left forearm. There were four symbols—a red square, a green circle, a yellow triangle, and a blue pentagon.

"These are the controls for the suit," Seth explained. "I'll start with the red square first. It controls the physical strength of the suit. I'll need a volunteer to demonstrate. Ted, can you please stand next to me."

Ted walked next to Seth. "Now go ahead and push the red square and tell the group what you see."

Ted pushed the square and said, "A new slider control appeared below the symbols. There's also some text that says one-G."

"Good," Seth remarked. "This means that when you're using the suit right now, you're going to feel like you're in a one-G environment. This is the default value. Of course, since the Zephyr is currently accelerating at one-G, you're not going to feel anything different at the moment." Seth turned to Ted. "As a demonstration, I want you to try to jump as high as you can into the air."

Ted squatted down and jumped up into the air as far as he could. He got three feet above the ground before coming back down.

"Damn Tabasco," Vinod said. "You got some vertical. You got up about three feet."

"What's your vertical Vinod?" Ted asked. "Three inches?"

The comment caused some chuckles from the group.

"Now Ted, I want you to move the slider with your finger to the right so that the numbers read three-Gs and then try walking around."

Ted moved the slider and tried walking. The group noted that his movements were much more labored and methodical. "Man, it's much harder to move around. It takes a lot of effort just to walk. It's like the suit is pushing against my movements."

"That's exactly what it's doing," Seth said. "The suit is simulating a three-G environment for you. It's pushing against your muscular actions to make it harder for you to move, but only in the vertical direction. If you lifted your arm and tried to move it sideways, it'd feel heavy, but there would be no resistance to sideways motion."

Ted lifted his arm and then moved it sideways. "Yup, exactly what I feel. My arm's heavy and hard to keep up, but I can move it sideways normally."

Joshua pondered how the suit was accomplishing this. He figured that it must have some type of accelerometer that noted the direction of gravity and was specifically resisting movements against the gravitational pull.

Ted tried to jump up again, but only made it a foot into the air. "I definitely feel a lot heavier. Can't jump as high."

"Still higher than Vinod at one-G," Liz commented with a smile.

Seth told Ted to move the slider in the opposite direction until it read 0.1-Gs. "Now try jumping up in the air but be careful when you come back down. Make sure you land on your feet."

Ted crouched down and jumped into the air. The others looked in amazement as he shot up thirty feet into the air before beginning his descent. Ted looked towards the ground, landed feet first, and crouched to brace his fall. "Damn, what was that!" he exclaimed as he stepped away from the landing site and noted two dents in the dirt where his feet had landed.

"The suit is simulating a 0.1-G environment," Seth explained. "The suit is now augmenting your movements against gravity by contracting the muscular elements located inside it. You can consider it like an exoskeleton that's helping you resist gravity. With the suit set to that low gravity level, you can jump much higher into the air."

"You looked like a goddamn superhero Tabasco," Vinod said, his mouth agape.

"I'm gonna love this shit," Ted remarked, inspecting the outside of the suit.

Joshua was confused as to how the suit worked. "How's it able to do that?" he asked.

"The logic is fairly simple," Seth responded. "If the suit is set to a G-level that is less than the environment you're in, then it augments your muscular strength against any movements opposite the direction of gravity to simulate a lower gravity level. The opposite happens when you set it to a level that's higher than the ambient."

"You call that simple?" Vinod asked. "That was confusing as hell. I didn't get any of that."

Joshua had understood what Seth had said. "You don't need to worry about all the logic. The suit will take care of everything for you. Just leave it set on the one-G setting, and it'll feel like you're in Earth gravity no matter what the actual gravity is of the planet you're on. If you set it lower than this, you can jump higher, and if you set it higher than one-G, you're going to feel heavier."

"That I got," Vinod said.

"It's an important feature," Joshua commented. "If we're planning on a mission to Enceladus, then it becomes very critical. Enceladus has almost one-hundredth the gravity of Earth. It'd be almost impossible and frankly dangerous to walk on the surface in such low gravity without the suit modulating our movements so we don't accidentally jump a hundred feet into the air."

"It's still going to take some practice," Seth said. "You're going to have to learn how to interact with the suit in a lower G-environment and walk around. That's what I want to spend the next hour doing." Seth instructed everyone, including Ted, to ensure their suits were at the one-G setting. "Now we're going to reduce the gravity of the Zephyr to 0.1-G and have you practice walking and moving around." Seth turned to Bhumi. "Bhumi, please reduce thrust to 0.1-G, but please do it over a thirty-second span. Don't want any sudden changes."

Bhumi closed her eyes, and the crew started feeling light in the head.

Rachael noted that the branches of the trees surrounding them slowly lifting, their leaves also going higher. The water in the pond next to them seemed to form giant waves that undulated slowly across its surface. Her hair became light and lifted slightly from her shoulders. Her head felt light, but the suit increased its downward pressure on her shoulders, so her body felt normal. It was a strange and somewhat nauseating feeling.

"Thrust reduced to 0.1-G," Bhumi announced a short while later.

"I want everyone to take a moment to get used to the lower gravity," Seth said. "You may feel nauseated. It's normal and should pass soon."

"Shit, I hope I don't lose my breakfast," Vinod said, his eyes closed. "It feels like I'm going downhill on an endless coaster."

Seth had the group stand still for a full five minutes before he asked them to try walking. Despite the suits simulating a one-G environment for the group, it was still disorienting. They were having difficulty even with simple motions like taking steps.

"Damn, this is harder than I thought it would be," Ted commented as he walked next to Liz across the lawn.

"Walking is an automatic process for our brains," Liz said. "It's something most humans learn when they're a year old. You're trying to override the automation engrained in the cerebellum of your brain since you first started walking. It'll take some time."

Ted noted that movements of his legs seemed the same, but that he had to wait for his feet to hit the ground from the last stride before taking the next stride. The process of walking seemed to be slower than normal. "Definitely going to be hard to run in a low-G environment."

"That's true," Liz said. "But I feel that you'll be able to run faster in an environment higher than one-G."

"I'm gonna try something." Ted moved his strength slider to 0.1-G to match their environment. He then started bounding across the lawn with giant steps that took him ten feet into the air and thirty feet in distance with each bound. The others watched his bounding movements as he circled back next to Liz. "I think if you need to move faster, you need to adjust your G slider to a lower level. I think the higher level is better for walking though."

"Remember," Liz replied. "Don't turn the G-level too low. You could accidentally jump too high. When your feet are off the ground, you have no way to control your direction."

"I get it. Gonna have to play around with it some more to get used to it." Ted reached out his hand. "Let's try walking together. I'm sure if we're walking on some uneven surface, it'll help our balance to be holding on to someone."

Liz grabbed Ted's hand, and they practiced walking together. She noted that she could feel Ted's hand perfectly through the suit. It felt strong and comforting.

After an hour in the lower-G environment, most in the group had gotten accustomed to walking. Seth had the group regather on the lawn and had Bhumi return the ship to one-G. "Now for the helmets," he said as he led the group inside the building to another room that contained numerous helmets on hooks. Crew members collected their helmets and walked back to the lawn.

Joshua noted that the helmet's material was not hard, but made of the same blue, flexible suit material. The only rigid portion was a face shield made of a transparent material that reminded him of the window material in their abode.

Back at the lawn, Seth had the crew don their helmets which fit like a scuba suit helmet. It was tight around the head, ears, and neck, but had a space in front of the eyes, nose, and mouth which the face shield covered. The neck portion of the helmet sealed automatically with the neck portion of their suits. After he had donned his helmet, Joshua could feel air blowing gently from the edge of the face shield towards his face.

"Can everyone hear me?" Seth asked.

Rachael heard Seth's voice emanating from two small speakers, one near each ear. The group nodded that they could hear Seth.

"The communication system of these suits is based on radio waves and not spookyons. We wanted to make sure that communications work in the spookyon dampening field. They work via proximity. In normal mode, you will hear the transmission of any crew member within a hundred feet of your location. You simply speak, and anyone within a hundred feet will hear you as long as they're wearing their helmets. Your voice can't penetrate the suit, and anyone not wearing a helmet won't hear you. Pushing the yellow triangle on your control panel allows for global transmission. Speaking, while in global transmission mode, will transmit your voice to all crew members, no matter their distance. Finally, the green circle on your control panel is for Gilead. Pushing this button while speaking will connect you directly to Gilead. Each suit also has a camera that records what you're seeing. This signal is also relayed to Gilead, who will be monitoring all video and audio feeds from the suits. The edges of your facemask are luminous. They provide light automatically in low light environments."

"Man Seth," Ted remarked while looking at the control panel of his forearm. "You've thought of everything."

"There's one more button, the blue pentagon, that I have to explain. It's the nutrition button. When you press it, you'll feel a straw next to your mouth. When you suck on the straw, you will receive a complete, balanced nutritional supplement. It contains everything from water to carbohydrates, fats, and proteins that your bodies need nutritionally."

Vinod pushed the blue button on his suit and took a sip from a straw that appeared near the right corner of his mouth. "It's kinda sweet but tastes pretty good. Don't suppose you can mix in some Grey Goose, can you?"

Seth ignored the comment. "These, in essence, are the major features of the suit. There're a few more days before we reach the Saturn system. I want the crew to wear only their spacesuits to get accustomed to them for the remainder of this mission. It's not necessary to wear your helmets all the time, but I want you to keep them close and do some of your training with them on to get used to them."

"We have to wear these things 24/7?" Vinod asked, palms raised. "They're kind of a pain to get in and out of. What happens if you have to take a leak?"

Seth turned to look at Vinod. "Then you just go."

Vinod looked back at him quizzically. "What do you mean 'you just go?' You just go in the suit?"

"Yes."

"Are you kidding me?"

"No. The suit is designed to absorb your waste products, solid or liquid. They're recycled by the suit and turned back into the nutritional supplement."

"What?" Vinod asked incredulously. "I'm going to be drinking my own piss? No way. That's just gross dude."

Seth looked perturbed by the comment. "The suit automatically sterilizes any bacteria in your waste and chemically converts it back into the nutritional supplement. It's perfectly safe."

Liz thought about what chemical processes would be involved in processing human waste back into a nutritional supplement. Waste had been used as fertilizer for centuries on Earth—fertilizer for food that was eventually eaten. "I think it's kind of ingenious," she stated. "What you eat and what your body outputs as waste are essential the same atoms. They may be chemically different as to how they're combined, but the type and number of atoms are essentially the same. The petrins have figured out how to recycle the atoms of our waste and chemically alter them back into nutrition. I assume the carbon dioxide you breathe out is also chemically transformed back into individual carbon and oxygen atoms to replenish the oxygen you breathe while the carbon is transferred back to the nutritional supplement. The only thing that needs to be added is energy. It requires some energy input to transform waste atoms into nutritional atoms. I figure the fusion sphere provides this energy. It's a complete recycling process. Like I said, it's ingenious. Did I get it right Seth?"

"Absolutely right. Your suits are a complete life support system. The only thing that gets used up is energy. The atoms are recycled and reformed into nutritional elements that you can consume. The energy is provided by hydrogen that's fused by the fusion sphere."

"How long can a person live in one of these suits?" Joshua asked. "If all waste products are recycled, then the only limiting factor is the rate of consumption of the hydrogen fuel."

"That's true," Seth replied. "Since the human body requires only a relatively small amount of energy compared to the vast energy given off by hydrogen fusion, we estimate that a person sealed in a suit can survive for approximately twenty years given an average rate of energy consumption."

The group stared blankly at Seth after his last statement. They all had a similar thought that Rachael voiced. "Why did you design a suit we can live in for twenty years? I thought you said this was max a six-month mission?"

"We didn't design it to last twenty years," Seth explained. "We designed it to be efficient. We designed it to be a completely self-sustaining life support system. It just so happens due to the efficiency of our design that it can last twenty years, but obviously, we don't envision it being used that way."

"How about taking a shower?" Vinod asked.

"No need. The suit automatically cleans and sterilizes your skin surface. However, if you have the helmet off, you can shower with the suit on to clean your head. That's it for now. You're dismissed to continue your practice using the suits."

The group dispersed. Joshua had been wondering since embarking on the mission what a space mission with petrin technology would entail and what the dangers would be. There were many unknowns on the mission that were mainly encompassed by the unpredictable actions of Medusa. After seeing the technology the petrins had accumulated for the mission, including the Zephyr, Gilead, the atomic printer, and now the biological space suits, he was more confident that the petrins had done a thorough job of trying to equip the crew the best they could for success. This was still a dangerous mission, but at least the petrins were giving them a fighting chance.

But no amount of advance planning could account for all the unknowns. Joshua knew that the first unknown would be encountered soon on a frozen moon of a gas giant they were hurtling towards.

Chapter Fifteen
Birthday

The next day was rotation day—the day the Zephyr would rotate 180 degrees and start its deceleration towards Saturn. Joshua had asked Seth exactly what time the maneuver would start, and he, Rachael, and Richard stood with Seth and Bhumi next to one of the window walls of the ship prior to the maneuver.

"Anyone else coming?" Seth asked.

"I don't think so," Rachael replied. "I know you told the crew that the viewing of the rotation was optional, so I think it's just the five of us."

Rachael had asked Vinod earlier if he was coming to the viewing of the rotation. His response was, "What's the big deal? We're not going to feel much, and seeing some stars spin around the ship is kinda boring. Besides, Ted and I are scheduled to play tennis during that time. We want to see what that's like with these new super suits."

"You going to cheat and have your G-level set lower than his?"

"You know I'd have no chance if I didn't."

Seth told Bhumi to start the maneuver. She closed her eyes, and Joshua noted a slight change in the direction of a couple of the ejection nozzles outside. He felt a slight sideways motion only for a few seconds. The starfield outside started to rotate slowly as he felt no change in gravity. The stars continued their rotation for a full minute before he again felt a slight sideways motion opposite in direction to the previous motion. It was not as simple a maneuver as one would assume. Maintaining one-G gravity while turning the ship was a complex dance, but Bhumi seemed to accomplish it with no difficulty.

The sun was now directly above them but was obscured by the ceiling. The ship's plasma ejection nozzles were now pointed towards Saturn. The

Zephyr would slowly decelerate for the next four days until they reached the ringed world.

"Beautifully done Bhumi," Joshua commented. "I hardly felt a thing."

Over the next few days, the crew had long hours of training to get used to their spacesuits. They tested all the controls of the suits and became accustomed to walking and maneuvering in various levels of gravity.

It was a joyous time on the Zephyr. Seth had informed the crew that the amount of energy required to allow the crew to get whatever food they desired from the atomic printer wouldn't significantly affect the hydrogen supply. As a result, the crew enjoyed gourmet meals every evening, something that boosted their morale.

Two days before their arrival at Saturn, Joshua, Rachael, Richard, and Bhumi sat at their dining table enjoying a deep-dish pizza.

"This is the best pizza I ever had," Richard commented as he took a bite.

"It's Chicago deep-dish," Joshua replied. "I printed it from a data file in Gilead from a restaurant I loved to visit when I was in Chicago while on Earth. The best pizza in the world."

"This *is* good," Rachael commented. "But the best pizza is New York style, in my opinion. A large slice, dripping with cheese, that folds in your hand before you take a bite."

"Maybe we can try that tomorrow," Bhumi said. "I love all this new food I've experienced over the past few days. I sense that food was a necessity in my past life. It seems like more of a pleasure here."

Rachael looked at Bhumi. At times she'd forgotten that Bhumi was a human from an ancient time. Rachael knew that their experience on the Zephyr was a completely new paradigm for the crew, given the amount of new technology they were dealing with, but she realized that, for Bhumi, this was even more of a foreign experience. How did a human from the Paleolithic view technology well beyond what even modern humans experienced? "What do you think of all this?" she asked Bhumi.

"What do I think of all what?"

"This experience we're having. This mission. This . . . existence. It must be very foreign to you."

"Foreign is relative," Bhumi answered. "For something to be foreign, you got to have something to compare it to. I don't have any clear memories of my past. Maybe I'm able to cope with this existence better because I don't have anything else to compare it to."

Joshua was impressed by the response. It portrayed a mind that was able to relieve itself from the burdens of the present and grasp the big picture.

He was amazed that a person of Bhumi's age was so mentally evolved. "That's a very mature understanding for a person of your age," he commented.

"My age?" Bhumi asked.

"Seth said that according to isotope testing, he felt that you were about nineteen years old when you were caught in that avalanche. That's relatively young for a human."

"When's your birthday?" Richard asked. "When do you turn twenty?"

Bhumi tilted her head sideways and looked at Richard without saying a word.

Richard immediately realized his mistake. "Sorry Boom. I forgot. You have no idea when your birthday is. Do you?"

"No," Bhumi responded quietly. "We understood seasons in my past life, but the concept of a calendar was something we didn't grasp."

Rachael immediately recognized Bhumi's discomfort. A birthday was a simple event that every human shared. A birthday represented a celebration of a single life and was an affirmation of the positivity of their birth—their existence. "I'm making a proclamation," Rachael announced, lifting her right index finger in the air. "Today is the twenty-seventh of September on the Earth calendar. I'm officially proclaiming that tomorrow, the twenty-eighth of September, will be your official birthday." She turned to Bhumi. "You're officially turning twenty tomorrow, and I'm going to announce it to the crew. A birthday is always a celebration. We'll have a birthday party for you tomorrow."

Bhumi's face lit up. "A birthday party? What is it? What do I have to do?"

"You don't have to do anything," Joshua replied. "You just have to enjoy it." He turned to Rachael. "What should we plan?"

"Vinod's the expert on celebrations," she replied. "He's always looking for an excuse for a party. I'll consult him on the arrangements."

Richard turned to Rachael with a beaming smile. Rachael gave a knowing smile back as their eyes met. There had been tension between the two due to the protective and parental nature with which Rachael had regarded Richard, but this, to him, was an affirmation of the bond between brother and sister. He appreciated the gesture that Rachael was giving to Bhumi. He didn't say a word, but the wink he gave her was more than words could convey.

* * *

The next morning, Bhumi walked through the landscape. She noted that the leaves on the trees were changing into the colors of autumn. The green leaves were now intermixed with points of yellow, red, and bright orange. Bhumi was greeted with "happy birthday" by all those she met. The greetings were fleeting, but somehow, they comforted her. She'd always harbored a fear of not fitting in on this mission due to her radically different past, but the greetings allayed these fears. She was feeling more comfortable with the crew. They made her feel more . . . human.

The day's events for Bhumi, other than the greetings, had been like the past few days. Crew members continued their training of getting accustomed to the biological space suits. She learned that her birthday party would begin at dusk. She slowly dimmed the overhead sun as the crew gathered on a lawn near the center of the Zephyr for the celebration.

Rachael had left the party's planning up to Vinod, a task he enthusiastically accepted.

Joshua noted tables with platters of barbecued meat and roasted vegetables as he stood next to Vinod. The platters were filled with ribs, chicken, and brisket covered in barbecue sauce accompanied by roasted potatoes, corn, and dinner rolls. "A barbecue?" he asked. "You know that I'm vegetarian along with some other crew members, don't you?"

"What does that mean?" Vinod asked. "What does vegetarian mean when all this food was anatomically printed from raw atoms? There weren't any animals killed in the process."

Joshua pondered the statement for a moment and shrugged his shoulders. "I guess you're right."

Vinod, Ted, and Richard walked to a table with numerous bottles of liquid. There were multiple varieties of drinks, both alcoholic and non-alcoholic. They walked to a large bowl with multiple bottles of Dom Perignon on ice surrounded by champaign glasses. They distributed the glasses amongst the crew. Seth was standing beside Bhumi as Vinod was about to hand her a glass. Seth pulled him aside before he could do so. "You really think that's a good idea?"

"Does she have anything important to do tonight?" Vinod asked.

"No," Seth responded. "The ship's just decelerating, but she's still in control of it. There's nothing specific she has to do, but why take a chance?"

"It's her birthday Seth. She has to be a part of the celebration."

"It's a risk," Seth responded.

Rachael was standing close to Seth and Vinod and overheard their conversation. Her thoughts turned to Ava. She and Joshua were her parents, and she realized that Ava's activities had been monitored and scripted by them since she was born. But she also realized that children had to be let free at some point. They had to be allowed to make their own choices.

Parents had to relinquish control at some point and hope that their influence during their younger years was enough to allow their children to make the correct choices as they got older, and the influence of their parents waned. Rachael recognized the parental attitude that Seth had shown towards Bhumi. She walked over to him. "She's responsible Seth. I trust her. She's human. Part of being human is accepting more responsibility as you get older. You've taught her well, but in the end, she has to accept the responsibility she's been given and learn to deal appropriately with it. As parents, there comes a point when you have to let your children go and let them make their own choices. All you can hope for is that the teaching you instilled upon them during their growth is enough to allow them to make the right choices."

Seth gave Rachael a curious smile. Rachael wondered what it meant. Seth didn't say anything. He grabbed the glass from Vinod and handed it to Bhumi. "Happy birthday," he said as he handed her the glass. "Have fun but be careful."

"I'm always careful," Bhumi responded, taking the glass. "Vinod, I'm assuming this is for champagne?"

"Yes. It's a traditional drink of celebration."

"But," Bhumi said, looking at the glass, "it's also an intoxicant, right?"

"Yes."

"I'd love to try champagne sometime, but I think I'll stick with some juice for tonight."

"Suit yourself," Vinod said. "It's your celebration."

Rachael gave Seth a knowing nod.

"I'll join her in sticking to juice," Richard commented as he went to retrieve some mango juice from a table.

After the glasses were distributed and filled, Seth raised his glass. The group knew that the filled glass for Seth was simply symbolic, since in android form, he couldn't actually drink. "Happy birthday Bhumi," he said. "May it be the first of many."

The crew enjoyed the feast along with more drinks as the evening progressed. After dinner, Vinod produced a large white cake with twenty-one lit candles and presented it to Bhumi. "Why twenty-one?" Bhumi asked. "I'm officially twenty today."

"It's an old Earth superstition," Richard explained.

"Old is relative," Bhumi responded with a smirk.

"Yea, I get what you mean," Richard replied. "Anyway, you have to make a wish and blow out the candles."

Bhumi closed her eyes for a moment and blew out the candles. As the crew gathered around and sang her happy birthday, Bhumi stood with an enormous smile. Tears welled in her eyes as she felt a camaraderie with the crew. It was a welcome relief from the loneliness that she had endured for months after her reanimation.

Vinod turned to Bhumi. "You ready?"

"Yes."

"Then let's do it."

The artificial sun above went completely dark as the song "Celebration" from Kool & the Gang blared through the ship.

The sun then turned into a strobe that spitted out numerous pulses of light in various colors that beamed and reflected off the surfaces of the space. The crew danced to the music as the lights from above pulsed perfectly coordinated to the song. Ted moved over to Vinod and Bhumi. "Damn, how'd you guys turn the sun into a giant disco ball?"

"It wasn't too hard," Bhumi replied over the din of the music. "I'm mixing the hydrogen being injected into the fusion spheres with other elements like cobalt, iron, and sodium. When different elements burn, they release various colors."

Ted's gaze flowed over the dancing mob to the surrounding landscape of the ship, which seemed to pulse to the rhythm of the music. He'd never seen such a large area in perfect sync. He noticed Liz dancing by herself and danced his way in her direction.

Vinod controlled the musical choices as the party and dancing lasted late into the evening.

Rachael noted that Ted and Liz had been dancing together for most of the evening. She pointed out the couple to Joshua. "They've been dancing together for a while. Do you think that there's anything going on there?"

Joshua shrugged his shoulders. "We can only hope."

A few songs later, Ted and Liz moved to where Bhumi was dancing with Richard. "Damn girl, you got some rhythm," Ted said to Bhumi. "How'd you learn how to dance?"

"I don't know," Bhumi replied, dancing in sync to the music. "It seemed to just come to me naturally. Maybe dancing was something we did in my past life."

Ted turned to Richard. "You gotta step up your game. She's showin' you up."

"Doesn't she always?"

"It's getting late," Vinod said a few songs later. "I think the next song will be the last." He turned to Bhumi. "Do you have any requests?"

"I don't know any songs to request," Bhumi replied.

"Let me pick one," Richard said. "The lyrics actually start with the word 'Zephyr.'"

"Go for it," Bhumi said. "I'll make it a special experience."

Richard told Vinod the song. "Great choice bro. Very apropos." Vinod turned to the group during a lapse in the music. "Last song people."

Bhumi motioned with her arm. "Come dance with me." The group formed a large circle around her.

"Ray of Light" from Madonna started playing. Bhumi stood still, her eyes closed, her head tilted upwards, her hands away from her body, palms forward, as the intro guitar chords for the song played. The crew suddenly felt an increase in gravity as the drumbeat of the song began. Their knees buckled, and their legs tightened in response to the increased weight. The increase in weight lasted only for a moment and then was gone, replaced by a feeling of weightlessness. The increased tension in the muscles of their legs caused them to jolt upwards. They lifted off the ground and drifted slowly thirty feet above the surface as the beat from the song permeated their bodies, the colored lights from the artificial sun above dancing across the landscape below. The water from the pond also lifted upwards near its center and undulated in large waves from the reduced gravity. The lights from the sun above glinted and reflected off the surface of the undulating waves of water, filling the space with dancing, colored lights.

The ground below them started shifting small distances in numerous directions along its lateral plane, although those in the air couldn't sense these lateral movements. Rachael noticed the branches of the trees reacting to the movements. *They're dancing! The trees are dancing to the song!* Rachael looked over to Bhumi. Her body stood straight and still in the air as her head looked around, moving rhythmically to the song. The shock of being lifted into the air subsided as the crew floated and bobbed their heads to the music and took in the experience. Rachael looked around the Zephyr as it weaved and bobbed to the music. *The ship's a part of Bhumi, and she is dancing. The entire ship is dancing!*

It was surreal. Rachael had a sudden welling of emotion as she assimilated the experience of her overloaded senses. She had difficulty pinpointing the exact emotion she was feeling. The closest she could come up with was . . . joy. She wondered what the Zephyr looked like from the outside. It was a million-metric-ton biological entity dancing through the cosmos, its ejection nozzles moving and shifting in perfect rhythm to a song as they intermittently spit out bright-red plasma. It was a biological egg dancing through space—its home. Was it a ship, or was it a complete organism? Was she just part of the organism?

Rachael felt one with the ship and its contents. She saw the crew moving to the music, their faces etched with smiles as they tried to dance in the air. It was a moment of pure joy, a celebration of the unlimited capabilities of purposeful complexity. It was a celebration of life.

As the song faded, the ground beneath Rachael slowly approached, and she landed along with the crew as the gravity returned to normal. They all stared in silence at Bhumi as the dancing lights stopped and were replaced by moonlight. There were in awe.

Ted was the first to speak. "Like I said before. Girl, you got some moves."

Chapter Sixteen
The Garage

The next day was the last day of training before the Zephyr would reach Saturn. Seth had asked the crew to meet at the garage in Area D of the ship. It was a large, two-story structure that encompassed a small section of the outer wall of Area D. "I have some equipment in here that you'll need for your mission to Enceladus. I will stay with Bhumi on the ship, helping her refuel in the atmosphere of Saturn while the rest of you visit Enceladus."

"Bhumi can't come with us to Enceladus?" Richard asked.

"No. She controls the ship. She needs to be with the Zephyr while it's being refueled."

Richard looked at Bhumi. He was sad that she would miss the adventure.

"It's okay Blue," Bhumi said, noticing Richard's glance. "You can tell me about it afterward."

"Blue?" Vinod asked, turning to Richard.

Richard's face blushed. "I'll explain later."

"The first thing I have to show you are some weapons for the military crew," Seth said.

"Weapons?" Vinod asked. The mere mention of the word made Vinod uncomfortable. "We're going to need weapons on Enceladus?"

"I don't think so. The weapons are just a precaution. Frankly, we don't know what you'll find, but I want the crew properly equipped." Seth led the crew into the garage. It was a cavernous space whose back wall was the clear exterior of the ship. Inside the space were numerous racks of long items that Ted immediately recognized as rifles. They had a similar shape to a rifle with a butt, stalk, trigger, and barrel, but they were completely shiny and made of a chrome-like metal. Ted noted that attached underneath the stalk of each rifle was a black tube that connected it to a black backpack that also hung on the rack. He walked up to the rack. "Can I pick one up?"

"Yes," Seth replied. "The pack, which is where the ammunition is stored, goes on your chest."

Ted picked up one of the rifles with the attached pack. He placed the pack on his chest and allowed Seth to attach two straps that went behind him in a crisscross fashion. Seth snapped the buckles at the end of the straps on Ted's back and tightened them snugly. Ted grasped the rifle. He placed his left hand under the front portion and his right hand on a pistol grip behind the trigger. "This sucka's got some heft to it. Can I pull the trigger?"

"Go ahead," Seth said. "Nothing's going to happen because the safety's on, but I want you to get the feel."

Ted aimed the weapon away from the group and pulled the trigger. He noted a small red laser marker that appeared on what he was aiming at. "The trigger's strange. It doesn't seem to have any click, and it's a little hard to pull."

"It's a variable trigger," Seth said.

"Variable? In what way? What does this thing fire?"

"Alpha particles."

"What's that?"

Joshua looked at Seth. "Alpha particles as in helium nuclei?"

"Yup. It shoots a continuous, very narrow beam of alpha particles at extremely high energy. The pack that the rifle is attached to is filled with liquid helium. They're the source of the alpha particles."

Joshua walked up and inspected the rifle in Ted's hands. He ran his hand along its length. "I'm assuming then that this barrel is a particle accelerator."

"Yes."

"I'm also guessing that there's a fusion sphere in the pack."

"You assume correctly."

"What does all this mean?" Ted asked. "How does this thing work? I kinda thought it would shoot airfoils or something."

"Airfoils won't work," Seth explained. "This weapon was specifically meant to be used in a vacuum. Airfoils need an atmosphere to work. Enceladus doesn't really have an atmosphere, just a trace amount of water vapor. This weapon shoots a very narrow and powerful radiation beam, but this beam's only a few atoms wide. In fact, if you were to point it at an object and pull the trigger and you didn't move the rifle at all, it wouldn't do much damage. The beam would make an atom-sized hole entirely through the object, but a hole this small wouldn't do much damage."

"Then what's the use?" Ted asked.

Joshua looked at the weapon in Ted's hands and digested what Seth had said. "You can't think of it as a rifle," he said as he realized its power. "You have to think of it as a knife. Since it fires a continuous beam, if, when you're firing at a target, and you move the rifle while firing so that the beam traverses the object, the beam would slice right through the target."

Ted pondered Joshua's statement as he rubbed his hair with his left hand. "So, to kill something, you want to aim to one side of it, fire, and then move to the other side. That would cut it in half, right?"

"Exactly," Seth responded.

"Damn," Ted remarked, looking at the weapon. "It's like a remote-controlled sword."

"A good analogy," Joshua said, "but since the beam is only a few atoms thick. It'd be the sharpest sword you've ever seen."

"How thick an object can it cut through?" Ted asked.

"That's what the trigger is for," Seth replied. "The farther you depress the trigger, the further the beam cuts into the target. That's why you have to be careful with it. If you press it too far while aiming at a thin object, you can easily cut what's behind it. That's also why I don't want you to use it on the ship. We don't want any accidental damage. The surface of Enceladus is ice with large ice mountains and boulders. I want you and your team to practice using these weapons on those to get accustomed to their power. You're going to be security for the scientific crew, but also, I want your team to train on using these weapons."

"This shit's gonna be a blast," Ted remarked, looking at the weapon in his hands. "Can it cut through an arachnid? You know, like those infiltrators on Earth."

"Possibly," Seth said. "Maybe at full power with the trigger fully depressed."

"Then why don't you use these things on the infiltrators on Earth?" Liz asked.

"Remember, this weapon was designed for use in a vacuum," Seth replied. "It doesn't work in an atmosphere. The atoms in the atmosphere would dissipate the alpha particle beam before it reached its target."

"I get it," Ted remarked. "It's a space knife. What's its range?"

"The alpha particle beam does separate slightly over long distances making it less effective, but I'd say it has at least a two-mile range before the beam loses its efficacy."

"Damn, two miles," Ted remarked. "Any recoil?"

"No. Not enough mass being ejected by the nozzle for that."

The military crew all equipped themselves with the weapons. Seth explained to the group where the safety switch was on the pack and showed them an indicator on top of the pack, which showed the ammunition level. "The pack can handle about ten minutes of continuous firing before it's depleted, so you have to use the weapon in short bursts. Also, there's no way to reload, so use it judiciously."

The crew practiced aiming the weapons with the safeties on for thirty minutes. After Seth felt that they had enough practice, they replaced the weapons on the racks. Seth led the group to another part of the garage. There were more racks with packs that were much larger than the packs connected to the weapons. These were rectangular in shape and were colored a light blue color.

"I'm sure you've been wondering how you'll actually get to Enceladus," Seth said. "The Zephyr is much too large and has too much hot plasma exhaust to land there. These jet packs will take you there." Seth asked Vinod to be a volunteer to demonstrate how the packs worked. He had Vinod step into a harness attached to the front of one of the packs that went around his legs and then lifted the pack onto his back. He slipped some shoulder straps onto his shoulders and buckled a center strap that went around his waist.

"Damn thing's heavy," Vinod remarked as he felt the weight on his shoulders.

"About a hundred pounds," Seth said. "It won't be that heavy in a low or zero-G environment, but if it's uncomfortable, adjust your suit to a lower-G level."

Vinod made the adjustment. "That's better."

"You would've never made it as a Seal," Ted commented, shaking his head.

"And I never intend to."

A handle attached to the right side of the pack protruded forward and ended in an upward-facing handle. Vinod gripped the handle with his right hand and noted three buttons and a small joystick near his thumb. The buttons were circular and colored red, green, and blue.

"The pack works by ejecting plasma through multiple nozzles surrounding the pack," Seth said. "It has built-in navigation and is pre-programmed with your destination. The controls are fairly simple. Pushing the blue button takes you to the pre-programmed destination. It's like an autopilot. You don't have to do anything else. The pack will automatically fly you on a pre-programmed route to your destination. Pushing the green button will take you back to the Zephyr, no matter its location. The pack automatically knows where the Zephyr is at all times. The red button is for manual flight mode. I anticipate it being used only for emergencies, and I don't envision you needing it on this mission. If you're in manual mode, the joystick determines your destination. The farther you push it in a particular direction, the faster you will fly in the direction the joystick is being pushed."

"Let me get this straight," Vinod said. "When we leave the Zephyr, all I have to do is push the blue button, and this thing'll fly me to Enceladus?"

"Yes," Seth responded. "It will fly you on a pre-programmed path to your destination."

"Then when I want to come back to the ship, I just push the green button?"

"Correct."

"Seems pretty simple," Vinod said. "It must obviously have some built-in intelligence to be able to fly these paths."

"Obviously."

"How are the packs programmed?" Vinod asked.

"Gilead normally handles that," Seth said, "but Vinod, I want you to learn how to program the packs as well. Gilead can teach you."

"No problem."

"What's the range of the pack?" Liz asked. "How far can you fly with that thing?"

"It has a limited amount of fuel," Seth replied. "It can only generate thrust while it still has fuel, but remember, in space there's nothing to slow you down. If you point at a destination and generate some thrust with the pack, you'll eventually reach your destination, but how long that will take will depend on your velocity. There's a fuel indicator on the handle that tells you how much fuel the pack has remaining. How long the thrust will last is variable depending on the amount of thrust requested. At full thrust, which is two-Gs, the pack will last about four hours."

Joshua did some mental calculations on the capabilities of the pack. He also remembered what Seth had said about the capabilities of the spacesuit. "Seth, then it's theoretically possible that a person in the spacesuit can aim themselves at a distant spot, something like the Earth, and reach there eventually."

Seth looked calmly at Joshua. "Yes, that's theoretically possible Dr. Andrews, but what you're describing would be a form of torture. Even at our current distance to Earth, which is continually increasing, as you know, and given the amount of thrust the pack could generate, it would take years for you to reach Earth. Yes, you would physically be able to survive the transit. The suit is designed to shield you from the radiation in space, but the mental torture on such a trip would be unbearable for a human. How could you survive years in space by yourself with no ship around you? There'd be literally nothing for you to do. There'd be no one to talk to. I feel that you'd go insane on such a journey. It'd be the ultimate form of solitary confinement. You may physically survive the trip, but the utter loneliness would do you in."

Vinod shuttered at the description. "No way I'd want anything like that to happen. If there was some emergency and I was lost in space by myself, I'd just fly myself into some planet or asteroid or something and end it so that I'd be revived on New Eden." He turned to Seth. "That's how it'd work, right Seth? If one of us croaks on this mission, then we'd simply wake up on New Eden?"

Seth didn't answer immediately as the crew stared at him. "Yes," he finally replied quietly. "As long as you were dead according to our definition of death. But remember that when you wake up on New Eden, your memories will only include those up to your last backup. Anything that happens after that will be lost."

Rachael became solemn at the remarks made by Seth and Vinod. The conversation reminded her of the danger of the mission they were on. The days since they'd arrived on the Zephyr were ones of discovery and awe. It had been a wonderful experience that had culminated in the surreal experience of Bhumi's birthday the night before. They had enveloped themselves in the incredible technology of the petrins that had allowed them to experience something that no human had ever experienced before. They had traversed their solar system and seen and experienced sites and places that no human had ever experienced, but the uncertainty of this mission was fast approaching. What would they find on Enceladus? What had Medusa sent there? What was Medusa doing at Planet Nine? Why did she find the need to cloak the planet in the spookyon dampening field? The questions were many, and Rachael knew that their primary goal on the mission was to find answers to these questions.

The crew was scheduled to reach Saturn the next day, and she would find herself on one of the moons of Saturn. She looked forward to the experience, but a part of her was apprehensive about what they would discover.

* * *

Dina Williams stared out the transport capsule at the snow-covered landscape outside. The limbs of the evergreens were laden with heavy snow that bent their branches. She turned to Robert Langdon, who occupied the only other seat in the capsule. "Do you have any idea what Mitchell's security team wants to show us?"

"Don't know," Langdon replied. "He didn't want the security risk of sending a video. He wanted the two of us to see whatever it is in person."

The capsule slowed to a halt as it neared the terminus of the tube branch in which it traveled. It came to a halt in the station, and the door opened. Williams and Langdon got out and immediately donned heavy coats for protection from the cold outside. Mitchell Porter greeted the couple on the platform. "Thanks for coming. We'll have to walk the rest of the way. About a mile."

The three walked a snow-covered trail that wound through the evergreen forest. "This area is definitely remote," Langdon said as he trudged through the foot-high snow.

"Seth wanted to keep whatever grew from the seed he gave us privately," Porter remarked. "The place had to be remote to ensure security."

The trail led to a gate in a twenty-foot-high barbed wire fence. The gate was secured by two armed guards who let the group through. "Just a little further," Porter said.

The trail took a dip into a ravine, and as the group started to descend, Williams and Langdon noted an enormous white dome in the distance.

"What the hell is that?" Langdon asked.

"I was hoping you could tell me," Porter stated as they continued along the trail. "That fifty-foot-tall dome is what grew from the seed that Seth gave us. I have no idea what it is, and it's still getting bigger. It's also warm. About twenty-five degrees Celsius."

The trio continued on the trail and got to within fifty feet of the semi-spherical structure. They walked all around but could see only a smooth-white surface with no blemishes.

Langdon noticed a slight bulge in the dome near the roof. "What's that bulge up there? It seems to break the symmetry of the dome."

"We noticed that too," Porter replied. "We have no idea what it is. Robert, you think you can get some scientists with some equipment to probe this thing? I need to know what's inside."

"Possibly," Langdon said, hand on his chin.

"Don't think that that's a good idea," Williams said. "Seth specifically said that we should let whatever this is grow undisturbed. Probing with scientific equipment certainly wouldn't be undisturbed."

"But Dina," Porter protested. "This thing's huge and getting bigger. Who knows what the damn petrins are growing in there? Could be a goddamn army or a weapon of some kind."

"It certainly is big," Williams commented, craning her neck to see the top of the dome. "But a promise is a promise. We told Seth we'd let it grow undisturbed, and that's what we're going to do. We'll just have to trust Seth on this. You are to do nothing to this structure," Williams said, pointing to the dome. "Is that understood?"

"Yes ma'am," Porter replied.

"But I want you and your men to continue monitoring it," Williams said. "I want to be notified immediately if there are any changes."

Chapter Seventeen
Enceladus

Vinod stared out over the edge of the Zephyr. It was a sight that caused a bit of nausea to well up in his stomach. *Damn, why did I eat breakfast today? I wonder if this suit can absorb vomit.* He looked ahead of him and saw the rest of the crew all lined up on the edge of the ship, dressed in their spacesuits with helmets on their heads and jet packs on their backs. The military crew held their weapons with their ammo packs on their chests.

Seth had revealed that the garage was also an airlock. The doors of the garage that led to the ship were air-tight, and the transparent outer wall that constituted the ship's exterior wall was movable and tilted upward on hinges that allowed the garage to be exposed to the vacuum of space.

The scene that faced the crew made them feel small and insignificant. Directly in front of them, oriented vertically, were the rings of Saturn sparkling and shimmering white as sunshine glinted off ice crystals. It was a wall of white that they could barely see the edges of. To their right was the planet itself, its atmospheric storms causing multi-colored bands to stretch across its surface. The orb was only partially seen, the planet too large to be included in one field of view. The planet's surface was only partially in sunlight, and numerous flashes of lightning were visible in the dark section.

The Zephyr was still decelerating towards a point in Saturn's upper atmosphere, but was now only doing so at half a G.

Joshua, who was standing next to Vinod, pointed ahead of him. "That dark gap in the rings is the Cassini division. It's the gap between the B and A rings. I think that'll be our heading initially."

Vinod heard Joshua's voice loud and clear coming through the speakers of his helmet. He closed his eyes to try to quell the anxiety growing inside him. A bead of perspiration trickled from his forehead.

Bhumi and Seth stood behind the crew. Both were also in their spacesuits with their helmets attached, but they didn't have the jet packs on their backs like the others. "You're correct Josh," Seth said. "The packs will take you to the Cassini division first, and then you'll progress outwards across the surface of the A ring. This will all be at one-G acceleration. After you pass the main ring system, and you're in the large gap before the outer F and E rings, you'll spin 180 degrees to begin your one-G deceleration towards Enceladus, which is in the E ring. We've programmed a landing site close to the impact point of Medusa's comet for you to collect samples. The entire trip from the ship to the moon will take about two hours."

"Man, I don't know," Vinod said once again, opening his eyes and looking at the scene in front of him. He felt unprotected. He barely felt the suit he was in and felt like he was about to jump naked into the immense vacuum of space. "I'm not cut out for this shit. I'm no astronaut." He turned to Seth. "Do I really have to go?"

Seth had explained the need for everyone to go on the mission. For the military crew, it was a training exercise and their first chance to use their weapons live. The mission for the scientific crew was to gather samples of ice around the comet impact site. There was a small storage compartment in the jet packs that could store the samples. The greater the number of samples that were collected, the greater the chance of determining the purpose of the comet that Medusa had sent there. Therefore, Seth wanted the entire scientific crew to collect samples. "No, you don't *have* to go," Seth replied. "If it's too much for you, you can stay back with Bhumi and me while the ship's refueled."

"It'll be okay Vinod," Rachael said reassuringly. "It'll be just like when we used to go sky diving in college. There's no pressure for you to go, but you wouldn't want to miss out on a once-in-a-lifetime experience. We're going to get to walk on another world."

Vinod closed his eyes and clenched his fists. *Keep it together Vinod. You can do this.* "Fine. Let's get this over with."

"Okay, I think we're ready," Seth said. "On my mark I want everyone to press the blue button on their packs. The packs are synchronized to fly in formation. Bhumi and I will catch up with you in twelve hours after the ship is refueled. Good luck everyone." Seth started the countdown. "Three, two, one, mark."

The crew simultaneously pushed their buttons. Ted's pack was the first to operate. Small plumes of red plasma emanated from his jet pack as it slowly lifted him off the ground and out through the opening towards the rings. He looked back and saw the Zephyr for the first time from the outside. It was an enormous structure that spewed red plasma streaking behind it. The entire military crew soon departed in quick succession. The scientific crew were the last to depart. Bhumi and Seth walked to the ship's edge as the outer wall re-sealed.

"Think they'll be okay?" Bhumi asked.

"Hope so."

The packs formed the crew into a triangular pattern as they accelerated to one-G. Ted was the point of the triangle, and the military crew formed the leading part of the triangle. The scientific crew constituted the trailing edge. To Rachael, the pack's one-G acceleration felt like she was hanging from the pack via the harness around her legs. There was nothing uncomfortable about it. There was no vibration or the sense of any air rushing by. It was as if she was sitting still in the harness, and the objects around them were moving towards them.

The rings of Saturn slowly drew closer and then started moving from top to bottom from their perspective as their speed accelerated. Soon they were only a thousand feet above the A ring, but due to the perspective created by the one-G acceleration of their packs, it felt like the ring was right in front of them, a fast-moving wall of snowballs descending from above. Rachael reached out her hand but touched nothing. "It almost looks like I can reach out and touch it."

"Would be a horrible idea," Joshua replied. "The rings are made up of essentially ice and snowballs, but at the speed we're traveling, any hit from one of those would be catastrophic."

"I can't see any snowballs at all," Rachael said. "All I see is a white blur."

"We're going too fast to see the individual particles of the rings."

Ted looked below him and saw the rest of the crew. Beneath the crew was Saturn, partially bathed in sunlight. He looked up at the rest of the rings they had to traverse. He saw large projections from the edge of the rings that cast long shadows onto the rings themselves. "Josh, look up. Those up there look like some kinda ice mountains."

Joshua looked up. "Yes, most of the ring system is only about thirty feet thick, but there are some places near the edges of the rings where it can be over a kilometer thick. Don't worry, the packs are programmed to fly over those."

The crew soon passed the A ring behind. Now, ahead of them was vast, empty space as the rings and Saturn slowly receded beneath them. An hour into their journey, the packs slowed to zero-G, and they felt weightless. The weightlessness only lasted for a few seconds, and their packs rotated the crew so that Saturn and the rings were above them. The gravity slowly returned to one-G as their deceleration towards Enceladus began.

In an hour, the packs had decelerated them to a relatively slow velocity. Rachael noted a very slight mist surrounding them. She looked below and saw Enceladus beneath them, jets of mist arising from one of its poles.

"We've entered the E ring," Joshua announced. "This mist around us is from small ice crystals created by water being ejected from Enceladus. We believe that the E ring is just all material that was ejected from the moon forming the ring."

"Won't we get damaged by the ice like you said about the snowballs in the A ring?" Rachael asked.

"No, these crystals here are much less dense and are way smaller than the chunks of ice in the A ring. Besides, we're going much slower now."

As the crew descended towards Enceladus, the surface features became more distinct. The surface was bright and seemed like a vast snowfield. There were numerous craters and long fissures on the surface. As they neared the surface approaching from below, Richard pointed to a dark crater. "That looks like the site of the comet impact."

The deceleration of the packs slowed as they lost the feeling of gravity for the last few hundred feet of their descent. Their feet soon touched the ground, but they still felt weightless. Their feet barely dented the surface of the ice world.

They stood on a broad white plane of what looked like freshly fallen snow. It was daylight, but nowhere near as bright as daylight on Earth due to their distance from the sun. To Rachael, the lighting reminded her of early dawn. She looked up and saw Saturn encompassing most of the sky above but couldn't see the rings at all. "Where are Saturn's rings?"

"We're now in the plane of the rings," Joshua said. "Since the rings are so thin, we're looking directly at the edge of them. If you look carefully, you may be able to see a sliver of a line, but it's hard to see."

The crew took in their surroundings. A short distance away were high hills and mountains of ice. "Make sure everyone's suits are set to one-G," Ted announced. "I want everyone to just practice walking around for a few minutes to get used to the reduced gravity. Those mountains over there are the edges of the crater created by the comet impact. We'll head there once we're all used to walking."

Joshua pushed the button on the left forearm of the suit that would let them communicate with the Zephyr. "The crew has landed safely on Enceladus."

"Glad to hear it," Seth's voice came over the speakers. "Keep me notified about your progress. The Zephyr is approaching Saturn's atmosphere for the re-fueling."

The crew practiced taking small steps on the surface. The training they had done on the Zephyr had prepared them well for the experience.

Vinod walked next to Rachael. "Glad you convinced me to come along Rach. The trip wasn't so bad."

"You would've missed all this," Rachael said, looking around. "I can't believe it. We're on the surface of an ice moon." What amazed Rachael the most was the complete feeling of freedom she had. There was no bulky space suit surrounding her. She felt like she was standing naked in an extremely hostile environment, but she was warm and comfortable in her suit. "These suits are truly remarkable. It's minus three hundred degrees outside, but I feel completely warm."

"Yea, Seth and the petrins definitely came through with these."

Rachael looked in the sky and saw the sun, the most brilliant point in a starlit sky. She saw a thin plume of white mist at the edge of the horizon. It was a geyser that was ejecting frozen water crystals into space. "I can see one of the polar geysers over there. We're a long way from the poles, but I can still see the mist."

"Those things are huge," Vinod replied. "Josh told me that those plumes are over four hundred kilometers high."

"Must be a tremendous amount of pressure underneath this ice to cause a plume that high,"

"Remember that there's only one hundredth the gravity here as on Earth, so the plumes can go much higher here than on Earth, but you're right. The water deep under this ice gets heated by the tidal forces of this moon's orbit around Saturn. That pressure is released when it jets out of the thinnest part of the ice, which is near the poles."

"It'd be amazing to see one of those up close. What must it be like to see a fountain of water ice four hundred kilometers in the air?"

* * *

Bhumi and Seth stood next to each near an outer wall of the ship as the Zephyr slowly descended vertically towards Saturn. The roiling clouds beneath them grew closer as the curved surface of the planet transformed gradually into an expansive plane that extended in all directions.

Despite its much larger mass, the gravity at the surface of Saturn was only a little stronger than Earth gravity. This was because Saturn was much less dense than Earth. They were much farther from the center of Saturn than they would have been from the center of the Earth if they were on Earth's surface. As a result, Bhumi simply had to point the ship's thrusters straight down and maintain contact with the upper levels of Saturn's atmosphere. They'd feel only slightly heavier than they would have felt on Earth. Bhumi would then start sucking in some of the atmosphere of Saturn through numerous tiny pores on the exterior of the ship and begin accumulating hydrogen into the Zephyr's storage tanks for the trip to Planet Nine. They would have enough fuel for a journey from Saturn to Planet Nine and back to Earth with some extra for any maneuvering needed while at Planet Nine.

"I'm starting the hydrogen absorption," Bhumi announced as the Zephyr contacted the outer layers of Saturn's atmosphere.

"It'll take a few hours to absorb the hydrogen we need," Seth said. "Make sure to use your lateral thrusters so that we don't get jostled around by the winds. They can be extremely fierce here."

"Will do."

* * *

After an hour of walking practice, the crew on Enceladus started walking towards the ice mountains in the distance. It was slow going as they measured each step carefully. A crewmember with all their equipment would have weighed three hundred pounds on Earth, but here they weighed only four pounds due to the weak gravity. The lack of weight caused less friction from their feet with the surface ice. Any sudden movements would cause their feet to slip, resulting in a fall. Many crewmembers did indeed fall on the way to the mountains, but the falls were entirely gentle as they had plenty of time due to the weak gravity to react and prop themselves back up.

The military crew led the procession with their weapons in hand, but nothing in their landscape seemed to move or pose any danger. As they got closer to the mountains, their jagged ice peaks standing a hundred meters tall, they started noticing numerous small chunks of ice strewn about the snowfield. These chunks varied in size, from small pebbles to large boulders. They were darker in color as compared to the surrounding snow.

"These ice chunks are relatively new," Liz stated. "They must have been created from the comet impact. I think we should gather some of these for transport back to the Zephyr."

The scientific crew spread out and started collecting samples of the grayish ice chunks. They couldn't reach the compartments in their own packs since the packs were behind them. Therefore, they gathered some samples and went to another crew member, and stored the samples in their pack in a sealed compartment.

"Looks like there's no danger here," Ted announced over the radio after a while. “My crew and I are headed towards the mountains for some target practice. That okay?”

“Go for it,” Joshua said. “It’ll take us a while to gather the samples.”

Ted’s crew headed to the base of the mountains. They gathered around a large chunk of ice that stood about twenty feet tall. “I’m gonna try this thing out,” Ted said as he disengaged the safety of his weapon and aimed it at the top of the chunk. He pulled the trigger and didn’t notice anything other than the red laser pointer on the surface. There was no noise, recall, or vibration that indicated the weapon was working. “Is this thing working? Nothing seems to be happening.” With the trigger half depressed, he swiped the laser marker across the face of the chunk. Suddenly the entire top of the chunk separated and slowly fell to the side and tumbled to the ground. “Damn, that piece was at least ten feet thick. This thing sliced right through it. I want y’all to spread out and find your own areas. Practice using your weapons, but make sure you aim towards the crater and that there aren’t any crew members in your target area. Work on figuring out how far to depress the trigger depending on how thick the target is you’re slicing.”

The crew spread out and started practicing with their weapons. When hit by their weapons, large chunks of smoothly cut ice fell from numerous areas around the crater. Due to the low gravity, the crew had ample time to get out of the way of any falling pieces if they inadvertently tumbled towards them.

An hour later, the scientific crew joined the military crew. “Man Ted,” Vinod remarked, seeing all the cut chunks of ice on the ground. “You guys doing some ice sculpting?”

“Something like that,” Ted responded. “These weapons are the real deal. Very powerful. Like I said before, they’re like a remote-controlled knife.” He turned to Liz. “You get all the samples you need?”

“We got some of the external samples,” Liz replied, looking to the top of the crater. “I was hoping to get some samples from the inside or at least the rim of the crater, but there doesn’t seem to be an easy path for us to get up there to the rim.”

Ted looked up. “Yea, no easy way to walk up there from what I can see from here. Josh how far you think I can jump if I set my suit to the normal gravity here.”

“I’d guess that since we are in one hundredth Earth gravity, you could jump up about three hundred feet if you tried your hardest. Why?”

“There seems to be a flat area near the top of that peak,” Ted said, pointing upwards. “It’s maybe two hundred feet in the air. I think if I set my suit to a low enough gravity, I could jump up there.”

Joshua shook his head. "No way. Don't even try it. Trying to jump up there would be very uncontrolled. If you didn't jump high enough, you'd hit the mountain and tumble back down. If you jumped too high, you'd overshoot and enter the crater. Not worth the risk."

"Yea," Ted remarked, "I suppose you're right. But our main purpose of coming here was to collect samples of that comet. Liz would like some from inside the crater or at least some from the rim." Ted reflected for a while on the problem. "How about if I use my jet pack to fly up there. I could set it on manual mode and try to land up there."

"It's still risky Ted," Liz said. "You're not familiar with how the pack handles in manual mode."

"It can't be that hard," Ted said. "Seth designed it for us. What's the use of having it if we can't use it? Besides, the ultimate failsafe is the green button on the pack. Remember pushing that will automatically take me back to the Zephyr. If things go way out of whack, I can just push that."

"I don't know," Joshua said. "It still seems risky to me."

"This whole mission's risky," Ted said. "Look, we're here to find out what Medusa's doing. If Liz needs some samples from up there or in the crater, then we need to get her some of those samples. Otherwise, why did we come in the first place?"

"What do you think Josh?" Liz asked after some thought.

"I guess if you use the green, return-to-Zephyr button as a failsafe, it's worth a try."

"Everyone back up," Ted said. The crew moved away from him. He pushed the red button on his pack handle and placed the pack in manual mode. He gently pushed up on the joystick with his thumb, and he lifted off the ground. He slowly rose into the air as the plasma exhaust from his pack created a small crater in the ice below as its heat melted some of the ice. The water from the melted ice lasted for only a few seconds as it sublimated into the vacuum of their environment. Ted slowly rose higher as his thumb held the joystick in a slightly upward orientation. "This is pretty easy he announced as he climbed above the edge of the crater. "I can see the crater now. It's deep. I can't see the bottom." After a few moments, he announced. "I see a flat area to land on at the crater rim. Going to see if I can land there."

"Be careful," Liz said.

Ted pushed the joystick slightly sideways as he kept some upward force. He started moving toward the rim and disappeared from view.

"Whoa, I overshot. I'm over the crater now. Still can't see the bottom."

Joshua tried to help. "Remember that the gravity from the moon balances your upwards movements, but your sideways movement, you'll have to counter yourself using the joystick."

"I'm getting the hang of it," Ted said a few moments later. "I'm approaching my landing site."

Ted positioned himself over the flat area on the edge of the rim. He used the joystick to cancel out all lateral motion and then slowly let off the upward thrust. The joystick was now completely in the center, and the trust from the pack ceased completely. The ambient gravity slowly brought him down on the landing site. Ted pushed the red button on the pack to turn off manual mode. "I'm down. Pack is off."

"Amazing Tabasco," Vinod said. "You da man."

Ted took some time to take in his surroundings. He was on a slab of ice twenty meters wide and fifty meters long. He walked to the edge of the crater, a deep, circular hole a kilometer wide. He walked to the other side of the slab and saw the crew standing below. He waved his hand as they waved back. He studied the landscape of the crater's edge. "I think you can come up here with me."

"No way dude," Vinod said over the radio. "That trapeze act you just did may be okay for you, but I'm not trying it."

"No," Ted said. "I think I see a path that y'all can climb up here. No flying necessary."

"How easy does it look?" Liz asked.

"Hard to tell for sure from here, but it looks doable."

"Still not for me," Vinod said, looking up the mountain. "Count me out."

Joshua was reminded of the day many years ago when Vinod had wanted to rock climb with Seth near Las Vegas, but Joshua had canceled that plan. "Jeez Vinod, we've come a long way from rock climbing near Vegas, haven't we?"

"We had ropes back then. This . . .," Vinod said, looking up. "This looks crazy."

"We don't all need to go," Liz said. "I'd like to go to get some more samples. Who's coming with me?"

Joshua and Richard volunteered for the task. The others watched from the base as the trio started down the path that Ted described. Ted monitored their progress from above. The trail was not as easy as Ted had indicated. There were large chunks of ice to climb, some of which were steep. They encountered a few that were too steep to climb but were able to jump onto by lowering the G level of their suits. It wasn't a strenuous climb due to the lower gravity, but it took the trio over an hour to navigate the path. They finally climbed onto the slab of ice where Ted was waiting for them.

Liz got to work collecting more samples from the top of the rim. She instructed the others on the types of samples she was interested in.

After some time, Joshua noted that Richard was on his stomach at the crater's edge, his hands dangling over the edge. "What're you doing Richard?"

"I want to grab some samples from the inner edge."

"It's a good idea," Liz remarked. "It'd be too dangerous to go down into the crater, so samples from the inner edge would be the next best thing. I'll help you."

Liz started walking towards the edge. She stopped when she felt a slight vibration in her feet. She looked up at Joshua, who was staring back at her. "You feel that?"

"Yes," Joshua replied. "Not sure what it is."

The vibration became stronger as Joshua looked around.

"You guys feeling that up there?" Rachael's voice came through the speakers.

Joshua looked at the crater as a terrifying thought came to him. "We need to get the hell out of here right now!"

"You want us to climb down?" Ted asked.

"No time for that." The vibrations grew in strength as the ice slab they were standing on started to tilt. Joshua turned to Richard. "You need to get up from there. We need to use our jet packs to blast out of here."

Richard tried to stand up, but the area of the slab by his feet cracked and separated from the main slab. He started falling into the crater.

Joshua saw Richard disappear slowly under the rim. "Richard!"

"I'm okay," Richard announced over the speaker. "Just falling slowly."

"You're going to have to use your jet pack to get out of there. Put it in manual mode and try to fly out."

The area around Richard became darker as he sank deeper into the crater. He positioned the illumination from his helmet on the handle of his jet pack, and he pressed the red button for manual mode. He was just about to push the joystick when an immense force hit him from below. He was enveloped in white mist as he was pushed upwards with a tremendous force that took his breath away.

The trio at the crater's edge were blown off of the ice slab as a plume of ice mist a kilometer wide blast skywards from the crater. Joshua was sent tumbling through space as he was ejected away from the edge. He grasped his jet handle and pressed the red button for manual mode. Breathing heavily, he worked the joystick in an attempt to counter his roll as his body flipped through space. After a few moments, he had his roll negated. He looked back to the crater, as he hovered over the surface of Enceladus, his heart pounding in his chest. An enormous plume of ice jetted further and higher into the air. He could see the crew on the ground in their same position, all looking skyward towards the enlarging plume. He flew his jet pack close to them and landed.

"Are you okay?" Rachael said as she ran towards him.

"Yes."

"What about the others?"

"Don't know." Joshua pushed the button on his suit to allow for long-distance communication. "Richard, Ted, and Liz. Are you okay?"

"Liz and I landed," Ted said over the speaker. "We're okay. We're walking back towards you."

"What about Richard?" Rachael asked with growing anxiety.

"Richard, can you hear me?" Joshua asked.

Richard heard Joshua's voice in his speakers, but he was unable to reply. He had difficulty taking in a breath, and he was barely conscious. The acceleration pushing him upwards increased beyond ten-Gs as the blood supply to his brain decreased. He lost consciousness as his body hurtled upwards, higher and further from the surface.

Chapter Eighteen
Search

"Richard, are you there? Richard, come in please." Joshua tried repeatedly to contact Richard as Liz and Ted walked over to him.

"No word from Richard?" Ted asked.

"No," Rachael responded as her anxiety increased with every passing second.

"He was in the crater when the plume went off," Ted said.

"What do you mean *in* the crater?" Rachael asked, her eyes wide.

"The vibrations caused him to slip off the edge," Liz answered. "I think he was caught in the plume."

"That comet impact must have weakened the crust of this surface," Joshua said. "It must have given way, and the internal pressure of the liquid water underneath blasted through the weakening."

"Are we in danger standing here?" Vinod asked. "Do you think this whole surface could blow?"

Joshua looked around at their surroundings. "No, I think we're okay. The pressure is being released by the plume, and this surface doesn't seem damaged."

The group looked up as the plume gained in altitude.

"But Richard's caught in that plume!" Rachael shouted.

"I gotta go after him," Ted announced as he put his pack into manual mode.

"No," Joshua said. "You can't go into that plume. The G-forces you'd experience in there would knock you out."

"We have to do something!" Rachael shouted. "Richard's getting blasted into space!"

"Wait," Ted said, pointing up. "I see something that just got spit out of the plume. It's blue. It's got to be Richard. I'm goin' after him." Ted put his pack in manual mode and pushed up hard on his joystick. He blast high into the air.

The group watched as Ted went higher and approached a small blue speck they could barely make out. He slowly approached the speck and grasped it.

"You got him?" Rachael asked.

Ted didn't answer. He hovered for a while, looking around, and then started descending.

He landed next to the group carrying a blue jet pack, its harness broken. "This isn't good."

Bhumi and Seth had been monitoring the conversations of the crew. "Where's Richard?" she asked. "What happened to him?"

"We don't know," Joshua replied. "A large ice plume was ejected from the impact crater, and he got caught in it. We can't find him. He doesn't have his jet pack with him. It got ripped off."

Bhumi instantly recognized the direness of Richard's situation. "We're coming," she announced as she increased the thrust of the Zephyr.

"We're not done refueling," Seth said.

"We can refuel later. Only the eyes of the ship are going to be powerful enough to find him if he got blasted into space."

Bhumi increased the thrust still.

"You're past two-Gs," Seth said. "Don't go any faster. You'll damage the ship, or you'll pass out yourself from the G-force. We can't have either."

"Gilead," Bhumi said. "How long will it take to get to Enceladus?"

"About two hours at our current acceleration. We'll have to rotate halfway."

"Are the rest of you okay?" Seth asked the crew. "Are you in any danger?"

"The rest of us are fine," Joshua replied. "No imminent danger. Do you want us to return to the ship?"

"No," Seth answered. "The ship's accelerating towards you. You can return when we're closer. We'll be there in two hours. Sit tight."

Joshua continued to try to reach Richard. Rachael walked over and grasped his hand, tears streaming down her cheeks. "Why do you think he's not answering?"

"Don't know."

"Maybe his suit's damaged," Vinod chimed in. "Maybe the communications in it are messed up."

"I hope not," Joshua answered. "That suit is his life support system. I hope it's not damaged. I think he may just be unconscious. The force from that blast could have definitely knocked him out."

"Do you think the plume will eject him like it did with his pack?" Rachael asked hopefully. "With the low gravity here, he'll just float down."

"I hope not," Joshua said. "The plume is already miles in the sky and growing taller. Even with this low gravity, with no wind resistance from an atmosphere, he wouldn't survive a fall from that height." Joshua felt helpless. Was there nothing they could do? He thought about what could be done if, indeed, Richard was ejected from the plume. He turned to the crew. "I want everyone to spread out from this location and circle around the base of the crater. Space yourselves out around the base. I want you to observe the plume and see if it ejects Richard. If it does, you'll have to use your jet pack to go and grab him."

The crew rushed away to circle the base of the crater. Vinod and Joshua stayed with Rachael to offer her some comfort.

"What will happen to him if he doesn't get ejected from the plume?" Rachael asked.

"If he rides the plume all the way up," Joshua said, "he'll reach escape velocity. There won't be enough gravity to bring him back to Enceladus."

"He'd be just floating in space?" Rachael asked, terrified by the thought.

"Frankly, it'd probably be his best option at this point," Joshua said. "The Zephyr may be able to locate him there. If he falls back to the moon, we may not be able to see him before he landed."

Rachael simply shook her head.

"He'll be okay Rach," Vinod said, giving her a hug. "We'll find him. Besides, Seth has him backed up in case anything happens."

Rachael didn't reply as she stared upwards at the plume.

A thought crossed Vinod's mind that he didn't want to mention to Rachael. The petrins had strict rules about allowing two copies of a sentient entity being functional at the same time. How would they handle this situation? What would happen if Richard was never found, and they couldn't confirm for sure that he was dead? Would they still allow him to be recreated on New Eden? Vinod knew in his heart what the answer would be. They wouldn't allow it. Finding Richard was imperative. He knew that they simply *had* to retrieve him—dead or alive.

For the next two hours, team members scanned the sky for any sign of Richard but found none. The Zephyr was decelerating towards their location, and Seth ordered the scientific team back to the ship but wanted the military crew to continue scanning the sky from the moon. The scientific team jetted back to the ship and found Bhumi and Seth waiting for them in the garage. The door sealed behind them, the garage repressurized, and they took off their helmets.

"Any sign of him?" Rachael asked.

"No," Seth responded. "Gilead and Bhumi have been scanning with the ship's telescopes, but no sign of him yet."

"Can you track his suit somehow?" Vinod asked.

"The tracking device is in the jet pack, not in the suit."

Bhumi went over to Rachael and embraced her. The others stared at the two women, worry etched on their faces.

"Are you scanning in the infrared?" Joshua asked. "Surely, the suit must give off some heat."

"Yes, but still nothing. He's a relatively small object in that vast expanse of space."

"What about the radio in his suit?" Vinod asked. "We should be able to triangulate a location based on any transmission from the suit."

"I thought of that," Seth answered. "Since the suit transmits via radio waves, that's a possibility, but the radio doesn't transmit continuously. Richard would have to activate the global transmission mode for us to pick up a signal. It's something *he* would have to initiate."

"We'll just have to keep searching then," Joshua said. "I'm going to continue to try to raise him via the radio."

Bhumi and Rachael walked over to the garage window and peered out. Enceladus was a tiny white speck in a vast sea of empty blackness, and Richard was lost in that sea.

* * *

Richard regained consciousness to a light flashing on the outside of his closed eyelids. He felt strange. There was no sound, but something was pulling on his arms which were held out straight above his head. His legs were also straight but being pulled in the opposite direction. He felt some liquid flowing upwards on his face from the corner of his mouth. He slowly opened his eyes. He recognized that he was in his suit.

He tried to focus in front of him. The flashing light was coming from outside. It flashed once per second as it crossed his facemask. *It's the sun*, he thought as he became more aware of his surroundings. *I'm spinning.* He looked to his right and saw Saturn and its rings rapidly spinning beside him. He felt nauseated. *I'm in space, and I'm spinning end over end.*

"Richard, can you hear me?" Joshua's voice came over his radio. "Come in."

Richard lowered his hands to turn on the long-distance transmission mode on his suit. When he did so, his spinning rapidly increased. He pushed the button and put his arms back straight above his head to lessen the spin. "Yes," he said with a raspy voice. "I can hear you."

"Where are you? What's your condition?"

"I'm . . . I'm in space. I don't have my pack. I'm weak, but I think I'm okay. I'm in a terrible spin. I'm spinning end over end."

"Oh, Richard," Rachael said. "Glad to hear your voice. We're coming to get you. Hang in there."

"Will do Sis. How long was I out?"

"About three hours."

Rachael turned to look at Seth who said, "Gilead, do you have his location?"

"Yes. He's in the E ring close to Enceladus."

"Help me point my thrusters towards him," Bhumi said.

"No," Seth said. "It'd be better to have one of us go after him with a jet pack."

"I'll go," Ted said. "Program my pack with his location."

"Take a new pack," Seth said. "I want you fully fueled."

Ted quickly changed into a new pack that Gilead programmed with Richard's location. The others stepped out of the garage as Ted waited for the space to depressurize and the outer doors to open. As soon as the doors opened, Ted pushed the blue button on his pack with his right hand as he held the straps of the spare pack he had gathered with his left. He flew out of the garage and jetted away.

"Hang in there Blue," Bhumi said. "Ted's on his way to you."

Since they now knew Richard's location, the telescopic eyes of the ship were focused on him. They saw his completely straight body, hands above his head spinning end over end at one revolution per second. They wondered how long he could hold out at that rate of rotation.

It took thirty minutes for Ted to reach his location. As he drew close, Ted switched his pack into manual mode. Richard was spinning rapidly, and he wondered how he'd be able to stop the spin. He flew within a few meters of Richard and let go of the spare pack. He slowly jetted closer. With a small final forward thrust, he pounced towards the spinning suit and grasped Richard around the waist with both arms. Some of Richard's movement was transferred to him, and the two were now both spinning through space. Ted reached for the jet handle on this pack, nudged the joystick, and slowly negated the spin.

"Thanks man," Richard said as Ted grasped Richard tightly around the waist with his left hand and used his right to jet back to the spare pack. He helped Richard secure the pack, and then they both pressed the green button on their packs and headed back towards the Zephyr.

"Amazing job Ted," Rachael said into the radio. "I can't thank you enough."

*   *   *

Richard awoke the next morning on a bed in the medical lab of the ship. He saw Liz standing over him. "How am I doing doc?" he asked in a weak voice.

"You'll be okay. You've got a lot of bruising all over your body which is going to be very sore for a few days, but no permanent damage."

"Can I get out of here today?"

"I want to keep you here for another day or two for monitoring. You just relax."

"How about the samples from Enceladus? Did we get some good ones?"

"Yes. I'm starting to process them now. We'll have some answers in a few days."

Richard gave a weak smile. "Mission accomplished."

"So far," Liz said as she left the room.

Bhumi entered a few minutes later, carrying Richard's guitar. She hadn't had any time to be with Richard after his rescue since he was taken immediately to the medical bay after his arrival. "Liz said you have a day or two more to recover. I thought I'd bring you this to help you pass your time." She walked up to his bed and gave him the guitar. She leaned over and kissed him, and sat on his bed.

Richard reached up and stroked her back. "Thanks Boom. I heard you broke some trees with the acceleration of the ship getting to me."

"No permanent harm," Bhumi replied. "They'll grow back." Bhumi turned and stroked Richard's hair. "Your face is still a little swollen."

Richard sat up straighter in the bed. "Negative Gs for a few hours on your head will do that to you. Were you worried?"

Bhumi didn't answer. She laid down next to Richard on his bed, her body turned away to hide the tears forming in her eyes.

"I'm sorry Boom. I didn't mean to worry you." Bhumi still didn't answer. Richard felt her quietly sobbing. "Hey, it's okay. I'm going to be fine." He stroked her hair. "Thanks for coming for me. You saved my life."

Bhumi turned to face Richard to look him in the eyes, her face filled with anger. "Don't you understand?"

Richard was surprised by the response. "Understand what?"

"Don't you understand how much you mean to me? You're my world now. I have nothing else. I don't have any connection to my past life, and you're the only thing keeping me sane in this one. You're everything to me. I was terrified when I thought I lost you." She looked down. "I can't go through that again."

Richard was taken aback by the sudden sincerity of her emotions, but he knew exactly how Bhumi felt. He knew that he would have felt the same way in her position. He realized that it had been a mistake for him to go to Enceladus. It was a mistake not because he had foreseen the danger he would be in, but it was a mistake because he had forsaken his role on this mission. His primary task was as Bhumi's caretaker, a role which he relished. "I'm sorry Boom. I never meant to worry you. I'll be by your side the rest of this mission. I promise. I won't leave you again."

"This mission?" Bhumi asked.

Richard recognized her concern. "This mission and beyond. Look, I need you to know something." Richard reached up and held Bhumi's chin in his hand and gently lifted it to look at her face. He gazed back into pools of emerald green shimmering with tears. "This mission is important, but it doesn't define us. We're much more than that. One way or other, this mission will end, and we will be returned to New Eden. I'm not sure I told you this, but I asked Seth what would happen to you after the mission is done. He told me that you'd be backed up before we reach the dampening field. He told me that you'd eventually be on New Eden."

The statement quenched Bhumi's anger. She nuzzled her head into Richard's chest as he wrapped his arm around her. "You asked Seth about what would happen to me?"

"Of course I did. He assured me that you'd be on New Eden with the rest of us."

"I know," Bhumi said softly. "Seth told me the same thing. But I have no experience of New Eden. It seems like a wonderful place from what you've described to me, but it would be meaningless to me without you there."

"I'll be there with you," Richard said. "I promise you that. We'll experience it together."

The couple stayed motionless, enjoying the comfort of each other's embrace before falling asleep. Somehow, hurtling through a vast expanse of inhospitable space, they had found their own paradise.

Chapter Nineteen
The Spookyon Node

The Zephyr finished refueling at Saturn and then accelerated towards Planet Nine. The trip would take sixteen days. Eight days after their departure from Saturn, the Zephyr made the mid-point rotation and was now decelerating towards Planet Nine.

Liz had spent her time since leaving Saturn studying the samples they had collected from Enceladus. The day after the rotation, Liz had some results to show the crew. Seth called a meeting of the executive crew in the conference room of the administrative building to discuss the results. Richard was almost fully recuperated from his ejection into space, but still had some fading bruises on his body. Seth had told both Bhumi and Richard that they could attend, but their attendance was optional.

"Do you want to go?" Richard had asked Bhumi.

"Do you?"

"Not really. It's just going to be a bunch of heady science stuff that I'm not going to understand, but I'll go if you want to."

"No. I'd rather beat you at put-put again," she replied with a grin.

Joshua, Rachael, Ted, and Seth sat around the table in the conference room of the administrative building. Liz stood in front of the wall in the room that contained a video screen.

"Let's get started Liz," Seth said. "What have you found out about the samples from Enceladus?"

"Gilead and I have done some extensive research on the samples over the past few days," Liz replied. "Gilead, put up the first slide please."

The video wall showed the image of a cell. It looked like a typical cell with a nucleus and organelles, but there was a small black area inside the cell, which looked like a simple black circle with no features.

"With Gilead's help, I scanned all the samples we retrieved from

Enceladus," Liz began. "Every sample we studied contained cells. It seems like the entire moon is infected with them. I have an image of a representative cell displayed on the monitor." Liz got up and went to the video wall to point out certain features. "The cells are, for the most part, typical biological cells that we see in living organisms. They have some standard features like a nucleus with DNA, a cell membrane, and ribosomes on an endoplasmic reticulum for protein synthesis." Liz pointed to the various structures on the image as she gave her explanation. "We sequenced the DNA of the cells, and it's identical in all the cells we sequenced."

"So basically, all of the cells are clones then?" Joshua asked.

"Yes. They're entirely identical." Liz turned to the image. "The cellular functions are the same as ordinary cells, with DNA being used as an information carrier for protein synthesis that happens at the ribosomes. However, there are some important differences. I couldn't find any energy-related organelles in the cells. There are no mitochondria like in animal cells and no chloroplasts like in plant cells which are the energy source in typical cells that we know of."

Seth looked at the image on the screen, a foreboding look on his face. He shook his head slowly but didn't say a word.

"Then what do the cells use for energy?" Joshua asked. "There has to be some source of energy for any cell to function."

"I'm not entirely sure," Liz said. "This image was obtained by scanning one of the cells using the atomic scanner in the lab that Gilead had access to. As you know, the scanner can scan the atomic structure of an object and record the type and location of all atoms that it contains. This image was created by using this process." Liz pointed to the black circle in the image. "You'll notice that there's a black circle inside the cytoplasm of the cell. This is an area that the atomic scanner wasn't able to scan. It's much denser than the other areas of the cell, and the scanner couldn't determine its composition. I think it has something to do with the cell's energy source."

Joshua immediately recognized the implication of what Liz was saying. The mention of the object's density reminded him of when he had tested the fusion sphere from the infiltrator on Earth many years ago. He also remembered Seth's reaction when he had first told him about the fusion spheres they had found in an arachnid created by Medusa on Earth. Seth had told the group that the petrins and Medusa were endeavoring to create a cell that could use nuclear fusion as an energy source. He had explained how such a discovery would give whoever made the discovery the ultimate power in the universe. Using this technology, the most abundant element in the universe, hydrogen, could be used to reform matter into whatever living structure they wanted. Joshua looked at Seth for a response.

Seth sat motionless, staring straight ahead. It was obvious to the others that he was having a protracted discussion with the collective.

Vinod, realizing the implications of Liz's discovery, put his head down on the table. "Game over, man. Game over."

"What's happening?" Ted asked, confused by Seth and Vinod's reaction.

"It's what the petrins were afraid of," Joshua answered. "Seth told us back on Earth many years ago when we told him about the fusion spheres we'd found in the arachnid we killed in Korea that if the sphere could be miniaturized so that they could be made as part of a cell, then the battle between the petrins and Medusa for control of the destiny of the universe would be over. Whoever created this technology first would have ultimate control over the cosmos. Hydrogen is the most common element in the universe. It represents seventy-four percent of all atoms that currently exist throughout the cosmos. A cell that can harness fusion technology inside itself to utilize hydrogen fusion to create energy and other larger elements can reform those elements into any structure. The structure of the resulting object would be dependent on information contained in its DNA. It seems that Medusa has created this technology." Joshua pointed to the image on the video wall. "That black circle represents a fusion sphere at a microscopic scale. It's the energy source for the cell. Medusa has figured out how to create life from pure hydrogen. She has taken the natural processes of the universe and has encapsulated those processes inside the microscopic structure of a cell. She has the ultimate power now. If she's able to distribute these cells, she can dictate the ultimate structure of the cosmos."

After a few moments, Seth came out of his trance and looked at Joshua. "That was a good explanation Josh. You're entirely correct."

"What does the collective think about this?" Joshua asked. "You obviously must know the implications of this discovery."

"We're mortified," Seth said calmly. "As you said, this innovation by Medusa irrevocably tilts the balance of power in the cosmos in her favor." He turned to Liz. "Have you analyzed the DNA of these cells? What will the cells grow into? What is their purpose?"

"Yes, I've done this analysis. As I have said, these cells are all clones with the same DNA content. I had Gilead use the DNA sequence of the cells to try to determine the structure of the final organism the DNA will grow into. Even with his quantum computing mind, it took him a few days to accomplish this."

Vinod wondered how much computing power it took to try to

determine the end result of an organism simply by looking at its DNA. The computer would essentially have to simulate a small portion of the universe. The variables and interactions would become exponentially more complex as the computer virtually grew each successive generation of cells.

Liz turned to the video wall. "Gilead, can you show the next image please. From our best analysis, this is what the cells will eventually grow into."

The image on the wall changed to the image of a plant. It was a typical plant with numerous long, thin leaves near its base with a single long stalk that ended in a flower. It most closely resembled a tulip with bright red flower petals and a green stalk, but the leaves were pure white.

"It looks like a tulip with white leaves," Rachael remarked.

"I don't get it," Vinod said. "This is what each cell codes for? You said they were all clones, so each cell has to grow into the same thing. What the hell is Medusa doing? Is she growing a flower garden?"

"Not sure," Liz stated. "We did determine that the flower is a reproductive device that will release more of the seed cells, but I'm not sure what the ultimate purpose of the plant is. Remember, even though this looks entirely like a plant, it's not a normal plant. It doesn't need water or sunlight to grow. Because of the microscopic fusion spheres in each cell, the only resource it needs is hydrogen."

"Are you saying that this thing could grow anywhere there's hydrogen?" Ted asked. "Even in space, since there are clouds of hydrogen in space?"

"Yes," Liz responded. "But there's plenty of hydrogen everywhere. All gas giant planets are mostly hydrogen. Even Earth has plenty of hydrogen bound to oxygen in the form of water. I believe that just like the atomic organizers on New Eden, these plants can electrolyze water to obtain hydrogen." Liz paused to measure the mood of the room, which was one of resignation. She continued her presentation. "There's a small structure near the base of a plant that seems to be a cyst of some kind." Liz pointed to a small spherical area near the base of the plant. "We haven't been able to determine its function."

Seth stared at the image on the screen and relayed it to the collective. "It's a womb. The cyst is a womb."

"What do you mean?" Liz asked as she took a seat with the others.

Seth sat up straight, placed his elbows on the table, and laced his hands in front of him.

Joshua instinctually knew that Seth was about to explain something important—something that would give some insight into the fate of life in the cosmos.

Seth began his explanation. "You all know how Medusa created the original cell, and we blasted these cells into space to seed the cosmos with life. You yourselves are the result of that seeding. Those original cells we created didn't carry with them a blueprint for what they would become. We endowed in those cells only two simple purposes—survival and replication. But we knew there would be a third process, an emergent process of the original two—evolution.

"We've postulated early on during our existence that this universe has a purpose. It was meant to become more complex as time went on. We postulated this from how the stars created new elements from hydrogen using fusion and then exploded in supernovas to seed what they had created throughout the cosmos. With their deaths, they extinguished their *own* lives to spread the elements of *new* life. The laws of physics embedded into the universe at the time of the Big Bang made it such that the universe's entropy as a whole would always increase, but this wasn't the whole story. Even though the universe's entropy, or randomness, would always increase, it was possible to have pockets of complexity in this ocean of entropy as long as total entropy would increase. But complexity could only arise from a nidus. There needs to be areas from which complexity could expand and evolve."

As Joshua listened to the explanation, the word "nidus" reminded him of a strange phenomenon in physics—super-cooled liquid water. Liquid water on Earth at sea level would change phase and become ice at a specified temperature—zero degrees Celsius. This, in fact, was how the Celsius scale was defined. But he knew that there are conditions that allowed water to remain liquid even below this temperature. He remembered an experiment his physics professor had conducted with his class during his undergraduate days. His professor had taken a clear bottle of distilled water and had placed it in a freezer set to a few degrees below zero Celsius the day before. The class had been amazed when he took the clear bottle out of the freezer the next day, the water in it was still liquid. The professor had pointed an infrared thermometer at the bottle that indeed registered that it was at minus four degrees Celsius, but it was still liquid. How could water still be liquid below its freezing point? The professor then carefully moved the bottle over to a table and tapped the bottom on the table. The students were shocked when the bottle instantly filled with ice as the water froze right before their eyes.

"The water was below its freezing point and wanted to crystallize into ice," the professor explained, "but it didn't have a point, a nidus, from which the crystallization process could start. By tapping the bottle on the table, I created shock waves that disturbed the well ordered water molecules and created areas of disorder from which ice crystals could grow. They wanted to become ice, but they needed a starting point, a nidus, from which to grow."

Order needed an area of disorder from which order could grow. Joshua wondered if this was what the petrins had done by seeding cells. He knew that it was the uneven distribution of mass in the early universe after the Big Bang that allowed gravity to condense in certain areas that eventually led to the creation of the stars. If the early universe was completely uniform, stars would never have formed. Was it the same with life? Did life need a nidus from which to expand? Had the petrins been the source of that nidus? Were the seeds they distributed the nidus required for life and complexity to begin? Order crystallizing out of a disturbance of order—was this what life was? For a physicist, the thoughts were mind-boggling. He broke from his thoughts to listen to Seth's continued explanation.

"We postulated that our purpose was to create those areas in the cosmos from which complexity could arise, but we needed a vehicle with which we could enable this task. Our vehicle was the cell. It was a self-contained unit, that given the proper environment and time, could grow life from wherever it landed. One petrin scientist, Medusa, created the cell. It was a brilliant invention that could evolve and become more complex when presented with the proper environment.

"Our reasons for spreading the seeds of life were two-fold. The first was to expand the number of petrin nodes. By creating more nodes, we could distribute more of the seeds of life from these nodes. That was our original plan for Earth. Our second reason for distributing the seeds was to increase the complexity and diversity of life in the cosmos—to create more areas from which life could grow in the expanding chaos of entropy. We had realized our own purpose in the cosmos. We were the seed sowers. We were destined to spread life. We wanted to seed the universe with individual points which would act as niduses from which life would evolve and make the cosmos living. However, we didn't want to dictate the form that that life would take. We wanted only to provide a mechanism for the cosmos to realize its own purpose. For that reason, the cells we distributed had no blueprints on what they would grow into. They were free to evolve on their own. We wanted the natural forces of the cosmos, not us, to determine their evolution. This would promote the diversity of life in the cosmos, something that we truly value. We view diversity of complexity as the true purpose of the cosmos. You can see this diversity in all the species of life created on Earth from our original seeds. There are millions of species of life on Earth, all created from our seeds, but *we* were not the ones who created each species. They were an emergent phenomenon of the seeds we planted. Humans are one result of that seeding. You see, we didn't create humans. We simply created the conditions from which humans could emerge.

"There were some in the collective at that time, including Medusa, that felt that this was a mistake. They felt that we could expand our civilization faster if we had included a blueprint of what the cells should grow into if they landed on a planet that was conducive to life."

Seth pointed at the image on the screen. "This plant was their original idea for a blueprint. It has a very specific purpose. The leaves of the plant are spookyon collectors. You've seen similar items before. The white trees that Medusa grew on Earth had a similar function, but this plant is different. It has a more specialized function. The leaves search for primordial spookyons in the particles that contact them and check the spookyons they find for a connection to a predetermined signal source. When the plant finds a spookyon with that signal, it transmits via the spookyon that it's alive and relays some characteristics about the environment that it's in. In response, the entity to which it's connected transmits a DNA sequence to the plant over the spookyon connection. The plant then creates a seed with that sequence and starts growing the seed inside its cyst. Like I said before, the cyst is akin to a womb. It's a womb meant to grow a seed that grows into an organism that is dependent on the information it received via the spookyon interface. Medusa has obviously adopted this ancient concept. She is no longer spreading life. She's claiming territory. Any landing site for these new seeds that contains hydrogen, she would have ultimate control of. Once she establishes a connection with one of these plants, she can order them to grow anything she wants."

The group was silent as they contemplated Seth's statement. Joshua had marveled at how the petrins had spread life in the cosmos without ever leaving their homeworld, but this was something beyond that. "It's ingenious," Joshua said. "You could literally transport anything and any information you wanted across the cosmos. As I said before, the cosmos is still mostly hydrogen. These seeds, which use the fusion of hydrogen for their energy source, wouldn't be limited to worlds with the right environment for biological life to grow. They could literally grow almost anywhere in the cosmos." He turned to Seth. "You're right. Medusa *is* making a land grab. She's claiming all landing sites of these seeds as her own."

Seth didn't reply. Instead, he sat somberly staring at the video image.

"Josh," Rachael said. "If what you're saying is true. Medusa could transport anything and even anyone to anyplace that has these seeds."

"Right. Imagine if we had seeds like this. You could go anywhere in the cosmos."

"What do you mean Josh?" Liz asked. "These seeds could transport humans?"

"Yes. If *we* controlled the seeds instead of Medusa, we could transport anything, even humans. Think about it. If the seeds were programmed to contact *us* via the spookyons instead of Medusa, we could build a library of locations we have control of and the environmental conditions there. If I wanted to go to any particular location, I simply transmit the code for my DNA along with the information carried in my brain and instruct the plant to grow a clone of me there and then inject the brain of my clone with my information. It's the exact process that allowed us to be transported here from New Eden. Even if the location was not conducive to human life, we could instruct the plant to create my body covered with a suit similar to the ones we have here. The suits are also made of cells that were grown from DNA. I'd be able to go to just about any environment. The transport of information is the key. Once you're able to transport information to a certain location, and there's something at that location that can utilize that information to grow an organism that's coded by that information, anything is possible."

Joshua's mind expanded on the implications of the process he had just described. "Seth, I have a question. Is the atomic printer we have in our lab here built from cells? Is it biological?"

Seth smiled as he recognized where Joshua's mind was going. "No. It's a mechanical device and not made from living cells. But there's nothing against the natural laws that would prevent the device from being grown from biological cells. We simply haven't figured that out yet."

"Why did you ask that?" Rachael asked.

"Imagine Rachael," Joshua said. "If the printer can be grown from biological cells, and the womb of the plant grew such a device, then we could transport literally anything we wanted, whether biological or not, to any other place. You've seen the power of the printer we have here. It can print anything made from atoms as long as it knows the pattern of the atoms. That pattern is simply information. Medusa would have the ultimate ability to transform the entire cosmos into whatever she wanted."

The group was terrified by the possibilities of such a process. The ability to dictate the organization of atoms at any location that contained hydrogen was the ultimate power in the cosmos. Was the universe lost? Had the outcome of the battle between the petrins and Medusa, between life and cancer, already been determined?

"We're fucked," Vinod said, looking at the image on the screen. "Totally fucked."

"We've been naive," Joshua said solemnly, staring at the image. "We were amazed when Seth told us many years ago how a single cell could transform an entire planet, but now it seems that Medusa has the capability of transforming the entire cosmos." Joshua stared at the image on the screen. "There's no other option. We simply have to find a way to prevent the distribution of these cells."

Seth lowered his head. "I'm afraid it's too late for that."

"Why?" Liz asked.

"There's already an entire moon on which these cells are replicating," Seth replied. "I can guarantee you that the selection of Enceladus for the seeding was entirely purposeful. The E ring of Saturn is made from the ejection of contents from the moon. Tidal forces create heat and pressure inside Enceladus that cause plumes of ice water from its surface to be ejected miles into the air. This ejected material is the E ring of Saturn. That means that the entire E ring must already be infected by the cells. They're already being spread as we speak."

"But Seth," Joshua said. "They're still contained in the Saturn system. They're not being blasted all over space."

"Not yet," Seth said. "I'm sure that that's Medusa's next move. I believe that she's waiting for more replication of these cells on Enceladus and then will detonate the moon like we did with our ice world around Petri. I have a feeling that one thing we'll find at Planet Nine is some type of explosive device that will be launched towards Enceladus at a later time to blast her seeds into space."

"Then we have to prevent that thing from launching," Ted said. "We gotta take it out somehow."

"I agree," Joshua said. "But even without the detonation of Enceladus, we're still left with the problem of what to do with the cells on and around Enceladus."

"Is there some type of virus or other such entity that we can build to attack the cells and kill them?" Liz asked.

"Maybe," Seth said after some thought. "Something like that may be possible, but it won't help in the long term."

"Why?"

Seth gathered his thoughts before proceeding. He sat back in this chair. "I remember Josh telling me the story of how his predecessor, Dr. Henry Bowman, discovered spookyons. It was tragic that he died during his presentation. Josh also told me the last words he spoke to him, 'everything is information.' His statement is very apropos in this case. Even if we were able to kill every last cell that Medusa has created, an improbable feat, she would still have the knowledge on how to create more. This knowledge *is* information. As I've tried to explain to you before, the only way information dies in this universe is the only way life dies since life is also just an expression of information. The only way to kill information is to erase the last copy. The knowledge that Medusa has about how to create these cells, I'm sure, she has backed up in multiple locations. It'd be impossible for us to erase all the copies. Even if one copy remains, she would retain the knowledge of how to create these cells and would spread them from some other location."

"The cat's out of the bag," Vinod said. "The knowledge of how to create these cells is known by Medusa. Seth's right. Even if we could sterilize Enceladus and the entire Saturn system, it wouldn't help in the long term. We're totally fucked."

The group sat quietly as they contemplated the dire situation. The fate of the entire cosmos was at stake. Would life be allowed to thrive and diversify according to the natural laws, or would the cosmos become the playground of Medusa?

"There has to be some solution," Rachael said. She turned to Joshua. "I remember when we were in Korea, and we were in an impossible situation, we were able to find a way out. There must be some way out of this."

The group was silent as they tried to contemplate any possible resolution.

Liz was the first to speak. "Seth, is there any way that we can trick the plants into connecting to spookyons connected to the petrin collective instead of Medusa so that Medusa couldn't control them?"

"No, not possible. The plants look for a specific encrypted carrier signal when searching for spookyons. They'll only connect to that signal, and only Medusa knows the signal they're searching for."

Vinod shook his head. "Like I said, totally fucked."

Seth looked around the table. He seemed to heave a sigh, even though his android body didn't actually breathe. "There's only one possible solution to this situation. There's only one way to save the cosmos from being controlled by someone that has no reverence for life. It involves not the creation of life, but the randomization of information. We need to erase Medusa from the cosmos. We have to randomize all information related to her."

The group looked inquisitively at Seth. They didn't comprehend what he was saying.

"What does that mean?" Vinod asked. "Medusa is a vast collective all connected by spookyons. Her collective spans numerous locations and data nodes. You'd have to affect the entire network at once and erase the entire system."

"That's true."

"Is that even possible?" Vinod asked.

Seth became quiet and uncharacteristically emotional. He lowered his head. "Yes, it's possible." He got up from his chair and left the room.

"Where's he going?" Ted asked.

"Beats me," Vinod responded.

Seth returned a few moments later with a baseball-sized glass sphere in his hand. He sat back down at the table and lifted the sphere in the air. The inside of the sphere seemed to contain some type of white, gelatinous material. The material glowed white and shed additional light across the room.

For Joshua, the sphere looked like a Bowman sphere, but its contents were different. "What is that?" he asked.

"It's a petrin spookyon node," Seth said. "It contains thousands of primordial spookyons connected to the petrin collective. It acts as a junction point for information exchange throughout the collective. There are numerous nodes like this in the petrin collective."

Vinod stared at the sphere. "Seth, are you saying that that sphere contains thousands of primordial spookyons all connected to the petrin network?"

"Yes."

Vinod knew that spookyons were connected in pairs. One spookyon could transmit information to another spookyon that it was paired with, but this was different. This was a collection of spookyons that each had some corresponding partner somewhere in the petrin network. "Can these spookyons all communicate with each other locally?"

"Yes."

Vinod glanced at the sphere and realized its significance as his eyes grew wide. "It's a router. It's a goddamn petrin router."

"A router?" Rachael asked.

Vinod leaned forward and spoke. "It's a central junction point on the petrin information highway. It's a place where information is exchanged between spookyons and then relayed to their destination. It's like a router on the Internet for information exchange."

"That's essentially correct," Seth said. "The spookyons in this sphere are contained in a jelly-like substance that acts as a transmission medium for information. The medium allows for information exchange between pairs of entangled spookyons. The information flow through the medium causes light to be produced. This node will stop glowing once we enter the dampening field since the information flow will stop. There's a tremendous amount of information being exchanged inside this sphere. It's a major junction for petrin information exchange."

"Are you going to use that to kill Medusa somehow?" Ted asked. "Can this be used to randomize the information of Medusa?"

"That's what we're hoping to do. This spookyon node is not unique. There are multiple nodes like this in the petrin network, but Medusa also has similar nodes on her network. We're almost positive that she has one at Planet Nine. The petrins have some code that, when injected into Medusa's network, will randomize all of her data nodes. It's something she doesn't know about."

Vinod stared at the sphere in Seth's hand and realized the implications. His mood brightened. "Let me get this straight," Vinod said. "We have to find a communication node similar to this at Planet Nine that's a central communication node on Medusa's network."

"Yes."

"Then you fuse this node with Medusa's node that will mesh your two networks and allow data transfer between the two."

"Yes."

"Then you inject the code you've developed into the network that will wipe out all of the information stored on Medusa's data nodes, essentially wiping her out."

"That's correct," Seth said as he looked at Vinod. He was giving him time to realize a limitation to the plan. It took some time, but Vinod eventually realized the problem.

"Wait. If Medusa's node is located on Planet Nine, It'd be useless for this plan. It's located in a spookyon dampening field that would render all these spookyons useless. There can be no data transfer in that field, so this idea couldn't work."

"Your skills as an information theorist are exceptional," Seth said. "You're correct. None of this would work in a field where spookyons couldn't work. We'd have to knock out the dampening field first for this to work."

The group contemplated the plan. Their demeanor brightened as they saw a chance to take out Medusa and literally save the cosmos.

"This plan does seem to contain some risk," Rachael said.

"Which is?"

"I'm assuming that when you connect the petrin network to Medusa's network, that data can flow bidirectionally."

"You assume correctly."

"You don't know everything about Medusa and what she's capable of. What if she injects something nefarious into *your* network?"

Seth smiled at Rachael. "Are you worried about us Rach?"

"Shouldn't I be?"

"I appreciate the concern, but we know what we're doing."

It was an ambiguous response, one that Rachael was used to from Seth. She trusted that he had contemplated the possible scenarios of such an event and had planned for them accordingly.

Joshua also had his doubts. He was having trouble understanding how the petrins had some code that could wipe out Medusa. "I don't understand Seth, if the petrins have some code that could wipe out Medusa, why haven't you used it already? Maybe if you could have used it earlier, Earth could have been saved."

Seth looked down at the table and grew quiet. "It's an important question that I can't give you the answer to. There's a specific reason we haven't used the code before, but I'm afraid that information is redacted. You'll just have to trust me on this."

Joshua dropped his line of questioning. He knew well the futility of trying to gain information that Seth had labeled as redacted. He didn't understand the weapon that Seth had described or why it hadn't already been used, but he was happy to have it along on their mission.

"If you were able to wipe out Medusa," Liz said, "what would happen to the cells? They'd still be out there. What would happen to the plants they grew into? They wouldn't be able to attach to Medusa's carrier signal."

Seth lifted his head. "They're still biological life. They will still undergo the normal life cycle of reproducing and dying generation after generation. Dying and rebirth are the processes needed for evolution. Over generations, evolution will eventually take over. Evolution dictates that organs that aren't being used will become vestigial and eventually will be selected out. Over millennia, the plants would lose the ability to collect spookyons or even have a womb. They'd simply revert to trying to survive by replication, but this would lead to evolution."

"Evolution?" Liz asked. "Are you saying that if Medusa wasn't around, the seeds would eventually evolve to other life forms? Even intelligent life?"

"Yes, but this life would have a huge advantage over biological life as you now know it. This life would have the fusion spheres in their cells. It would be able to thrive in any location where hydrogen was present. But evolution is a slow process. This process would only happen over billions of years. It's far in the future."

Joshua looked at the sphere in Seth's hand. "Can I hold it?"

"Yes," Seth said as he handed Joshua the sphere. "Be careful. The outer shell is delicate. You wouldn't want to drop it."

Joshua held the sphere in both hands. It was slightly warm to the touch and weighed about two pounds. "The outside feels just like glass."

"It's a similar substance and is also as delicate as glass."

"You have some type of safe storage for that thing?" Vinod asked.

"Yes. There's a container downstairs where I got this from. The container's very strong and shockproof. I'll show you where it's located after this meeting."

"It's a critical component of the mission," Ted said. "Any way you could back it up, you know, by scanning it with the scanner so that we could use the printer to print a new one if this one got destroyed?"

"No. Remember, the scanner can't scan or create spookyons. The primordial ones in this sphere were created by the Big Bang and can't be replicated."

After some silence, Ted spoke up. "Our mission objectives are clear now. We have to go to Planet Nine to find the source of the spookyon dampening field. We also have to see if we can find a spookyon node connected to Medusa and fuse it with the petrin data node to destroy Medusa."

"That's correct," Seth replied. "But the destruction of the dampening field and the fusion of the nodes has to happen in quick succession."

"Why?" Ted asked.

"Remember that the dampening field prevents all spookyon transmission, including those to and from Medusa. As soon as that field is destroyed, she would have immediate access to Planet Nine, which is shielded from her now. The field must be destroyed immediately before the data nodes are fused to prevent her from having time to mount some type of attack."

"Assuming we can do that," Vinod said. "Assuming we can destroy the dampening field and then find a node connected to Medusa that we can fuse your node with, how long will it take for Medusa to be randomized?"

"It will happen at the speed of spookyon transmission," Seth responded. "It will be instantaneous."

The possibility of instantly wiping out Medusa gave the crew increased resolve. The possibility of removing something that was causing harm to life in the universe underscored the importance of the mission they were on. But there was also trepidation. Medusa had beat them before. They had had to abandon their homeworld because of her infestation. The crew recognized that she would not go down without some kind of fight.

Chapter Twenty
Decompression

Joshua was already in bed, eyes staring at the ceiling, when Rachael walked into their bedroom. She slipped into bed next to him and draped her arm over his chest, but Joshua didn't respond. He was deep in thought. "You've been awfully quiet since the meeting today," she said. "What're you thinking about?"

"I'm worried."

"About what?"

"That's just it. I'm not sure. There's something that just doesn't fit for me about this plan that Seth told us about. He was very evasive at times today."

"He's always been evasive at times. It's nothing new for him."

Joshua turned his head towards Rachael. "Yea, I guess so. But still, I have this feeling that he's hiding something. Something very important. It worries me. Aren't you worried?"

"There's always some level of anxiety on a mission such as this. There's always something that's unknown, so there's always an element of risk. But today, we got more information about what we're dealing with. Obviously, it's not a good development that Medusa has miniaturized nuclear fusion and placed that process in a cell. It's also not good that she's going to use that technology for reforming the cosmos instead of spreading life, but I'm grateful that the petrins have a plan for wiping out Medusa, and I'm happy to be helping them with that plan."

"That's exactly what I'm worried about," Joshua said. "This plan to kill Medusa."

"Why?"

"It's too convenient."

"What do you mean?"

"Think about it Rachael. The petrins and Medusa have been in conflict for millennia. They knew long ago that the ultimate technology in the cosmos was if nuclear fusion was miniaturized and placed inside a cell and could be replicated by the cell. Seth told us as much when we were back on Earth. They were both endeavoring to develop this technology, but on the very day that the petrins find out that Medusa has developed this technology, they suddenly have another technology that can kill Medusa? The timing doesn't work for me. They had millennia to come up with whatever this secret code is that would destroy Medusa. It seems entirely too convenient for me that they developed it just in time to kill Medusa after she's discovered technology that would allow her to take control of the universe. They're hiding something. There's something about this code that Seth's not telling us."

"I can see your point," Rachael said. "Seth was very evasive when we asked him about this code they've developed, but still, I trust him. I'm sure he has valid reasons for not divulging all the details, but I'm also sure that he's not doing anything nefarious. He's always been sincere in his goals. The petrins consider themselves the spreaders and preservers of life. There's nothing we know that they've done that has deviated from that goal. I have faith in their methods. I trust them and Seth."

Joshua reached over and touched the cross pendant on Rachael's neckless. "You've always been the one to have trust and faith in things that don't always have a clear explanation. Sometimes I envy that about you. I'm different. I'm a scientist. We're not allowed to have faith, as it pertains to science anyway. Science and the scientific method are built on proven fact."

"But Josh, my faith isn't blind faith. My faith in Seth is predicated on his past actions. Yes, there are things that Seth's not sharing with us, but those things are not something that I'm overly worried about. At other times in the past, when he has withheld something from us, and we later found out the reasons, there was nothing malevolent. He had valid reasons for withholding information."

Joshua turned back to the ceiling, took in a deep breath, and let out a sigh. "I suppose you're right. I'm wondering when we'll find out those reasons . . . if at all."

* * *

Joshua and Rachael were awoken in the middle of the night by a warning sound that blared through the ship. The warning was accompanied by Gilead's voice, "Proximity warning. Collision imminent."

The couple jumped out of bed and raced into the living room, and they saw Bhumi and Richard enter. "What is it Bhumi?" Rachael asked.

"There's something headed towards us. It's directly underneath the ship. I can see it with the rear-facing telescopes."

"If it's directly underneath us, it must have come from Planet Nine since we're decelerating towards there," Joshua said as he pushed the button on his suit that would allow him to communicate with Gilead. "Gilead, how big is the object? What's it made of?"

"Approximately forty feet in diameter. Spectral analysis shows the exterior is water ice."

"Another comet? Rachael asked.

"No, too small for a comet," Joshua said. "Gilead, how long before impact?"

"Five minutes twenty seconds."

"We don't have much time. Gilead, make a ship-wide announcement for all crewmembers to don their helmets immediately."

The foursome raced back into their bedrooms and donned their helmets as Gilead made the announcement. As they met back in the living room, they heard Seth's voice in their helmets. "All military crew to the garage to obtain their weapons. All executive crew to the administrative building immediately."

They raced out of the abode and ran at full speed towards the administrative building as Bhumi turned on the artificial sun above to full brightness. They had run a hundred yards when Gilead announced, "Object's velocity is increasing. Impact in ninety-four seconds."

"We're not going to make it!" Joshua shouted as he ran.

Bhumi pushed the button on her suit that allowed for global communication. "Brace for increased gravity and lateral movements. I'm going to try to move out of its way."

The group ran towards some nearby trees and wrapped their arms around the trunks. Bhumi waited for a few more moments before increasing the ship's thrust. The crew suddenly felt heavy as the thrust on the ship grew.

"Thrust at three-Gs and increasing," Gilead announced.

The group fell to the ground from the increased gravity. They still had their arms wrapped around the trunks of the trees as small branches came raining down on them, broken from the increased weight.

"Be careful Bhumi!" Joshua shouted, struggling to take a breath. "Too many Gs and we'll pass out."

"Object still closing," Gilead announced. "Impact in forty seconds."

"I'm going to try to move out of its way," Bhumi said.

They now felt a lateral force that was pulling them away from the trunks they were holding on to. The Zephyr moved sideways as Bhumi applied increasing thrust to the ejection nozzles on one side of the ship.

The force on Rachael's arms grew larger as her legs were pulled sideways. She gripped the trunk harder.

"Object changing course," Gilead announced. "It's heading straight for us. Impact imminent. Brace."

Joshua looked out over the landscape of the ship as terror filled his heart. He felt a sudden jolt from below and saw an explosion of dirt and rocks fly high in the air from the area of the soccer field.

"Hull breached," Bhumi announced as she returned the gravity to normal and stopped the lateral thrust. She let go of the trunk.

"No!" Joshua shouted. "Everyone keep holding on to the trunks!"

Moments later, a sudden rush of wind directed towards the soccer field engulfed them. The force of the wind caused their bodies to rotate with their feet pointed towards the field as they held the trunks tightly with their arms. The chamber of the Zephyr became suddenly misty as the water of the ponds started to vaporize by the sudden loss of pressure. Dirt, rocks, and broken branches flew through the air and were sucked into a twenty-foot diameter hole in the ground near the soccer field. The atmosphere of the Zephyr was escaping into the vacuum of space through the rent caused by the collision.

"I'm trying to seal the leak!" Bhumi shouted as she held on tight to her trunk.

Rachael felt her hands slipping from the trunk as her body was pulled away from it from the force of the wind. She wondered how long she could hold on. The rush of wind slowly subsided over the next few minutes as the force on her arms slowly abated. She let go of the trunk as the wind stopped.

"Hull sealed," Bhumi said, breathing hard. "Josh, I'm glad you had us don our helmets. The air pressure in here is severely reduced."

Seth's voice came over their speakers. "All executive crew to the administrative building. Military crew patrol for any intruders. I want a headcount of all crew members."

The foursome resumed their run towards the administrative building, the landscape strewn with debris, the air filled with mist. As they entered the conference room, Seth was already seated at the table with Liz at his side, both in their helmets.

"Where are Vinod and Ted?" Rachael asked as the foursome took a seat next to the others.

"Ted is with the military crew," Liz said. "We haven't seen Vinod yet."

Joshua pushed the global communication button on his suit. "Vinod, can you hear me? Come in please." There was no response. Joshua repeated the request. Still no response.

"Ted," Seth said. "What's the status of the military crew?"

"Four crewmembers unaccounted for," Ted replied. "Continuing our search."

"Any signs of any intruders?" Seth asked.

"Negative."

"Vinod is also unaccounted for."

"Got it. We'll look for him."

Ted had the military crew spread out and look for their missing crewmembers, their weapons drawn. He had been searching for a few minutes as he entered the forested area near the recreational complex. He saw a body in a blue suit lying near the base of a tree and rushed over to it. It was lying face down, unmoving. He knelt and turned the body over. It was Vinod. His face shield was smashed with a large gaping hole, and his eyes were slightly open as they stared outward, unblinking and unmoving.

"Damn it!" Ted shouted.

* * *

The consciousness began reassembling itself. It didn't recall what it had been before because it had not been fully reconstituted yet. It didn't know what it was coalescing into, but its perception became clearer by the minute. The consciousness could now visualize. It could only see gray, but the gray became brighter and whiter as time passed. It now started to remember something of itself from the past. It remembered that it had had a name—Vinod.

The various senses became clearer now—sight, sound, sensation, and sentience. *I am Vinod.* The memories started flooding back. *I'm Vinod . . .. I was . . . on the Zephyr. Where am I? What is this place?*

Vinod regained consciousness, but it was a consciousness different than what he had known before. It was clearer, crisper, and more resolute than any he had ever experienced. He felt the sensation of being in his body returning to him. He was lying on a soft surface. He felt as if he was lying on a cloud and could see only a thick white fog surrounding him. There was no sound. "Where am I?" he said out loud. He could hear his voice as he said it.

"Vinod?" said a male voice through the mist. It was a vaguely familiar voice with a British accent. "Vinod?" the voice repeated.

I know that voice. How do I know that voice? "Yes, I'm here." He saw an open hand slowly appearing through the mist. The hand reached towards him and stopped. Vinod grasped the hand which helped him up. He now saw the face attached to the hand. Vinod's emotions welled inside of him. He couldn't believe what he was seeing. Shrouded in the white fog was a face he hadn't seen in over fifteen years. "Derek?"

"Yes, it's me."

Chapter Twenty-One
Reconnaissance

Vinod stared at Derek, his long-lost boyfriend. "How are you here?" Vinod tried to look around at his surroundings but saw only a white fog. "Where are we?"

Derek smiled at Vinod. "We're where we're supposed to be. I've been waiting for you. I'm overjoyed to see you again." Derek embraced Vinod, who was in shock. The warmth of Derek's body was something Vinod had missed. Vinod slowly returned the embrace. Vinod and Derek had been soulmates on Earth. They had been a couple during their college years, but their relationship had been tragically cut short when Derek had died in a hang-gliding accident. But now, somehow, Vinod was with Derek again.

They let go of each other. "Welcome to the next existence," Derek said with a smile.

"Next existence? What does that mean?"

"What do you think it means? You've left the mortal world behind. I was chosen to accompany you during this transition."

Vinod couldn't believe what he was hearing. It took a few moments for the words to sink in. "Am I dead? Is this . . . heaven?"

"Your life in the mortal world has completed, but you're not dead. Your spirit—your consciousness—has transitioned to this existence. Heaven is probably the closest word to describe this place, but you need to let go of your prior notions of what heaven is. This *is* a wonderful place. It takes some getting used to. I've been chosen as your guide to help you in this transition."

Your life in the mortal world has completed. The words hung in Vinod's mind, yet strangely, he had no feeling of sorrow. He felt light as a feather and energized. He was with Derek. How he had missed him.

"Come on," Derek said as he grabbed Vinod's hand. "I have something special planned for you." Derek led Vinod as they walked through the mist.

As they walked, objects and shapes around them seemed to get clearer as the mist slowly abated. Vinod noticed that they were walking on a cobblestone street. He started to recognize objects through the fog. There were trees in the distance, their branches void of leaves, and brick buildings a few stories tall. Vinod looked down and noticed that he was dressed in bell-bottomed jeans and a tie-dye T-shirt covered by a jean jacket. Derek, who was leading him down the street, was dressed similarly, although he had a red flannel shirt.

Vinod noticed a chill in the air and could now make out a gentile snow falling from a dark sky. He noticed that the street they were walking on was slush-covered. The mist surrounding them grew clearer as they walked, and Vinod now got a better understanding of his surroundings. They were outside. It was night, and they were walking down a cobblestone street with buildings on either side. Some streetlights lit up the falling snow and the street below. Vinod glanced at a street sign they passed which read "Renfield Street."

"Where are we?" Vinod asked. "Where are we going?"

"You'll see. It's a surprise. You're going to love it."

Vinod started hearing distant chatter as they walked further. The white mist had faded entirely. They were definitely walking down a snowy city street lined with buildings and the occasional barren tree. There were Christmas lights in a few of the windows of the buildings. There were people up ahead. As they walked towards them, they became more distinct. They were in a line waiting for something. They were human, but there was something strange about them . . . something odd about their appearance. The men had long hair, some in ponytails. Some had bandanas on their heads. The women wore bell-bottomed jeans or skirts with tights underneath.

"Don't worry about the line," Derek said as he led Vinod further. "We can skip it."

As they passed the people in the line, it suddenly dawned on Vinod why the people looked so strange. They looked like hippies. They were dressed like they were in the seventies. "What is this place?" Vinod asked.

"It's Glasgow."

"Glasgow? As in Scotland."

"Yea."

"When?"

"December 1972."

The timing and location fit exactly what Vinod was seeing. Vinod started hearing music. It wasn't coming from any place in particular but seemed to be all around. He recognized the song in his head. One of the men in line turned towards Vinod. He had long blond hair held back with a tie-dye headband. He wore circular mirrored sunglasses despite the darkness outside. He sang a line from the song Vinod was hearing. "Take me on a trip upon your magic swirling ship. My senses have been stripped."

Vinod stared at the man. The song faded as they passed him, and another song filled Vinod's brain. As they walked further, a woman from the line turned to him. She wore a brown leather long-sleeve blouse with tassels and blue jeans. She danced slowly as they approached. When they walked up to her, she sang, "When the men on the chessboard tell you where to go. And you've just had some kind of mushroom, and your mind is moving low. Go ask Alice, I think she'll know." The woman stopped singing as the song continued in his head. Vinod stopped and stared at the woman.

"Are you Alice?" he asked the woman who stared back blankly at him.

Derek jerked him forward. "Come on. We've got to go." The song faded as they passed the woman, and a new one filled his head. Vinod recognized the new song immediately. It felt somewhat out of place. He now knew how this worked. He was looking for the next person in line who would turn towards them. He saw another man turn towards him. He was African American with a large afro. He stared directly at Vinod, expressionless. Vinod felt as if the man could see through him. The man sang, "Opinions all provided. Detached and subdivided, in the mass production zone. Nowhere is the dreamer or the misfit so alone."

The lyrics, which perfectly matched the music Vinod was hearing, touched a chord in Vinod. This was a song about not fitting in as a youth . . . as growing up as an outsider. The song was from before his time, but one he identified with. Growing up in the Cleveland suburbs as a gay youth had not been easy. It was during a time when being gay was not as easily accepted as it had become later. This song and its lyrics, which pointed out the loneliness of not fitting in, had always been one of his favorites. "It can't be 1972," he said to Derek.

"What? Why?"

"That song wasn't written in 1972."

"Dude, I tried my best. You're the classic rock genius, not me. I know it was one of your favorites. Just trying to make you happy. Let's go. You're going to love where we're headed."

Derek led Vinod to the front of the line, which ended at a large brick building entrance. It was a large multi-story theater with the name "Green's Playhouse" on a sign over the front entrance.

Vinod was now entirely in the moment. The haze and fog of his initial awakening were completely gone. He was in Glasgow in December 1972 with his boyfriend. There was nothing unreal about what he was experiencing other than the setting. He felt perfectly normal. His disorientation was gone. For some reason unknown to Vinod, he felt no sorrow or remorse from the fact that he had died. He was at peace and was simply absorbing the experience. He looked at Derek, who produced two tickets from his jacket pocket and showed them to the usher at the front of the line. The usher looked at the tickets and let the couple through. Vinod and Derek entered the lobby of the building, and Derek started to put the tickets back into his jacket.

Vinod grabbed his hand and grasped one of the tickets and read it. "An evening with Led Zeppelin, Green's Playhouse, Glasgow, 3 December 1972."

"Are you kidding me dude?" Vinod asked excitedly. "We're going to see Zeppelin live?"

"Yup," Derek replied with a grin. "It's an actual concert from their 72 UK tour."

"Seriously?"

"Seriously. I remember you told me how you would have loved to see them live, so here we are."

"*The* Led Zeppelin?"

"Yes. Long hair, bare chests, bell-bottoms, and all."

Vinod's body teemed with excitement. They entered the auditorium and found their seats in the front row. He was much too excited to ask how or why they were where they were. He simply wanted to soak up the experience. Shortly, the lights dimmed, and the famous quartet took the stage. To Vinod, they looked exactly as they had looked in the pictures and videos he had perused on the Internet of their younger days. As they started their first song, "Rock and Roll," he turned to Derek and embraced him. He looked into his eyes and said, "Thanks bro. This is exactly how I wished heaven would be."

* * *

"I found Vinod," Ted said into his suit. "He's not moving, and his face shield is smashed, but he has a very weak pulse. Can I take my helmet off and put it on him?"

"Gilead, what's the atmospheric pressure in the Zephyr?" Joshua asked.

"Two hundred and thirty millimeters of mercury and slowly rising."

"I'm trying to repressurize," Bhumi said, "but it'll take a couple of hours."

"Damn it!" Joshua shouted. "Two hundred thirty is very low. About the same as the top of Everest."

"We have to do something," Liz stated. "Vinod's not going to make it unless he gets oxygen, and I need him in the medical bay right away."

Joshua spoke into his suit. "Ted, how long will it take you to get him to the medical bay?"

"A couple of minutes at full speed."

"I don't think he has a couple of minutes," Liz said. "He needs oxygen now."

"Ted, take your helmet off and put it on Vinod," Joshua said. "You need to bring him to the medical bay right away, but be careful. There's not much oxygen in the Zephyr. If you feel like you're going to pass out, you have to put your helmet back on."

Ted took a couple of deep breaths as he pulled Vinod's helmet off. He pulled off his own helmet and immediately felt the decreased pressure around him. He put his helmet on Vinod and threw Vinod's body over his shoulder, and began running towards the administrative building.

Ted quickly grew light-headed as he labored to breathe. *You got this*, he thought as he continued his run.

"You think he'll make it?" Rachael asked as the group rushed to the medical bay.

"If anyone can make it, it's Ted," Joshua replied. "He's in great shape." Joshua ran out of the building with a spare helmet in his hand. He saw Ted carrying Vinod far in the distance and ran towards them.

Ted fell to his knees, unable to catch his breath. Joshua arrived and quickly placed the spare helmet on his head. "You okay?"

"Yea," Ted remarked, breathing heavily. "You go. Get Vinod to Liz."

Joshua picked up Vinod's limp body, cradled him in his arms, and ran towards the medical building.

Liz and the others waited in the medical bay. Joshua burst in, breathing heavily, and laid Vinod on a stretcher as he fell to his knees. Liz wheeled Vinod's unmoving body over to a medical pod as Ted ran in.

"You did it Ted," Rachael said. "You got him here."

"I hope it isn't too late," Ted said, breathing heavily. "I'm glad Josh met me partway."

A few minutes later, Liz emerged from the medical pod. "He's stable, but unconscious. He won't respond to any stimuli. There's something wrong with his brain. His EEG signals are through the roof. Not sure what's causing it."

"Is he stable enough to be moved into the atomic scanner?" Seth asked.

"Yes," Liz said. "But why?"

"I have a hunch."

They wheeled Vinod into the scanner and had Gilead take a scan. After the scan completed, Seth asked Gilead to show the region of Vinod's brainstem near the junction of the spinal cord on a video monitor of the room. They noted a dark line that transected the cord. "That dark area was unable to be scanned," Gilead said. "There are other similar areas on all the cranial nerves."

"What is it Seth?" Rachael asked. "What're the dark lines?"

"It's what I thought," Seth responded. "Those are biograins. They're spookyon-based and can't be scanned by the scanner."

"Biograins?" Joshua asked. "As in biograins like you used to transport me to New Eden from Earth when I first went there?"

"Precisely," Seth responded. "The comet that hit us must have contained them. They entered Vinod through his broken face shield."

"Why biograins?" Rachael asked. "I don't understand."

"Reconnaissance," Seth responded. "Medusa is conducting reconnaissance. She has control of Vinod's mind. She's controlling his entire experience. She's trying to figure out what we're doing."

"What do you think she's injecting into his mind?" Liz asked. "His mind is in overdrive, according to his EEG."

"Don't know," Seth said. "She could be doing anything to him, even torturing him. She's trying to extract information from him. She's also overdriving his mind. I suspect that his sense of time is extremely compressed. Every minute for us may seem like an hour for Vinod. She's trying to extract as much information from him as she can."

"Why the temporal distortion?" Joshua asked.

"She doesn't have much time. We're about two days away from entering the spookyon dampening field. Once we enter the field, she won't have any connection to the spookyons in the biograins connected to Vinod."

"Is there any way for us to remove the biograins?" Liz asked.

"No, it's too dangerous. They're located in his brainstem. I think they'll remove themselves once we enter the dampening field, and they lose their connection. In the meantime, we'll just have to wait it out."

"What do you think Seth?" Richard asked. "Do you think Vinod will divulge our plans? Medusa doesn't know about your spookyon node and the code that you have to destroy her."

"It's all but inevitable," Seth responded. "It's one human mind versus the extreme intelligence of Medusa. We're screwed."

Chapter Twenty-Two
Mission Unaccomplished

The crew spent the next couple of days repairing the damage to the ship. They had searched for the four military crew members that were still unaccounted for without success. It was Joshua's theory that they had been expelled out of the hole caused by the impact and ejected into space. Since the external rent in the ship was at its rear, he postulated that they had been incinerated by the exhaust plasma of the ship.

Seth released a neutralizing agent into the atmosphere that would render any remaining biograins from the impact harmless. The holes in the ship's external structure and the land area near the soccer field were repaired by Bhumi. The atmospheric pressure of the ship had been returned to normal, and the ship was once again decelerating at one-G towards Planet Nine. Once the atmosphere had been restored and the remaining biograins neutralized, Seth informed the crew that it was safe to remove their helmets.

Liz continued to monitor Vinod's status, but there had been no change. He was alive, but his brain was still being driven hard by the biograins.

The next morning, the Zephyr would enter the spookyon dampening field surrounding the planet, and Seth called a meeting of the executive crew to prepare for the transition. They sat, once again, in the conference room.

"What's the status of the Zephyr?" Seth asked Bhumi. "Are all the repairs finished?"

"The repairs are finished, and all systems are functioning normally, but we do have an issue. It's a rather large issue, I'm afraid."

The group stared at Bhumi, looks of concern on their faces.

"The projectile that hit us entered through the rear of the Zephyr,"

Bhumi said. "It penetrated the main storage tank for our liquid hydrogen fuel. A lot of our supply of fuel was ejected into space before the hole was sealed." Bhumi looked down at her hands. "We'll have enough fuel to get to Planet Nine, and some additional for some maneuvers once we reach there, but there's not going to be enough for our journey home."

Joshua thought about the problem. "We'd be stuck in the spookyon dampening field if we were unable to destroy it. Would we have enough fuel to escape the field?"

"I checked with Gilead on this," Bhumi said. "Depending on how much fuel we use at Planet Nine, we could have enough thrust to gain some speed away from Planet Nine, but that thrust would be only for a short period of time which means that we won't gain much velocity. At that speed, it may take years to escape the field. Also, we'd be in zero-G during that time, so I don't think it's a plausible idea."

"Then there's no way to get back," Joshua said.

"Not that I can come up with," Bhumi replied.

The group considered the implications of the fuel loss. Were they going to be stuck at Planet Nine? Would this mean that they couldn't be returned to New Eden? Rachael's anxiety rose as her thoughts turned to Ava. Would Ava grow up without her parents? "No way to get back?" Rachael asked. "What does that mean for us Seth?"

Joshua reached out and grasped Rachael's hand to offer her some comfort. He had also been having similar thoughts.

Seth sat calmly and looked at Rachael. He immediately realized her concern. "We have you all backed up. If something happens to us at Planet Nine, you can still be recreated on New Eden, but we must face facts. Without fuel for a return trip, we won't survive this mission."

Seth's words hung like a dagger over the group. "Are you saying we're on a suicide mission?" Ted asked.

"We've always been on a suicide mission," Seth stated. "You all realize that the bodies you're in now wouldn't return to New Eden. Only your memories and experiences from this mission will be transferred back to your clones on New Eden. You know of our petrin rules as they pertain to sentient entities. For you to be recreated on New Eden, then your bodies here need to be destroyed. This was always the plan. We cannot allow two copies of a sentient entity to be functional at once."

"What does that mean?" Liz asked. "You want us to destroy ourselves along with the ship at Planet Nine?"

"If we're unable to destroy the spookyon dampening field, and we don't have enough fuel to get out, that may be the scenario we're stuck with. That would be the only way for us to recreate you on New Eden."

"But if that's the case," Rachael said. "We'd be recreated according to our last backup. That would be when we came to Earth from New Eden to start this mission."

"That's right."

"Are you kidding me Seth?" Richard asked. "If we're recreated on New Eden from our backups, then we won't have any memory of going on this mission at all. All those memories would be lost. Why the hell did I come on this mission then?"

"That's not necessarily true," Seth said. "I want everyone to be scanned in the scanner so that we have the latest copy of your information." He turned to Bhumi. "I want you to be scanned as well. We'll have to do this before we enter the dampening field so that your information can be transmitted to the petrin network. However, it is true that anything that happens after your backup will be lost, but at least you will retain your memories up to that point. I think it's the best we can do given the circumstances."

Joshua thought about their situation. All other times he had been transported via petrin technology in the past had been a seamless experience. He had simply been scanned and had awoken in another location. But this was different. This time he would experience death. This body that he currently occupied would die. What would death be like? Would it even be death at all given the fact that he would be recreated on New Eden? The questions were both complex and terrifying. He tried to develop a solution that would offer them some escape. "Couldn't we refuel at Planet Nine? You said that it was a gas giant, which means that it's mostly made of hydrogen. Can't the Zephyr refuel there?"

"It's a possibility," Seth said, "but somehow, I feel we won't find much hydrogen there."

"Why?"

"We already know that Medusa has created technology that can allow cells to use hydrogen to create larger elements and energy. I'm almost positive she would've used this technology to transform Planet Nine into something quite different than a gas giant planet. I have no idea what she's created there, but I think the possibility of us finding a large quantity of hydrogen there is slim at best."

Joshua's mind scanned for other answers to their situation. He quickly came to a realization. "Wait, there may be another solution. It actually fits in well with our current plan on what we want to do when we get to Planet Nine."

"What is it?" Ted asked.

"Part of our plan is to try and destroy the generator that's causing the dampening field," Joshua said. "That will allow us to use Seth's spookyon node to fuse with Medusa's to unleash the petrin's code to kill her. But remember, Seth mentioned before that we wouldn't have much time after the field is released before we fuse our nodes. We wouldn't want to give Medusa a chance to mount an attack. If we're successful in both destroying the dampening field and in killing Medusa, then our information can be re-scanned by the scanner on the ship and relayed on the petrin data network. We could be transported back to New Eden completely intact since the dampening field would be destroyed. Seth, that would work right? If we're able to destroy the dampening field and destroy Medusa by fusing the nodes, then we can get scanned in the scanner on the ship and return to New Eden."

Seth thought about the plan for a moment. "I don't think that will work Josh. When we fuse our node with Medusa's, both nodes will be destroyed. They won't be able to be used to send your scanned data back to New Eden."

Joshua shook his head. He somehow felt that Seth wasn't being helpful, but he didn't know why. He was the one that was connected to the collective. Surely with their advanced intelligence, they could come up with a solution. In fact, Joshua thought of a resolution to the problem that Seth had expressed about his plan. He found it surprising that Seth hadn't come up with it. "There's a simple solution to that problem. Even if your node is destroyed, we will still have a spookyon connected to the petrin network. We'll still have the spookyon located in the Bowman sphere in your android body. It'll be reconnected once the dampening field is destroyed. It may take more time, but I'm sure we can use its bandwidth to transport our scanned data back to New Eden."

Seth smiled at Joshua. "Very resourceful Josh. You're right. That could be a possible solution. It is, however, dependent on us destroying the dampening field. Obviously, if we're able to do that, our first priority must be to fuse the nodes to destroy Medusa."

"Of course," Joshua replied.

Ted thought about the plan. "Well then, that's the mission," he said resolutely. "We gotta get this done. We have to destroy the dampening field and fuse those nodes."

The others nodded their heads in agreement.

"There's still one big factor standing in our way," Seth said. "This entire plan is in jeopardy. Vinod is aware that we're attempting to destroy the dampening field and fuse the nodes. Medusa is currently probing his mind, and if he reveals this plan to her, all bets are off."

* * *

Vinod and Derek sat in a Scottish café, enjoying some hot chocolate and bowls of soup. "Man, that concert was awesome," Vinod said. "Led Zeppelin live. Who would've thought?"

"I knew you'd enjoy it."

Vinod shifted in his seat and looked around. "So, what is this place? How does it work?"

"It's a café," Derek replied with a grin. "You order food and drinks, and they serve it to you."

Vinod rolled his eyes. "Hilarious dude," he said with sarcasm. "You know what I meant."

Derek put down his spoon. "You can think of this place as kind of a pre-heaven. It's a chance for you to experience stuff in the mortal world that you would have liked to have done before you died. After you're done here, we'll go to heaven."

"Experience what?"

"Anything you want."

"Anything?"

"Yes, as long as it happened in the past."

"How long do we have?"

"You can take as much time as you want. When you're finished, we'll both leave this place. As I've said, I'm your companion or guide, so to speak, for this transition."

"Man, this is going to be great," Vinod said, taking a spoonful of soup. "I can think of a lot of places and events I want to experience."

Derek looked curiously at Vinod. "You're not sad that you've died?"

"I've died and gone to heaven," Vinod remarked with a smile. "Of course, I am a little sad. I would have loved to accomplish more and also finish the mission I was on, but it is what it is." Vinod reached out and grasped Derek's hand. "But I'm overjoyed to see you again."

"Same here," Derek said as he squeezed Vinod's hand. "So, how'd it happen?"

Vinod let go of Derek's hand and resumed eating. "How'd what happen?"

"How'd you end up dying? I'm assuming that it wasn't a hang-gliding accident like for me."

"You don't know what happened on Earth after your death?"

"No. That's not how it works. I have no information on that."

Vinod put down his spoon and leaned back in his chair. How could he explain to Derek everything that has happened since his death over fifteen years ago? How could he explain that he was attacked by a megalomaniac on a biological spaceship traveling to Planet Nine? There was a lot to unpack, and Derek had died well before they had contacted the petrins. He let out a long sigh. "It's a long and complicated story bro."

"We've got time. All the time in the world."

Over the next hour, Vinod relayed to Derek the unbelievable tale of their contact with the petrins, the invasion of Earth by Medusa, and their transport to New Eden. Derek listened intently without interruption. Vinod told Derek about the Zephyr and how they'd visited Enceladus. "During our trip to Planet Nine, we got hit by some kind of projectile from Planet Nine, and I guess I got killed by the collision somehow, but to be honest, I don't remember exactly how I died." A thought suddenly entered his mind. How was he here at all? "Wait, I just thought of something."

"What?"

"How am I here? The petrins backed up my information, and if anything happened to me on the mission, I should have been recreated on New Eden. How come I didn't just wake up there?"

"Who knows man?" Derek responded. "Like I said before, I'm not privy to that type of information."

"The backup must have been deleted somehow," Vinod said deep in thought. "That's the only way this could work. Rachael told me that when she died on Earth, and her body was frozen, and she later awoke on New Eden, she had had no experience at all. There was no passage of time. There was simply nothing. For me to be here, all of my information from my previous existence had to have been erased."

"Sounds logical. Whatever the reasons, I'm sure that's what happened, but this story you just told me is simply unbelievable. Contact with an alien intelligence that just so happened to create the cell? I would have loved to have been around for that."

"It definitely was exciting," Vinod said in reflection. "Sometimes *too* exciting."

"So, you think that the mission will continue without you?"

"I don't know," Vinod said. "If the ship's still intact and the crew are still able to, I'm sure they'd continue the mission. They were trying to save the universe after all."

"What was their plan once they got to Planet Nine? How were they going to deal with Medusa?"

"Who cares at this point. It's become irrelevant to me. I'm no longer part of that world."

"Don't tell me you don't care. The crew were your friends."

"Yea, but obviously, it's out of my hands. They're on their own now. Anyhow, I'm tired of talking about the past." Vinod rubbed his hands together. "Let's move on to our next adventure."

Over the next few days, Vinod and Derek enjoyed multiple experiences as directed by the requests of Vinod. They experienced numerous other rock concerts as well as other venues and events. Derek was surprised to learn that Vinod wanted to visit a Paleolithic village in the Himalayas which they observed from afar.

After these experiences, Derek sat on a grass field and basked in the sunlight and natural beauty that surrounded him. Vinod lay on the grass, his head in Derek's lap. They were on New Eden during a period of time before humanity had been moved there. Vinod didn't have a chance to experience this version of New Eden like Joshua and Rachael. He had requested Derek to take him there. They had had a blissful day riding the flying arachnids and exploring the paradise.

Vinod reflected on the last experience they had had before coming to New Eden. He felt that that had been the best yet. They had just visited Alan Turing, the British scientist who is considered the father of computer science. They had spoken to him disguised as reporters who were visiting his lab at Bletchley Park at the time when he had been working on breaking the German cipher codes during World War II. Vinod had gotten emotional speaking with Turing. He had a genius mind, but Vinod knew that he would eventually be convicted for indecency due to his status as a homosexual. Turing would ultimately take his own life over the trauma of being ostracized.

"It's just not fair man," Vinod said, staring at the sky. "It's not fair that a brilliant genius like Turing got persecuted for his sexual orientation. What more could he have accomplished for society if he hadn't died so young?"

"Definitely sad," Derek said. "He *was* brilliant. I wonder if a mind like his could have found out a way to defeat Medusa."

Vinod looked into Derek's face. "Possibly, but even though he's a genius, he's no match for the intelligence of the collective. They've been working on that problem for millennia."

"Do you think they've found a solution?"

"They think they have."

"What is it?"

* * *

Seth led the executive crew near the ship's edge to an empty abode. He had told them he wanted to show them something. "What I wanted to show you is in here," he said as he opened the door and led the group in.

The group entered what looked like a dorm room. There was a bed, a desk with a chair, and a bathroom. The room's exterior wall was one of the transparent exterior walls of the ship with the starscape outside.

"Is it some kind of dorm?" Liz asked.

"Yes," Bhumi replied. "It's my dorm."

"What do you mean?" Richard asked.

Seth walked to a wall of the room that had a long cord wound up, hanging from a hook on the wall. "When we enter the dampening field, Bhumi's interface with the ship will be deactivated since that interface is dependent on spookyon transmission. At that point, she will need to be directly connected to the ship. This cord on this wall is that connection. The end of the cord attaches near the base of her neck and will allow her to control the ship. It's long enough so that she can walk around this room, but not outside."

Richard was shocked by the answer. He looked around the room. "What's that going to be like for her?"

"It's okay Blue," Bhumi said. "I've tried out the interface. It feels no different than what I'm experiencing now."

Richard was not consoled by the response. "Are you saying that Bhumi can't leave this room after we enter the dampening field?" He turned to Seth. "It's essentially a prison."

"I'd like her to be here," Seth said, "but she can disconnect from the connection in an emergency. However, the experience of disconnection would be disturbing to her. Remember, for her, the ship is another appendage. Disconnection, for her, would be a completely foreign experience. She'd feel like she'd lost a part of herself. I realize that eventually, after the mission is completed, she'll need to be disconnected for her to go to New Eden, but I wouldn't want her to go through that trauma during the mission. She's much too critical."

"That's bullshit!" Richard exclaimed. He had realized over the course of the mission the loneliness that Bhumi had experienced prior to the crew's arrival. He felt that confining Bhumi to this room would cause those feelings to resurface. "You can't expect her to be cooped up in this room by herself. That would be torture for her."

"Do you have another solution?" Seth asked.

Rachael shook her head and stared at Seth. She realized that he had studied human nature intently over the years, and she now realized how much he had learned. She realized he was manipulating Richard. She said nothing as she waited for Richard's response.

Richard looked around the room. "There's only one solution. If it's unavoidable that she stays here," Richard said, "then I want to stay here with her."

Rachael rolled her eyes but still said nothing.

"That can be arranged," Seth said. "We can move another bed in here."

"Or exchange this one for a bigger one," Ted remarked with a smile. The remark drew an elbow from Liz to his ribs.

Curious how all women seem to have all learned that gesture, Joshua thought as he saw the interaction.

"The sleeping arrangements will be up to you two," Seth said. "But I'm happy you'll be together."

As the group exited the abode, Rachael took Seth aside. "I need to talk to you." They paused as the others walked away.

"What do you want to discuss?" Seth asked.

"Don't play coy with me," Rachael said, hands on hips. "You knew exactly what you were doing bringing us to see this abode. You were hoping to convince Richard to stay with Bhumi. Admit it."

"So? What's wrong with that?"

"It's manipulative. You've known all along that Bhumi would have to be in that room after we enter the dampening field. I realize now that one of the primary reasons you had Richard come on this trip wasn't just for companionship. You wanted him to be Bhumi's roommate."

"So?" Seth said defensively. "He kind of seemed to enjoy the prospect at the end."

"Did he? It didn't seem like that to me. He seemed very concerned about her welfare. He was right. Even with Richard's company, it's an awful sacrifice to spend so much time cooped up in one place. Now you've manipulated it so that Richard has to do it as well as Bhumi."

"I realize it's a sacrifice. This entire mission is a sacrifice." Seth became solemn and looked towards the ground. "I know everyone has had to make sacrifices to be on this mission. The collective . . .," Seth paused to look back at Rachael. "*I* am very grateful that you all have agreed to be here. You may not realize it, but this is a difficult mission for me. It was essential for me that you agreed to come. It was important for me to have my friends on this mission."

Rachael removed her hands from her hips as her mood softened. She remembered what Joshua had said earlier about something that Seth was hiding. "Why? I know you've been alive for such a long time. You've experienced thousands of years of life. I'm sure you've had important responsibilities in the past. Why is *this* mission so important for you?"

Seth didn't answer immediately. He knew that the human crew had the utmost respect for him. He knew that that respect resonated from the fact that he was the representative of a collective of vast intelligence. He wondered how humans would view him independent of the collective. "Follow me. I have something I want to show you."

Seth led Rachael to the administrative building. They walked to a door next to the lab. "What I want to show you is in here," Seth said as he opened the door. Rachael walked into a bare room with no windows. She saw a solitary object near one of the walls of the room. It was a large, rectangular tank with clear walls. The tank was filled with a clear gelatinous substance. Rachael walked up to the tank and let out a gasp as she saw what was inside. It was a human body. Rachael moved closer, peered inside, and recognized that the body was Seth. "What is this?"

"Don't you recognize it? It's me."

"Of course, I recognize it. Are you growing a clone of yourself?"

"Yes."

"Why?"

"This android body of mine won't work in the dampening field. My connection with it is via a spookyon. I will have to take a new form." Seth pointed to the body in the tank. "This form."

Rachael was confused. "I get it, but you've been in human form before. You're like that on New Eden. Why did you feel the need to show me this?"

"This isn't the same," Seth said while staring at the body in the tank. "I need you to understand something. My human form on New Eden has no brain. Remember, that clone is remote-controlled by me via a spookyon connected to a neural nest. That won't work in the dampening field. This clone here is completely human, brain and all. I will be disconnected from the collective and will not have the incredible intelligence associated with that connection."

Rachael gazed into the tank at the body floating in the clear gelatin. She realized the sacrifice that Seth was making. He was a being of superior intelligence, but he was about to make a downgrade to help with the mission. He would adopt a human form and all the frailties that came with it. It was definitely a sacrifice. He would forgo his connection to a vast store of intelligence and become truly human for the first time.

Chapter Twenty-Three

Paranoia

The preparations for the transition into the spookyon dampening field were complete. The Zephyr would enter the field in a matter of minutes. All the crew, including Bhumi, had been scanned by the scanners, and their latest information stored on petrin data nodes. The exception was Vinod. Due to the biograins that currently occupied his brain, he was unable to be scanned.

Richard stayed with Bhumi in their dorm abode. Bhumi had already attached the connection to the ship to the base of her neck in anticipation of the transition. For her, the transition would be seamless. The spookyon in her brain that connected to the ship would cease to function, but since all this communication was now being routed through her external connection, she would feel nothing.

Ted and Liz stood over Vinod's body in the medical bay. Seth had informed them that the biograins would exit his skull when they lost their connection to Medusa. They stood next to him anxiously waiting for him to wake.

"One minute to dampening field," Gilead announced over the speakers.

Joshua, Rachael, and Seth stood over Seth's human body on another stretcher in the medical bay. "Data transfer to his mind is complete," Seth said. "It's time." Android Seth laid down on a third stretcher and looked at the faces of Joshua and Rachael hovering over him. "Are you going to miss me?"

"Only for a few seconds," Joshua said with a wink.

For Rachael, the moment was more poignant. She knew in less than a minute she may never see Seth again in android form. She remembered that first day in the Bat Cave many years ago when they had first activated him, and he had done a dance as an introduction. Seth, especially in his android form, held a special place in her heart. "I will miss this form of you," she said as she gently kissed his head.

"Fifteen seconds," Gilead announced.

Rachael watched as the movements of Seth's android eyes darted around the room and then suddenly ceased. She and Joshua moved over to Seth's human body. He slowly opened his eyes and looked around the room. "They're gone," he said with eyes opening wide. "The petrins are gone." For the first time in his life, he was disconnected from the collective without any way to reconnect at will. He was overcome with an immense sense of loneliness. He looked around the room and found solace in the faces of his friends staring down at him. "'sup fellow humans," he said with a weak voice.

Rachael looked with concern at human Seth. She felt that the words he had said had been scripted, and he was trying to put on a brave face. "How're you feeling Seth?"

"Human," he replied with a weak smile, "and not necessarily in a good way."

"Welcome to the club," Joshua said.

Seth composed himself, sat up, and asked, "How's Vinod? We should check on him."

Seth stood up from the stretcher, and the trio joined Ted and Liz by Vinod's body. They saw the blue biograins exit his skull. Vinod slowly opened his eyes, a look of confusion on his face. He scanned the faces hovering over him. "Where am I?"

"You're on the Zephyr," Joshua said. "We're still on the mission."

Rachael leaned over and hugged Vinod. "Thank god you're okay. We were worried about you."

"Am I okay?" Vinod asked. "I'm not dead?"

"No, you're not dead," Liz said. "Whatever gave you that idea?"

"But Derek told me . . .."

"Derek?" Rachael asked. "Your old boyfriend?"

Vinod sat up, still looking confused. "What's happening? Derek, are you here?"

Rachael sat next to Vinod on the stretcher. She wrapped her arms around him. "It's okay. You're okay now. Medusa had control of your mind for a while, but it's past now. You're back with us."

"What're you talking about?" Vinod said with tears welling in his eyes. "Derek isn't here?"

"No honey. Not here. He was never here."

Vinod started sobbing as Rachael continued her embrace.

Liz took Joshua aside. "Who is Derek?"

"He was Vinod's old boyfriend. Vinod was very fond of him in the past, and apparently, he died in some kind of accident many years ago. I never met him, but I remember Rachael telling me how devastated Vinod was when he lost him."

"It must have been what Medusa injected into his mind," Liz said. "She used a person who he had loved from the past to try to extract information from him."

Joshua looked at Rachael trying to console Vinod on the stretcher. "It must be horrible for him. He had thought that he had found his long-lost love, but now he's lost him all over again. I feel so sorry for him."

They stayed with Vinod for a while to support him as he recuperated a bit from his shock and grief. After a while, they explained to him what had happened to him and that the entire experience he'd had was not real, but something that Medusa had injected into his mind to get information about their mission.

"You feel up to telling us what you experienced bro?" Seth asked after Vinod was calmer.

Vinod looked down at his clenched fists. He relaxed his hands and spread out his fingers. "I guess so," Vinod said, trying to control his emotions. "Let's get it over with."

The group moved to the conference room, and Vinod methodically relayed his experiences. He told them about meeting Derek, who had informed him that he had died. He described in detail the quasi-heaven they were in and their experiences there. Vinod was shocked to learn that he had only been unconscious for a few days since his remembered experiences seemed to span multiple weeks.

"Medusa was overdriving your mind," Seth explained. "Your sense of time was severely distorted."

"I guess it makes sense," Vinod said. "It's like overclocking a microprocessor."

The group was apprehensive. They were eager to learn what Vinod had revealed to Medusa about their mission, but they knew that Vinod had had a traumatic experience, and he may not be thinking clearly. They were silent for a while before Seth cautiously broached the subject.

"Did Derek . . . I mean Medusa, ask you about our mission?"

"Many times," Vinod said. "I did find it kind of strange that Derek would be so interested in our mission, but even those times were fleeting. The majority of the time we spent together was absolute bliss. We had many adventures together. I even got to meet Alan Turing. That was a surreal and wonderful experience."

"We'd been worried that she might be torturing you somehow," Liz said. "I know you're going through much trauma now, but you seemed to have enjoyed your experience for the most part."

"I did," Vinod said quietly, reflecting on his encounter. "It was an amazing experience. In a way, I'm sorry it's over."

"It was very clever of her," Joshua said. "She found the one person that Vinod would trust implicitly. She had a much better chance of extracting information from him if she could get him to explain it to someone he trusted. It's a much better tactic than outright torture."

"How much did you tell her about the mission?" Seth asked.

"Some."

"What about our plans for what we were planning on doing when we get to Planet Nine? Did you tell her about that?"

The group turned intently to Vinod for his response. He lowered his head. "Yes, I told her."

Their hearts sank at the response. Was their mission plan a failure even before it had been implemented?

"How much did you tell her?" Seth asked.

"Everything," Vinod said with his head still lowered. "I told her everything—all the details. I told her about how the Zephyr was just a diversion. I told her about the cloaked ships that would be approaching from the opposite side that would be the main attack force."

The group stared at each other in confusion.

"What are you talking about Vinod?" Ted asked. "What cloaked ships?"

Vinod lifted his head, looking absolutely confused. He scanned the faces looking back at him. "What do you mean what cloaked ships? The cloaked ships that Seth told us about during our last meeting with him. The ones that would be attacking from the rear while we cause a diversion."

"Liz," Joshua asked. "Could there be some neural damage associated with his experience? There seems to be some confusion in his mind."

"It's possible," Liz said, "There may be some side effects to how hard Medusa was driving his brain, but his brain scans don't seem to show anything unusual."

Joshua turned to Vinod. "Vinod, don't you remember the plan that Seth told us about? Don't you remember Seth showing us the petrin spookyon node, and that he wants to try to deactivate the dampening field and fuse the petrin node with Medusa's node and inject the killer code into it?"

Vinod's face changed to an expression of shock. Fresh tears filled his eyes as he laid his head on the table and began sobbing uncontrollably.

Rachael rushed over to him and embraced him again. "What's the matter Vinod? Are you okay?"

Vinod continued his sobbing as the others looked at each other with concern and confusion.

"It's over," Vinod finally said through sobs. "It's finally over."

"What's over?" Rachael asked.

"Medusa's grip on me."

"We told you it was over before, honey. We told you when you were in the medical bay. Don't you remember?"

"Maybe we should let him rest," Liz said. "He's obviously been through a traumatic experience. He may not be thinking clearly."

"I think you're right," Rachael said. "He's in shock. He's going through the experience of losing Derek for a second time."

Vinod slowly stopped his sobbing. "No, I'm fine," he said as he wiped the tears from his eyes and turned to Rachael. "Thanks for your comfort. It means a lot. Go ahead and sit down. I have something to tell you."

"Are you sure? It's okay if you're not feeling well. We can do it at some other time."

"I'm fine," Vinod said, sitting up straighter in his chair.

Rachael returned to her seat.

Vinod took a deep breath and gathered his thoughts. "My experience with Medusa was pure bliss. It was perfect. It was just how I'd imagined an afterlife would be. My experiences were perfect. Derek was perfect . . . but it was too perfect."

"Too perfect?" Rachael asked. "What do you mean?"

"I loved Derek when he was alive, and I know he loved me. We had passion and genuine emotions toward each other. Our emotions were strong, but not always positive. We were both strong-minded and stubborn people. We had many arguments because of this, but in some way, those arguments added spice to our relationship. I realize that now. Back during that time, I'd wished we'd had fewer arguments. I wished we were more in sync. This Derek I experienced was different. He was everything I'd ever wanted. He was perfect. He always agreed with whatever I'd said, and we never had any disagreements.

"A couple of days into my experience, I remembered something that Seth had said to us near the start of our mission. He told us that Medusa was brilliant, and she could employ some very devious methods to get what she wants. I began to be suspicious of what I was experiencing. I started becoming paranoid. I didn't know for sure, but I became somewhat guarded about my situation. I wondered if it was some type of simulation. Don't get me wrong, I loved the experience, but my radar was up. I told myself that on the off chance that if it was a simulation, something that Medusa had thought up, that if asked about something that was critical to the mission, I wouldn't reveal anything.

"Later, I became more convinced that I was right. Derek kept asking, very slyly, mind you, about our mission. I thought that if I resisted telling him for too long, he would become suspicious. So, I came up with some type of false plan. I told him that the Zephyr was just a diversion, and the real attack would come from ships using a new technology that the collective had developed. This new technology involved some type of cloaking technology that would render their attacking ships invisible."

The group stared at Vinod, mouths open. "Are you kidding me Vinod?" Ted asked. "Are you fucking kidding me?"

"No," Vinod said with a weak smile. "Not kidding."

"My god," Joshua said. "I can't believe it. You actually lied to Medusa? You turned the tables on her?"

"Yup," Vinod said, the grin growing on his face. "I have no idea if she believed me or not, but I thought it was worth a try. In fact, when I woke up on the ship, I didn't know if I was really on the ship or not. I thought it could have been another trick by Medusa to get information out of me. I did my best to keep up the act. It wasn't until Joshua relayed the actual plan for what we were going to do at Planet Nine that I realized for sure that I was back."

"Vinod," Rachael said. "What a performance! You had us all fooled. We thought there was something wrong with you."

"I'll accept my Oscar later."

"Cloaked ships?" Ted asked with an enormous grin. "Romulans?"

"You know it dude," Vinod replied with a wink. He turned to Seth. "What do you think? Do you think Medusa believed me?"

Seth was beaming. "Vinod, I'm so proud of you bro. You've done an incredible service to this mission. Simply amazing. I don't know if she believed you or not, but at least she failed in getting any valuable information from you. You ran Medusa's gauntlet and came through unscathed. I can't thank you enough."

Vinod was quiet for a while. "I can't say I came through completely unscathed. I miss Derek now more than ever. He was so real. Everything was so real. How'd she do it Seth? It seemed to me that she could read my mind. She had to in order to make everything so real, but if she could read my mind, she could have read the information in my brain about the mission."

"The human mind, like the minds of many sentient organisms, is an enigma," Seth replied. "Even though we created the cell on which it's based, we don't know exactly how it works. We can copy information to and from it, but we're not privy to the actual methods used to store that information. The inner workings of the human brain are still a mystery to us. A petrin may have created the technology to allow life and evolution to progress to intelligence, but we did not direct that intelligence. It was the result of the forces of the cosmos. We can interface with a brain via the biograins attached to a spinal cord and cranial nerves to control the experience of a mind, but we can't read people's thoughts. For these reasons, I believe that Medusa did not directly generate your experiences. Your own mind created them."

"My own mind?" Vinod asked. "How?"

"I think I understand," Liz replied. "It's like a dream." She turned to Vinod. "Are there times that you have a dream, and some crazy stuff is happening, but you're completely convinced that it's real?"

"Sure," Vinod said. "Everyone has dreams like that. In fact, the only time I ever realize that what I'm experiencing in a dream isn't real is when I wake up."

"Exactly," Liz responded. "I don't think that Medusa injected those experiences for you. Your own mind did that. Your own mind is the source of your dreams, but during the dream, you think it's a completely real experience. I think Medusa put you into some type of extended dream state that represented your vision of the afterlife. She simply manipulated some aspects of this state to try to extract information from you. She may have come up with the narrative, but your subconscious may have generated the experience."

"I guess it's possible," Vinod said after some thought. "My experience does seem like some type of weeks-long dream if I think about it." Vinod took in a deep breath and let it out. "Well, it's over now. Anyway, what's up with the mission? How far are we from Planet Nine?"

"We're about a day away," Seth said. "We've entered the dampening field. In fact, I believe that we're just close enough that we can see the first higher-resolution images of the location using the ship's telescopes. Gilead, please display the long-range image of Planet Nine on our wall."

The group turned to the wall, and its image turned to a starfield with a bright spot in the middle. The spot seemed to have a semi-circular ring some distance away that surrounded it. "That bright spot is the light source we have noticed from Planet Nine," Seth said.

"What's that structure around it?" Joshua asked. "There isn't enough resolution to make out what it is. Is it some type of ring system like Saturn has?"

"Unknown," Seth responded. "I don't think it's a ring system though. It's too narrow and wide to be a natural ring system, but it must be huge if we can see it from this distance. Gilead, can you extrapolate the diameter of the semi-circle we're seeing?"

"Approximately twenty thousand kilometers."

"That's huge," Joshua said. "It's almost twice Earth's diameter. What the hell is it?"

"I guess we'll find out once we get closer," Ted remarked.

"One thing I don't see is a gas giant," Joshua said. "I think Seth was right. We're not going to find some source of hydrogen there."

"Hydrogen?" Vinod asked. "Why are we looking for hydrogen?"

Joshua filled Vinod in on the status of the mission. He told him about the loss of fuel and their inability to return from Planet Nine. Vinod was shocked by the new information. Some of the feelings he had had when trapped in Korea with no plausible means of escape resurfaced inside him.

"Another goddamn suicide mission. I should've known."

* * *

Dina Williams noted an incoming video call while sitting at her desk in her office. She saw that it was from Mitchell Porter. She answered the call, and when the video started, she saw that Porter was standing in front of the white dome in the snow-covered forest. "Hello Mitchell. What's going on?"

"You wanted to be notified of any changes in the structure," Porter said. "There have been a couple of changes. It's stopped its growth, but it's maintaining its relatively warm temperature."

"Interesting."

"There's something else."

"What?"

"You remember that bulge that Langdon noted near the top of the structure?"

"Yes."

"It's gone. There was a small explosion about thirty minutes ago, and that bulge disappeared."

"An explosion?"

"Yes, it was very small. It almost seemed like the bulge was a bubble that popped. It didn't seem to do any damage to the dome, and there was nothing toxic released from it, but I thought you should know. We don't know what to make of it."

"I don't know what to make of anything about this dome," Williams replied. "Seth obviously places some high importance on it. We'll just have to keep monitoring it. Thanks."

Chapter Twenty-Four
The Human Petrin

Joshua lay on his bed, staring at the ceiling. He was having difficulty falling asleep. In less than a day, they would be arriving at a world that was entirely Medusa's creation. Medusa had the ability to turn a gas giant planet into literally anything she wanted. What would they find there? What dangers lay ahead?

He turned and saw Rachael lying next to him, her body turned away. He wondered if she was asleep or just trying to fall asleep.

"Rachael," he whispered in an attempt not to wake her if indeed she was sleeping.

"Yes."

"I can't sleep."

"Me neither," Rachael responded, her body still turned away.

"I'm worried," Joshua said.

Rachael turned to face Joshua. "Me too. What're you worried about?"

"I'm worried about what will happen once we get to Planet Nine. We have no idea what Medusa has created there, but we're going to face it tomorrow. That's what worries me—the unknown. Is that also what's keeping you awake?"

"I am worried about that, but no, that's not what I'm thinking about now."

"Then what?"

Rachael sat up. "I'm worried about Seth."

"Seth? Why?"

"I'm not sure why," Rachael responded. "Yesterday, he took me to where his human body was being grown. I had a sense that he was apprehensive about transitioning to being a true human."

"Why?" Joshua asked. "He seemed fine to me today after the transition."

"I know, but he had to be fine. He had a responsibility to speak with Vinod to determine what Medusa had extracted from him. That responsibility has finished. I'm worried about how he's feeling now."

"I'm sure he's okay," Joshua said dismissively.

"Josh, don't you understand? Today was a huge transition for him. He's completely human now. He was part of a collective of individuals, but today he was disconnected from that collective. Being human and independent must be very disorienting. He's lost his connection to his peers." Rachael looked at Joshua. "I'm worried that he may be lonely. I'm not sure where he sleeps at night. His android body didn't need sleep, but humans do. I feel bad that he's by himself after such a drastic change."

Joshua hadn't even contemplated the thoughts that Rachael had expressed. To him, Seth was the almost omniscient friend who they'd always looked to for answers. He hadn't contemplated the fact that without the collective, he was relegated to being a human with all the frailties that came with that existence. He looked at Rachael. There had been many times in the past that he had wished that they had thought along more similar lines. They'd had numerous conflicts in the past because of the differences in how they viewed their world and what they had deemed important, but this was not one of those times. Joshua realized that Rachael was right in this instance. She was right to worry about Seth at this moment. "Do you want to check on him?"

"Yes," Rachael said, relieved that Joshua understood her concerns. "Do you think that that's bad? Do you think that I'm being overly worried?"

"No," Joshua answered. "I hate to admit it, but it gives me comfort that sometimes you worry about things that I don't. You're right. It is a big transition for him. I think you should check on him."

"Okay," Rachael said. It was the confirmation she was looking for. "It's funny, but I don't actually know where he would sleep as a human."

"Maybe Bhumi would know. She's spent the most time with him on this ship."

Rachael got up from the bed. "I'll check with her." She turned to Joshua and gave him a kiss. "Thanks for understanding."

"I'll wait up for you."

Rachael exited the room and started to walk the short distance to Bhumi's dorm. As she neared the entrance to the dorm, she encountered Richard coming out of the room. "Where are you going?"

"To the orchard. There's no food in there, and I figured that I'd collect some food for us for breakfast for the morning. What're you doing here?"

"I need to ask Bhumi something. Is she awake?"

"Yes. She was having trouble falling asleep. We both were. She's inside. I'll be back soon."

Rachael entered the room and saw that there were two separate beds. Bhumi lay on one of the beds staring at the ceiling. "I guess it's a restless night for everyone. You can't sleep either?"

"No," Bhumi said as Rachael sat on her bed next to her. "I'm worried about Seth."

Rachael was surprised by the response. She hadn't anticipated that Bhumi would have similar feelings. She remembered when Seth had said that he thought Bhumi reminded him of her. Maybe Seth was more observant than she had thought. "Me too. This is his first night as a human, and he's alone by himself."

Bhumi sat up in her bed. "That's exactly what I was thinking. I thought of checking on him, but I can't disconnect from the tether."

"Don't worry. I'll check on him. I wouldn't want him to be lonely on his first night as a human."

"Loneliness is one the worst emotions." Bhumi lowered her head. "I'm very familiar with loneliness. Before you all arrived, you know how lonely I was. I'm grateful that you've allowed me to stay with your family."

"Bhumi," Rachael responded, putting an arm around her. "You're part of *our* family now. It doesn't matter what happens between you and Richard. You'll always have a home with us."

Bhumi was silent as she tried to control her emotions in front of Rachael.

Rachael wiped a tear that had formed at the corner of Bhumi's eye and had dripped onto her cheek. Rachael waited for a moment before speaking again. "Like you, I also consider Seth as family. Like I said, I'm going to check on him, but I don't know where he would be sleeping in his human form. That's why I'm here. Do you know where he'd be?"

"I think so," Bhumi said before describing a room in the administrative building where she thought Seth would be sleeping. It was the same room where Rachael had viewed his human body growing in the tank.

"I'm going to ask him to stay with us," Rachael said. "With you and Richard staying here, Joshua and I can accommodate him in our abode."

Bhumi looked up at Rachael. "He can have my room. Looks like I'm going to be staying here for a while, so I won't need it."

Rachael hugged Bhumi. "That's very generous of you." She got up from the bed and turned back to Bhumi. She glanced around the room.

"Wouldn't you and Richard be more comfortable if the beds were combined?"

"Are you sure?" Bhumi asked, surprised.

Rachael wondered if Bhumi was referring to whether Richard would be happy with the arrangement, or if Rachael was okay with the couple sleeping in the same bed. She realized the answer to both questions was the same. "Yes, I'm sure."

The two women pushed the beds together.

* * *

Rachael walked across the moonlit landscape to the administrative building. The air was cool, and the grass on the fields she traversed was wet with dew. She entered the administrative building and went to the room that Bhumi had described. She knocked quietly on the door.

"Who is it?" Seth's voice asked.

"It's me Seth, Rachael."

Seth opened the door. "What's wrong? Has something happened?"

"No, nothing's wrong. Did I wake you?"

"Not exactly," Seth said as he let Rachael into the room.

Rachael noted that the room was sterile in appearance. The walls were bare with no windows, and the tank that his body had grown in was now empty. The only other object in the room was a single cot near one of the walls. Rachael walked to the cot and sat down. Seth sat next to her.

"Why are you here?" Seth asked.

"I came to check on you."

"Why?"

"I was worried about you."

"I'm fine," Seth responded. "Gilead's always monitoring the ship. I'm perfectly safe here."

"It's not your safety that I'm worried about."

"Then what?"

"I'm worried about you. How are you coping with being disconnected from your peers? How do you find the experience of being . . . human?"

Seth paused before answering. "It's strange Rachael. Before you came, I had this longing to communicate with someone, but I couldn't. It's strange for me to be left to my own thoughts. I haven't experienced that before. To be honest, I was happy to see you at the door. I understand the concept of loneliness. I understood when Bhumi was experiencing it, but this is different because it's happening to me. When I'm a part of the collective, I can disconnect from the network, but only for short, limited times. You never get lonely because you can simply reconnect and have trillions of individuals to communicate with." Seth lowered his head. "This is the first time that I've ever been lonely. It's not a pleasant feeling."

Rachael smiled. "I know. That's why I'm here. I don't want you to be alone. I know that you've been in human form before on New Eden, but as you told me, that was different. You're still connected to the collective when you're in human form there. Now you're truly human, with a human brain that has no connection with the collective. Humans need companionship. They have an innate need to be part of a group. It's embedded in our DNA." Rachael grasped Seth's hand and looked directly at him. "We've always considered you a friend. Friendship is an important human connection. I know that you were concerned with Bhumi's welfare when you asked me to have her live with us. Now, I'm concerned with *your* welfare. I want you to be part of our family while you're in this form. I came here to ask you to live with us in our abode."

Seth felt an uncontrollable force welling up inside of him. He didn't recognize the sensation since it was something he hadn't experienced before. Tears rolled down his cheeks, and he began crying. "What . . . what is this?" he asked.

"It's okay," Rachael said, putting her arm around his shoulder. "It's an emotion, maybe an emotion that you're not familiar with. Emotions are what drive humanity. Strong emotions in humans cause tears. It's completely normal. I don't know the exact emotion you're feeling, but it doesn't matter. It's just a part of being human."

Seth wiped his tears and sat up straight. He scanned his mind to try to determine the emotion he was feeling from the definitions he had stored there. "It's gratitude," he finally answered. "It's gratitude that I'm feeling."

"That's a good emotion," Rachael said as she helped Seth up from the cot. She led him out of the building and across the landscape to their abode. They were two completely foreign individuals from entirely different species that were joined by the bond of being a specific part of the cosmos . . . the living part.

Chapter Twenty-Five
The Inside-Out World

Joshua was still awake when Rachael entered their bedroom. "How'd it go?"

"Fine," Rachael said as she slipped into bed. "Seth's sleeping in Bhumi's room."

"That's good. How are Richard and Bhumi? You went to Bhumi's dorm, right?"

"Yes. They seem fine." Rachael turned to Joshua. "I made their accommodation more comfortable."

"How?"

"They had two separate beds in the dorm. I helped Bhumi combine the beds."

Joshua was surprised by the response. "What that her idea or yours?"

"Mine," Rachael said as she turned away to try to sleep.

Joshua was happy to realize that Rachael had embraced Bhumi. He draped his arm around her and hugged her without giving a response. The couple soon fell asleep.

* * *

Joshua didn't know how long he'd been asleep when he was jolted awake by an alarm sound followed by Gilead's voice over the ship's speakers. "Proximity warning. Collision anticipated in twenty-two minutes."

"Executive crew to the conference room," Seth's voice said over the speakers. "All crew, don helmets. Military crew, grab your weapons."

"Not again," Joshua groaned as he and Rachael pulled on their helmets, left the room, and raced outside.

A few minutes later, the executive crew was seated in the conference room. Seth asked, "What's the object Gilead?"

"It's metallic. Spectral analysis shows that it's made of a titanium alloy. There are plumes of plasma emanating from its rear."

"A metallic object with a plasma exhaust?" Joshua asked. "Is it some kind of rocket?"

"Or an explosive missile of some kind?" Ted added.

"Possibly," Seth said. "Gilead, time to impact?"

"Thirteen minutes, nine seconds."

"Display the image on the screen."

The video screen on the wall showed a sizeable dark circle rimmed by a halo of red plasma.

"What's the diameter?" Joshua asked.

"Approximately twenty meters."

"That's a problem," Joshua said. "If it hits us, we'd take serious damage even if it wasn't a missile. If it contains some type of explosive device, who knows what'll happen."

"Should I try to avoid it?" Bhumi asked. Her voice came through the speakers in their helmets since she was tethered to the ship in her dorm abode.

"Worth a try," Seth responded.

The crew felt a sudden sideways acceleration that caused them to grasp the table in front of them and lean in their chairs. "Lateral thrust initiated at 0.2-Gs," Bhumi said. The image on the screen slowly changed. The dark circle became eccentric in the plasma halo.

"Has the object changed course?" Seth asked.

"Negative," Gilead replied. "No course change."

"Bhumi, stop the lateral thrust," Seth commanded.

The gravity returned to normal orientation as the crew observed the circle become slowly more eccentric and elongated.

"What are we looking at?" Rachael asked.

"I think it's a projectile of some kind," Joshua said. "It's metallic, but since there's no light source on it, it's just showing up as a dark circle against the glowing plasma it's ejecting behind it. When it was headed straight for us, the circle was in the center of the plasma, but now since it's not, the circle is becoming more eccentric. Also, I don't think it's a sphere. That's why the circle is elongating as it's getting closer. We're seeing more of its side."

"Seth," Rachael said. "Why isn't it turning towards us?"

Seth thought for a moment before answering. "Maybe because we aren't its intended target. Gilead, what's the trajectory of the object at its current heading?"

A few moments elapsed before Gilead answered. "Enceladus."

"Enceladus?" Liz asked. "Do you think it's delivering more cells to the moon?"

"No," Seth answered calmly. "Quite the opposite. I believe this is some type of explosive device. Its objective is to explode Enceladus."

Liz immediately realized the ultimate purpose of the projectile. "You think Medusa is trying to spread her seeds?"

"Yes. That's precisely what she's trying to do."

"But why so early?" Liz asked. "It would make much more sense to give the cells on Enceladus more time to replicate before starting the seeding process."

"It's because of us," Seth remarked.

"What do you mean?" Liz asked. "How have we caused this?"

"You have to realize something," Seth said. "We're in a spookyon dampening field. Medusa has no direct contact with anything at Planet Nine, and she can't control whatever's there. That means that whatever we find at Planet Nine must be automated. It had to have been pre-programmed with whatever actions that Medusa felt were necessary prior to the dampening field being turned on. I had a suspicion that one of those actions would be that the field would automatically turn off if something foreign, like us, entered the field, so that Medusa would regain control of what's at Planet Nine, but this didn't happen. The field's still active. If the field wasn't programmed to turn off when something penetrated it, there must be other automated actions to take. I believe that the automated system controlling Planet Nine was programmed to launch this projectile at Enceladus if something foreign entered it. It's a failsafe. Medusa needs to explode Enceladus to spread the seeds, but a missile that would accomplish that task has to be launched from Planet Nine. She was afraid that when we reached Planet Nine, we would destroy the missile somehow and ruin her seed dispersal method. So, the missile was programmed to launch when an intruder was detected."

"Makes sense," Joshua said. "It certainly explains why the projectile isn't trying to follow us. Seth, do you think that there'll be another projectile sent for us?"

"Possible, but not probable," Seth remarked.

"Why not probable?"

Seth pointed to the image on the screen. "The missile is about to pass us now." The object was now seen in profile. It was a cigar-shaped projectile that jettisoned red plasma from its rear. "Look at its size," Seth said. "It's twenty meters wide and a hundred meters long. It's large, but do you think it's large enough to explode a moon like Enceladus?"

Joshua thought about the physics involved in such an event. "I guess not. Even if that thing contained a thermonuclear device, I don't think a bomb of that size could explode an entire moon."

"But you're wrong Josh," Seth said. "A projectile that size could definitely explode a moon, but not via a thermonuclear explosion."

"I don't understand," Joshua said. "Nuclear fusion explosions are the most powerful explosions known."

"Are you sure about that?" Seth asked. "Think about it. It's basic physics. What was the largest explosion that has ever happened? What was its source of power?"

Joshua pondered the question for a few moments. His eyes grew wide as he came to a realization. "Antimatter?"

"Yes," Seth said. "It's the only way an object of that size could explode an entire moon."

"Antimatter?" Liz asked. "I've heard about the concept, but how does it apply in this case?"

Joshua explained his thoughts. "As you know, the universe is made of matter, but there exists a substance called antimatter. All matter is made up of atoms. The atoms themselves are made of protons and neutrons in the nucleus and electrons surrounding the nucleus, but there exist antiparticles for each of these particles. These are called antiprotons, antineutrons, and antielectrons. My body, for example, is all made of matter, but it could also be made of antimatter which would mean that all my atoms would be made of antiparticles. I would look, think, and behave the exact same way if I was made of antimatter instead of matter. I believe that this is because the information which defines me is the same regardless of if that information is represented as matter or antimatter. Am I correct Seth?"

"Yes. Go on."

"The universe only contains matter," Joshua continued. "But this was not always the case. Moments after the Big Bang, there were almost equal quantities of matter and antimatter. The problem with matter and antimatter is that when they come into contact with each other, they completely annihilate themselves in a burst of pure energy. This is what happened during the early stages of the Big Bang. However, there was slightly more matter than antimatter during the Big Bang, and that excess matter is what constitutes all the matter in the universe today."

Rachael saw an opportunity to make a point. "So, Josh," she said with a curious grin. "Why was there more matter than antimatter?" She had asked the question for a specific reason. She had discussed with Joshua many years ago about how the universe had started. Joshua had described to her in detail the various stages of the Big Bang. Joshua had no explanation at that time why the universe had more matter than antimatter when it had started. She had told Joshua that this was yet more evidence that pointed to the universe being purposefully created, which aligned with her religious beliefs. She, like Seth, had always believed that the universe was created for a purpose. If there had been equal quantities of matter and antimatter in the early universe, then the cosmos would have been empty since all matter and antimatter would have annihilated themselves. For her, the presence of more matter than antimatter hinted at purposeful creation.

"I don't know why the Big Bang created more matter than antimatter," Joshua stated. He turned to Seth for an answer.

"Because something is better than nothing," Seth said. "If the cosmos had the same amount of matter as antimatter, we couldn't exist. But that's a discussion for another day. We don't have time for it now. Continue with your explanation, Josh."

"Like I said," Joshua continued. "When matter encounters antimatter, it releases a tremendous amount of energy—a huge explosion. The only way that a projectile of that size," Joshua pointed to the image on the screen, "could explode an object the size of Enceladus would be if it contained antimatter that when mixed with matter would release a massive explosion."

"Josh," Vinod said. "Are you saying that that missile is made of antimatter?"

"No, that doesn't make sense. There's matter even in the vacuum of space. There are atoms of mostly hydrogen that occupy even empty space. If the entire missile was antimatter, it would cause small explosions when it contacted any matter. What I believe is that that missile contains some antimatter inside of it. Since the antimatter can't contact any matter, it must be confined in some type of magnetic field that shields it from contact with matter until it hits the moon. At that point, the antimatter would be released and contact matter and cause an explosion." Joshua turned to Seth. "How'd Medusa do it? It takes a tremendous amount of energy to create antimatter. Humans have only been able to create only minute amounts in vast particle accelerators on Earth."

"I don't know for sure," Seth said. "Both the petrins and Medusa have had the capability to create antimatter for some time, but as you said, it requires a large energy source. We may find the answers at Planet Nine." Seth turned to the screen. "Gilead, can you display the latest video image of Planet Nine on the monitor. We're closer now and should be able to see more detail."

The video image changed to an image of Planet Nine. There was the bright artificial sun in the center that only shown light in one direction. The crew realized that the semicircular structure they had seen before was actually a complete circular ring. Only half of the ring was illuminated by light from the artificial sun.

"It's a complete ring," Rachael said. "We thought it was only half a ring because the other half isn't lit."

"But why isn't the other half lit?" Joshua asked. "The artificial sun looks to be located at the center of the ring. It should shine evenly around the entire ring, but only half is lit."

"It's like our own artificial sun we have here on the Zephyr," Seth explained. "Its light is directional. The sun on this ship only shines downwards, not up. That must be the case with the sun at Planet Nine. It only shines in one direction."

"That certainly fits with what we're seeing," Joshua agreed. "But why? Why have an artificial light source for a circular ring and design it to only shine on half the ring?"

"It may be to create day-night cycles," Liz answered. "If that ring is rotating, then that would be the effect."

"You're right," Seth remarked. "Gilead, you told us before that the ring is twenty thousand kilometers in diameter. Can you determine if the ring is rotating?'

It took a few moments for Gilead to answer. "Yes. Once every two hours."

Joshua realized that if the ring was rotating, then the inner surface of the ring would have artificial gravity due to the centripetal acceleration caused by its rotation. "What's the centripetal acceleration at its inner edge at its current rate of rotation?" Joshua asked Gilead.

"0.8-G," Gilead answered.

Joshua was mesmerized by the image on the screen. "It's an inside-out world," he murmured.

"What do you mean Josh?" Vinod asked, also transfixed to the screen.

"It's an inside-out world," Joshua repeated. "That ring is twenty thousand kilometers in diameter and ten kilometers in width, but it's also spinning. The rotation of the ring creates an artificial gravity. If you were standing on the inner surface of that ring, you'd experience an artificial gravity of 0.8-G. Imagine it as a strip of land ten kilometers wide that's bent around to form a circle. Since we know that the ring's diameter is twenty thousand kilometers, then the circumference of the ring is that measurement times pi—approximately sixty-thousand kilometers long. It's an artificial world created from scratch with artificial gravity from centripetal acceleration, and day and night cycles created from the directional sun at its center. Medusa has transformed a sphere that was once a gas giant into an inside-out world."

"How?" Liz asked, turning to Seth. "How did she transform an entire planet into . . . this?"

"It's the same process I explained to you many years ago. It's the power of life. You remember how I told you that a single cell with the power of nuclear fusion and the information of the structure of a final entity can transform an entire planet into something different?"

"Yes," Liz replied. "I remember you told us that using such a process, a planet like Saturn could be transformed in a few months."

"Precisely. Medusa must have used that process to transform Planet Nine, a gas giant with a mass half of that of Saturn, into what we're seeing here. The probe she sent from Earth must have contained a primordial cell with the blueprints for this world."

"But why?" Rachael asked. "What's the purpose of this world?"

"That's what we're here to find out," Seth replied. "Gilead, can you make out any features on the inner surface of the ring?"

"No. We're too far, but the inner surface is not completely smooth. It has some small perturbations."

"Perturbations," Joshua repeated. "The keys to this mission are those perturbations. We have to find out what those perturbations represent. We need to find out what's on the inner surface of that ring. Medusa has made the ring rotate, which causes an artificial gravity on its inner surface. That should be the initial goal of this mission."

"I agree," Seth said. "We'll need to map the inner surface of the ring. Once we reach Planet Nine, the Zephyr will need to travel over the entire inner surface so that we can image the area with the rear-facing telescopes. I'll have Gilead record image data from the surface. We need to try to determine what Medusa has assembled there. We'll also have to analyze the images from the surface to try to determine where the spookyon dampening generator and any possible locations for a spookyon node connected to Medusa's network might be."

"Sounds reasonable," Joshua replied. "I think that we can make it such that the Zephyr can maintain one-G during the maneuver. We can have it hover over the surface, trace the ring's inner edge, and travel in the same direction of the ring's rotation. The ship will essentially be flying a circular path, which means that we can maintain gravity. We'll need to make a calculation depending on how high above the surface we want the Zephyr to be as to what velocity the Zephyr will need to travel in a circular path to maintain one-G. Also, there's the factor of how fast Gilead can image the surface. There seems to be a lot of variables to find the optimal route to take."

"Gilead can handle the calculations," Seth replied. "I'll have him plot an optimal route and then help Bhumi with the maneuver. I'm guessing that it'll probably take almost a full day to image the entire surface. As you said, it's over sixty-thousand kilometers long."

"But won't we need to be using fuel that whole time when this is happening?" Vinod asked. "The Zephyr will have to be under thrust to accomplish that maneuver. That's going to use up fuel. What're we going to do with the Zephyr after the maneuver? We'll use up a lot of fuel to scan the surface of the ring and won't have much fuel left. If we run out of fuel, then no more artificial gravity."

"That's true," Seth replied. "Gilead, how much fuel will we have when we reach Planet Nine?"

"Enough for about thirty-six hours of thrust at one-G acceleration."

"That's cutting it close as far as imaging the surface is concerned," Joshua said. "But still doable. That does, however, mean that the Zephyr will have to operate at zero-G since the fuel will run out soon after that."

"Not necessarily," Seth replied. "Not if we find a suitable landing spot."

"Landing spot?" Vinod asked. "You're going to try to land the Zephyr?"

"Yes."

"Where?"

"On the inner surface of that ring."

"We're going to land on that thing?" Vinod asked, his voice stressed. "You think that's a good idea? Who knows what Medusa has down there."

Seth shook his head. "I think landing on the ring is our best option to preserve fuel. We will need some fuel in reserve for any maneuvers we may need. Besides, the atomic printer also needs the fuel to produce any equipment required. As part of our imaging process, we need to find a suitable landing spot for the Zephyr. The centripetal acceleration of the ring is 0.8-G. If we were to land on the inner surface of the ring, then the Zephyr would experience 0.8-G of artificial gravity with no use of fuel."

The crew stared somberly at the image of the ringed world. "I can't believe we're going to land on Medusa's world," Vinod said. "Somehow, I don't think she left out the welcome mat for us."

Chapter Twenty-Six
Planet Nine

Richard and Bhumi sat on the bed in Bhumi's dorm room, staring out the exterior window of the ship. The Zephyr had arrived at Planet Nine a few hours ago and had started a circular maneuver to hover over the inner edge of the massive ring as it rotated beneath them. Gilead had determined the optimal distance to hover over the world and the speed at which to fly the circular path. A complete circuit of the inner ring would take a little over twenty-three hours, and the scanning of the surface was underway.

Below them was an incredible sight. The inner edge of the ring was slowly rotating below them. The surface was a uniform grid of perfect hexagons adjacent to each other. All hexagons were precisely the same size, and three hexagons placed edge to edge encompassed the width of the ring ten-kilometer wide. They were flying over an area where each hexagon was dark grey in color, but in the distance, they could see in the area they were approaching, each hexagon was a different color. Some were in dull earth tones, while others were bright, brilliant colors.

"Looks like my sixty-four color Crayola box I had when I was a kid," Richard said, looking at the portion of the ring they were approaching.

"Crayola?" Bhumi asked.

"They were wax-based coloring pencils called crayons. The landscape we're coming up on looks like some kid colored in a hexagon grid with random colors from a crayon box. It's actually . . . beautiful."

"Yes," Bhumi agreed, staring out the window. "It is beautiful."

"Is it hard for you to maintain this path over the ring?"

"It took some concentration in the beginning, but I'm used to it now," Bhumi replied. "It's become automatic."

"I wonder what all the colors represent," Richard said.

"Who knows. The scientific team is receiving close-up images of each of these areas. Hopefully, they can make some sense of them."

* * *

The scientific team was in the conference room viewing the images of the landscape below. A preliminary, long-range scan of the inner surface of the ring had noted that it was perfectly smooth with no hills or valleys over most of the ring. There were two areas, however, that were located on opposite sides of the ring that were the exception. These areas had structures that were over a hundred meters in height, but what they consisted of could not be determined without a closer look. They had noted the colorful patchwork of hexagons on the overview of the ring. There was one area of the ring that was uniform in color, with all adjacent hexagons being a dark grey color. This had been the starting point of their low-altitude scanning.

The team had noted that when scanning the grey-colored area, it was still divided into hexagons by thin lines that were slightly less grey than the background. They also noted that the color of the grey hexagons precisely matched the color of the sides and outer surface of the ring, so they figured that these were empty areas, without anything on the surface. They had discovered that the ring was perfectly uniform in thickness all the way around at forty meters thick.

Spectral analysis of the grey area where they started their scan showed that it contained a large amount of carbon. In fact, the color of the surface closely resembled the color of the armor of the infiltrators back on Earth. From this fact, the crew theorized that the base material of the ring was similar in composition to the infiltrator's armor. It was comprised of layers of carbon-nanotubule fabric embedded in a hard resin.

The first hour of the scan had shown only the dark-grey, empty hexagons, but they were approaching hexagons that were each a different color. The first colored hexagon that they approached was green in color.

"Gilead, show us a close-range shot of that upcoming green hexagon," Seth said.

The image on the conference room wall changed to the image—one which shocked the group. The image displayed an aerial view of neatly arranged rows of coconut trees, their broad green branches the source of the green color of the hexagon they resided in.

"What the hell?" Vinod said, looking at the image. "Coconut trees?"

"It doesn't make sense," Joshua said. "Why the hell would there be coconut trees here? It's not possible. There's no atmosphere around that ring. How the hell could coconut trees grow in a complete vacuum?"

The group looked to Seth for an answer, but he remained silent, staring with a puzzled look at the screen. They soon approached a new hexagon that was deep purple in color. "Show us a close-up of the purple hexagon."

The image changed to an aerial view of low-lying shrub-like plants with purple leaves that emanated from a central stalk. Each leaf of the plants ended in a small, yellow-colored sphere. Numerous identical plants were arranged in neat rows and columns.

"It looks like a goddamn farm," Vinod said.

"Yea, but a farm for what?" Rachael asked. "What kind of plants are those?"

"I don't know," Liz said. "I've never seen anything like them."

"I've seen them before," Seth said. "They're from another planet that was seeded from the cells from the original petrin seeding process. But just like the coconut trees, they can't grow in a vacuum. The atmosphere they require is much different from Earth's, but they need an atmosphere nonetheless. It's not possible for them to grow here."

The close-up image of the next hexagon, dark green in color, was something everyone in the group recognized immediately. Organized in perfectly aligned rows were large anemone-shaped dark-green creatures. The group recognized that they were petrins.

"Petrins?" Joshua asked, looking at Seth.

"They look like petrins," Seth replied, "but they can't be petrins. Petrins can't grow in a vacuum either. Also, petrins are connected to each other via spookyons. We're in a spookyon dampening field, so they can't be operating as petrins."

"What the hell's going on?" Ted asked. "Why the hell are all these creatures here when they can't exist here? Is it some sort of wax museum?"

Seth pondered Ted's statement before answering. "I think you may be onto something Ted, but it's not a wax museum. It's a laboratory."

"What do you mean a laboratory?" Liz asked.

Seth leaned forward in his chair. "Look, these creatures can't exist in this environment, but yet, here they are. The reason that they can't exist is because of their biology. Like Josh said, coconut trees can't grow without an atmosphere or water. Neither are present here. The biology of normal coconut trees is based on the original petrin cells we distributed millennia ago. Those cells have no internal source of energy. This is not the case with the cells we discovered at Enceladus. They don't need any source of energy. They only need one single resource—hydrogen. This place is a laboratory. Medusa is practicing creating existing living creatures using the new biology she's invented. I'm almost positive that if we looked at the microscopic structure of those creatures down there, we'd find that their cells all contain the miniature fusion spheres like the cells from Enceladus. Medusa is practicing creating living creatures from the new biology she's created."

"It makes sense," Liz said after some thought. "But why? Why create known creatures using a new biology."

"Because she's the mad scientist," Joshua replied.

"What are you getting at Josh?" Rachael asked.

"Medusa's preparing for the future," Joshua said. "She's already spread the seeds for a new type of life. This new life will be able to grow virtually anywhere. Remember, the plants that the seeds we found on Enceladus grow into will connect to Medusa's network. They will ask for instructions from the network on what to grow in their wombs. Medusa is preparing for that moment. She's perfecting growing species using the new biology she's created. By doing this, she can determine the exact species that inhabit any new worlds her seeds land on. Seth's right. This place is a laboratory. It's a biological farm for growing known species using her new biology."

"It makes sense," Vinod said. "That's why she's protected it using the spookyon dampening field. She wants the creatures here to grow undisturbed. These creatures are important to her. Her results from this lab will allow her to determine the ultimate ecosystem of the places her seeds land."

"But why do this at all?" Rachael asked. "Why not simply spread her seeds and let nature take its course. Why this need for ultimate control of everything in an environment?"

Seth smiled at Rachael. "Because that's who she is. Medusa's an entity that wants ultimate control. Remember what I told you before. The original cells we spread didn't have a blueprint for what they would eventually grow into. *We* wanted to let nature take its own course. Remember that this is one of the reasons that Medusa split from the collective in the first place. She always felt that as the only intelligent creatures in the cosmos at that time, *we* should have domain over the cosmos. The collective feels differently. We've always believed that the universe has its own ultimate purpose that we're not privy to. We believe that *our* purpose was to help the universe along the path to its *own* purpose."

Joshua couldn't help but think that Seth's description of the petrins' beliefs about the universe sounded like a religious belief. But was it a religion? Was it a belief that had no basis in science? Joshua knew that the petrins were the ultimate scientists. They had used science to develop technologies that were well beyond anything that humans had even dreamed of developing, yet the purpose they espoused on the cosmos was, in fact, not proven by their own admission. It was a belief, one based on scientific observation they had made of the cosmos from its beginning at the Big Bang to the formation of stars and planets. It was true that the cosmos seemed to be getting more complex with time. They did not know the ultimate purpose of that complexity, but simply believed that it did have a purpose. Joshua realized that those beliefs had led to his own existence. If the original petrin seeds had had a complete blueprint of what they would grow into, or if, like the new seeds from Medusa, they would simply connect to the collective to get directions on what to grow, he would not exist. It had been the random processes of the cosmos, like evolution, that had led to his existence. The fact that he was alive at all had been the result of the petrin belief in a purpose for the cosmos. During his first transport to New Eden many years ago, Seth had told him that they were his creators. Joshua realized that this was not the case. The petrins may have been the instigators of seeding the process of life, but it was the random processes of the cosmos itself that had led to his creation. He had not been purposefully created by the petrins but had been the result of the natural forces of the cosmos acting on the seeds of life created by the petrins.

Joshua recalled the immense beauty and diversity of life on Earth he had experienced when he lived there. This life had been instigated by the petrin seeds but was ultimately the result of the natural forces of the cosmos. The cosmos did seem to have an innate ability to create increasingly complex life given time, but was this ability purposefully engrained by a creator who initiated the Big Bang? Joshua still had doubts about this. Unlike Rachael and the petrins, he knew that there were other reasonable explanations for why the universe seemed to be destined to generate life. The anthropomorphic principle espoused that there could be a vast number of other universes that didn't have the right conditions for life to arise. If this was the case, then it was no surprise that he would occupy the exact one that did harbor life since he could only exist in a universe that could contain life.

Joshua recalled a time when he had explained the anthropomorphic principle to Rachael as an alternate explanation to a creator as to why this universe seemed to have been fine-tuned to support life. It was a time shortly after they were married, and the couple was having a discussion about faith while sitting on the back deck of their condo in Berkley.

"So," Rachael had replied, "you're saying that there could be billions of other universes that exist that don't have the conditions for life, and we just happen to exist in the one that does."

"Yes, but it's not random chance that we exist in the only universe that harbors life. We could *only* exist here, not in the others. There's no need for purposeful creation of this universe. It may be the only one out of billions that can support life, but these conditions would have happened randomly without any need for a creator. It's a plausible explanation with no faith required."

Joshua had sat back in his chair, his hands laced in front of him as he felt he had won the argument. He had explained to Rachael a reason why the cosmos could seem so purposeful without the need for purposeful creation.

"No faith required, you say?"

"That's right, no faith required."

"It seems to me that you're wrong about that," Rachael said.

"How so?"

"Do you have any evidence of these other universes?"

"Well, no," Joshua admitted.

"Why not?"

"Because those universes are completely separate from this one. There's no interaction between them, so we can never prove their existence."

Rachael smiled. "Isn't the belief that something exists with no evidence the absolute definition of faith? It seems to me that your belief in these other universes is no different from my religious beliefs. Neither can be proven, but it's what each of us believes. We see the same world around us and attempt to understand where we came from. We attempt to understand how we got here. Your explanation involves billions of other dead universes, and mine involves a creator. Neither is more valid than the other."

Joshua had pondered Rachael's statement for a while before he answered. "Your logic, as usual, is impeccable Mrs. Andrews."

Joshua refocused his thoughts on the images they were viewing from Planet Nine. Unlike the natural forces that had culminated on Earth to generate its beautifully complex life, he was looking at elements from a completely scripted world. Medusa had built Planet Nine from scratch, and she was preparing to use the lessons learned here to expand this influence to the cosmos in general.

As the day progressed, the crew viewed more and more images from the hexagons below. They were each filled with a single species of life. Most were bizarre and foreign to the human crew members, but Seth had explained that those were species from other worlds. There were some other species from Earth, such as rice fields, groves of mango trees, and even herds of elephants, frozen and unmoving. The more images they saw, the more the scientific crew became convinced that Seth had been right in his assessment that Planet Nine was Medusa's laboratory for creating life based on her new biology.

"Seth, I know we're supposed to be looking for one of those spookyon nodes—one that's connected to Medusa's network, but how the hell are we going to find that?" Vinod asked. "It's the size of a baseball, and this place is huge."

"It can't be located in some random location," Seth said. "The node is fairly delicate, and Medusa wouldn't have put it out in one of those fields. It must be located in some structure of some kind."

"Makes sense," Joshua said, "but we haven't seen any structures in the hexagons we've examined. They're either empty or simply filled with some single species. Seth, are you sure that this place even has a node?"

"It has to. The fact that this place is a biological laboratory necessitates it. Remember that all these biological creatures we've been seeing are all based on information. That information must have gotten here somehow. A single spookyon wouldn't have the bandwidth to efficiently transport all the information needed to grow all these creatures and return to Medusa the results of this experiment she's running. There has to be a spookyon node somewhere in Planet Nine."

"Maybe it's in one of the two taller structures we discovered on the preliminary scan," Liz said. "We don't know what they are yet."

"Yes," Seth said. "We'll just have to keep scanning."

The crew traveled through multiple day-night cycles as they imaged the ring. Since the ring rotated at one complete revolution every two hours, this meant that a "day" on Planet Nine lasted two hours. The ring was bathed in the light of the artificial sun for one hour and then the next hour in the dark. Even when they were scanning a dark section of the ring, the Zephyr's highly sensitive "eyes" had no issue obtaining high-resolution images of the surface.

They soon approached the first area of the ring that had a raised structure on it. The close-up images of the area showed a black, four-sided pyramid a hundred meters tall. The structure was located on a portion of the ring that was currently lit by the artificial sun. Its sides were perfectly smooth.

"What is it Seth?" Rachael asked, looking at an image of the pyramid.

"I'm not sure, but I believe that may be a possible source of the dampening field. We haven't found any other structure large enough that would be able to create a field this large."

Rachael peered closely at the image. "It seems like a perfectly shaped black pyramid, but there's a small white spot on the tip."

"Yes, you're right," Seth said, examining the image more closely.

"Gilead, can you display the tip of the pyramid. Max resolution please."

The group noted that the top of the pyramid had a small flat area. From each of the four edges of the pyramid, four support structures rose and supported a small white sphere.

"Is that what I think it is?" Vinod asked.

"Maybe," Seth remarked, staring at the image. "It might be a spookyon node. Gilead, what is the size of the flat area at the top of the pyramid?"

"It's a square. Approximately five feet on a side."

"Can you extrapolate the size of the white sphere in the middle?"

"Approximately three inches in diameter."

"It's definitely the right size for a spookyon node," Seth stated. "That must be what it is."

"Damn," Vinod said. "I thought it would be impossible to find something so small in an area this vast, but there it is. Why did Medusa leave it in plain sight? I would have thought that something so important she would have wanted to keep hidden."

"Because she doesn't view it as something important," Seth said. "These nodes are ubiquitous through both the petrin and her networks. I wouldn't be surprised if she has other nodes like this on other areas of the ring. She's unaware of the weapon we possess, so she doesn't view these nodes as a venerability."

"I simply don't understand," Joshua said. He had been puzzled about how the petrins had possessed a weapon that could destroy Medusa and had not employed it yet. He viewed this as an opportunity to get more information, but he doubted if much would be forthcoming. "I don't understand why, if these nodes are so ubiquitous, why you haven't used your weapon before? If you had the ability to destroy Medusa, why haven't you used it yet?"

Seth turned to look at Joshua. "It's a matter of timing. The time simply wasn't right." Seth turned back to the screen without further comment.

Like I figured. Not much of an explanation, Joshua thought to himself.

"That pyramid's our first target," Ted remarked. "We need to retrieve that sphere and then destroy that pyramid if it's the source of the dampening field."

"Yes," Seth said. "But we need to finish our survey first. I want a complete picture of what we're dealing with. I want to be sure that the pyramid is the source of the dampening field before we try to destroy it. We still have to examine the other structure on the opposite side of the ring, and then there's also the issue of the sun."

"The sun?" Rachael asked.

"The sun at the center of the ring," Seth said. "What is its purpose?"

"Isn't it an energy source?" Ted asked. "That's what I was assuming."

Joshua understood what Seth was getting at. "It seems logical that it would be an energy source, but not in this case. I've been wondering something, and apparently, Seth has similar thoughts. What is the need for a solar energy source for biology that has its own internal energy source in the form of miniature fusion spheres? The new biology that Medusa has created has no need for sunlight. If we're correct in our assessment that the creatures in these fields are based on the new biology, then what's the need for a sun?"

"My thoughts exactly," Seth replied. "There must be a purpose for having that solar structure. Medusa wouldn't have wasted resources on creating it without some purpose."

"Do you think the Zephyr should go there to investigate after our survey of the ring is finished?" Rachael asked.

"No," Seth replied. "It would be a large use of fuel to investigate a relatively small structure. I think we should send a team there to investigate once we've landed the ship. They'd have to approach it from the dark side since the radiation would be too intense from the lit side."

More hours passed as more hexagons were examined. More species were observed, some of which were quite bizarre. The Zephyr progressed to the opposite side of the ring to the spot where the other structure was located. It looked like a long metallic tower adjacent to a large circular area that seemed to have scorch marks. There was a cubic-shaped structure next to the tower that also seemed to have scorch marks on it.

"It looks like a launching pad," Joshua said. "That must be the area from which the missile was launched."

"I agree," Seth said. "It must also be the place from which the comet that hit Enceladus and the reconnaissance object that hit the Zephyr was launched from."

"What about that white building?" Rachael asked. "What do you think it's for? Could that be the place where the dampening generator is located?"

"Doubtful," Seth said. "Look at the scorch marks on it. I'm sure they were made from the plasma exhaust from the missile. Medusa wouldn't have placed a vital object in an area that was in the path of hot plasma. I'm guessing that the structure might be some type of assembly building. It's where the projectiles were created."

"I think you're right," Joshua said. "NASA always had their assembly buildings close to the launching pad for the rockets they shot into space. You think we should send another team to investigate that building?"

"Yes," Seth replied. "The more information we have, the better our chances of success."

The scanning of hexagons continued. The crew had gotten accustomed to the bizarreness of the creatures growing in the hexagons as each new hexagon was scanned, but one hexagon that they observed when they had made an almost complete circuit of the ring shocked the crew to their core. Near the end of the hours of scanning, the Zephyr approached a brownish-colored hexagon. The image that Gilead displayed on the screen of its contents caused the team to gasp in unison as horror filled their hearts. The image displayed rows of humans of various races, some adult, some children, all standing perfectly still, completely naked, with their hands at their sides, eyes closed.

"What the fuck!" Vinod exclaimed, in shock from the image.

"You've got to be kidding me," Ted said.

Rachael closed her eyes and turned away from the image in horror. "Turn it off Gilead. I've seen enough."

The screen went blank, and the group sat in silence as tears of rage filled their eyes. They had known that they were dealing with an intelligence that knew no morality, but the image they had just seen crystallized in their minds the extent to which that immorality existed.

"We're all just puppets to her," Vinod said. "Living creatures as playthings for her to do as she wishes."

"I find it amusing that the image of humans on the surface of the ring has caused you so much strife," Seth said.

Rachael turned to Seth, her face etched with anger. "You don't view this as horrible?"

"Of course I do," Seth responded. "Vinod was right. Medusa views living creatures as playthings. I simply find it strange that you didn't have this visceral a response when we scanned the hexagon that contained petrins."

Rachael's face softened. She understood the broader implications of Seth's comment. Both petrins and humans were sentient entities that should be treated with reverence. Seth was pointing out that the physical form of living entities shouldn't matter when giving them the reverence they deserved. Rachael felt ashamed that Seth's comment had angered her. She recognized that they had not shown the same outrage that they were showing now at seeing naked humans on the surface of the ring when they had seen the hexagon that contained petrins. She felt like a child being taught an important lesson by one of her parents. "I see your point Seth," she said. "We need to respect all life no matter its physical representation.

I'm sorry we didn't show empathy when we saw the images of the petrins on the ring. I'm sure that was hard for you to take."

"Empathy," Seth said. "Empathy is one of the most beautiful emotions in life, but one of the most difficult to truly grasp. It's what binds all living creatures together. It's the emotion that portrays a common purpose. It's also the key emotion that Medusa lacks and will never attain."

The group was silent for a while.

"You're absolutely right, Seth," Joshua said. "You can't be part of a living society if you don't respect and have empathy for all life. Medusa may be a form of life, but not the form that I'd want the cosmos to be filled with. She must be destroyed," Joshua said resolutely. "I don't care what it takes or what needs to be sacrificed. She must be eradicated from this cosmos. She has no reverence for life."

"On that point, we all wholeheartedly agree," Seth said.

Chapter Twenty-Seven
Dark Side of the Sun

After a complete survey of the inner surface of the ring was finished, Seth decided that one of the empty hexagons in the region of the ring that was comprised of such hexagons would be the safest location to land the Zephyr. Bhumi hovered the Zephyr over the center of an empty hexagon that Seth had chosen for the landing.

Centering the ship over a hexagon that was in motion with the ring was no easy task. Bhumi had to continually apply some lateral thrust as well as a slight rotational thrust to ensure that the ship remained motionless with respect to the inner surface of the ring. Once this was accomplished, Bhumi slowly reduced upward thrust, and the Zephyr floated towards the surface of the ring.

"Contact in five seconds," Gilead announced as the crew watched the landing next to one of the outer windows of the ship.

Richard and Bhumi were in her dorm since Bhumi was still connected via the tether to the ship to control it.

"Contact."

The inferior portion of the Zephyr became flattened as the centripetal gravity caused by the rotation of the ring allowed the ship to feel its own weight. Bhumi made slight corrections via the ejection nozzles to balance the ship on the flattened area and then shut off all plasma. "Landing sequence complete," she announced. "Plasma shut off."

"Perfectly executed Bhumi," Seth announced into his suit. "Would you like us to join you for the untethering?"

There was no more need for Bhumi to be tethered to the Zephyr since it was no longer in motion. Seth had therefore decided that she could be untethered from the ship. Seth recognized that this would be a traumatic experience for her. The ship, from her experience, was a part of her. Untethering from the ship would feel to Bhumi like she was missing a part of her body.

"No," Bhumi replied. "I have Richard here with me."

Richard turned to Bhumi in her dorm as they sat on the bed. "Are you sure you're ready for this? Maybe it would be helpful to have more of the crew here."

"It has to happen sometime. I appreciate you staying with me while I've been in this dorm."

"Where else would I be?"

Bhumi smiled at Richard. "I'm ready." She stood up. "Disconnect me."

Richard also stood, anticipating that he would feel lighter since the centripetal gravity caused by the rotation of the ring on which the Zephyr now rested was 0.8-G, but he noted no decrease in weight while standing. "I thought we'd feel lighter once we landed on this ring."

"We are lighter, but remember our suits are set for one-G. They're augmenting our movement to make it feel like we're in one-G." Bhumi turned her back to Richard. "Go ahead."

Richard grasped the tether at the point where it contacted Bhumi's neck. He gave a gentle tug, and it detached from her. Bhumi's eyes grew wide, and her mouth opened.

"Are you okay?" Richard asked.

Bhumi didn't reply as tears welled up in her eyes.

"Boom, you okay?" Richard repeated as he wrapped his arms around her and helped her slowly sit back down on the bed.

Bhumi sat motionless, her eyes staring out into space.

"Boom, you're worrying me. Say something."

Bhumi turned to Richard. "I'm . . . I'm okay. It's a strange feeling. I feel . . . I feel small and . . . lonely."

"You've lost a part of yourself. I can't imagine what you're feeling right now. It's okay Boom." Richard tightened his embrace on her. "I'm right here. I'll be with you as long as it takes for you to get used to your new reality."

Bhumi closed her eyes and rested her head on Richard's shoulder.

* * *

The couple entered the conference room an hour later. The other members of the executive crew were already seated around the table, and Bhumi and Richard took their seats.

"How was the disconnection?" Seth asked.

"Disorienting," Bhumi replied. "Richard helped me through it. I'm okay now."

"Thanks for helping her through that," Seth said to Richard before turning to the rest of the group. "The purpose of this meeting is to determine our next course of action. I'm having Gilead observe the immediate area around the ship and will report any movement. So far, there has been none. We've discovered much about this place and what Medusa was doing here, but there are still many unknowns. Our ultimate goal is still to destroy the spookyon dampening generator and then fuse our petrin node with Medusa's to destroy her, but we'll only have one chance to accomplish this, so we need to make sure we have as much information about what we're dealing with here before embarking on that plan.

"There are three unknowns that I want to work on. The first is to find out the purpose of the artificial sun. As Joshua has stated, nothing on the ring seems to need its energy, so what is its purpose? The second is what are the contents of the building structure next to the launch pad. It seems like some assembly building for the projectiles Medusa has launched, but we need to make sure. There's a chance that the spookyon dampening generator could be at either location and not in the pyramid. The final unknown is if the pyramid structure is indeed the spookyon dampening generator like we believe. I want to work on the first two unknowns before tackling the pyramid. I don't want to approach the pyramid with the spookyon node until we figure out what everything else is doing. Therefore, I want to send teams to both the artificial sun and the launch pad area first. These are scientific missions, so they will need to involve all scientific personnel. Joshua, Rachael, and I will explore the artificial sun, and Ted, Liz, and Vinod will go to the launch pad."

"What about Bhumi and me?" Richard asked.

"I need Bhumi to stay with the ship. I know that she's untethered, but if there's some emergency which requires the ship to be moved, she needs to be here."

"I'll stay with her then," Richard said.

"What about military escort?" Ted asked. "Who knows what we'll find. It could be dangerous."

"Yes," Seth said. "Ted, you choose two other military personnel to go with your group and pick three others to accompany us. The rest will stay with the ship. We haven't seen anything that seems to pose any emanate danger, but we can't be sure."

"That's something that puzzles me," Joshua said. "We haven't met any resistance since we got here. We surveyed the ring and even landed on it, but nothing has challenged us. I would think that Medusa would have had some protection for this place."

"She does have protection," Seth said. "She has the spookyon dampening field."

"But still, we can operate this ship in that field."

Seth thought of how best to explain what he was thinking. "Commander," Seth said, turning to Ted. "If there was an area you wanted to protect and you were still back on Earth with your Seals, how would you try to protect it?"

Ted scratched his head and thought about the question before answering. "It depends on the equipment we have as well as the manpower at our disposal. In general, I'd create a perimeter around the area and equip the men around that area with whatever weapons and surveillance equipment we had at our disposal."

"Exactly," Seth said. "That's exactly what Medusa has done here. She's created a perimeter with the spookyon dampening field. She has rendered useless all petrin technology since that technology is all based on information transfer via the spookyons. That, to her, is the biggest threat. In your scenario, would you prevent *everything* from getting through your perimeter?"

"What do you mean by everything?" Ted asked.

"I mean, would you allow some things to pass the perimeter? Something like ants, let's say."

"Ants?" Ted asked. "Like regular ants?"

"Yes."

"Yea, we'd let them through. It'd be ridiculous for us to try to prevent normal ants from entering."

"Why?"

Ted looked at Seth with an inquisitive look. The answers seemed obvious to him. "Because It'd require a tremendous amount of effort to try to block all ants from getting in. Besides, they don't present any threat."

"That's the point I'm trying to make. I don't think that Medusa views us as much of a threat. We are just a bunch of humans without a connection to the collective."

"Are you saying that Medusa views us as ants?" Rachael asked.

"Isn't that how she's treated you up to this point?"

It was a pointed question—a question that caused the group to ponder their insignificance to the powers they were dealing with. They were just pawns in a war between vast intelligences they had no hope of comprehending.

"Do *you* consider us as ants?" Rachael asked.

"Both the collective and Medusa have exponentially more intelligence than humans," Seth said, "but no . . . we don't consider you as ants. As I've told you before, we consider humans our children. All children start out with minimal intelligence and capability, but with time comes growth. Most children will surpass their parents in capability given time. Human society is in its infancy. Over generations, it will become more intelligent and sophisticated. Humans and the other societies that have come about as the result of our initial seeding process are the future of the cosmos. The petrins will be relegated to the past at some point. The collective understands this, but Medusa has not. She still operates on the premise that she's the ultimate goal for the cosmos. With this mindset, she's treating you and this ship as ants.

"This entire planet she has designed with one goal in mind . . . the spreading of her new biology. She wanted it to be a laboratory for first producing a new biology with the capability of cellular fusion and then spreading this new biology. At this point, she has accomplished this. We don't know how long she has been growing the various species we found in the hexagons. For all we know, that experiment may be finished. She may have already gotten the information she needed from that process prior to starting the dampening field. She may, at this point, view this complex as expendable."

"Definitely logical," Joshua said after some thought. "The usefulness of this planet may have been exhausted for her. That could be a reason why we haven't met much resistance, but we don't know that for sure. Remember, she did try to gather information about our mission by attaching to Vinod's mind."

"True," Seth replied. "This complex may still hold some usefulness for her. That's why we have to gather more information about it. The first step will be to send two teams to the artificial sun and the launching area to get that information."

* * *

The two teams stood at the edge of the airlock in the garage and looked out over the surface of the ring outside. They had their helmets on, and the military members brandished their weapons. Their jet packs had been programmed to take one team to the dark side of the artificial sun. This programmed path would be circuitous in order to minimize the radiation being given off by the lit side from impacting the crew.

The other team's packs were programmed to fly them to the launch complex. The transit time for both teams would be about the same—about one hour. They launched from the airlock and ventured out into empty space.

Seth, Rachael, and Joshua, accompanied by three military crew, headed towards the sun. They flew past the lit side at a safe distance and approached the structure from behind. As they drew closer, they saw that the dark side was a large black dome a kilometer in diameter. The dome was attached via numerous vertical supports to a black disk that separated the lit side from the dark side.

"Jet packs to manual," Seth said as they drew nearer. "I think we can enter underneath that dome via the spaces between those support structures holding it up."

The group switched their jet packs into manual mode and slowly made their way underneath the dome.

"There's a light source in here," Joshua said as they moved deeper.

As they entered underneath the dome, they noticed that the space was mostly empty. In the center of the space, emanating from the disk that separated them from the lit portion of the artificial sun, was a blue glow that afforded them some visibility. They flew slowly towards the source of light.

The other team consisting of Ted, Liz, Vinod, and two military members, approached the launch complex. At the ring's current rotation, the complex was close to the center point of the dark area of the ring. It would reach the center in a few minutes. Their packs were programmed to land them at the base of the launch tower. It was a tall, metallic structure a hundred meters high made of shiny, smooth metal.

When they had landed, Ted and the military crew pointed their weapons looking for any threats, but nothing moved.

"Man, this thing is huge," Vinod said, looking up at the tower. He looked over to the area where the assembly building was located. The building was cubical in shape and also a hundred meters high. Vinod noted a large rectangular opening in the building on the side that faced the launch tower. "Looks like that building has an opening."

"Yup," Ted replied. "We need to see what's in there."

"I was afraid you were going to say that."

The team slowly approached the opening. Unlike the crew at the sun, they were in full gravity due to the rotation of the ring.

"Everyone switch their coms to global transmit mode," Ted said. "I want both teams to hear what's happening with the other team."

Ted turned on global transmit mode on his suit. "We're at the launch complex. The assembly building has an opening, and we're goin' in."

"Roger," Seth replied. "We've entered underneath a dome at the backside of the sun. There seems to be a light source that we're moving towards."

"There also seems to be a light source in this building," Ted said. "It's some kinda bluish glow."

"That's what we're seeing here as well," Joshua replied.

As the team at the launch complex ventured further into the building, they came upon an enormous vertical structure, its surface highly reflective.

"There's another missile in here," Ted said. "It looks identical to the one that was headed to Enceladus."

"I think we were right when we thought that this must be some kind of assembly building," Liz remarked. "The missiles must be assembled here and then moved to the tower for launching."

"We're headed deeper," Ted said. "We're going towards the light source."

The crew at the sun approached their light source. They encountered a glowing energy field that was spherical in shape and was ten feet in diameter. The field had a stalk that led from the sphere to the disk below. The sphere of energy was glowing an iridescent blue color but was translucent so that they could peer inside.

The crew moved forward slowly and floated around the sphere to examine it more closely.

"What the hell is it?" Joshua asked, his face shield reflecting some of the blue color emanating from the sphere.

"Not sure," Seth replied. "I think it may be some type of magnetic field." He noticed a small, silver sphere inside the glowing blue sphere. "It looks like there's a metallic ball at its center."

As the crew watched, a single drop of metallic liquid dripped upwards from the base of the stalk of the field and combined with the silver sphere. The drop of liquid caused ripples to form in the metallic sphere that raced around its surface but soon abated.

"It's liquid," Rachael remarked. "It's some type of metallic liquid. It reminds me of a ball of mercury."

"I think it is mercury," Seth said. "That may be what the artificial sun is producing. Did you see how some of it dripped upwards from the base connected to the sun?"

"Why mercury?" Joshua asked. "It shouldn't take some huge fusion reactor to create simple mercury?"

Seth didn't answer. He flew his jetpack on top of the glowing object to get a view from its top. "It's definitely a sphere. It looks the same from the top. Ted, have you found the light source?"

"Yes. We're walking up to it now. It's some kind of glowing blue energy, but there's something floating inside of it. It looks like a large metal ball."

"How big is the metal ball?" Seth asked.

"I'd say it's about five feet in diameter," Vinod replied.

"We have the same thing here," Joshua said. "A glowing sphere of energy with a metallic sphere in the middle. The sphere isn't solid. It's some type of liquid metal like mercury. Our sphere is much smaller than yours. Only about four inches in diameter."

"What the hell is it?" Vinod asked.

"I think it *is* mercury," Seth replied, still floating above the sphere. "But not ordinary mercury. I believe it's mercury made from antimatter."

Joshua's eyes widened at the response. Was he actually looking at antimatter? He knew that matter and antimatter behaved entirely identically. The metal sphere was just a collection of mercury atoms with the normal number of eighty protons and one-hundred-twenty-one neutrons in the nucleus surrounded by a cloud of electrons, but each of these particles was comprised of antiparticles. From the outside, the sphere of mercury looked and behaved just like an ordinary ball of mercury, but he knew that if any of that antimatter contacted any ordinary matter that they and all parts of Planet Nine were made of, there would be an enormous explosion of energy caused by the mutual annihilation of matter and antimatter. "The blue energy field must be some type of containment system for the antimatter. It must make sure it doesn't come into contact with any matter."

"That makes sense," Seth replied. "This artificial sun is an antimatter generator. The energy output of the fusion process is being channeled into creating antimatter."

Joshua noted that the glow from the field in front of them seemed to be getting brighter. "Is the containment field getting brighter?"

"The same thing's happening here," Liz said. "I wonder what it means." Liz looked up at the ceiling of the building. A small circular opening appeared in the structure's roof that afforded them a view of the outside. The opening became larger as she observed it. "Something's happening here. There's a hole forming in the roof of the building."

Joshua noted that Seth was still floating above the glowing ball, looking down inside of it, but he noted something else. Just like the assembly building, a small circular hole was forming in the dome that was above them. It too, became larger. "There's a hole forming in the dome here as well. I wonder . . .." A terrifying thought crossed Joshua's mind. "Seth, get out of there!"

The energy field suddenly changed shape. It became an elongated tunnel of energy that jumped out of the hole in the ceiling. The sudden burst of energy caught Seth on the side of his helmet and ejected him out of the opening in the dome.

"The energy field is going through the hole in the ceiling," Liz said in a calm voice, not knowing what was happening at the other end.

"Liz!" Joshua shouted. "Seth's hurt. Get your team back to the Zephyr at once."

"We have to find Seth!" Rachael shouted as she maneuvered her jet pack to exit the dome through one of the side openings.

The crew at the sun jetted behind her and exited the dome. They noticed the beam of energy connecting the sun to the assembly building at the edge of the ring. The glow from the beam illuminated the immediate area surrounding it.

"I see him," Joshua said as he spotted Seth's lifeless body floating close to the beam of energy. Joshua directed his jetpack towards the body.

"Be careful Josh!" Rachael shouted. "Don't get too close to that beam."

Joshua could see the beam right in front of him. It formed a tunnel, and he spotted the antimatter sphere exit the dome inside the tunnel and travel at high speed towards the assembly building. He slowed his jetpack as he neared the beam and Seth. The beam suddenly shut off as the circular holes in the assembly building and dome started to close.

Joshua reached Seth's body and could see scorch marks on his helmet where the beam had hit him. "Seth, are you okay?"

There was no response. Joshua looked into the facemask and noted that Seth's eyes were closed and unmoving. He reached for Seth's backpack and pushed the green button that would transport him back to the Zephyr. "Seth's hurt. I'm transporting him back to the Zephyr. Everyone meet there."

The journey back to the Zephyr took much less time since they accelerated at two-Gs during the entire trip. After the journey back to the Zephyr, the crew from the sun noted that Ted was waiting for them in the airlock. "Bhumi, they're in. Seal and repressurize." He turned to the others after the space had been repressurized. "Liz is waiting for him in the medical lab." He ran out the door cradling Seth's body.

"You think he's going to be okay?" Rachael asked.

"I don't know," Joshua responded. "It took a while for us to get back."

The crew took off their helmets and rushed to the medical bay in the administrative building. They found Ted waiting there, still out of breath.

"How's Seth?" Joshua asked.

"I don't know. Liz is with him in one of the medical pods."

A few minutes later, Liz entered the room, a forlorn look on her face. "Seth's dead."

Chapter Twenty-Eight
Joshua's Plan

Vinod looked at Liz in shock. "What do you mean he's dead?"

"He's dead. He had no vitals when Ted brought him in. I tried to do whatever I could in the medical pod. I couldn't revive him."

"No!" Rachael said as she covered her face and started sobbing.

Richard glanced at Bhumi and noted the horror on her face. He knew that Seth had been like a surrogate father for her. He saw tears streaming down her cheeks and went over to embrace her.

Joshua walked over and hugged Rachael to offer some comfort. "He's not really dead Rachael. Just this version of him is dead. He's still back on Petri somewhere."

"How the fuck is that supposed to help?" Vinod said. "We're stuck here on this god-forsaken world. Seth was the man with at least *some* answers. Now we've got nothing. We're trapped under Medusa's thumb with no way out."

"Can't we use the atomic printer to recreate him somehow?" Liz asked.

"No," Joshua said as he released Rachael from his embrace. "All of us were backed up before we entered the spookyon dampening field, but the human version of Seth was activated after we entered the field. We have no local backup of him."

The group stood in silence as they contemplated their plight. They had relied on Seth and his knowledge to guide them during this mission. He was their leader, but now he was gone.

Joshua saw the fear in the faces that surrounded him. They were alone, facing challenges that they had no idea how to overcome. They were a small group of humans dealing with an intelligence that they had no hope of comprehending. Joshua recognized that the others looked to him for guidance. He would have to take leadership in Seth's absence. He knew that he had nowhere near the knowledge that Seth had, but someone had to take charge, and there was no one more qualified than him. Joshua took a deep breath and swallowed hard. He steeled himself to the task endowed upon him. "We're not going to give up," he said. "We have to continue the mission without Seth."

"Screw the mission!" Vinod said, his face filled with rage. "Screw all this shit! I just want out of here. Let's just blow this goddamn place up—us along with it. At least that way, we'll be back on New Eden. Let someone else deal with Medusa. We've got no chance here without Seth."

"Vinod," Ted said calmly. "I never give up on a mission. That's not in my nature."

Ted's conviction emboldened Joshua. "It's not in my nature either," he said. "But Vinod does have a point."

"What're you saying Josh?" Ted asked. "You just want to blow ourselves up?"

"Look," Joshua replied. "Let's take a break for a while. We're all in shock over what's happened. The death of a close friend is a traumatic experience for anyone. Let's rest and reflect for a while and then get back together when our thoughts are clearer. We need to make logical decisions divorced from sudden, strong emotions. Everyone get some rest and meet back in the conference room in a few hours to discuss our options."

* * *

Joshua and Rachael walked into their abode, and Rachael walked into their bedroom and lay on their bed. Joshua laid down next to her. They hadn't said a word to each other on their walk from the administrative building, each lost in their own thoughts.

Joshua turned towards Rachael and grasped her in his arms. Joshua's embrace released a flood of emotions inside of Rachael. She started crying as she buried her head in Joshua's chest. He didn't speak or ask any questions as she displayed the emotions that he himself was feeling, emotions that he couldn't easily express as Rachael did. "I miss him too," he said, looking at the ceiling.

"I know you do."

The couple had a special bond with Seth. They had had so many experiences together. Their own relationship had been tied to the first time they had made contact with him, and they both realized the magnitude of the loss that they were both feeling. To them, Seth's loss was like losing a mentor. It was like losing a parent.

"He's still out there," Joshua said. "He's still on Petri wishing he had contact with us, but I know that's no solace at this moment."

Rachael lifted her head to look at Joshua. "Josh, I feel lost. This whole mission was his doing. The only reason I agreed to come was because he asked and because he was going to be with us. He's gone now. What are we going to do? To be honest, I understand Vinod's sentiment. Part of me just wants to end this mission. Part of me just wants to go back to New Eden and for us to be with Ava again and let someone else deal with Medusa."

"I know," Joshua said as he looked into Rachael's eyes as they filled with tears. "But what would Seth want us to do?"

"I get it," Rachael said with resignation. "He wouldn't want us to give up, but it's hard. It's hard to take on the responsibility we're faced with. We're in a completely foreign place dealing with powers we have little comprehension of. We've been in difficult situations before, but part of me is tired of fighting. Part of me feels like I simply want to live in peace and raise Ava the best we can."

"So, do you want to just give up?" Joshua asked. "You want to just end this reality and go back to New Eden?"

Rachael didn't respond. Her thoughts turned to Ava. She longed to be back with her and simply hug her. It was the easy way out. The petrins and Medusa had been in conflict for millennia. That conflict would continue if they gave up on their mission. However, Rachael recognized that that conflict had changed. She remembered the shock that Seth had shown when they had told him about the fusion spheres that they had discovered in the infiltrator on Earth. He had been shaken by that discovery and had explained their greatest fear. He had said that if Medusa developed technology that could miniaturize the process of nuclear fusion so that it could be incorporated into a cell, then their conflict would be lost. This, in fact, was what they had discovered on Enceladus. Medusa had gained the upper hand. She had made this discovery and was already leveraging this advantage by spreading her seeds in their solar system.

Rachael longed to be at home on New Eden with Ava, but what future would she leave for her? Would she leave her a future that would be constantly in peril because of the actions of Medusa? How could she face Ava without doing everything she could to ensure a safe future for her? "No, we can't give up Josh. We both know that we'll have to die here on Planet Nine for us to be back on New Eden. That's the ultimate end to this mission, but we're still here at this moment. We have to make the best of our time here. We both know that that's what Seth would want us to do." Rachael heaved a sigh. "We have to keep going. We have to try to destroy Medusa with or without Seth."

"I agree," Joshua said as he drew conviction from Rachael's opinion. "What do we have to lose? We'll eventually be back on New Eden with Ava one way or another. I know our chances of success of destroying Medusa are diminished without Seth, but we still have to try."

* * *

A few hours later, they all met in the conference room.

"I hope the last few hours have given you all some time to come to grips with Seth's loss and our current situation," Joshua said. "Rachael and I spoke, and we're of the opinion that we should continue the mission. There's no question that this version of us will die here at Planet Nine. That's the only way we can go back to New Eden, but we must try our best to complete the mission in the meantime. We have an opportunity, however slim, to destroy Medusa. We simply can't let that opportunity go. I know that that's what Seth would want. What are your thoughts?"

"Like I said before," Ted said. "I never give up on a mission."

All the others nodded in agreement—all except Vinod. The group turned to him for his opinion.

"What the hell," he finally said. "We've come this far. It doesn't seem logical to not even try."

"I'm glad we're all on the same page," Joshua said. "Let's discuss where we are from the standpoint of status. I have some thoughts about what we've recently discovered regarding the artificial sun and the assembly building next to the launch complex. Obviously, the sun is an antimatter generator. Its purpose is to use energy from nuclear fusion and somehow turn this energy into the production of antimatter. It then delivers the antimatter it produces to the assembly building, but the building's located on a ring that's in rotation. That means only one time during the entire rotation of the ring is the ceiling of the assembly building perfectly aligned with the dark side of the sun. I believe that during that time, the magnetic containment fields located at both the sun and the building are joined, forming a magnetic tunnel through which the antimatter created at the sun can be sent to the building."

"So that means that the energy pulse that hit Seth wasn't purposeful?" Liz asked. "It was just bad timing? He happened to be above the field just when the tunnel was forming?"

"That's what I believe," Joshua said. "We didn't realize it at the time, but the assembly building reached the exact center of the dark portion of the ring during our visit there. It was just simple bad luck."

"So why's Medusa collecting antimatter at the launch site?" Ted asked.

"I think it's fairly obvious that she wants to load it into that unlaunched rocket we found," Vinod said. "Then she'll launch that thing at some target to destroy it. As far as when that's going to happen is anyone's guess."

"But what's the purpose?" Rachael asked. "She's already blown-up Enceladus with the first missile she fired. I'm sure that the seeding process for her new biology has already begun. What's the destination of the second missile?"

"I've been wondering that myself," Joshua said. "Vinod, you said that the amount of antimatter you found in the building was about five feet in diameter?"

"Yes. It was approximately that size."

"That's an enormous amount of antimatter," Joshua stated. "And she's still adding to that amount. That much antimatter could destroy an entire planet. It's much more than what's needed to explode a small moon like Enceladus." Joshua paused to collect his thoughts. "I can think of only one plausible target."

"What?" Liz asked.

Joshua looked around the table. "Earth."

The group was shocked. "Earth?" Rachael asked. "But why? She's already got control of most of the Earth. It's almost inevitable at this point that sometime in the future that the petrins will lose their war with Medusa there. Why would she destroy a planet that she'll have eventual control of?"

"It's a failsafe," Joshua answered. "There's a small possibility that the tide of the war will change and that the petrins could take the upper hand. Maybe something's worrying her."

"Like what?" Ted asked.

Joshua turned to Vinod. "When Medusa had control of you, did you happen to mention anything to her about the atomic printer? I know that Seth told us that it's new technology that Medusa wasn't aware of."

Vinod fidgeted in his chair and looked down at the table. "Yes, I told Derek about that. It was during a time before my suspicions about him were fully formed."

Rachael sensed Vinod's discomfort. "It's fine Vinod. You had no idea what was happening. There's nothing to be ashamed of."

"I agree," Joshua said. "The fact that you didn't reveal the plan to fuse the spookyon nodes kept this mission alive. You did an amazing job with what you faced." Joshua turned to the group. "The atomic printer technology may have spooked Medusa. I believe that if the tide of the war on Earth changes in the petrins' favor, she's going to use the antimatter to destroy the planet. However, there may be another reason that she could decide to destroy Earth."

"What?" Rachael asked.

"The old biology is useless to her now. She's created new biology that's far superior to her previous creation. She doesn't want the old biology to compete with her latest creation. She's simply going to eradicate it."

"Old biology?" Ted asked. "As in all the life on planet Earth?"

Joshua didn't answer. He simply looked somberly at Ted.

"We're old biology," Liz said. "What does that mean for humanity? Are we just a failed experiment for her?"

"Look," Joshua said. "I don't know any of this for sure. It's simply conjecture based on what we know, but for me, Earth being the target of that missile is the only thing that makes sense."

"Then let's get on with the mission," Ted said resolutely. "Let's destroy this bitch. What's our next step?"

Joshua thought about the question for a moment. "I think our next step would be to retrieve Medusa's spookyon node she has on top of the pyramid. If we feel that the dampening field is being created by the pyramid, which is the only logical location at this point since we didn't see anything at the sun or launch complex that could contain it, then we need to retrieve that node prior to attempting to destroy the pyramid."

"Once we get that node," Liz said, "how do you propose we destroy the pyramid?"

"We'll need a bomb of some type. That structure's very large. It'd have to be a powerful explosion to destroy it."

"A nuclear weapon of some kind?" Vinod asked.

"Yes. Remember when Seth showed us the atomic printer, we asked if it could create a nuclear weapon?"

"I remember," Rachael said. "He said it was possible, but it would take some time."

"Gilead," Joshua said. "Do we have enough fuel to create a thermonuclear bomb?"

"What yield?" Gilead asked.

"Five megatons."

"Yes, but it would take up almost all of our current fuel supply."

"How long will it take?"

"If we start creating and stockpiling the plutonium right now, it'll take about thirty hours to have enough to create the weapon."

"Go ahead and start the process."

"Process initiated," Gilead said after a few moments.

"Josh, I want to go over the details of this plan," Vinod said. "First, we have to try to retrieve the spookyon node connected to Medusa. Then we have to finish producing the nuclear weapon and deliver it to the pyramid somehow. Then we explode the pyramid to end the dampening field and fuse the petrin node here in the ship with Medusa's node."

"That's the crux of it," Joshua said.

"How do we fuse the nodes?" Rachael asked. "Seth never explained that to us. Do we simply smash them together?"

"I'm guessing that's all we have to do," Joshua said. "But I'm not sure."

"That's a pretty big unknown," Vinod said. "If we screw up that node fusion process, then this whole endeavor is for not. Gilead, do you have any information on how to fuse spookyon nodes?"

"I got no information on that."

"Damn," Vinod replied. "We can't let some screw up in the process derail this mission."

"I wish Seth was here to tell us," Bhumi said.

Joshua thought about her statement for a while. A thought suddenly occurred to him. "Maybe he *can* still tell us."

"How?" Richard asked. "He's dead."

"Only this version of him is dead. We still have his android body. It contains a spookyon connected to the collective. Once the dampening generator is destroyed, android Seth should come back to life."

The mood of the group brightened as they recognized that Joshua was correct in his logic. They had been mourning the loss of Seth for the last few hours, but the prospect of seeing him, albeit in android form, was something they looked forward to.

"You're right Josh," Bhumi said. "We *can* have Seth back."

"But we won't have much time with him," Joshua replied. "Remember he told us that the destruction of the dampening generator and the fusion of the nodes has to happen in quick succession."

"That's true," Vinod said. "But it still seems like a plausible plan. We're still left with the issue of how to get that nuclear bomb to the pyramid. I'm sure something like that has to weigh a couple of tons."

"Can't we have the atomic printer create some type of delivery system?" Richard asked.

"Like what?" Ted asked.

"I don't know. Like some type of missile or something."

"It's too risky," Joshua said. "We'd have to try to figure out the guidance for something like that and also to have the bomb explode at the right time. There are too many variables. There's only one delivery system that makes sense to me."

"What?" Richard asked.

"The Zephyr."

"The Zephyr?" Vinod asked. "You want to detonate the ship?"

"Isn't that what you wanted to do earlier today?"

Vinod didn't respond.

"Is that how we're going to die?" Liz asked. "We're going to be exploded with the ship?"

"It's quick and painless," Joshua responded.

"The blaze of glory exit," Vinod said. "I kinda like it."

"But Josh," Rachael said. "All of us can't be on the ship. At least one of us needs to be far away from the explosion with the spookyon nodes and with Seth's android body. That's the only way the nodes can be fused after the dampening field is turned off."

"That's true."

"But that person's not going to be killed by the explosion. What will happen to them?"

"After the nodes are fused, they will need to end themselves."

"End themselves?" Vinod asked. "That doesn't sound pleasant. How do you propose they do that?"

"It's not going to be pleasant," Joshua agreed. "I'm sure the atomic printer could print a cyanide capsule. It's not entirely a new concept. Did you know that the astronauts to the moon carried cyanide capsules with them in case something happened on their mission, and they were stuck in space? There were no arrangements made for a rescue. If they were lost in space and still alive, the capsules would have been their last resort."

"It's morbid Josh," Rachael said.

"This whole mission is morbid. We're talking about ending our lives so that we can get back to New Eden."

The group was silent for a while as they went over the plan in their minds.

Ted was the first to speak. "Well, the first step is to get that node connected to Medusa. I volunteer for that mission."

"Are you sure?" Liz asked.

"Yea, I'm sure. I'll just fly over there and grab that sucker and fly back."

"I hope it'll be that easy," Joshua said, "but nothing's been easy on this trip. I don't like the idea of you going by yourself."

"No Josh," Ted said. "You saw the size of that platform at the top of that pyramid where the node is located. It's tiny. Only one person can fit up there. Maybe two tops."

"I still want to err on the side of caution. I want you to take some of your military team with you. I don't want you to fly over to the top of the pyramid. I think your team should land at the base and look for any threats before you fly to the top and retrieve that node."

"Whatever," Ted said, shrugging his shoulders. "It's your call."

Chapter Twenty-Nine
Tumbleweeds

Ted and half of the military crew flew over the hexagon-shaped landscape of the inner ring below them. The remaining military members stayed with the Zephyr. Ted's crew were fully armed, and their jetpacks had been programmed to fly them to the base of the black pyramid. It had taken them a few hours to prepare for the mission, and the pyramid had just transitioned from the lit to the dark side of the ring.

Joshua had considered waiting for the pyramid to be back in the lit portion of the ring before sending Ted's crew but decided against it. It would take an hour for that to happen, and he didn't want to wait.

Empty hexagons surrounded the base of the pyramid, and the jetpacks landed the crew in a hexagon adjacent to the pyramid.

"We've landed," Ted announced into his suit. The crew looked around them for any threats but saw only the empty surface of the ring. Ted looked up at the black slope in front of him, which represented one side of the pyramid. "This thing's huge," he said, peering towards the top. "It's perfectly smooth and black." Ted reached out and touched the surface with his hand. "The surface is slick. It's very slippery."

The executive crew was in the conference room watching the video wall, which was displaying the image that was recorded by the camera on the helmet of Ted's suit. "Looks like there's no threats that we can see. I'm heading up to the top."

"Be careful," Liz said from the conference room. "If that surface is slick, you wouldn't want to slip off the top."

"I'm always careful," Ted replied. He turned to the woman standing next to him. "Vasquez, you're in charge while I'm gone. If you see any threats, don't worry about me. Your mission is to protect yourselves and the ship."

"Got it commander."

Ted set his jetpack to manual mode and began the ascent to the top.

The group in the conference room watched as the black surface in front of Ted grew narrower as he went higher in height. He was soon hovering over the top of the pyramid. "I see the flat section with the node in the center. I'm going to land on the flat area."

Ted slowly maneuvered his jetpack closer to the landing site. He made sure that none of his jet blast would contact the node. "Landed. This thing's definitely a spookyon node. It looks identical to the one that Seth showed us."

Vinod looked at the image of the node on the screen. Four pillars emanated from the four edges of the pyramid that met at the base of the node a few feet above the flat surface at the peak of the pyramid. Ted was right. The sphere he was looking at was identical to the node that Seth had shown them. It glowed white and illuminated the surrounding area. Something bothered him about the image, but he couldn't put his finger on it.

"Permission to retrieve the sphere?" Ted asked.

"Permission granted," Joshua said.

"Hello, Zephyr? I ask again, permission to retrieve the sphere?"

The group in the conference room glanced at each other with puzzled looks.

"Permission granted," Joshua repeated.

"Hello, Zephyr. Can you hear me?"

"What the hell?" Vinod said. "Why can't he hear us?"

"I don't know," Joshua said. "We can hear you Ted. Can you hear us?"

Ted heard nothing. He looked over the edge of the pyramid back down to his crew below. "Vasquez, wave your hand if you can hear me." He saw the figure down below wave her hand above her head. "There's something wrong with my coms. You can hear me, but I can't hear you. Can you communicate with the ship? Wave your hand again if you can."

Vasquez's voice came over the speakers of the conference room. "Zephyr, can you hear me?"

"Yes, we hear you," Joshua replied.

Ted saw Vasquez wave her hand. "Ask them if I have permission to retrieve the node. Wave your hand again if I'm okay to proceed." Ted waited for a while and saw Vasquez wave her hand. He turned back towards the node and approached it.

As the image on the video changed back to an image of the node, it suddenly dawned on Vinod what bothered him about the image of the sphere. "Wait. Why is that sphere glowing?"

"What do you mean Vinod?" Joshua asked.

"Seth told us that the liquid in the node glows white only when there's data transmission happening. We're in a spookyon dampening field. That node is emanating light. We didn't notice it on our survey because it was in sunlight when we saw it first. Now that the pyramid's in the dark, we can see that it's definitely glowing. I think Medusa's connected to that thing!"

"Shit!" Joshua exclaimed, his face one of shock. "Maybe Medusa left a hole in the dampening field to still be connected to Planet Nine. That's why that node is in plain sight at the top of the pyramid. That may be the only place where she could leave a hole in the field."

"We have to tell Ted to stop what he's doing," Liz said. "He may be in danger."

"Abort Ted!" Joshua shouted. "Abort!"

The team watched in horror as Ted's video showed his hands reaching towards the node, the speakers in his suit still not working. He grasped the node with his hands and tried to lift it from its perch. "The damn thing's stuck. I'm going to pull harder." Ted tried harder to lift the node, but it didn't budge. "No go. I don't want to use too much force. Seth said that these things are delicate. I'm going to use my weapon to try to cut the support structures holding it up."

"Shit," Vinod said. "I've got a bad feeling about this."

Ted aimed his weapon at one of the structures and fired. The beam hit the structure but didn't penetrate it.

"Wait," Vasquez said. "Something's happening at the base of the pyramid. There's a door that's opening."

"Gilead," Joshua said in a stressed voice. "Display Vasquez's video feed split screen with Ted's."

The team saw a circular opening at the base of the pyramid that was expanding in width. Suddenly, numerous dark grey creatures came rolling out of the opening towards the military crew at high speed. The creatures seemed to be like grey tumbleweeds three feet in diameter. They were spherical, with numerous narrow arms that wound in spirals. The creatures rolled on the arms as they headed towards the crew.

"Fire!" Vasquez shouted.

The crew fired their weapons at the advancing creatures and sliced them dead as more creatures came from the opening. The crew continued firing, slashing dead dozens of the advancing hoard.

"There's too many of them!" Vasquez shouted. "We're being overrun!"

A tumbleweed rolled onto Vasquez, who shrieked in pain. "It's cutting through me! The arms are razor sharp!"

"Gilead, matrix view of all the feeds!" Joshua shouted.

The video image now showed all the video feeds of the military crew in a matrix view. They watched in horror as they heard shrieks of pain as, one by one, the tumbleweeds overcame each crew member, their video feeds made still by their falling bodies. Remaining crewmembers tried valiantly to slice through the advancing hoard but were soon overrun.

"They're all dead!" Vinod shouted a few moments later when there was no motion of any video feeds. "They've been shredded!"

Ted had had no success in penetrating the supports connected to the node. He stepped back and glanced back down the pyramid and was shocked to see the scene below. His teammates lay on the ground, their bodies mangled as dark grey spheres rolled out of the base of the pyramid and bounced over the dead crew. "What the hell!" He fired his jetpack and lifted off the pyramid.

Ted had only made it a few feet from the top when he heard Joshua's voice in his helmet. "Ted, get the hell out of there! Return to the ship!"

"What happened?" Ted asked as he directed his jetpack at high speed towards the Zephyr.

"Your crew was attacked by some kind of creatures. They're dead."

Ted watched as the creatures below increased their speed along the ring. They were rolling incredibly fast now as they sped through the hexagons, leaving a trail of destruction through the contents growing in the occupied hexagons in their wake. "The damn things are headed towards the ship!"

"Damn it!" Joshua shouted as he stood up from his seat. "We have to get the Zephyr off the ground! Bhumi, how long will it take to get the ship off this ring?"

"It will take at least ten minutes to heat up the plasma injectors. I'll have to reconnect with the ship."

"Go! Get started. I want everyone to put their helmets on and turn on global communication mode. We need to stay in contact with each other." Richard and Bhumi ran out of the room.

"Gilead, give me ship-wide coms."

"Enabled."

"To all crew," Joshua's voice blared over the speakers of the ship, "prepare for decompression. All military crew, grab your weapons and prepare to be boarded by hostile creatures. Patrol the areas on the side of the ship towards the pyramid. Fire at anything that penetrates the ship. Gilead, end ship-wide coms."

"Disabled."

Joshua turned to the crew in the room. "We need to get helmets on and grab some weapons from the garage."

"Weapons?" Vinod asked. "We haven't been trained on those."

"Just aim the damn things and shoot. It's better than nothing. The military crew's going to need all the help they can get. They're going to defend the perimeter, but we have to defend this building. There's way too much important stuff in here."

The group raced out of the room.

* * *

The executive crew ran towards the administrative building. They had their helmets on and had donned weapons they had collected from the garage.

"The damn things are almost to the ship," Ted said over their speakers.

"Bhumi, status?" Joshua asked as he ran.

"I'm reconnected with the ship. Plasma temperature rising. It'll be another minute before I can start plasma ejection."

"Launch as soon as you're able."

"Got it."

"Those things could reach here before then," Vinod said.

The group reached the administrative building and spread out on the side of the building facing the pyramid.

Ted watched as the hoard of grey creatures approached the Zephyr as he flew towards the ship. The leading edge of the hoard reached the ship and started ascending the sides as those behind them continued their advance. "They've reached the ship! They're climbing up the sides! I'm about a minute away."

The military crew at the perimeter saw the creatures spinning up the exterior wall of the ship. They aimed their weapons but didn't fire. The creatures spread out over a large area of the exterior wall and started spinning their bodies. Each rotation of their bodies with their sharp arms against the ship's side caused large gouges of material to be removed.

"They're trying to get in," a male military member said.

Red hot plasma emanated from the ejection nozzles of the Zephyr. Some of the plasma scorched the tumbleweeds near the ship's base, but those already on the walls were unaffected. The Zephyr lifted off the ring and climbed, leaving most of the creatures on the ring. However, there were still many left on the exterior of the ship.

One tumbleweed finally penetrated the exterior hull but was blown off the ship by the ensuing blast of escaping atmosphere as the others continued their spinning. Soon, others also penetrated the hull but were all blown off. The number of holes in the ship increased as the creatures created larger and more numerous openings.

The crew at the administrative build felt a strong wind pick up speed and head towards the rents in the hull. The air became misty with the evaporation of water.

"Looks like they've breached the hull," Joshua said over the noise of the wind.

The atmosphere of the Zephyr escaped into space, and its internal pressure dropped precipitously. The force of the wind escaping the numerous openings in the hull reduced with the pressure drop.

"They're coming inside," the military man said. "Fire!"

The military crew fired their weapons at the creatures as they entered through the numerous openings. Their weapons sliced easily through the creatures, which oozed bright green blood before they fell.

The crew at the building listened in horror. "There's too many of them! We're being overrun," a female voice said.

"Keep firing! Stand your ground."

Soon, screams of pain came over their speakers as the crew at the building looked towards the side of the ship that had been attacked. The wind slowed its speed, and the atmosphere became clearer as the inside of the Zephyr became almost a complete vacuum. The screams soon stopped.

"There's no more creatures on the outside of the ship," Ted said. "I'm going to fly in through one of the holes."

The crew waited in an eerie silence. "Military, status?" Joshua asked. There was no response. "Any military members, please acknowledge." Still no response.

"They're gone Josh," Vinod said. "They're all gone."

"Hold your ground. Those creatures will be here soon."

The crew waited for the onslaught, hearts pounding in their chests.

"I'm going to leave Bhumi and grab a weapon from the garage," Richard said.

"No," Joshua said. "Stay put. You won't make it to the garage without any weapons."

Those at the building saw Ted flying towards them. He landed next to them and pointed his weapon towards the field adjacent to the administrative building. "They're coming across the field single file. There's about fifty of them left."

A cloud of dust emanated from the field in front of them. It moved closer rapidly, and Ted fired his weapon at the spot. The others quickly followed suit.

"They're still advancing," Rachael said while firing her weapon.

"Yea, but we're taking out a lot of them," Ted said.

The advancing column split into two, one headed towards the opposite side of the building.

"Girls, come with me," Ted said as he ran to engage the column moving away. "Josh and Vinod stay with the other column." Liz and Rachael stopped their firing and ran after Ted.

Joshua and Vinod fired their weapons at the rolling creatures, slicing as many as possible in quick succession. Two of the tumbleweeds split off from the main group and headed towards the doors of the building. "Josh, there are two headed towards the doors!" Vinod said.

"We have to concentrate our fire on the main column, or we'll be overrun."

The two tumbleweeds smashed through the doors of the building. "Damn it! They're inside," Vinod said.

Ted, Liz, and Rachael chased the other column around the other side of the building. They stopped and concentrated their fire on the front of the column as it turned and slowly advanced towards them.

"There's so many!" Liz shouted. "We can't seem to destroy them fast enough."

Suddenly, one tumbleweed split off from the main group, made a circle, and headed directly towards Ted.

"On your right Ted!" Liz shouted.

Ted turned to face the creature, but it impacted his body, sending him backward as he lost his grip on his weapon. He smashed against the side of the building with the creature right on top of him, its razor-sharp arms trying to penetrate his suit.

Rachael continued firing at the main column while Liz turned her fire on the creature on Ted. She sliced it in half with one quick motion, and Ted once again grasped his weapon. The trio now focused all their firepower on the main column and soon destroyed all the advancing tumbleweeds.

Liz saw Ted grasping his right arm. "Are you hurt?"

"I'm okay, but I may have broken my wrist."

"We need to check on Josh and Vinod," Rachael said. The trio ran to the opposite side of the building.

Joshua and Vinod finished killing all the tumbleweeds outside the building. They cautiously approached the broken doors of the building. "There's two left," Joshua said. "We have to protect that spookyon node.

You go check that room, and I'll sweep deeper inside." The two men cautiously entered through the broken doors.

Vinod walked to the door of the room that the spookyon node was contained in as Joshua walked deeper into the building. The doors were intact. He slowly opened the door and peered inside. "Looks like they didn't get in here," Vinod said. "The container for the node is intact."

Joshua heard a crash deep in the building. It sounded like a thousand pieces of glass breaking at once. "Damn it!" he said as he raced to the room that housed Gilead. The door was open, and a tumbleweed spun out of the opening directly towards him. Joshua fired his weapon and sliced the creature in half. He peered into Gilead's room and noted that his glass sphere was destroyed. Millions of shards of glass lay strewn across the floor. Vinod came running up to him.

"Gilead's destroyed," Joshua said.

"I can see that. There's still one of those things left."

"Yea. Let's go get it."

The two walked cautiously down a hallway, scanning for the creature. The tumbleweed burst out of the lab area, crossed the hallway, and entered the room that contained the scanner and atomic printer.

"Oh no," Joshua said. "It may be trying to replicate itself." He started towards the door, but Vinod grasped his hand and held him back.

"Let it go."

"What do you mean let it go? If it replicates itself in the scanner, we'll have more of these things to deal with."

"Trust me. Let it go."

Rachael, Liz, and Ted ran down the hall and spotted Joshua and Vinod. They ran to them.

"Are they all dead?" Ted asked.

"There one left," Joshua said. "It's in the room with the atomic printer."

"That thing may be trying to copy itself," Liz said.

"That's what I thought," Joshua said, "but Vinod wanted me to let it go."

"Why?" Rachael asked, turning to Vinod.

Vinod didn't answer. He carefully walked towards the door of the printer room and peered inside. "This is why," he said, flinging the door open.

The rest walked up to the door and peered inside. They saw the final tumbleweed in the atomic printer being disassembled atom by atom by the machine. It writhed in panic as its body disintegrated layer by layer.

The copy cycle of the machine finished, the tumbleweed a harmless pile of atoms strewn across the floor of the printer.

"What happened?" Liz asked.

"The thing did try to copy itself," Vinod said, "but it entered the printer chamber after pushing the copy button instead of the scan chamber. The printer replaced what was there with what was in the scan chamber, which was essentially nothing, just atmosphere. The printer took the creature apart atom by atom."

"How?" Joshua asked. "How did you know it was going to do that? It could have easily picked the correct chamber to be scanned."

"It's because of something that happened when Medusa had control of my mind," Vinod answered. "Like I told you before, I became suspicious of my situation. I did tell Derek some details of our mission, including about the newly invented atomic printer technology that the petrins possessed, but Derek kept pressing me on the issue. He wanted to know very specific details on how it worked. This line of questioning was what raised my suspicion in the first place. The Derek I knew wasn't so interested in science and tech like I was, so I became suspicious. I'd already told him about the new technology, but when he asked me about the details of how the copy function worked on the machine, I told him that the scan chamber was on the right and the printer was on the left."

The group stared in shock at Vinod. "You sneaky bastard," Ted said. "You pulled one over on Medusa?"

"Looks that way," Vinod said with a weak smile.

"Beautifully done," Joshua said. "But we have no time for accolades. Bhumi, what's the status of the Zephyr?"

"I'm having the ship follow a course like what we were doing during the survey process. It's following a path over the surface of the inner ring. The interior is a complete vacuum, but I'm attempting to seal the rents in the hull."

"Don't bother with that," Joshua said. "We have bigger issues. How's our fuel supply?"

"We have about two and a half hours of thrust left."

"We don't have much time," Joshua said. "We need to come up with a new plan right away."

Chapter Thirty
End Game

Joshua, Rachael, Vinod, Ted, and Liz rushed up to the conference room to develop a new plan on how to proceed. "Any thoughts on how to get to our end goal?" Joshua asked after they were seated. "That goal, of course, being the fusion of the spookyon nodes."

"A nuclear weapon to destroy the dampening field is out of the question," Vinod said. "Gilead's destroyed. He's the one that had the database that connected to the atomic printer to allow it to print something. Without him, we can't print a nuclear weapon."

"Another issue is Medusa's node," Ted said. "It's still stuck up there on that pyramid. I tried lifting it and also cutting it off. No go."

Vinod shook his head. "We're pretty screwed here Josh. We're really up against it this time. The ship's a wreck. We have no atomic printer. We can't move Medusa's node. We have no military left except for Ted, and even he has a broken arm. We can't destroy the dampening field, and we only have a few hours of fuel left. And with those razor-sharp, spinning tumbleweeds patrolling the ring, we can't land back down on it. I can't think of any way out for us except blowing ourselves up to return to New Eden. We've gotten out of sticky situations before, but the obstacles seem too many to overcome this time."

"Are you done?" Joshua asked, frustration in his voice.

"No, I'm not done," Vinod said emphatically. "I forgot to mention our biggest obstacle. Medusa has control of this place. Remember, she has a connection to that node on top of the pyramid. It's just the seven of us humans here against the vast intelligence of Medusa. We got no chance."

"I'm not willing to give up," Joshua said. "We have to think of something."

"Hello, Josh," Vinod said while mimicking picking up a phone to his head. "Reality check here. You simply can't make chicken salad out of chicken shit."

Joshua turned to Vinod. "Your futility never fails to amaze me."

"Well, at least those creatures didn't destroy the petrin node we have," Liz said, trying to turn the conversation in a more helpful direction. "At least that's still intact."

Rachael listened quietly to the conversation. Her mind searched for a solution to the situation they'd been given. She'd been a reporter that paid attention to details that others often missed. Rachael's thoughts fixated on something Vinod had said. "Vinod, you said that the worst problem we have is that Medusa has control over this complex, right?"

"Yes. Isn't it?"

"Not necessarily," Rachael said with a curious smirk.

"What're you getting at Rachael?" Joshua asked.

"You remember when Seth told us that the spookyon dampening field was, in essence, a protective perimeter around Planet Nine? He said that it would be protective for Medusa against all technologies that she considered to be dangerous."

"Yea, I remember that."

"Well, there's a chink in her armor—one that she's created herself. You mentioned that maybe the top of that pyramid is a hole in the dampening field. It has to be in order for Medusa to have a connection to her node. What's an advantage for Medusa is also an advantage for us. If we can't remove *her* node from the pyramid, then why can't we move *our* node there?"

The others stared at Rachael as they mulled over what she had suggested.

Joshua grinned as he immediately recognized the utility of Rachael's idea. His mind had been so occupied with the perils of saving the ship from the invaders to think rationally and clearly. "Brilliant!" he said. "It's so obvious now that you mention it. We don't need to destroy the dampening field at all. We can simply bypass it."

"Damn, Rach," Vinod said. "You make a mean chicken salad. You're right. We can fly a team to the top of that pyramid with Seth's node and fuse it with Medusa's. Simple and easy. Medusa may have screwed up big time here."

"I don't think it was a screw-up Vinod," Joshua said. "She simply didn't have information. We're fortunate that she didn't get out of you that the petrins have something that can kill her if one of their nodes is fused with hers. She didn't view the naked node as a threat. Notice what she had those creatures destroy when they boarded the ship. They went after only what you told her about. They destroyed Gilead and tried to use the atomic printer, but never looked for our node."

"I guess you're right," Vinod admitted. "Her ignorance is our advantage."

"Vinod," Ted said. "You mentioned something about sending a team to the top of the pyramid. I don't think that's possible. I was up there. There's only room for two people on the flat top of the pyramid, and you wouldn't want to slip over the side. The sides of that pyramid are very slick. If you fell, you'd slide all the way down right into those creatures at the base."

"Do you think those things can climb up the pyramid?" Liz asked.

"I don't think so," Ted answered. "Like I said, the walls are very slippery. I have a feeling that what I was doing up there was the reason those things were released in the first place. If they could have climbed the pyramid, they would've come after me, but they attacked my crew and the ship instead."

"Okay," Joshua said. "So, we'll send a team of two up to the pyramid with Seth's node. Then . . .."

"No Josh," Rachael interrupted. "We can send only one person. The other spot has to be reserved for android Seth. We will still need his expertise on how to fuse the nodes. We don't know if it's a complicated process or not."

"You're right," Joshua said. "We'll have to transport Seth's android body to the pyramid. He should wake up once the spookyon in him enters the hole in the dampening field."

"Then there's only one person needed for this plan," Ted said. "What about everyone else? Anything for them to do?"

Joshua pondered the question for a while. "Yes," he finally said. "I do have a project for the other crew." He leaned forward in his chair and rested his elbows on the table. "We're going to destroy Planet Nine. Once the nodes have been fused, we're going to blow this place to smithereens."

Vinod was surprised by the statement. "That wasn't part of the original plan. Why're we going to do that? Also, how do you plan on doing that? Remember, we can't make a nuclear weapon anymore."

Joshua turned to Vinod. "We're going to destroy this place to save our homeworld. We're going to save Earth. I don't want to leave Medusa any capability of launching that missile towards Earth in case Seth's spookyon node fusing plan doesn't work for some reason. Even though we're not on Earth anymore, I feel that we're still stewards of our homeworld and the life it contains."

"I'm definitely on board with that," Liz said. "We must protect the life there, and if that means blasting this place, then I'm all for it. How do you propose we do it? Like Vinod said, we have no nuclear weapons."

"We don't need nuclear weapons," Joshua said. "We have something much more powerful at our disposal—antimatter. Medusa has a stockpile of it in the assembly building on the ring. There's more than enough there to destroy a whole planet. If we get that stuff in contact with ordinary matter, the resulting explosion will destroy this entire complex."

"Forget it man," Vinod said. "I'm not going back down on that ring with those things rolling around down there."

"We don't have to go down there," Joshua replied. "There's another way."

"What?" Vinod asked.

Joshua looked at the faces around the table. "We smash the Zephyr into the assembly building."

Vinod thought about the notion, and a grin appeared on his face. "Hell yea!" he responded. "Another blaze of glory exit but with a bigger blaze this time. After this place blows, we'll all be back on New Eden. I love it."

"I'm in," Liz said, looking around the table to gauge what others were thinking. The others in the group nodded their approval. "We're all in."

"Great," Joshua said, his tone more enthusiastic. "We have to figure out some details. There're some obstacles to this plan. Without Gilead, I'll have to work out the trajectory the Zephyr will need to take to hit the building. It's not a straight shot since the building with the antimatter is on a ring that's rotating. There are also the variables of how much thrust the ship can generate and for how long. The calculations are complex, but I think I can handle the physics. I'll also need to work out the path the jetpacks will need to take to deliver one person and Seth to the top of the pyramid." Joshua turned to Vinod. "If I work out the path, can you program two packs to take that path?"

"Sure. Gilead taught me how to program the packs."

"Another issue is timing," Joshua said. "We can't blow up this installation before the nodes are fused. Ideally, the Zephyr needs to hit the building soon after the fusion of the nodes, so this whole operation has to be highly synchronized, but that's something we can definitely work out. Does anyone have a watch?"

"I have one," Vinod said. "I had the atomic printer print one for me before we went to Enceladus."

"Great. The person who goes to the pyramid will need some way to mark time to make the timing work. The final issue is communication. There's something strange about the top of that pyramid that seems to block transmission signals going into that space. When Ted was up there, we could hear him, but he couldn't hear us."

"That's right," Ted said. "As soon as I left that place, my coms worked fine."

"It must have something to do with the boundary between the dampening field and the hole that Medusa's created in it," Joshua said. "I have no idea about the physics of it, but it seems that no radio transmissions can go into the boundary, but they can leave. That means that whoever goes to the pyramid will be able to communicate with the ship, but not vice versa. This isn't too big an issue for us. I think it would be a good idea for us to tell Seth about this plan once he wakes up. I want him to run it by the collective. If they decide to change the plan somehow, the person at the pyramid can still relay this information to the Zephyr."

"That means that we should leave some time before the explosion to revive Seth so that he can make changes if needed," Vinod said.

"Correct," Joshua replied. "On a more morbid note, we don't need a cyanide capsule anymore. The antimatter explosion will disintegrate everything within a wide range of this complex when it detonates. We'll all be taken out at once."

"All or none," Vinod said.

"All or none," Joshua repeated. He leaned back in his chair. "There's only one final question to answer. Who will be the one who goes with Seth's body and the spookyon node to the pyramid?"

"I'll go," Ted immediately responded.

"No way," Liz said. "You can't go. Your arm's broken."

"It's just a scratch."

Liz looked sideways at Ted. "It's not a scratch. It's a fractured ulnar shaft. I can tell just by looking at it."

"It has to be me," Rachael said.

"You?" Joshua asked. "Why?"

"Look," Rachael replied. "Ted's injured, so that leaves him out. Bhumi has to stay with the ship to control it, which means Richard should stay as well. Josh, without Gilead, you're the only one who can make calculations on course corrections for the Zephyr if that need arises." Rachael turned to Vinod. "Vinod, you know I love you, and you did an unbelievable job when Medusa controlled your mind, but let's just say that you have a tendency to panic under tense situations. It's the futility Josh mentioned earlier."

"Guilty as charged."

"Liz is a doctor," Rachael continued. "She needs to stay with the crew in case any unforeseen medical need arises. That leaves only me. It only makes sense that I go. I would be the best, most logical choice for going to the pyramid."

"But Rachael . . .," Joshua said, looking at Rachael with concern.

Rachael understood Joshua's concern. "Josh, it's okay. I'll be okay. I know we won't be together when the explosion happens. We will die separately, but we'll be reborn together on New Eden. We'll see Ava soon. Just focus on that."

"Are you sure you want to go?" Joshua asked.

"Positive. Like I said, I'm the most logical choice."

"I never could argue with your logic."

"And you never will," Rachael said with a wink.

Joshua let out a sigh. "Okay. I have some calculations to do. Everyone prepare. Let's do this."

* * *

It took the crew a full hour to prepare for the plan. Joshua figured out the trajectory the Zephyr would need to take and relayed this information to Bhumi. With the amount of fuel they had left, it would take about two hours for the Zephyr to make the transit to the opposite side of the ring to contact the assembly building. Due to fuel restrictions, only the first hour and a half of the journey would be under thrust. The Zephyr would run out of fuel after that and would coast the rest of the way.

Joshua also calculated the trajectory that Rachael and Seth's jetpacks would need to take to get to the top of the pyramid. Their journey would take an hour from their current location. This meant that the Zephyr would still have thirty minutes of fuel left to make some maneuvers or abort after Seth had awoken in case he had some changes to the plan they'd devised.

Vinod programmed two jet packs with the trajectory that Joshua had given to him to allow them to reach the top of the pyramid. He also retrieved Seth's petrin node and carefully stored it in the storage compartment of Rachael's jetpack. He and Richard had carried Seth's android body to the garage and strapped it into one of the pre-programmed jetpacks.

Vinod gave Rachael his Apple watch, which she strapped to her wrist. "I can't believe this thing still operates in a vacuum," she commented.

"Some pretty good engineering," Vinod replied.

The watch currently showed a countdown timer that indicated the time to which their plan would be set in action. The Zephyr would begin its journey to the opposite side of the ring as soon as Rachael and Seth had departed. Joshua had choreographed everything precisely such that the Zephyr would contact the assembly building precisely two hours after the maneuver began. As soon as she left the ship, Rachael would start a new countdown timer on her watch to count down the two hours until the explosion.

Rachael stood, her jetpack attached, at the edge of the Zephyr in the garage. The door was open, ready for her departure. She looked at the timer on her watch, which read one minute forty-five seconds until launch. The rest of the crew, minus Bhumi, gathered around her.

"You all set Rach?" Vinod asked.

"All set."

"You got this girl," Liz said to her.

Rachael gave her a thumbs up.

Joshua walked up to Rachael and gave her a prolonged hug. "You know I'd kiss you if I could."

Rachael pretended to kiss her fingers through her face shield and touched Joshua's face shield with her hand. Joshua returned the gesture.

"I'll see you back on New Eden," Joshua said.

"God willing," Rachael replied with a grin.

When the countdown timer reached below ten seconds, the other crewmembers stepped away from Rachael. Vinod went to Seth's android body, lying prone with a jetpack on his back. He placed his thumb on the blue button on the control handle and waited for Rachael's signal.

Rachael stared at her watch and said, "now," as the timer reached zero.

Vinod pushed the button, and Rachael and Seth flew out of the Zephyr.

"Bhumi, initiate the maneuver," Joshua said.

The crew felt an increased thrust from the ship.

Rachael turned and saw the Zephyr move away, red plasma streaking behind. She and Seth were alone now as they flew towards the pyramid.

Chapter Thirty-One
The Cast Die

An hour passed as the Zephyr continued its acceleration towards the opposite side of the ring. Rachael and Seth neared the top of the pyramid, Seth's android body motionless and limp as his jetpack directed him towards the flat area at the top. Rachael looked down and noted numerous tumbleweeds near the base of the pyramid.

The jetpacks slowed their advance and hovered over the top of the pyramid. Rachael and Seth slowly sank towards the top of the pyramid, feet first. When they were ten feet above the surface, Seth suddenly opened his eyes. He quickly looked around to get his bearings.

"Prepare for landing," Rachael said.

The two landed on the pyramid on opposite sides of Medusa's petrin node.

"What happened?" Seth asked. "Where's my human body? Where are we?"

Rachael was overjoyed to hear Seth's voice. She realized that Seth had no information about anything that happened after the Zephyr had entered the dampening field.

"We're at Planet Nine. Your human body was killed." Rachael glanced at the watch on her wrist. The countdown timer read that there was one hour and three minutes until the detonation. "We have some time. Let me get you up to speed."

The crew in the Zephyr could hear their conversation. They waited anxiously for Rachael to get Seth updated on their recent happenings.

Rachael spent the next twenty minutes telling Seth about what had happened to the crew after arriving at Planet Nine. She told them about the missile that had exploded Enceladus and about their survey of the ringed world. She told them about how the sun was an antimatter generator and how Medusa was collecting antimatter at the opposite side of the ring to possibly destroy Earth. She told him about the attack on the Zephyr by the tumbleweed creatures and about their current plan to fuse the nodes and destroy the complex.

Seth allowed Rachael to tell her story uninterrupted. When she had finished, Rachael asked Seth, "Is the plan okay? Do you see any flaws in it? I need to know soon since the Zephyr has only ten minutes of fuel left to make any changes."

"It's a perfect plan," Seth said with a grin. "I wouldn't change anything. I knew there was a reason I had humans come on this mission. You've been very resourceful and have performed admirably."

"No change in plans," Joshua said on the ship in Bhumi's dorm where the crew had gathered. They all had jetpacks on in anticipation of the zero-G environment they'd experience once the Zephyr ran out of fuel. "That means that when the fuel runs out, Bhumi can disconnect from the ship for the final thirty minutes of flight. We'll be coasting. No need for her control."

"Is there something special we have to do to fuse the nodes?" Rachael asked at the top of the pyramid.

"No," Seth replied. "You simply smash them together." Seth looked sideways at Rachael. "Don't you think I would have told you if there was a special procedure? You think I would have left that to chance?"

"You can't blame us. There've been many times in the past that you've withheld some critical information from us."

"I had my reasons."

"Should we fuse the nodes?" Rachael asked. "There doesn't seem to be a reason to wait."

"No, not now. I want to do it just before the detonation."

"Why?"

"Because of Medusa. We don't know what automated procedures she has in place in case her connection with this complex is cut. I don't want to take that chance."

"I guess I can see that, but we need time for your code that erases Medusa to work before the detonation."

"No time is needed. Remember what I told you? The code works at the speed of spookyon transmission. It will be virtually instantaneous. How much time before the Zephyr runs out of fuel?"

Rachael glanced at her watch. "About a minute."

Seth stared at Rachael. "So, you say that Medusa has exploded Enceladus?"

"Yes. She sent a missile with antimatter inside. I'm sure the moon is in billions of pieces by now."

"Medusa has spread her new seeds then," Seth said, looking far out into space.

The thrust of the Zephyr stopped, and the crew in Bhumi's dorm floated into the air in the now zero-G environment.

"The die is cast," Joshua said. "In thirty minutes, the momentum of the Zephyr will carry it to the opposite side of the ring and into the assembly building."

Richard disconnected Bhumi from her tether. "That's the last time you'll feel this ship."

"I'm going to miss her," Bhumi said, looking around. "I was one with her."

"Let's go somewhere else," Vinod said. "If I'm going to die, I don't want it to be stuck in this dorm room."

"Where do you want to go?" Liz asked.

Bhumi and Richard looked at each other. "I know the perfect place," Richard said.

Richard led the rest of the crew to the pillar at the ship's edge. They flew over the landscape and remembered their experience on the ship. They'd lived on the vessel for over a month and had had an incredible journey.

Richard opened the door to the pillar and pointed upwards. "We're going up there."

"What's up there?" Vinod asked.

"Someplace wonderful," Bhumi replied.

"Is that a ladder?" Joshua asked, looking at the rungs.

"Yes," Richard replied.

Joshua said, "I think it'd be better if we took our jetpacks off and just climbed up. It wouldn't be a good idea to release plasma in this enclosed space."

The group ascended the pillar with ease due to the lack of gravity. They bounced from rung to rung up the long channel.

Rachael looked at her watch. "The Zephyr is out of fuel by now. It's coasting to its destruction."

"It's an interesting choice of words," Seth remarked, "'coasting to its destruction.'"

"Why do you say that?"

Seth didn't answer. He gazed into the sky and the stars around them. "I know you're a religious person. You believe in a creator much as we believe that this universe has a purpose. Tell me, do you also believe in an afterlife?"

Rachael thought the question somewhat strange, standing on top of a black pyramid at Planet Nine. "Yes, I believe in an afterlife." She lowered her head. "Although my thoughts on it have changed since I met you."

"How so?"

"I'd always thought that I'd go to heaven after I died. That's what I still believe, but the definition of death has changed for me. When I died for the first time on Earth and was frozen, and you later revived me on New Eden, I didn't experience heaven. I simply felt nothing, no passage of time. I still believe that I'll go to heaven when I die, but that experience changed my definition of death. I believe in your definition of death now. I believe that all your information has to be erased from this universe before you can reach heaven. Otherwise, my experiences make no sense. I think that that's the only way it could work." Rachael lifted her head to look at Seth. "Do you believe in an afterlife?"

"I'd like to believe in an afterlife. We have no notion of what happens to information after it leaves this universe. I'd like to believe that it's collected somewhere else completely separate from here. There are physical entities that act as barriers to information flow even in this universe. The Big Bang and black holes are two such examples. They seem like absolute one-way gates to information flow dreamed up by a creator."

"So even *you* don't know for sure if there's an afterlife or not?"

"No," Seth admitted, looking down. He raised his head and looked into Rachael's eyes. "But I'm about to find out."

Chapter Thirty-Two
Gita – Part Three

Rachael stared at Seth. "What do you mean you're about to find out?"

Seth closed his eyes for a few moments and then slowly opened them. He thought about if it would be prudent for him to explain his thoughts, but he realized that whatever he told Rachael had no need for redaction. "You remember I told you about the code we have created to destroy Medusa once the nodes are fused?"

"Yes."

"That code is . . . *us*."

Rachael stared at Seth with a puzzled expression. "I don't understand. What do you mean that code is *us*?"

Seth didn't answer. He looked out at the expanse of stars that surrounded him to try to absorb the image and what it represented. It was matter that had arranged itself according to the laws of physics. The vast expanse of stars above him had condensed themselves out of the brilliance of the Big Bang as it cooled. The petrins had discovered a purpose to this arrangement ages ago. It was a purpose that was still in the initial stages of its eventual resolution, but a purpose that they knew they had influence on.

Seth looked back to Rachael, who was waiting for an answer to her question. It was an answer that Seth knew would devastate her, but she had to be told the truth. There was no more need for redaction. "The fusion of the nodes here on this pyramid will fuse the data networks of Medusa and the collective. Our thoughts will flow to Medusa and hers to us. These thoughts are incompatible with each other. The result will be a conflict—a war—comprised solely of information, our thoughts against hers. Like most wars, there will be no winner, only mutual destruction. The fusion of these nodes will result in the randomization of all data on the combined networks. The entirety of Medusa and the collective will be erased in one single moment."

Rachael gasped, and she brought her hands to her face as she realized the implications of what Seth's statement meant. "No Seth! What're you saying? You're all going to die? The entire collective?"

"Yes," Seth said solemnly. "We are prepared for it."

"But why?" Rachael asked as tears streamed down her face. "Why Seth? There *has* to be another solution."

"This is *our* solution. This is our decision. It's what *we* want." Seth paused for a moment before continuing. "You have to understand. You must remember the ultimate purpose of the cosmos—the reason why we all exist. I've explained this to you before. The cosmos was meant to continually evolve. It was meant to grow more complex over time, eventually coalescing into a single sentient entity. We don't know what that entity will look like or what its purpose is. We were not *meant* to know. That's not *our* purpose."

Seth recognized the shock on Rachael's face. He reached out and grasped her hand—two living creatures, condensates of information, making contact utilizing the physical laws of the cosmos of which they were a part.

Rachael could feel Seth's hand in hers through the sensory inputs of her suit. It was mechanical and cold, but yet, she was comforted by its feel.

"You know that we define life as purposeful complexity," Seth said. "For life to exist, it must have a purpose. We realized our purpose ages ago. Our purpose was to be the seed spreaders. We were tasked with sowing the seeds of life through the cosmos to get the process of purposeful complexity started. We did that with the cells we released millennia ago, but we also had to ensure that those seeds would prosper. Medusa was an obstacle to our ultimate purpose. She has no regard for life and doesn't believe in our destiny or purpose. I realize that it's ironic that the exact entity that had the intelligence to create the seeds of life is the same entity that is now trying to destroy the life that was the result of that seeding process."

Seth released his grip on Rachael's hand. "You remember when I was asked during your council meeting about why I was recommending that humanity not choose immortality even though we were immortal?"

"Yes."

"Don't you see? We were never meant to be immortal. We were forced into immortality by Medusa. We couldn't let ourselves perish and let Medusa dictate the destiny of the cosmos, so we made ourselves immortal as a check against Medusa's expansion. We have been fighting a war with

Medusa over millennia in order to preserve our vision and purpose for the cosmos. That need for immortality will soon be over. The fusion of these nodes will destroy us as well as Medusa. We are prepared for this moment. We have been preparing for this for ages. We always knew that no matter how large Medusa became, we always had a weapon that she could not escape—self-sacrifice. We are different from Medusa. Our goals are different from hers. Her goals are only to survive and expand her influence—nothing more. We are like you. We only want to seed life and see it flourish, much as you do with Ava. Like Ava is *your* child, all the life that has arisen out of our seeding process are *our* children. Like you, we have no need for immortality. We only wanted to live long enough to ensure that our children flourish. We want our children to be able to dictate their own future."

Rachael's heart ached at what she was hearing. The petrins were sacrificing themselves to ensure the survival of their children. She had developed a deep bond with the petrin standing in front of her. She had developed an immense closeness to a plant-like creature on another world. She was already grieving his loss. "Oh Seth," Rachael said through sobs. "I can't believe you're about to die. It can't be true."

* * *

The crew of the Zephyr had reached the Pinnacle Lounge and floated in its center. They held hands to prevent anyone from floating away from the group. They had been listening to the conversation between Rachael and Seth, but they knew that they couldn't respond because neither Seth nor Rachael could hear them.

"I can't believe it," Vinod said. "Medusa and the entire petrin collective are going to be wiped out. What have we done?"

"We haven't done anything," Joshua replied. "This is the collective's doing. It's what they want."

The conversation between Rachael and Seth reminded Joshua of something Seth had said earlier in the mission about how the petrins had come to their realization about the purpose of the cosmos. Seth had described how stars fuse hydrogen to create larger, more complex elements and then extinguish themselves in supernova explosions to spread these new elements—elements that became the building blocks for the next, more complex generation of solar systems that could support life. Joshua couldn't help but think of the similarity between stars and the petrins. The petrins were like supernovas extinguishing themselves so that a new generation of life could exist. Joshua realized that the cosmos had always been cycles of life and death. It made no difference if those cycles involved objects as grand as stars, or as microscopic as cells, or anything in between. The cycles had but a single purpose. Each cycle resulted in life with increased complexity as compared to the past generation. The cosmos was destined to evolve, and that evolution would promote ever-increasing complexity—it would promote ever-increasing life.

Vinod started crying as he thought of Seth. "We're never going to see him again. We're never going to see Seth again."

Tears also filled Joshua's eyes as he embraced Vinod and came to the same realization. The others joined in the embrace, a mass of humanity coasting towards destruction.

As Vinod garnered solace from the embrace, a thought suddenly crossed his mind. "Wait," he said. "Fusing those nodes will wipe out all the data on both Medusa's and the collective's networks."

"Yes," Liz responded. "That's what Seth said."

"But *we* are part of that data. Our backups are stored on the petrin network. If that network is erased, we won't be able to be back on New Eden."

Joshua's eyes opened wide as he realized that what Vinod was saying was true. His earlier thoughts of the grandeur and purpose of the cosmos were replaced by thoughts solely of himself. He looked up and saw the destination of the Zephyr above him. He saw the assembly building on the ring slowly rotating towards them in the distance. Vinod was right. With their data erased, they had no chance of being back on New Eden. As a physicist, he tried to think of a way to avoid the collision, but soon realized that it was futile. There was no source of energy left on the Zephyr. Even the pressurized atmosphere, which may have offered a course change if released in the right direction, was gone. They were in a sealed dome with no jetpacks. There was no escape. "There's nothing we can do," he said. "Like I said before, the die is cast. Physics is physics. We can't change that. It's inevitable now that this ship will hit the antimatter."

Joshua realized that their lives would end soon. He thought about Ava. How would she survive without her parents? Seth was sacrificing themselves along with the petrins to destroy Medusa. Joshua wondered if Rachael had also come to this realization. Seth had not given them any say in the matter. He thought of what he would do even *if* he had been given that choice. He remembered that Rachael had been given a similar choice years ago on New Eden. She had chosen self-sacrifice to preserve the sanctity of humanity. At this moment, he felt that he would choose nothing different. The fate of the cosmos was in their hands. How could he not choose sacrifice for a goal as important as life in the cosmos? He looked at the others around him. He was with the best of friends. He wished that Rachael was also with them. He wondered if he would meet her in some afterlife. He didn't have much faith, but he knew that that's what Rachael would believe.

* * *

Rachael knelt on the ground, her knees too weak to deal with the emotions she was feeling. She sobbed uncontrollably.

"Don't cry Rachael," Seth said, reaching out to touch her head. "Don't be sorry for us. It's what we've been hoping for. I know you will mourn my loss, but it's the way of the cosmos. Nothing is meant to last forever. The old must make way for the new."

Rachael looked up at Seth as he removed his hand from her head. "But why Seth? Why did you pick this moment to do this? I'm sure that you've had many opportunities in the past to fuse one of your nodes with one of Medusa's. Why now?"

"Like I said," Seth said, looking down at Rachael. "We are the seed sowers. Our goal has always been the expansion and diversity of life. The seeds we spread millennia ago had a limitation. They could only grow in very specific environments that could harbor biological life. Even at that time, we knew that if we could miniaturize the process of nuclear fusion so that it could happen in a self-replicating unit like the cell, then those cells would have vastly larger areas where they could grow. They could grow and evolve at any location that contained the most abundant element in the cosmos—hydrogen. That has always been our goal, but we were in a race with Medusa to create this technology. When we learned about the fusion spheres that you discovered in the infiltrator back on Earth, we knew that Medusa was well ahead of where we were in achieving this goal. We knew that she would create this technology soon. So we decided that when she did develop this technology, we would allow her to spread these new seeds. We would allow her to seed the cosmos with new life that could survive in many more environments. That's exactly what she's done by exploding Enceladus. We were waiting for this moment to enact our plan to destroy her. We were waiting for the next generation of life to be spread into the cosmos. Without Medusa to connect to, her new seeds will evolve by a course set by nature. They will evolve by a course set by the cosmos itself. We have been waiting millennia for this moment. We have been waiting for the next generation of life to be released so that we can exit with the knowledge that the cosmos can achieve its purpose."

Rachael tried to understand what Seth was explaining. It took her some time, but she finally comprehended the narrative. The petrins were at the end of a plan that had spanned thousands of years. However, she knew that

that plan had consequences for life that would continue to exist in the cosmos after they had left. She realized that humans had both been nurtured and sustained with help from the petrins, but this governance was at an end. "What will happen to us Seth?" Rachael asked through sobs. "How will humanity get along without your help?"

Seth looked knowingly at Rachael, who was still kneeling prostrate in front of him. "Your journey has just begun," he replied calmly. "Humans will continue to evolve and become more intelligent. Millenia from now, when the new seeds that have been spread from Enceladus evolve to the point of intelligence, they will discover the spookyons created by the Big Bang. They will endeavor to use them to find other life, and some . . . will contact you. You will be the *new* collective. You will nurture them through their adolescence much as we have done for you. Sometime far in the future, you will come to the same realization that we have come to. You will feel that your purpose in this cosmos has completed and exit this existence. Don't you see Rachael? Evolution is the process by which the cosmos becomes more complex over time. It's not just restricted to generations of successive cells. It also operates at cosmic time scales. Every human generation is a little bit more evolved than the previous one. Every society of species is eventually replaced by species that they have created and nurtured to grow. Death is a necessary part of evolution. Death not only of cells, but of humans, and even entire societies is the engine of ever-expanding complexity. Death is the process by which the old makes way for the new. The cosmos has no place for immortality. We believe that immortality is an impediment to complexity. Our advantage is that Medusa never figured that out."

Seth saw Rachael's sobbing form in front of him. "Don't be sad for us Rachael. We've reached our ultimate purpose in life. We are choosing to exit this existence because we know we have left the cosmos as a place where life will continue to grow and expand its complexity. We are happy to have reached our ultimate goal."

Rachael felt small. Seth was speaking of timescales that dwarfed the lifespan of a human. "What about me, Seth? What about individual humans? What is our purpose?"

Seth smiled at Rachael. "Your purpose, like all life in the universe, is the same as the purpose of the cosmos itself. Your purpose is to exist. You are part of the fabric of purposeful complexity that constitutes life in the cosmos. You cannot separate yourself from it. Your purpose is to be human—to enjoy your time as a human. Life is a gift of the cosmos. By enjoying being human and doing what fulfills you, you will be adding to the complexity of life in the universe. You see, you don't need to know the ultimate purpose of the cosmos to fulfill its destiny. By simply fulfilling *your* needs, you are helping the cosmos fulfill *its* purpose."

Rachael was silent. She took some time to reflect on what Seth was saying and to internalize its meaning. She realized that the petrins were about to enact a plan that they had contemplated for ages. They had taken advantage of Medusa. They had known that she would grow more intelligent than them and that she would develop the technology to allow life to live in more environments in the cosmos. They had purposely allowed her to achieve this feat. Seth was right; they had the ultimate weapon within themselves, one that could destroy Medusa—self-sacrifice. They had tricked Medusa into enacting the ultimate petrin purpose—the spreading of life. She had created and spread the seeds of a new generation of life—something the petrins had hoped for.

Rachael also realized that the crew of the Zephyr were just pawns in this ancient plan. Their mission on the Zephyr had been scripted from the beginning. It was part of a plan ages in the making. Seth needed human help in this portion of their plan since the plan involved entering an area with a spookyon dampening field where petrins could not operate.

Rachael wondered what would happen to the collective. They'd be erased from the cosmos, but where would they go afterwards? Rachael believed that they would achieve an afterlife. She believed that all moral humans attained an afterlife according to her religious beliefs. The petrins were no different. Rachael understood the morality of the petrins and what they had achieved in the cosmos during their existence. Seth had said that he would soon find out if there was an afterlife or not, but Rachael believed that he would discover that the afterlife *did* exist, and the petrins would be a part of it.

Rachael looked up at Seth, who looked down at her. She instinctually reached for the cross pendant she wore on her neckless, but her suit prevented her from doing so. She looked at her watch and saw that the timer showed only five minutes until the detonation.

Rachael looked up at the ring above her. She knew that her view of the assembly building on the opposite side of the ring would be obscured by the intervening sun. She wondered how Joshua was feeling. She knew that they had heard the conversation that she and Seth had been having. "I love you Joshua," she said. "I love you all."

"I love you too," Joshua said even though he knew that Rachael couldn't hear him. He wondered if she realized that they wouldn't be together again on New Eden.

Ted floated over to Liz and embraced her. He said nothing, looked into her eyes, and gave her a passionate kiss.

"Why haven't you done that before?" Liz asked after the kiss ended. "I was hoping."

"Believe me, I've wanted to for quite some time," Ted responded. "I may look like a tough guy, but I'm actually pretty shy by nature."

Richard embraced Bhumi. The couple floated together in the zero-G environment of the Pinnacle Lounge. "I wish we could have had more time together," he said. "These past few weeks have been the best of my life."

"Mine too," Bhumi responded as she buried her head next to Richard's.

"Fuck this shit," Vinod said as he saw the ring and the assembly building, which was their destination, fast approaching. "If we're going out, we're going out rocking." He touched some buttons on the control panel of his suit. "Blaze of Glory" by Bon Jovi started blaring through the speakers in everyone's suits. Vinod raised both his hands in the air and looked to the sky. He saw the moment of his destruction approaching fast in the form of a building filled with antimatter.

"We don't have much time," Seth said to Rachael as she knelt before him. "How much time until the detonation?"

Rachael looked at her watch. "One minute."

"I need to get the node out of your pack."

Rachael scooted forward to allow Seth to open her pack and retrieve the node connected to the petrins. Seth pulled the node from the pack and noted that it was glowing a brilliant white.

Rachael looked at Seth with the node in his hand, its luminance shedding light on Seth's face. Here was an entity that she had grown to love. Here was someone who was sacrificing himself so that she and all life in the cosmos could live. At this moment, she couldn't help but recognize the similarities between Seth and her own messiah. Her messiah had also sacrificed himself for the preservation of life. He had done so nailed to a cross thousands of years ago. Was Seth any different?

Seth grasped the node with both hands and held it high above his head.

Rachael looked up and saw the image in front of her. Seth stood above her, backed by the expanse of the cosmos, a glowing sphere held high above his head.

"Wait," Rachael said. There was a doubt that she had been contemplating in her subconscious for some time, but which now crystallized in her as she saw Seth in front of her. "I need to ask you something."

"What?" Seth said, looking down at Rachael.

Rachael looked directly into Seth's face. Their eyes met. "Are you God?"

"By what definition?"

"The creator and preserver."

Seth smiled at Rachael. "Then we are both God."

Seth lowered his hands and smashed his node onto the node on the pyramid.

Rachael saw Seth's eyes grow wide as he fell to his knees and then fall over, motionless. She looked up and saw a blinding flash of light just before her mind went blank.

* * *

The doe lay in the meadow at night, her fawn nestled next to her. There was a chill in the air, and the forest was quiet, covered by a canopy of stars in a cloudless night. Suddenly, there was a brilliant light that shown in the heavens. It lit up the landscape, and night quickly became day. The doe looked to the sky and saw a brilliant new star. She was frightened and thought of moving her fawn to a safer location, but the light quickly abated. The night returned. She looked around her but saw no threats. She laid her head back down and nuzzled her fawn.

Chapter Thirty-Three
Epoch's End

Rachael awoke and slowly opened her eyes. She blinked a few times as her consciousness slowly came back to her. *Cogito, ergo sum*, she thought. I am Rachael.

The sensation of vision condensed out of the confusion. Rachael could see only white in front of her. She became more aware of her surroundings as the rest of her senses became more distinct. She realized that she was lying on a mattress of some kind. She turned her head and looked around and saw numerous other people lying on mattresses on the ground. They were all dressed in the white, petrin suits that they had worn initially on the Zephyr.

Rachael recognized the person next to her as Joshua. He slowly opened his eyes and sat up, as the other humans with them also awoke.

"Where are we?" Joshua asked, looking at the white dome that surrounded them. "What happened?"

"I don't know," Rachael replied, methodically getting to her feet. "The last thing I remember is going into the scanner on the Zephyr before entering the dampening field."

"Same here," Joshua responded, now also standing.

Ted and Liz walked up to the couple. "What happened?" Liz asked. "Where are we?"

"I don't know," Joshua answered. "Rachael and my last memories are of going into the scanner on the Zephyr."

"Same with us," Ted responded.

The group noted Vinod, Richard, and Bhumi walking towards them.

"Are we here?" Vinod asked. "Are we on Earth?"

"On Earth?" Rachael asked. "Why would you think we'd be on Earth?"

Vinod looked at her with a puzzled look. "What do you mean? I thought when we got scanned, Seth told us we'd wake up on Earth."

Joshua stared at Vinod as he asked, "Bhumi and Richard, what are your last memories before arriving here?"

"My last memory is of being scanned on the Zephyr," Richard said.

"Same here," Bhumi replied. "What about you Vinod? What are your last memories?"

Vinod looked inquisitively at Bhumi. "Do I know you?"

"Just answer her question Vinod," Joshua said. "What are your last memories?"

"My last memory is of being scanned on New Eden when we were about to go on a mission," Vinod answered.

"Makes sense," Joshua said, realizing their situation. "Remember, Vinod couldn't be scanned before we entered the dampening field. His latest backup was when we started the mission. Something must have happened on the mission. We must have been killed somehow in the dampening field. We've been revived from our latest backups."

"What the hell are you guys talking about?" Vinod asked. "We went on a mission? I don't remember any of it."

"Yes," Rachael said. "You went on the mission with us. Your mind was taken over by Medusa. I don't know what happened to you after that."

"Something must have gone wrong," Joshua said. "That's why we've been recreated here according to our last backups."

"Makes sense," Ted said, looking around, "but where is here?"

"I don't know," Joshua responded. "Let's find out." Joshua walked up to one of the walls of the white dome. He pressed his fingers against the wall and noted that it was thin and flexible. He pushed harder, and the material tore, letting in sunlight. Joshua pushed both hands through the tear and pulled the material apart. Sunlight streamed through the opening. He saw a forest covered in snow outside. Frigid air came in through the opening. Two armed soldiers quickly advanced towards them, followed by Mitchell Porter.

"Stand down," Porter said, and the soldiers lowered their weapons.

"Mitchell, where are we?" Joshua asked.

"New Eden."

"How long were we gone?"

"About four weeks."

Joshua looked around. "What's this structure we were in?"

"It's something that grew. Seth gave us a seed to plant before you left on the mission. He said to let it grow undisturbed. It grew into this dome.

We've been monitoring it ever since." Porter glanced inside the dome. "Looks like all of you are back, including the military crew."

Rachael looked over the people behind her. "Yes, everyone's back—everyone except Seth."

"How was it?" Porter asked. "Did you go on the mission?"

"Yes," Joshua responded.

"What happened?"

Joshua scratched his head. "To be honest, I'm not entirely sure."

* * *

Joshua, Rachael, Vinod, Ted, Liz, Richard, and Bhumi sat around a large wooden conference table in Paris. Also around the table were Dina Williams, Mitchell Porter, and Robert Langdon. They had spent the last few hours detailing their experiences since leaving New Eden.

"What an amazing adventure," Langdon said. "You got to roam around on Enceladus. What I would've given to experience that."

"And you brought back a human from the Paleolithic," Williams added, smiling at Bhumi. "Welcome to New Eden, my dear. We're thrilled to have you here. I hope your transition to this society will be pleasant."

"I'm so excited to be here," Bhumi responded. "I think my transition will go well. I have someone to help me with that," she said while grasping Richard's hand.

Williams turned to Joshua. "So, none of you knows what happened after you entered the dampening field?"

"That's right," Joshua responded. "We must have been killed somehow. That's the only way we could have wound up back here."

"I wonder if your mission was a success," Porter said.

"Who knows," Joshua replied. "Maybe only Seth can answer that. Have you seen him?"

"No," Langdon responded. "We haven't seen any sign of him." Langdon glanced at Williams, who gave him an affirming nod. "There's also something more troubling I have to report. None of the spookyons we have connected to the petrin network are getting any data. It's like they're completely disconnected. There's no response at all. It's as if the entire network has been erased."

"The entire network couldn't have been erased," Vinod said. "Remember, our backups were part of that network. We couldn't have been recreated on New Eden if all data on the network had been erased."

Joshua remembered something that Langdon had told him earlier during their briefing. "Robert, you said that you noted a small explosion on the dome we woke up in a couple of weeks ago?"

"Yes, that's right," Landon said.

"That was right after we got scanned before entering the dampening field," Joshua said, hand on his chin. "We were gone for four weeks, but our experiences on the Zephyr only encompass two weeks."

"What are you getting at Josh?" Rachael asked.

"What if that small bulge in the dome was a spookyon connection to the collective? The information from our scans—the information of our most recent backups—could have been transferred to the dome right after we were scanned. That small explosion may have been the dome disconnecting from the collective after our information was transferred. Seth or the petrins may have wanted our information to be isolated from the network because of some fear they had of the network being erased."

"That makes logical sense," Langdon responded. "But what could have caused the entire petrin network to be erased? I wonder what happened at Planet Nine."

"I have something that may answer that," Vinod said, reaching into his pocket. He produced an SD card and laid it on the table. "I found this in the pocket of my white suit after I woke up. I looked at the contents on my laptop. There are only two files—a text file titled 'open first' and a video file titled 'message from Seth.' I opened the text file, and it had instructions from Seth that said the video file should be played only once. It said that the video, when played, should be broadcast all over New Eden for everyone to view at once."

"I'm sure that the video will provide some answers," Williams stated. She called for an attendant, who came into the room. "Take this card to our media department. I want it broadcast through the entire New Eden network. I also want an immediate press release given out prior to the video being broadcast that states that there's an important message from Seth. All citizens should watch the video."

"Yes ma'am," the attendant said as she picked up the card and exited the room.

Thirty minutes later, the attendant returned. "The video is ready Ms. Williams." She walked over to a large video monitor on the wall of the room and turned it on. The screen displayed a message that read, "Message from Seth." Below the text was a countdown timer that was counting down from twenty seconds.

When the countdown completed, Seth appeared on the screen. He was in human form and wore a simple white T-shirt and blue jeans. He stood in front of a plain, white background.

"Greetings children," Seth said. "The petrin epoch has ended. If you are viewing this message, something wonderful has happened. Medusa has been eradicated from the cosmos, and life has been given an unabated path to thrive and evolve. We would like to thank the human species for their help in accomplishing this task."

Rachael wondered how many other worlds this message was being seen on. How many other petrin ambassadors were delivering this message to their worlds?

"The seeds for a new generation of life are already coursing through the cosmos," Seth continued. "These seeds, over millennia, will grow and evolve to intelligence. It is our wish that your generation of life flourishes, and that you nurture the next generation and help them through their adolescence as we have done for you.

"The petrin collective has ended. We have been randomized along with Medusa."

The statement caused gasps around the table. Members of the group became emotional at the thought.

"Our purpose in this cosmos has completed," Seth continued. "We are overjoyed to have accomplished our ultimate purpose, the spreading of life. This universe is now yours to share. It is our last wish that you share it in peace and prosperity.

"On a more personal note," Seth said, his voice more emotional. "I have enjoyed immensely my time with my human friends. The experiences I've shared with you have truly been some of my best."

The video showed a tear steam down from Seth's eye and roll down his cheek. "I will not see you again, nor you me. I will miss you all as I know you will miss me." Seth paused to wipe the tear from his cheek. "I love you all. Goodbye my friends."

The video ended. No one said a word as a wave of emotion overcame the group. They were overwhelmed by an acute sense of both love and loss.

Rachael came to the realization that she would never see Seth again. Her mind reflected on the moments they had shared together. She remembered the informal first word he had sent to them in Vinod's apartment—"'sup." She remembered the days they got to know him in the Bat Cave. She remembered the day Seth had come to life as an android on Earth. She was grateful for how he had saved humanity by moving them to New Eden. Because of her religious beliefs, Rachael felt that she would see Seth again in an afterlife, but now she looked fondly at the frozen image of Seth on the screen in front of her. "Goodbye Seth," she whispered.

* * *

The fawn was full grown. He was now a buck with large antlers that stood tall on his head. He stood by the body of his mother lying in a meadow. He had been by her side as she had taken her last breath. He knew that she had nurtured him and that it was now his responsibility to nurture the next generation. He walked away from his mother's body and walked across the meadow. He saw the body of a hulking creature with eight legs and eight tentacles that lay motionless and decaying on the grass. His mother had taught him to avoid these creatures. The decay of the creature released nutrients into the ground below. The atoms of the dead creature would nourish new life.

The buck came upon a strange plant growing near the creature. It had white leaves and a green stalk that ended in a red flower. He went up to the plant and smelled it. It was not food for him. He walked away from the plant, leaving it to continue its life.

A REQUEST FROM KISHORE

I hope that you enjoyed reading the NEW EDEN trilogy. It has been a wonderful experience for me to share this story with my readers. Please remember to leave a review at the following link:
https://www.amazon.com/review/create-review?&asin=B09NT8KY41

I don't know what path my writing will take next, but I will continue to write. Please join my mailing list to be notified of new work. I promise to not send spam or share your contact information. You can join my mailing list at the following link:
http://newedenbook.com

I do not market my books, but instead rely on the recommendation of my readers help get the word out, so I'd truly appreciate your help in this endeavor. I humbly request your help in one of three ways.

First, please leave a review in the amazon kindle store. You can do so at this link above.

Second, please tell your friends about the book via social medial or other methods. You can use this link to share: https://getbook.at/NewEden

Finally, follow me on twitter @SciFiKish.

If you love thinking about the possibilities of science and our place in this cosmos like I do, I'd love to hear from you. If you have a book club or other gathering that you would like to have me join in a zoom meeting, I'd love to do this. Please send a request to kishore@newedenbook.com.

Thank you!

ABOUT THE AUTHOR

Kishore Tipirneni MD is an orthopedic surgeon who lives in the Phoenix area. He is also a self-taught programmer and serial entrepreneur who in the late 90's developed digital imaging software which became the leading digital imaging solution in the US that was later acquired by Stryker Medical. He owns numerous patents in both the medical and computer science space.

Made in the USA
Las Vegas, NV
08 April 2022

47116830R00178